After a breathless moment of silence, she made the connection.

A burst of energy rushed past Caylee. Then, bolt after bolt of bluish white lightning arced across the sky, lighting the meadow and casting shadows in the trees surrounding it. The sound of thunder was so loud it caused the ground to shake. She would've fallen to her knees if Haden hadn't been standing behind her, holding her in his strong arms and anchoring her against his solid body. She blinked to focus on a pitch-black cloud of smoke forming several feet in front of her.

Holding her breath, she watched as the smoke dissipated and a huge, shadowy image appeared. Squinting, she struggled to make sense of what she was seeing. It was an animal. A very large animal.

A colorful series of explosions, similar to fireworks, started at the top of the animal's head and continued all the way to the tip of its tail until brilliant shades of red, gold, silver, and purple shimmering streaks illuminated what appeared to be a black dragon.

To Caylee's horror, the dragon turned and fixed its gaze onto hers. It slowly moved toward her. With each step it took the ground rumbled beneath its weight. Stopping directly in front of her, it bowed its massive head reverently at her feet.

Seeking Haden's protection, Caylee took a step back, only to realize he was no longer behind her. How could he just abandon her? She would've screamed, but she couldn't even breathe.

"Breathe, little love. I would never abandon you."

"Huh?" She blinked. Did the dragon just smile at her? She shook her head. Did it just talk to her? She tilted her head to the side, studying its eyes. It didn't make sense. Its eyes were so familiar, so comforting. After a breathless moment of silence, she made the connection.

"Oh, oh my God." She swallowed hard. "Haden?" It had to be an illusion. "No." It was a magic trick of some sort. She'd seen him do many strange, impossible things. She'd seen him appear from out of nowhere and disappear several times. The dragon wasn't real. Hoping to prove it, she reached out to touch it. Her fingers felt warm, hard scales. "It's you."

ETERNAL BREATH
OF DARKNESS

By

Candice Stauffer

Hi Michael,
Best wishes to you
& your lovely
wife! C Stauffer

Edited by: Karen Babcock
Cover Artist: Rae Monet

All rights reserved

Candice Stauffer
www.candicestaufferparanormalromanceauthor.com

Published In the United States Of America

October 2011

Dedication

I would like to dedicate this to a wonderful friend and
fabulous author, Claudy Conn.

~ *One* ~

TAKING A DEEP breath, savoring the sweetness of her lingering scent, Haden Drake watched Caylee Adams walk toward Mia's Clothing Boutique. He shifted, repositioning the seam of his pants, attempting to lessen the terrible ache that was becoming his most loyal, frustrating as hell companion. There was a small chance his attempt to get a little more comfortable would've worked if she hadn't dropped her phone and bent over to pick it up. Shuddering, he uttered a curse, his cock swelling until it was impossibly hard, nearly bursting out of his pants. She was sexy in anything, but nothing compared to the way the worn fabric of those tight, low-rise jeans hugged her ass at that moment.

He, a demon, was the furthest thing from a saint, and pretending to be one was no longer an option. For a year he'd battled against his powerful, volatile sex drive, but day after day the torment of wanting her and not having her had been building into a fierce, unstoppable storm of raw lust. Every night he dreamed of her writhing beneath him, calling out his name in sheer ecstasy as he plunged deep inside the tight, silky heat of her body. She wasn't ready for him to stake his claim on her, but the season for moving slowly, seducing her gently, was long gone. Despite his great power, he was utterly powerless to deny his insatiable hunger for her any longer.

Just before entering the boutique, she glanced over her shoulder and smiled at him. It was a naughty, wickedly sexy smile. If he didn't know her better, he would've thought she'd purposely bent over to torment him. Had she? Rejecting the thought, he shook his head. "Nah." Teasing wasn't her style. Once she was out of sight, he was unable shake the feeling something wasn't quite right. Every second that went by the feeling of uneasiness increased in him so much that his centuries-learned ability to remain absolutely calm under pressure failed. It was her smile. Something about it was raising a red flag. He would never admit it, but the moment she turned to smile at him, chasing after her was inevitable.

While getting out of the car he tried to merge his mind with hers, but she was blocking him. He could easily use more force to penetrate the barrier, but he wouldn't do it. Not yet anyways. He would if it proved necessary, but for now, knowing it would cause her pain, he decided to wait.

A terrible, should've known better feeling churning in his gut, he approached the boutique, hoping she was inside. He really wished she wasn't so skilled at blocking him. She was uncomfortable with his ability to touch her mind at will so he permitted her to build a wall to keep him out. Hindsight was a particularly brutal thorn in his ass. He was an idiot for allowing her wall to become so solid the only way to get through it was to cause her pain.

Taking a deep breath, he released it with a frustrated groan as he entered the building.

"Well, Mr. Slick, it definitely took you long enough to figure it out." Mia approached from behind.

Her sharp voice slicing deep gouges into Haden's skull, he cringed as he slowly turned toward her. His eyes brows drawn together, he flashed her an uneasy smile. "Hello, Mia." The instant he saw the wicked look in her eyes, his heart stopped. "Where's Caylee?"

"Oh, I get it." Hands on her hips, Mia narrowed her gaze on him. "It's a man thing. You couldn't possibly comprehend what has just happened without further explanation. Oh my, you poor, miserable boy. There's no reason to pout. It's your lucky day. I just happen to be feeling quite charitable."

He suppressed the urge to growl. She was smiling too sweetly, showing way too much teeth for any demon's liking. The woman was a wolf. Literally. She was lycan, though she didn't know it. She had been orphaned at young age and raised in foster homes and eventually group homes. He wasn't sure why, but the true essence of her wolf remained dormant. However, when she was riled, the temperament of the wolf was always present. She never hesitated to follow through with a bite after baring her teeth.

"She ditched your pathetic ass," she whispered.

"What?" Things like this didn't happen to him. "No." He was a powerful, immortal warrior. "No." He was a demon, a master of deception. "No." He'd live too many lifetimes, acquired too much knowledge to be so easily duped. "Where's Caylee?" It was joke. She was hiding somewhere, having a good laugh at his expense. Laughing was good. It was great. But enough was enough. Feeling uncharacteristically bewildered, he glanced around. Spotting the dressing room area, deciding it was a perfect hiding place, he walked toward it.

"Just what the hell do you think you're doing? Don't you dare open that door." Mia followed him. "You're going to scare the hell out of my customers." She grabbed his arm and yanked it as hard as she could. "She isn't here."

Turning, he glared at her. "Where is she?"

Mia glared right back at him. "She … ditched … your … pathetic … ass." She smiled, lifting her chin defiantly, obviously enjoying the moment. "Was that clear enough for you? If not, I'm sure that I could look around and find some crayons to draw you a picture."

"Why?" Nah. It was much more than enjoying the moment. She was clearly savoring it.

"Why do you think?" Snorting indignantly, she glanced down at his groin. "You haven't even tried to make it worth the aggravation you put her through day and night. Try using the most valuable tool God gave your gender." Smirking, she shrugged. "Maybe, and, yes, I know it's a highly unlikely maybe, if you manage to use it correctly she'll learn to look beyond the fact you're a seriously flawed, arrogant bastard."

Fists clenched at his sides, Haden nodded. Yep. The woman was a wolf. Rather than bite and release, she clamped down to bury teeth bone-deep to rip and devour. She clearly had some really messed-up, unresolved issues with men. He wanted to strangle her, but unfortunately, no matter how infuriating women happened to be, he never strangled them. He was a demon of great strength, integrity and valor. A warrior. A guardian. Demons like him didn't strangle women. Not even if they were lycan. Grumbling, because it was the only thing he could do, he turned to walk away.

"Leave her alone, Haden." She managed to get in front of him, using her body to prevent him from leaving. "I'm serious. You can't continue whatever sick game you're playing with her. It's wrong, and you know it is."

He stared down at her. "What are you talking about?" Wonderful. She was willing to take him on to protect Caylee. Now, despite the fact she irritated the hell out of him, he actually respected the woman.

"Look, Haden, it's totally cool if you're gay. It's not a big deal. Really, it isn't. I swear. Just be honest with Caylee. Introduce her to your lover. You can still be her friend." She shrugged. "Unless—" She tilted her head to the side. "—your lover boy is the controlling, jealous type and he doesn't allow you to engage in other relationships."

"Huh?" His jaw dropped. "Caylee thinks I'm gay?"

"No," she lied. Smiling, she softened her expression, attempting to use kindness to manipulate him into continuing the conversation. "That's my assumption," she lied again. "You're a very wealthy man. You're not all that hard on the eyes. You're always clinging to Caylee. I've never seen you give any other woman a second glance. And, here's the big one—you've never tried to get down her pants. Oh, and don't try to lie to me about it—she would've told me. She always shares her greatest disappointments with me." She waited for a few seconds, but he didn't respond. "Look, I don't have all day to play games with you. Just tell me the truth, are you gay or not?"

Haden really wished he didn't know Mia was lying. He didn't even want to consider the possibility Caylee believed he was gay. For the first time ever, he truly regretted having the ability to hear the thoughts of another person. A few women, peeking at them from behind a manikin, giggled and whispered to each other. He glanced over at them and then, shaking his head, he looked down at Mia. "No."

"Oh crap. It figures. She won another one." She waved a twenty-dollar bill in his face. "You know, I'm starting to think it's time to take that girl to Vegas. Well anyways, give this to her when you catch up to her." Dismissing him, she turned and walked away.

The moment Haden stepped out of the boutique he tried to call Caylee, but her phone was turned off. Driving to the secluded trails where she jogged, he reviewed everything that had happened. Fearing for her safety, he'd told her to stay out of forest. As expected, she refused to listen. She loved using the scenic trails to jog in the afternoon. He was ready for the argument, ready to win. He'd offered to jog with her. How could she refuse? And, she didn't. She looked up at him with the mysterious, sexy smile that always heated his blood and wreaked havoc in his body, and she agreed.

Caylee *smirked* at him, Haden suddenly realized. She wasn't teasing him. Opening the door to the boutique, she'd glanced over her shoulder to smirk at him. She was flipping him the bird in her own special way. He would've known it if he hadn't been obsessing over her ass. Accelerating through the last curve, pushing the car to its limits, he punched the dash with so much force he left an impression of his fist in it. If she were anyone else, he would've happily abandoned her.

He sure as hell wouldn't be chasing after her to protect her, completely helpless to do anything else.

Throwing gravel, he sped into the parking lot and slammed on the brakes. Sliding sideways, the car abruptly stopped when the rear end crashed against a boulder. From time to time, she accused him of being a control freak. To be fair, he was a bit overly protective of her, but he wasn't a control freak. His behavior wasn't due to a lack of respect for her. It was his responsibility, his right to ensure her survival. If she would just be honest with herself, she would accept the fact she didn't always make the best decisions. It wasn't her fault. Not really. She was a woman. Women needed men to lead them. Women commonly made bad decisions based on overly sensitive emotions. It was a hormone thing. Hopefully she would eventually learn to rely solely on his flawless wisdom. It would sure as hell make life a whole lot easier.

He opened the car door and stepped out. Hoping to find her more quickly, he checked his phone, just in case she'd left a message. "Of course not," he growled, clenching his fist, crushing the phone. "Why make anything easier?" The woman was stubborn as hell. He had until the end of time to train her, but deep down in his heart he knew it wouldn't be long enough for him to teach her to submit.

There were miles of trails in every direction, and he needed to find her now. He never should've let her out of his sight. Slamming the car door, he moved quickly, allowing his finely honed tracking skills to lead him. The warm, muggy air reeked of old blood and decayed flesh. Surely, despite being human, she could smell it, couldn't she? He grumbled unintelligibly; questioning her ability to detect the presence of danger was senseless. It was his responsibility to guide and protect her. What pissed him off was that he'd told her to stay out of the forest and now, deliberately defying him, she was jogging directly into the path of a vicious predator.

Haden stopped. The vampire was hunting. Swinging his head to the left, he clenched his jaw, drawing his lips back in a soundless snarl. All senses on alert, he scanned the ever-darkening interior of the forest. Standing completely still, he was silent, barely even breathing, focusing on the vampire, studying the creature's venomous thoughts. He felt the ferocious, relentless thirst for blood driving it far beyond a state of madness. He felt its depraved anticipation for the kill.

Then, Haden saw the vampire's intended prey.

"Caylee."

Absolute fury welled up, stirring the deepest, darkest portion of his essence, the dragon, the living force of destruction feared by even the most powerful, deadly immortals. A deep, ominous growl, a promise of swift, violent retribution to the undead pursuing her, rumbled in his throat as he expanded his mind to pinpoint her exact location. But he felt nothing. No hint of her location.

Terror instantly replaced fury. It slammed into him so hard and so quickly that he did what a fearless, unfaltering immortal never resorted to doing: he panicked. Heart pounding, he took to the sky, ripping the atmosphere apart, creating a thunderous boom while an enormous mass of black, swirling clouds that completely covered the sun hid his ascent. As he traveled with supernatural speed, he covered her with a hedge of protection, but he quickly realized that he still didn't know where she was. His heart stopped. With his enormous power and strength, he'd never experienced fear or doubt in his ability to defeat adversity of any kind. But now with her life in jeopardy, fearing he wouldn't reach her in time, he froze.

While he plummeted toward the ground, lightning exploded all around, violently crisscrossing the sky. He landed hard, jarring his bones, but ignoring the pain he remained on his feet. Lifting his face to the heavens, he closed his eyes and expanded his mind to search for her. *Caylee, where are you?* Normally, nothing ever rattled him to the core. He was utterly unshakable, but not now. *Show me!* He didn't have the strength to wait for her to answer or to willingly open her mind to him. Sending forth a brutal current of power, he forced his way into her mind.

Fully merging his mind with hers, Haden was able to see through her eyes. She was scared out of her mind, but she was safe and would remain safe as long as he reached her before the vampire breached the hedge of protection surrounding her. He should've felt some relief, but he didn't. As a demon, he was far more powerful than the undead, but with her life a stake it didn't matter. *You're safe, Caylee.*

* * *

Looking down at her foot, Caylee wiggled her toes. "Shit. Shit. Shit." She yanked on her foot, but it was too tightly wedged between tree roots to move it very much at all. "Oh, God." She had always joked about having the worst luck, but suddenly, thanks to the fact that Haden's bossy nature had finally pushed her too far, her lack of good fortune was no joking matter.

Okay. In all honesty, it wasn't Haden's fault. Not really. Sexual frustration was to blame. He wouldn't have the ability to irritate her so easily if she hadn't allowed her secret crush on him to spiral out of control. It wasn't his fault that she'd entertained countless sexual fantasies about him. During the past year, he'd never even pretended to be interested in more than a platonic friendship. He'd always, despite his habit of continually being present and bossing her around, behaved like a perfect gentleman.

He was a good friend. Besides Mia, he was her best friend. It wasn't fair, but his willingness to share a long-term platonic friendship with her was what irritated her the most. She craved so much more with him, but it wasn't an option. She'd suffered a horrifying, violent attack, and now she hated to be touched, so she hadn't exactly tried to seduce him, to act on her fantasies. Besides, she was fairly certain he was gay. He never dated. In fact, he never so much as even gave any woman a second glance.

Still, it wasn't his fault that she'd been too busy wondering how long he'd taken to realize she'd given him the slip to watch where she was putting her feet. She'd veered off the edge of the trail, stumbled, and somehow ended up with her foot wedged in the roots of a tree.

Caylee turned her head to look for a stick to use to pry apart the roots. She blinked. "No." Eyes wide, she stared in disbelief. "Oh, no."

She had never, not even in her worst nightmare, imagined anything so gruesome. There was so much blood. It was everywhere. The woman's throat was ripped out, her mouth gaped in a silent cry for help, and her lifeless eyes, opened wide, mirrored the terrible pain and suffering of a death that refused to come quickly. Screaming was Caylee's first urge, but she knew that making her presence known was the worst thing she could do.

She desperately wanted to look away from the carnage, but she couldn't even blink. She tried to take a breath, but the stench in the air was so bad her throat was swollen shut. How hadn't she noticed it before?

Gasping for air, she clutched her chest. It felt tight. It was worse than uncomfortable. It was extremely painful. Her heart raced far too quickly, pushing adrenaline through her bloodstream, causing her entire body to shake. Feeling the sharp pain of Haden's sudden intrusion in her mind, she winced, but she was too frightened to recognize his presence or to hear his voice. She needed to get away! She needed to run! She tried to stand up, but since her foot was stuck she fell back onto her butt.

Her vision narrowed and darkened. She tried to pull her foot out, but it was no use. Her head was spinning. If she ran, her foot wasn't going with her. Of course, leaving it behind wasn't feasible. She was having a panic attack. She needed to calm. She needed to think. It was easier said than done, but it was the only way she would have any hope of coming up with a plan.

Within seconds, she heard Haden's voice. She felt his presence enveloping her, surrounding her with protection and warmth. But it didn't really make her feel better. She knew he wasn't really there with her. In fact, she sensed he wasn't close at all. She knew he was able to use spells to create illusions, but an illusion of safety wasn't what she needed.Haden planned to use a spell to hide the dead body from her, but he needed to take her focus off it or it wouldn't work. *Listen to me, little love. I want you to close your eyes and take a breath.*

His voice was only a whisper, but it was a powerful command that forced her eyes to close, allowing her to escape the grisly sight. But dreading the thought of inhaling the stench of death, she struggled against the command to breathe. Panicking, she started to choke.

Please, Caylee, do not panic. Her fear pierced his heart so deeply that it was making him insane. He was moving faster than ever before, faster than he ever thought possible, but it wasn't fast enough.

The air surrounding you is pure. Just breathe, little love. I'm so very close to you now. But not nearly close enough. Driven by ancient, savage instincts to protect her at any cost, he wouldn't be close enough until he destroyed the vampire and she was safe in his arms.

Believing Haden didn't understand, Caylee continued to panic. The air wasn't pure. The stench of decayed flesh was so strong she could taste it. Stomach rolling, mouthwatering, she struggled to hold her breath.

Breathe.

His voice was a whisper, but it was so powerful there was no fighting his command this time. She took a deep breath, filling her lungs with his familiar scent. And just like that, defying the physical distance between them, she felt his strong arms holding her, protecting her.

That's it, little love—just keep breathing.

Knowing he was so close was comforting until she realized his voice was way too calm considering the situation. He couldn't fool her. She wasn't stupid. She knew he was mad. She'd ditched him to teach him a lesson in manners. Sneaking out the backdoor, she'd left him sitting in his car in front of her best friend's clothing boutique. It seemed like such a great idea at the time. Frowning, she bit her lower lip. It didn't seem like such a great idea now. She didn't want him to find her. Putting him in his place, challenging his self-proclaimed dictatorship over her every move was a great stress reliever and a distraction from what she really wanted to do to him. But she'd never pushed him this far before.

She considered trying to hide from him. She was a strong woman. She didn't need him. She could pull herself together and get out of the mess on her own. *If it makes you feel better, feel free to try to hide, but it isn't happening.* She looked down at her foot and rolled her eyes. He was right. She wasn't going anywhere. She looked over at the woman's remains, but there was a barrier hiding it. Still, she knew what was behind the wall of strange black and silver flames. She wouldn't even try to hide. Regardless of his mood, she didn't want to be alone any longer.

* * *

Lured by Caylee's mouth-watering scent, Paul was backtracking, returning to where he'd left the body of his last female victim. Cursed for all of eternity, he would never experience the peace of true contentment. His body would always crave more, need more, demand more. He was a vampire, a monstrous creature, a loveless, soulless, living corpse suffering the agony of a perpetual thirst for human blood.

Recalling his previous killing, knowing he would soon kill again, gave Paul the most perverse joy any being would ever experience. Groaning aloud, he clutched his chest, taking great pleasure in the fact that the blood of his last victim sustained his corrupt heart. Oh yes, nothing was more magnificent than the ecstasy of ripping a screaming woman's flesh to shreds and consuming every last savory drop of her blood. Lifting his head, he breathed deeply through his nostrils, inhaling the scent of his new quarry. It wouldn't be long. She was less than a mile away. Soon, he would taste the sweet, exhilarating fear in her blood.

Hearing Haden and feeling a surge of power, Paul stopped. There was no missing the fact that a demon was on the move. Closing his eyes, he inhaled deeply through his nostrils. Immediately recognizing Haden's scent, Paul opened his eyes. He'd gone to great lengths to avoid the demon for days. Paul smiled. It didn't matter. Thanks to his supply of ancient demonic powers and abilities, Paul was confident he was considerably stronger than most vampires and able to hold his own in any fight against any demon. Besides, Haden was moving away from the area, and he was nowhere near the woman. There would likely be no need to fight. He would have more than enough time to drain her blood and leave the area long before the demon was able to interfere.

Paul was about to attack Caylee, but he hesitated. Lifting his face, he studied the stormy sky. Something was off-kilter. Haden seemed to be moving away quickly. Too quickly. It was as if the demon didn't know a vampire was in the area. It was a trick. Perhaps it was a trap. Haden was an ancient. There was no way he'd overlooked the fact that a vampire was in the area hunting. Demons never allowed vampires to hunt in peace. Cloaking his presence from Haden, a feat very few of his kind could perform, Paul waited to see what his enemy was really doing.

~ *Two* ~

THE WIND PICKED up, pushing through the treetops, causing the branches to sway and a flurry of pine needles to fall down all around. The air electrified, causing her skin to tingle. Rolling her eyes, she wasn't surprised at the loud *swoosh* behind her and didn't turn to look. She knew it was him.

"Damn it, Caylee, what the hell are you doing out here?" Pulling her upright, his strong arms locked her body against his. With a gesture, he freed her foot from the tangle of roots.

Lifting her head, she looked up into his black, unblinking gaze. Even the whites of his normally dark blue eyes were black with flecks of silver. It was a startling sight. She would never get used to it. She tried to pull away from him, but he didn't allow it; in fact, he wrapped his arms around her, hugging her so close she could feel this heart thumping.

"What do you think you're doing, Haden?" He was an enormous man, and she could feel his frustration and his anger. She didn't like feeling so small and defenseless in his arms, feeling crushed. *Though I shouldn't have provoked him*, she admitted to herself. Any fool could see he was a dangerous man to cross. She struggled to pull away from him, but he didn't budge an inch. "Let go of me!" She squirmed in vain, using her palms to push at his heavily muscled chest.

She knew he was attempting to soothe her fear as he gently caressed the nape of her neck. "Why are you afraid of me? What have I done to make you believe the worst of me?"

"Please, Haden, just let go of me," she pleaded. "I can't breathe."

"You're breathing just fine." There was a long moment of silence. "I told you to stay out of the forest unless I was with you," he whispered between clenched teeth. "You agreed."

"I never agreed to anything, Haden." She lifted her chin and defiantly meet his gaze. "I didn't argue with you because I chose to ignore the fact that you were giving me another order. To be completely honest, your attempts to order me around are annoying."

That brought his eyebrow up. Claiming he wasn't mad wasn't a lie. He was quite furious. She definitely possessed a talent for provoking the hell out of him. "Really?" Obviously, she'd forgotten about stumbling across a murder scene because she hadn't listened to him.

"Yes, it is. No one likes to hang out with an arrogant jerk, Haden."

"Stop." He clenched his jaw, and a low growl of frustration rumbled in his throat.

"No. I won't. And, did you just growl at me?" She rolled her eyes. "Stop acting like an animal. I mean, get over it. So what if I dared to defy you? Big deal. Who really cares? You might think you're superior to everyone else, but you're not God." Biting her lower lip, she paused. "I have every right to make my own decision. I'm a grown woman. I have every right to take any risk I want to take."

For a moment, he stood there in silence, staring down at her. The fact that she didn't value her life broke his heart. Convinced the vampire wasn't nearby, believing it had retreated, he released her—not because he wanted to, but because she wanted him to. "I will never be strong enough to stand back and allow you to put yourself in danger. You're more than just important to me, Caylee. You are all that matters to me." He was a wreck. He needed to hold her more than he needed to breathe, but he would always put her needs and wants above his. "Time will heal your heart and soul. Eventually, the pain of the past won't be so great."

She shook her head. She didn't want to talk about the past. She didn't want to even think about it. Not with him. Not with anyone. "I don't want to argue with you. I won't. If you want to argue, go and stand in front of a mirror and do it."

She remembered where they were, and what she'd seen. "We need to do something for her. Can you help her?"

"I'm sorry. There's nothing I can do for her. She's dead."

"You didn't even look at her. You don't know she's dead," she whispered, despite knowing he was right. Her head was a big, jumbled-up mess. She should've felt better when he let go of her, but she didn't. She wanted him to let go of her, right? If so, why did she feel so miserable and so cold? "How could anyone be so cruel?" Hot tears streaming down her face, she stared up at him. "Oh Haden." Hands trembling, she wiped the tears from her cheeks. "She's so young."

He felt Caylee's agony churning in the pit of his stomach. A small part of him wanted to comprehend her empathy, but compassion for a stranger was foreign to his nature. He quickly shrugged it off. The woman didn't matter. Caylee was all that mattered to him. Needing the physical contact with her, he lightly placed his hand on the center of her back, but as expected, she flinched and moved away.

Feeling foolish, she held her breath, a blush rising from her neck to her cheeks. He was only trying to comfort her. He was her friend. He wasn't her lover. He wasn't asking her to get naked and have hot, passionate sex with him. She was the one with sex on the brain. And she didn't just think about having sex with him. Lately, her body ached for it, demanded it. Her hormones were spiraling out of control.

It might help if she could convince her eyes to ignore him. She glared at him. It was his fault. It was a sin to walk around looking like him. Just looking at him made her wet. How many hours did he spend at the gym sculpting his body? Way too many. Smiling, she nodded. Yep. Her naughty sex thoughts were entirely his fault. She was an innocent victim. More often than not, when her eyes wandered over him, she forgot the size and contours of his huge, muscular frame terrified the hell out of her. What woman wouldn't want to experience wild, hot sex with man like him? But it wasn't possible for her. She hated to be touched by anyone. A simple handshake was enough to send her into a full-blown panic attack. He was merely a dark fantasy. A sinful temptation. Mysterious. Powerful. Strange. He was the hottest, sexiest man she'd ever seen. But he was definitely strange. Besides, he was gay.

He shook his head. He refused to acknowledge the fact that she thought he was gay. Soon, very soon, he planned to prove to her he wasn't. But he wasn't all that strange, was he? Tilting his head to the side, he smiled, his gaze locked onto hers. It didn't matter if she believed he was strange. "You think I'm the hottest, sexiest man you've ever seen." It was great to know. It totally outweighed the fact that she might view some of his behavior as strange. Clearly, she was wrong—he wasn't strange at all.

She cursed beneath her breath. "I can't believe you were doing it again. And you didn't even have the decency to warn me." Looking quite fierce, she took a step toward him. "Stay out of my head!" Clenching her fists, she glared up at him. "And stop grinning at me like that!" A noise, a rustle in a nearby bush, startled her. Moving closer to him, she grabbed his shirtsleeve.

"It was only a bird." He looked down at her hand clenching the fabric of his shirt. It was so much more than her touching him. "You're safe with me." It was her trusting him to protect her.

It was an extremely delicate situation, and he was the furthest thing from delicate. Every single cell in his body yearned to react to her touch, to dominate and to possess her body and soul, but he couldn't. It would cause her to withdraw. She was touching him, she was in control, and that was the way she needed it to remain. Reining in his body's fierce need for her, not an easy feat by any means at all, he gathered enough strength to defeat his overwhelming need to stake his claim on her.

He looked down at the woman's corpse. If he hadn't realized in time that Caylee had deceived him, she too would've suffered a horrific death. Keeping her mortal was frightening as hell. Caylee was just as fragile as the dead woman. She was just as vulnerable to death. He couldn't take her last mortal breath and give her the breath of immortality unless she believed in his love for her. She needed to have complete faith, blind faith in his love for her. He couldn't warn her. He couldn't prepare her for it. He could only do it and hope for the best.

Many of his kind, if they knew anything concerning her violent past, would instruct him to walk away from her. They would argue her heart and soul could never be strong enough to believe in the unconditional love that would enable her to receive immortality from him. The immortality of his kind was only bestowed upon the strongest of the strong. To receive it she needed to endure a brutal and frightening ritual, but when he performed it she would die if she feared him too much to return to her body and receive his breath. He wouldn't do it until he was certain she knew what she meant to him. Proving his love and gaining her trust was the only way he could ensure that they would be free to be together for eternity.

For as long as she was still mortal, he simply needed to keep her alive. It should've been an easy task for a demon able to control the most violent forces of nature with a thought, but it wasn't. He could command the heavens and the earth to do his will, but he couldn't command her to believe in him. While he was fully aware of the fact that he would be in serious trouble when she realized how deeply he loved her, more than anything, he longed for the day to come.

Caylee stared up at him. "Haden." He turned his head, meeting her gaze, his attention focused solely on her. "I'm sorry."

"No." He frowned. "Don't be sorry. None of this is your fault."

"When you told me it was too dangerous to come out here, I overreacted. I was being stupid. You were only looking out for me. You've been such a good friend to me. I should've listened to you." She wrapped her arms around his waist and rested her forehead on his chest. "I should've trusted you."

He was so afraid he would do something to frighten her. "It's okay." Taking a breath, he held it, standing perfectly still. It was the first time she'd ever held him. He didn't want the moment to end.

She hugged him tighter, her body trembling against his. "Please, don't hate me for being so stupid."

Wrapping his arms around her slender body, he slowly pulled her closer, so grateful she didn't resist. Releasing his breath in a long sigh, he leaned down to tuck her head beneath his chin. "I could never hate you." Savoring the heat, the nearness of her body, he closed his eyes and breathed in her sweet scent, allowing it to fill his lungs. "And you're not stupid." His body was raging. "But I will say that you're stubborn as hell."

With each passing second he was more aroused by the sensation of her soft, feminine curves pressed so snugly against his hard, muscular frame. He needed to move away from her, but he couldn't. He remained silent, rocking her gently, knowing one moment of weakness would cause her to find fear instead of refuge in his arms.

Lightning whipped through him, heating his blood, sizzling over his flesh. Every muscle tightly bunching, he fought to keep his traitorous flesh from responding to the feeling of her breasts pressed so snugly against his body, but he lost the battle in a matter of seconds. There was absolutely no hiding the hot rush of desire that shot straight to his groin.

Muttering undecipherable curses, he pushed her away and took a step back, wanting to spare her, knowing the evidence of his body's need for hers would scare the hell out of her.

Blinking back tears, she looked up at him, nervously nibbling her lower lip. How could she be so stupid? "I'm so sorry." And she most certainly was. What was she thinking? Feeling like an absolute idiot, she lowered her head. Why had she expected him to want to hold her as a lover?

He reached out to gently lift her chin, forcing her to meet his gaze. "It's not what you think, little love." He bent down so his mouth was so very close to hers.

His mouth was way too close to hers. "I'm sorry," she whispered. She felt the heat of his breath on her lips. Her heart raced wildly. She knew she should back away from him, but she unintentionally moved a little closer, her body seeking the warmth of his.

"There's no reason for you to be sorry." They stood brow-to-brow, his fierce gaze locked onto hers. Something wickedly exquisite, like tiny flames, danced over her flesh and heightened her body's sexual awareness of his when his lips brushed across hers.

"We need to do something. We can't leave her here, Haden." Her voice was a breathless, husky whisper. "What should we do?" Why did her voice sound so funny?

A shiver ran from her toes, up her spine, and to the top of her head. Her flesh tingled. What was wrong with her? That was a silly question. She knew it was her body coming to life with desire. She tried, but it was impossible to ignore the way her most intimate places were aching, throbbing, crying out with the most agonizing need for him. She had serious issues. How could she be thinking about sex when he looked so mad?

"This is not me looking mad, little love." His voice was deeper, raspier than usual. "This is me looking frustrated." It was a soft growl, laced with lust, vibrating over every inch of her flesh. "Extremely frustrated."

"Why?" Grinning shyly, biting her lower lip, she stared up at him.

Having his mind so deeply merged with hers, feeling her desire, certainly wasn't making it easy to keep from ripping her skimpy jogging outfit off her body and showing her what he thought they should do. It was such a simple act, but it was so erotic. Oh damn, how he ached to feel her tiny white teeth nibbling his flesh. Hell, he wouldn't mind if she bit him hard. As he focused on her mouth, his heart stuttered as if to stop; then its pace quickened. Reaching around her waist, dragging her to him, and pressing her body against his, he bent his head to hers.

"You're starting to freak me out." Taking a breath and holding it, she blinked up at him.

"Good." He moved slowly, so very, very slowly, his gaze locked onto hers.

"Haden?" With his mind so deeply merged with hers, he knew she was excited and scared all at the same time, but he also knew she was most certainly, unquestionably more excited than scared. A sudden and drastic change in the atmosphere captured his attention. Taking her with him, Haden spun around and went completely still, protectively holding her at his side. Expanding his mind, he studied the area. At least three vampires and a number of ghouls surrounded them. Paul, the vampire responsible for most of the recent killings in the area, was considerably closer than the other two. Haden also felt the energy of his cousin, Zack Savage, moving quickly in their direction. Zack was a rogue of sorts, hotheaded and rebellious, but he was a capable and trusted warrior when push came to shove.

Under the shelter of his arm, lifting her face, Caylee quietly studied Haden. She didn't know what was wrong, but she knew he perceived a threat. He didn't need to explain it. She trusted his judgment. For now, she didn't dare distract him by pulling away. Under the shelter of his arm was right where she wanted to be. And while he was distracted, she could stop freaking out over the thought of him kissing her.

Haden took her hand and placed the twenty-dollar bill in it. "I'm not gay. And I don't really think it's a reason for you to freak out, but if being kissed by me is going to freak you out, I wouldn't stop freaking out just yet. The night is far from over, little love, and I intend to kiss you before it is."

Caylee opened her mouth to respond, but she settled for yanking her hand out of his and glaring up at him. For the time being she wouldn't scold him for invading her privacy or deny making the bet with Mia.

Lifting his head, Haden took a deep breath through his nostrils. The vampire's rancid odor, far worse than the corpse at his feet, filled his lungs. He, one of the most powerful demons in existence, had nearly missed the fact that the creature was hunting him. Haden was hiding the fact that he was a demon, pretending to be human, in hopes of luring the undead close enough to destroy it, but it never should've been able to sneak up on him. "We need to hurry." He reached for her hand again. "I'll take you home."

Moving too fast, he startled her. "What do you think you're doing?" She smacked his hand away. "I'm not a child. I'm not going anywhere with you right now." She stared up at him. "We can't leave her here."

Struggling to maintain some semblance of control, he lowered his brow, his muscles tensing to the point of pain. Miraculously, he resisted the urge to grab her and shake her. With a thought, he removed the veil separating her from the woman's remains. "Look at her, Caylee. Take a good, long look at her. It could've been you." The instant he said the words and exposed her to the woman's gruesome remains a tiny, weak part of him wanted to take them back, but he wouldn't. And damn her for making him feel so weak.

Taking a step back, she jammed her fist against her mouth, but she didn't come close to muffling her gut-wrenching sob. "That was an incredibly terrible thing to say to me, Haden. I apologized. I told you I was wrong." Trembling, she stared up at him, tears streaming down her face. "You're a ... you're just so ..." She stared up at him, her eyes mirroring the pain he placed in her heart.

"You need to understand the danger you placed yourself in today," he whispered, drastically gentling his expression and voice, secretly hoping it would be enough to stop her tears. He wouldn't apologize for being right. It could've been her. Damn it, why the hell was she still crying?

"Please, don't cry, little love." Slowly, he reached out to wipe away the tears that were so thoroughly kicking his ass. "I'm sorry." Damn her. Damn him. What the hell was he doing? Why was he apologizing when he was right? He held out his hand for her. "I'll make sure the authorities know where to find her."

At that precise moment, she heard howls and strange, inhuman screams in the distance. She sensed something different in the air. It was something evil. Bloodthirsty. Sadistic. And it was close. Her blood pressure skyrocketed; her mouth went dry. It was very close. They were being hunted. She didn't know how she knew it, but it didn't matter—she knew it. Whatever had killed the woman was coming for them.

"We need to go now." Refusing to give her a chance to argue, he took her hand and walked, pulling her along. He walked too quickly, causing her to trip over her own feet. In an instant, without missing a step, his powerful arms swept around her and scooped her up. Cradling her against his chest, he continued to walk.

Irritated, she muttered a few shocking curses and particularly brutal threats beneath her breath. She could walk. Being bigger and stronger didn't give him the right to manhandle her. "What are you doing?" She wiggled, attempting to force him to put her down, but he didn't even seem to notice. He just kept walking, and she just kept getting madder. "Put me down, Haden. I can walk on my own."

"Yes," he said, looking down at her, "but not fast enough for my liking." His eyes gave no hint of humor, but there was no hiding it in his voice. She was mad as hell.

"Come on, Haden. I'm too heavy. Put me down." She wiggled. Of course she knew how ridiculous she sounded. He didn't have any problem carrying her. He was a good foot taller than her, and he was built like a ... well, he was a very solid, well built man. And she wasn't going to elaborate on any other thought concerning his body. He was probably mucking around in her head, and his ego was already way too overly inflated. "You'll hurt your back." She couldn't resist saying it. Why? She wasn't sure. But she also couldn't resist giggling over it. But then, remembering she was mad because he was manhandling her, she doubled her fist and punched his shoulder. "Put me down!"

Amused, he stopped and stared down at her, laughter welling up, but he managed to hold it back. Lips curved down, her frown was so comically, obviously exaggerated as she met his gaze. "I'm starting to get the idea you're angry, little love."

His heart was so full of joy he was certain it would burst. "I can't believe you hit me." Somewhere along the line she'd missed the fact that his powerful presence demanded absolute respect. "I'm assuming it was supposed to hurt." He'd never known love. He'd never wanted to fall in love. Love was a funny thing, a wonderful thing, but a funny thing nonetheless. "If I tell you it hurt like hell, will you smile for me?"

"Nope. No way. But I will hit you again, and I will make sure it hurts if you don't put me down," she vowed, finding it very difficult to keep a frown on her face.

"Well then," he said as he started walking, "I'm most definitely not putting you down any time soon."

A shiver raced through her body. Her head was spinning. He wasn't gay. His voice was pure, dark seduction. A sensuous, erotic growl. Lust made it aggressive, but love made it gentle. It vibrated over her flesh like a hot, sinful caress, touching her, heating her everywhere at once. He wasn't gay. Before she could respond, Haden stopped.

"Don't be afraid," he whispered. "I need you to stay very still. The creature responsible for killing the woman is returning. No matter what happens, no arguments, you must do whatever I tell you to do."

Staring up at Haden, she opened her mouth, but nothing came out. He wasn't looking at her. His gaze was searching for something. She felt a rumble deep beneath the ground, but somehow it didn't bother her. Why would it? The ground moved when he was around. Why did he use the word *creature*? That's what bothered her. Was it a bear? A mountain lion? A wolf? Maybe she should jump out of his arms and climb a tree. Nah. She wasn't a very talented tree climber. Besides, she was definitely better off staying as close to him as possible.

~ *Three* ~

PAUL WAS A bit confused. Where was the demon? He was an expert hunter. His predator instincts were very well developed. Something was telling him to back off, but his thirst for human blood was too great to yield to the voice of caution. Believing Haden was human, Paul approached with the intent to kill him and then find woman he'd been tracking. "Come closer to me." Moving forward slowly, arms outstretched, he attempted to use his mind to control Haden. "Where's the woman?"

"There is no woman here," Haden replied.

Paul knew something was off. The man standing before him appeared to be an average human, but he didn't react like one. Paul was attempting to fill the man's head with fear, but he was showing no sign of distress. There was no fear in the man. Absolutely none. Attempting to figure out what was going on, Paul took a step closer. "You can't hide her from me."

Wondering how Haden was hiding her, Caylee turned her head to get a look at the other man. He had long black hair and glowing yellow eyes. He was downright creepy looking. He was too slender for his height, and his flesh was eerily pale.

She could easily see him. He was standing no more than twenty feet away. Why couldn't he see her? Not that she was complaining. The man was dangerous; hatred and violence flowed from him in dark waves.

Caylee suddenly realized her gaze was locked onto the other man's eyes. She tried to close her eyes, but she couldn't even blink. A strange, faint buzzing sound echoed in her head. She felt dizzy and nauseous. Her head was in a thick, murky fog. She felt drawn to the stranger, wanting to get close to him, needing to touch him.

There's no reason to worry. You're safe with me, little love. I'm hiding your presence, but he knows you're nearby. He was tracking you before I got to you. He's confused because he can't figure out what I am or where you are. He's using a compulsion to draw you to him. I will not allow him to succeed.

Haden had hoped to avoid using his power until Zack arrived, wanting to allow the other vampires to get close enough so he could destroy them too. However, it appeared the vampire was quite powerful, so he decided to make what he was clear. With any luck, it would flee rather than die. Then, after Haden took Caylee to safety, he would pursue and destroy the vampire.

Black flames swirling around him, Haden exposed his true identity and created the image with which he took an aggressive step forward. "What do you want with me, foul one?" A strong wind rose from out of nowhere. Stirred by Haden's rage, dark clouds streaked with lightning and billowed in the sky, accompanied by a constant roar of thunder.

Zack connected with Haden. *You're getting better at camouflaging your energy. I thought you were human. I didn't know you were out here at all. I'm close. Joseph is also headed your way. Your woman won't be forced to witness the vampire's destruction as long as you are able hold him back until we get there.*

There was no mistaking the surge of demonic energy in the atmosphere. Paul nervously glanced around. "Why did you hide from me? Why are you playing games with me?"

Haden laughed aloud. "Consider it to be a learning experience. Before killing you, I decided it would be enlightening to know what it felt like to be weak. Of course it didn't work. How could a demon as powerful as I know what weakness feels like? You've gone to great lengths to hide from me these past few weeks." His great power causing the ground to rumble deep below the earth, Haden created the image of his wings extending as he took another step toward Paul.

Looking around warily, Paul used his mind to call his ghouls to his aid. Then, he met Haden's cold, black gaze. He'd never actually encountered Haden face to face. He decided to test him. It was a dangerous situation, but he wasn't the type to give up easily. "I don't hide from anyone," Paul lied. Vampires always hid from and avoided direct contact with demons. They were natural enemies, as vampires had killed humans and demons have protected humans since the beginning of time. "And, Demon, understand you're going to die for interfering with my meal. The woman you're hiding belongs to me. You can't protect her. One way or another, I will eventually take her from you, and I will kill her."

Haden's expression remained emotionless. "You can try to take her." The deep, ominous sound of his voice echoed. "But you will fail. Regardless, you will die tonight."

Avoiding the fierce bite of Haden's black flames, Paul took a few steps back. "I will succeed." Paul knew he should flee, but curiosity and hunger kept him there. The fact that Haden hadn't already attacked him was odd. The demon was merely posturing, possibly stalling. But for what? Paul knew the woman he was tracking was still close by. He could feel subtle vibrations of her fear. And, although it was faint, he could still smell her sweet, tantalizing scent.

Haden laughed aloud again. The sound of it was even more menacing and ferocious than before. "The only thing you will achieve this evening is your destruction."

Pushed by powerful gusts of wind, horizontal rain fell heavily, saturating everything. Lightning crisscrossed the sky.

Be careful, Haden—it's true. He has the aid of a powerful demon. I've dealt with this one on several occasions. He's dangerous. He has no common sense, and he possesses more strength and power than most of his kind. Zack was using nature to make it very clear he was on his way, attempting to aid Haden by convincing the vampire to back off.

What demon? Haden asked.

I will explain as soon as I'm with you. Keep your focus on Paul.

Haden had never run away from a fight, but he started to consider taking Caylee through time and space to get her out of danger.

No! Zack warned. *Don't do it. There's a massive web of ancient demonic spells surrounding the entire area. They're deadly. She'll be destroyed if you attempt to take her through them.*

Burying her face against Haden's shoulder, Caylee held her breath. She really hoped Haden wasn't planning to fight with her in his arms. Lightning flashed everywhere, and deafening thunder echoed all around. If it weren't for the lightning, the idea of climbing a tree would be much more appealing than waiting for them to fight. She was shivering so uncontrollably her teeth were chattering. She was so afraid, so cold.

Just breathe, little love. There'll be no reason for you to climb a tree. I'm with you. I'm able to protect you. There's nothing to fear. I won't allow him to touch you.

The instant she heard Haden's voice in her head, peace enveloped her. It filled her with soothing warmth. She breathed easier, and her teeth stopped chattering.

Besides, Haden continued, *I won't need to fight him at all. We're not alone. Two friends are coming to help us. When they get here we will leave.*

Well, knowing they weren't totally alone helped. A little, but it helped.

Smiling, Paul tilted his head to the side. "You used your woman to draw me out? Normally using a female for bait is a little too risky for a demon's liking. And why is your mate still mortal?"

At that, Caylee glared up at Haden, totally missing the mate thing. He'd better not be using her for bait. She would definitely have a thing or two to say about that. But whether or not he was using her as bait, she wouldn't argue with him at that moment or insist he put her down. She wasn't an idiot. She was the safest person on the face of the earth as long as she was in his arms. Besides, there was no way he was using her as bait; he was way too much of an overbearing, know-it-all control freak to even consider allowing her to do anything even remotely dangerous.

Your opinion of me is very unflattering, little love. I'm not an overbearing control freak. I'm just a tad bit overly protective of you.

Whatever. She rolled her eyes. *Just stop mucking around in my head.*

Don't be alarmed. Our friends are about to show up.

"This is a very peculiar situation, is it not?" Paul smiled.

"Or else you're still as stupid as you look, and I used them both to bait you," a deep, booming voice echoed as a coppery mist appeared in front of Paul. When Haden's friends stepped out of the mist, Caylee's breath caught in her throat. She wanted to look away, but she couldn't stop staring at the men. She felt waves of enormous dark power flowing from them. Just like Haden they were well over six feet tall, with perfectly sculpted, muscular bodies. They were beautiful. They had the same strong, godlike facial features as Haden. They were perfect. Too perfect. They reminded her of ancient warriors.

Paul took a step back. "Why are you here?"

"What, you didn't miss me?" One of Haden's friends laughed aloud, seemingly mocking the vampire's startled reaction. "Don't feel bad. The feeling is mutual. I really don't like you very much at all. To be honest, running into you and seeing your face again and again has become an intolerable form of suffering I'm no longer willing to endure. I simply bore too easily to continue this game any longer. And please don't bother begging. It's pathetic. It turns my stomach. I won't tolerate it this time. It's over. You need to just come to terms with the fact that you're going to have to die today."

Hissing, the man that had threatened to kill her took another step back. Caylee almost laughed. She clearly saw by the look on his face that he was shocked and quite scared. She couldn't blame him. Haden and his friends looked extremely intimidating. Taking one on would be risky endeavor; taking three on would be just plain insane. It would be suicide. He fled so quickly that she didn't actually see him leave. One second he was there, and next he was gone.

One of Haden's friends disappeared too. His other friend stared at her. And she didn't like the way he was looking at her. She felt threatened.

What's wrong with you, Haden? Your woman is still mortal. You aren't handling her properly. She is weak. Vulnerable to death. You know what fear does to our kind. It's been a year since you found her again. Destiny will never bend to honor your weakness. You need to walk away from her or attempt to give her immortality now. She will make it, or she will not. You cannot keep putting it off. It's too dangerous. Besides, you need to get back to what's important. The days are far darker than ever before. Evil no longer hides in the darkest shadows of the night; it thrives even in the light of day, destroying the innocent we're expected to protect. We need you.

Caylee studied Haden's face. She felt his hostility toward the other man but saw no sign of it in his eyes. She certainly didn't want to be around if their dispute turned into physical violence. Zack was just as big and intimidating as Haden. Knowing they were secretly communicating, she decided to remain silent rather than interrupt, hoping they would work out whatever dispute was between them with words.

She didn't hear it, but she felt vibrations of a growl against Haden's chest. *Do not tell me how to take care of my mate,*

Zack. I will wait until I am absolutely positive she will survive it. She needs my undivided attention right now. She's all that matters to me. I've wasted far too many lifetimes protecting humans from their hatred and greed. I've come to the conclusion none of our efforts have truly mattered. Humans are too ignorant to benefit from our greater wisdom. They will continue to destroy each other no matter what we do or don't do.

You know better, Haden. Do you no longer remember the others you've counseled in this matter? Shaking his head, the other man's lips curved upward in a humorless smile. *In the span of just one short year, a woman you obviously believe is too weak to ever receive the immortality of our kind and to stand by your side as your mate for eternity has managed to ruin you.*

Enough! Another low, threatening growl vibrated through Haden's chest. But this time she heard it. *You will not speak poorly about my mate. Tell me about the demon that's helping the vampire.*

Obviously irritated, the other man glared at her for a moment. She was starting to get the feeling he was mad at her. To her relief, he rubbed the bridge of his nose and shifted his gaze to Haden. *You've been out of the loop for too long, Haden. The vampires in this area are extremely dangerous. They're working together with a group of female humans led by Mary Tate.*

That's odd. Vampires don't normally play well with humans. And don't look at her again. You're scaring her.

She should be scared. You've lost your fucking mind, and it's going to get her killed. Zack shrugged. *With Demetri guarding the bitch, the vampires have no other choice than to play nice with her. There's no way in hell any vampire would dare to challenge a demon as old and as powerful as Demetri. They act as if they're her pets.*

Haden took a deep breath. *I didn't realize Demetri was still with her. Why would he give any vampire his power?*

The only theory that makes any sense is that the combination of the magic and poison Mary uses on Demetri ensures his loyalty to her no matter what. He glanced at Caylee and then looked directly into Haden's eyes. *If his true mate ever appears he will kill her to please Mary. He will have no other choice. Mary will force him to do it. She seeks immortality above all else. She knows he won't ever be able to give it to her unless he takes the life of his true mate. It seems he will be lost to us forever. There's little to no hope for him. Mary's magic grows more powerful every day.*

There has to be more to it. Haden shook his head. *It doesn't make sense. Demetri is too powerful, too old to be held captive by a human's magic or poison. And he's far too honorable to side with the vampires. There's something else motivating him. Something we can't see.*

Zack shook his head. "Just get her away from here before more bloodsuckers catch her scent. Paul isn't far away. He won't give up. I will search for him and hunt the others that are nearby." He turned to walk away.

"Go after the others. I will take care of Paul."

Caylee blinked up at Haden. "Catch my scent?" Heart pounding, she wrapped her arms tighter around his neck, desperately clinging to him, praying he didn't put her down. "What does he mean?"

"There's no reason for you to worry about it." Haden placed a protective barrier around them an instant before they were surrounded by a pack of hideous, half-dead-looking pack of dogs.

She stiffened. "What are they?" They were so gruesome, snarling and growling, making strange cackling noises.

Despite Caylee's best effort to cling to him, he set her down on her feet. Heart racing, she started to panic. From behind he wrapped his arms around her waist, encouraging her to lean her back against his body. She didn't resist, but her body was as stiff.

"Relax, little love," he whispered in her ear. "They're nothing. They can't hurt you. They can't touch you." He raised her hands to the heavens and pulled the power of nature to them.

Exhilarating currents of raw energy surged through her body. She'd never experienced anything like it. Tilting her head back, she watched in awe as lightning swirled in a massive funnel above them. There were so many bright colors clashing together, exploding. Violent, turbulent power surrounded her, filled her. Her heart raced frantically. The power was too intense. It was too much. It was deadly.

He bent his head to kiss her cheek. "Don't be afraid. What you're feeling, what you're seeing is a part of me. No part of me could ever hurt you." The strange funnel of colorful lightning moved closer, completely surrounding them. Then, waves of something fiery and wild enveloped them.

* * *

Zack turned to watch. He was alone, always and forever alone. He chose to be alone. Having a woman would only bring him frustration and sorrow, but watching Haden and Caylee at that moment created a memory he wouldn't soon forget. Haden was a fool in love. He was a moron. He was way too old to be showing off like a teenage boy. Shaking his head, Zack cursed aloud. He never thought Haden would ever fall victim to love. A particularly sharp, painful stab of envy pierced his heart, but he would rather die than ever admit to feeling it.

Sighing aloud, he turned to walk away. Caught off guard by a blinding flash, Zack stumbled. "What the fuck are you doing, Joseph? Where's the vampire?"

"He got away. And sorry. I couldn't resist." Saving the picture on his phone, Joseph laughed aloud. "This sweet, sappy look on your face is priceless." He sent the picture to Zack's profile. "It makes you look all cute and huggable." He laughed again. "Check it out." He tilted the phone to show Zack. "Jacob likes it. Oh wow, take a look," he commented.

Squinting, Joseph read aloud, "Great profile picture, lover boy!"

"You're an asshole, Joseph," Zack growled between clenched teeth. "Put the fucking phone away." He turned and walked away.

"Just a minute. Oh, damn, Zack, you're a popular guy. There're already six … no, eight more likes and five more comments."

Zack turned suddenly. "I told you to put the fucking phone away!" He ripped the phone out of Joseph's hand, crushed it in his fist, and threw it. The pieces instantly burst into flames and turned to ashes.

"You dumb son of a bitch. Your temper tantrums really suck. And for your information, nobody likes to be around you. Nobody. I would recommend a good therapist to you, but you're seriously, irreversibly screwed up beyond any fucking hope," Joseph said.

"Agreed," Zack growled. "Now shut the hell up. We have vampires to kill. We can't allow any of them to get away. I think they have his woman's scent. What the hell is Haden's problem? I can't believe she's still mortal." He started to walk away but stopped and turned to face Joseph. "And if you know what's good for you, you'll stop changing my fucking status and posting profile pictures."

* * *

A burst of energy rushed past Caylee. Then, bolt after bolt of bluish white lightning arced across the sky, lighting the meadow and casting shadows in the trees surrounding it. The sound of thunder was so loud it caused the ground to shake. She covered her ears. She would've fallen to her knees if Haden hadn't been standing behind her, holding her in his strong arms and anchoring her against his solid body. She blinked to focus on a pitch-black cloud of smoke forming several feet in front of her. She wanted to run, but sensing she was about to see something spectacular, she remained still, waiting to see what would happen next.

Holding her breath, she watched as the smoke dissipated and a huge, shadowy image appeared. Squinting, she struggled to make sense of what she was seeing. It was an animal. A very large animal.

A colorful series of explosions, similar to fireworks, started at the top of the animal's head and continued all the way to the tip of its tail until brilliant shades of red, gold, silver, and purple shimmering streaks illuminated what appeared to be a black dragon.

Doing the rational thing, she shook her head, rejecting the idea that dragons existed. It was so beautiful. She wanted to move closer. She wanted to touch it. She shook her head. What was she thinking? Yes, it was beautiful, but there was no way she would ever dare get close enough to touch it.

The dragon lifted its head high and roared. It was unlike anything Caylee had ever heard before. It was so deep and loud she actually felt the sound in her belly. It echoed all around, causing the ground to shake violently.

It was shocking, but nothing could have prepared her for what happened next. Her breath caught in her throat as she watched the hideous doglike creatures turn on each other. It was such a terrifying, gruesome sight. Jaws snapping and claws slicing, they attacked each other in a rabid frenzy. It didn't make sense. Why would they attack each other? *I commanded them to destroy each other.* Haden whispered in her mind. And he sounded amused. Rolling her eyes, she frowned. Of course it was his doing. Her gaze shifted to the dragon. She wondered what Haden was planning to do with it.

She wanted to go back to believing there were no such things as dragons, but she couldn't deny what was right in front of her face. She would give anything to hit rewind and start the day over. Appearing almost disinterested, the dragon watched the brutal chaos for a few more minutes, and then, lifting its head high, it roared once more. The creatures, suddenly silent, turned to face the dragon and froze. Eyes wide, Caylee held her breath as flames shot out of the dragon's mouth and reduced the creatures to an unrecognizable pile of smoldering ashes at the dragon's feet. Shaking her head, she took a breath. She now knew the rumors of fire-breathing dragons were not rumors at all.

To Caylee's horror, the dragon turned and fixed its gaze onto hers. It slowly moved toward her. With each step it took the ground rumbled beneath its weight. Stopping directly in front of her, it bowed its massive head reverently at her feet.

Seeking Haden's protection, Caylee took a step back, only to realize he was no longer behind her. He'd left her? Her mouth went completely dry. Her heart actually stopped. How could he just abandon her? She would've screamed, but she couldn't even breathe.

"Breathe, little love. I would never abandon you."

"Huh?" She blinked. Did the dragon just smile at her? She shook her head. Did it just talk to her? She tilted her head to the side, studying its eyes. It didn't make sense. Its eyes were so familiar, so comforting. After a breathless moment of silence, she made the connection.

"Oh, oh my God." She swallowed hard. "Haden?" It had to be an illusion. "No." It was a magic trick of some sort. She'd seen him do many strange, impossible things. She'd seen him appear from out of nowhere and disappear several times. The dragon wasn't real. Hoping to prove it, she reached out to touch it. Her fingers felt warm, hard scales. "It's you."

"Yes." Obviously proud of the havoc it was wreaking in her mind, the dragon grinned at her.

"No." Her head was spinning out of control. "It's not possible." Making a small, whimper-like sound, she bit back a scream. "You're not a dragon." Swaying from side to side, she took a clumsy step back. "How?"

Before she could blink, Haden returned to human form. "It's a secret," he teased, wrapping his arm around her shoulders to hold her steady.

"That's it! I can't take it anymore! Get away from me, Haden!" Hoping to do some real damage, she jabbed her elbow against his ribs as hard as she could.

"Ouch." Hunching over, he grabbed his side, laughing aloud. "You have such nasty temper."

"You're making me crazy." Closing her eyes tightly, she shook her head. "This isn't real. None of this is real. You're not real."

He reached out to her. "Come here."

"No!" Crossing her arms over her chest, she glared at his. "Don't you dare ever touch me again!"

He wrapped his arm around her shoulders. "There's no reason for all the hostility."

"No reason? Are you serious? You should've warned me before you turned into a dragon." She jabbed him again, harder than before. "And for your information, I hate secrets."

"I considered warning you, but then I thought it was one those things you wouldn't believe without seeing." Nuzzling her ear, he whispered, "And I never said I wouldn't share the secret with you." He scooped her up in his arms and started walking. "In fact, there are many things I plan to share with you in the near future."

"I don't want to hear about any of them right now. Go ahead, do what you're most talented at doing. Muck around in head, and you'll discover why I don't want to hear about them."

"I would never want to trespass," he teased.

Her eyes narrowed on him. "Whatever. It doesn't matter anyways. I hate you, Haden." She instantly felt bad. Tilting her head back, she looked up at him. "I don't really hate you. I don't like you very much right now, but I don't hate you. I'm just a little freaked out right now."

"I wasn't worried about it." Looking way too pleased, he smiled down at her. "As long as you think I'm sexy, I'm happy. Sexy is good. It's wonderful. As far as I'm concerned it's a fabulous foundation for you to build your love for me on."

Groaning, she rolled her eyes. "Thank you for booting the stupid out of my head." Closing her eyes, she rested her face on his chest, soothed by the steady, strong rhythm of his heart. "I'm now one hundred percent positive I hate you." She yawned. "I'm tired. I want to go home."

* * *

Haden took Caylee to her uncle's home. He wasn't sure why Emmett bothered him, but he didn't like the man. He figured his bad feelings toward Emmett were related to not liking Caylee's living arrangement. Naturally, Haden wanted her under his roof, in his bed every night, but she wasn't even ready to admit they belonged together. Before leaving her to go hunt for Paul, Haden gave Caylee strict orders to stay out of the forest. Then, doing what any all-powerful demon would do in the same situation, he begged her to obey. Thankfully, with all that had happened, she agreed. And this time, he knew she meant it.

Within an hour, Haden had returned to the crime scene and was following Paul's scent. The vampire was making many mistakes. Haden discovered his trail too quickly, too easily. He was obviously being led into a trap, but it didn't bother him. It certainly didn't intimidate him. A trap was a good thing. It meant he wouldn't be forced to waste any time or energy chasing after the creature to destroy it.

~ *Four* ~

CAYLEE WOKE UP suddenly, struggling to catch her breath as blasts of intense pain beat at her temples. A foul, misty fog hovered over her bed and filled her lungs. Violent, overwhelming fear slammed into her heart, and it raced frantically, pounding in her ears. It was too dark to see anything, but she sensed the presence of something wicked drawing closer, preparing to strike. Thunderous shrieking and howling erupted. She covered her ears to muffle it, but the volume increased. The air rushed in and out of her lungs in horrified gasps.

She gripped her head hard as a dark figure, cruel and wholly evil, moved in her mind. A bone-chilling breeze drifted into the room and swirled all around. For a moment everything was silent. Relief washed over her. It was a bad dream.

Rise and come to me. Paul's voice, resembling a hiss, seemed to come from every direction, but she knew it was coming from inside her mind. *Come to me.*

Increasingly severe bursts of pain jabbed at her skull. The pain was so intense she feared her head was going to explode. She gripped it harder, tangling her fingers in her hair.

Several invisible arms, similar to tentacles, slowly but surely wrapped around and squeezed her body. She struggled to get free, but it was useless. Yanked out of her bed, she was forced out of her room and down the hall. The front door burst open, and she was shoved outside. She tried to stop moving, but her attempt only caused her to stumble. She rubbed her throbbing temples, struggling to rationalize the situation. The volume of the whispering increased, becoming a steady roar, repeating her name over and over again as she continued to walk.

Her heart beat wildly, painfully. She needed to calm down. She needed to focus. If she was going to survive, she needed to figure out what was happening. Taking a deep breath, she held it for a few seconds, focusing on her legs, trying to stop them, but it was no use; her legs continued to move.

The hot, humid air caused her t-shirt to cling to her body, but she shivered uncontrollably. She knew beyond any doubt she was going to die. Heat lightning silently crisscrossed the sky, casting eerie shadows all around. She was unhappy with her life, but she didn't want to die. She feared the unknown waiting for her beyond the grave. Teeth chattering, she continued to walk, struggling to breathe as the stench of death filled her lungs.

Wait. Why hadn't she thought of Haden? Closing her eyes, she reached for him. Merging her mind with his, she instantly, to her horror, saw Haden attacking, raping a woman. She was confused. Their mental link had never been visual. It had always been verbal. Caylee withdrew from him, grief and disgust welling up to the extent she couldn't stop the cry that escaped her throat. She shook her head, attempting to erase the vile image, but it remained so very vivid in her mind. She swallowed hard, her body trembling as she walked to her death.

* * *

While tracking Paul, Haden came across Caylee's scent, immediately detecting the scent of her blood combined with it. A terrible explosion of rage ripped through his body, causing the ground to shift as the deepest, darkest portion of his essence emerged. Black flames swirled around him. From deep within his soul his other half, the dragon, roared.

Merging with her, Haden immediately discovered the images of him raping a woman. He took a deep breath, filling his lungs with the remnants of her lingering scent. For a moment, his dark, icy gaze melted away, replaced by strange, black, iridescent flames as he fully merged with her.

He tried to place a hedge of protection around her, but he failed. The vampire had full control over her. Her mind was severely fragmented, but he quickly, a silent shadow in her mind, sorted through her thoughts and retrieved bits and pieces of information. She was barefoot. The scent of her blood was from scratches on the bottom of her feet. Paul was hiding her location in a maze of confusion in her mind. It would take time for Haden to work his way through it—time, he feared, he didn't have.

* * *

An icy gust of wind blasted Caylee. *Caylee, stop and turn around.* Dark clouds, streaked with blinding flashes of lightning, billowed in the sky. The ground heaved and rumbled. Haden's voice was a whisper, but it held enormous power. *Haden?* She stopped walking; images of him raping the woman replayed in her mind, causing her to go completely still. A wall of black flames formed directly in front of her, and then a thunderous boom echoed all around and the flames disappeared. She knew it was Haden, searching for her, reaching out to her. Part of her wanted to go to him, but when she thought about him raping the woman, every muscle in her body cramped in protest.

You're nothing to him. Come to me now!

A sharp pain pierced Caylee's skull directly between her eyes. Defying Paul's command was impossible. Once more, she continued to walk toward him. The reality she was facing death grew in her. There was no one to help her. The streets were abandoned. She was alone, completely and utterly alone. Haden, her only hope, was with another woman, doing terrible things, brutally raping her.

* * *

Haden's heart was breaking. What was the point? Would she always believe the worst of him? If so, what future would she have if he continued to pursue a life with her?

Listen to me, Caylee—what you saw wasn't real.

She should know the truth. There shouldn't be any doubt in her mind. How deep was her fear? How far would she go to hide from him? Would she actually allow herself to be killed by a vampire because of her fear of the man who loved her more than anything?

Don't allow him to deceive you, little love.

Haden wouldn't allow her to die. He would save her. He would kill the vampire. But then, perhaps it was time to face the fact that letting her go was the most merciful thing he could do for her. He could secretly watch over her and protect her for the rest of her human life. She didn't even need to know he was with her.

Your mind is confused, but your heart knows the truth. You're not alone. Merge with me. Help me find you. I won't allow him to harm you.

* * *

Haden's voice was so calm. It was a comforting embrace. She wanted to believe him, but doubt crept into her mind. She'd seen him attacking a woman, hadn't she? She gripped her head hard, her knuckles turning white. Her temples ached so severely her vision was blurred, and her stomach was rolling. Waves of hopelessness washed over her. She was going to die. She entered a dark alley and stood completely still. She didn't want to die. Not yet. Not like this. She needed to turn around and run away, but her legs wouldn't move.

You don't need to move. You don't need to run. You simply need to trust me to protect you. I won't allow you to die. The pain gets worse when you attempt to resist his compulsion. Stop pulling away from me. You're not strong enough to fight him, but I am. Merge with me. Allow me to protect you.

Trust him? Paul's mocking laughter filled her mind. *He left you alone, knowing I would come for you, knowing you would be helpless, and knowing you would die. And why? He abandoned you so he could be with a more desirable woman.*

Devastated, Caylee didn't know what to believe. Lifting her face to the heavens, she whimpered. She was so very confused, so very afraid.

Since Paul had control of Caylee's mind, Haden had no other choice but to use an open mental path to communicate with her. It allowed the vampire to hear everything he said, but it also allowed Haden to hear every lie the vampire uttered.

Do not believe his lies, little love. You know me. You know I would never abandon you. I will always protect you. You are my life. There could never be another woman for me.

The ground split open, and a dark, shadowy image of a man burst out of it. The air rushed in and out of Caylee's lungs in short, violent gasps. Dirt and stones rained down several feet in every direction. Every muscle in her body tensed. Hoping the man was a figment of her imagination, she blinked. In an instant, he was directly in front of her. His black hair fell over his shoulders. It was stringy, tangled, and matted with dirt and other debris. His flesh was a sickly, bluish gray. He was very thin, his eyes sunken deep into his skull, and he stank of decayed flesh. He appeared to be the corpse of an old, malnourished man.

Caylee tried to back away, but she couldn't budge an inch. She knew he was the same man from earlier, but he looked different. More frightening. And so very repulsive. She opened her mouth to scream, but she didn't have the ability to make a sound. Just the sight of him sickened her, causing her mouth to water and stomach to cramp and twist. Gagging, she tried to look away, but his gaze held hers captive.

Caylee, I need you to merge with me. Do it now. Please, if only this one last time, trust me to protect you. Haden fought to keep his voice calm. He couldn't risk her misinterpreting his fear and frustration for anger. Tracking her as a man was taking far too much time. *Reach for me so I can find you.* Despite her attempts to hide, he continued to work through and unravel the maze of confusion in her mind.

"He is lying to you. He won't leave his woman to protect you." Paul thrust the image of Haden raping the woman into her mind. "You're nothing to him. If you mattered to him at all, he wouldn't have allowed you to remain a helpless mortal."

He plunged deeper into her mind, savoring her fear, hammering her with his violent lust for her blood. "You're nothing to him."

He listened to the frantic, seductive rhythm of her pulse. He took a deep breath and released it slowly with a hiss. Fear made blood hotter. Sweeter. And so entirely satisfying. His mouth watered. His stomached clenched.

"No!" She shook her head. "You're lying!" She knew Haden better. She might not be Haden's lover, but she was his friend. He would never rape a woman, and he would never abandon her.

Finally, through the power of sheer desperation, Caylee broke eye contact with Paul. She immediately wished she hadn't. She stared at his mouth. He smiled wide, revealing his serrated teeth and razor-sharp fangs. She had to be trapped in a nightmare. None of it could be real. She wanted to wake up, she wanted to run, but she couldn't do anything. She fought to regain control over her mind and body, but it was useless. Paul was too powerful to fight.

I need your help, little love. I've tried to find you through your thoughts, but he has distorted your memory. You need to trust me. You need to stop trying to fight him and reach for me. Look around and show me everything you see.

Paul reached out and lifted a section of her hair to his face. He breathed deeply, inhaling her sweet scent.

She was so afraid, but she couldn't allow Haden to die for her. *If you find me, he will kill you too. I know it wasn't real, Haden. I know you would never hurt a woman. I know you would never abandon me. Please forgive me—I'm so very sorry. I never should've believed any of it.*

Paul rubbed her silky hair against his face, twirling and tangling it around his fingers. Very slowly, he leaned toward her to nuzzle her neck. Groaning aloud, he inhaled deeply, savoring her scent.

Damn it, Caylee, he can't fucking kill me! Open your eyes! Haden was so beyond furious. *Do it now, Caylee!* He didn't care that he was causing her pain.

His booming voice hurt her ears. Echoing in her mind, his voice sounded like the rushing water of a mighty river. Like an avalanche racing down the side of a mountain. Her head hurt so badly she knew it was going explode.

Open your eyes! It was a powerful command, utterly impossible for any being mortal or immortal to defy.

She opened her eyes and scanned her surroundings. The fear of being cornered was terrible, but the icy chill of Paul's rancid breath on her flesh caused her stomach to twist. She felt weak, lightheaded, and nauseous. A split-second before she collapsed, she felt an unmistakable shift in her body and mind. Haden was closer to her than ever before. He was part of her. Their souls were united as one. She felt his enormous, dark power gathering in her, strengthening her.

Squaring her shoulders, she glared up at Paul. He planned to kill her, but she planned to make it as difficult as possible. She wasn't a child this time. She wasn't weak anymore. She would fight this time. She wouldn't allow herself to be victimized. Vampire or not, he was going to be sorry, extremely sorry.

No! Do not provoke him, Caylee! Through her eyes Haden studied her surroundings. *Wait for me!* In a matter of seconds, he recognized the alley. In an instant, he launched himself into the stormy sky, black wings erupting from his back. He moved incredibly fast, forcing the wind to shift direction so it added to his speed.

Combined with the sweet taste of her fear, the spiciness of her courage promised to make her blood more delectable. Her defiance stirred to life the most primal, deadly urges of Paul's predator nature. He craved but seldom enjoyed foreplay with a strong woman. Most of his victims quickly wilted and died. He wished he could play with her for a while longer. He would enjoy using her to satisfy his other physical needs. But he wasn't stupid. He couldn't afford to be caught with his pants down. He needed to feed. Paul knew Haden was close. He needed her blood to restore his strength before he faced the demon.

Catching Paul off guard, Caylee kicked him in the groin, hard. Roaring in pain, he went down on all fours. She ran, but he jumped to his feet and tackled her to the ground. She fought with every ounce of her strength. She clawed, scratched, hit, and kicked him. But it was all for nothing. He easily overpowered her, wrapping his hands around her throat, squeezing until she could no longer breathe.

Her thoughts racing, she thrashed wildly. She was dying. Seconds before she blacked out, she heard Haden's voice. *My strength is yours. My life is yours. You will not die—I forbid it. I am with you, Caylee. You have my breath. Feel it inside your body, sustaining your life. My heart beats for yours, steady and strong. Feel it and know you will not die.*

There was no way to hide the terror in his voice. Haden was so very aware of her frailty at that moment. Why had he waited? Why was she still mortal?

Black clouds billowed overhead, and lightning streaked across the sky. Earsplitting thundered rumbled between the buildings. Rain pelted down on her. She looked up at the stormy sky and smiled. It was Haden. The lightning, thunder, wind, and rain were all manifestations of his power. He was so extremely intense. He was mysterious and powerful beyond belief. One day she hoped to know each and every one of his secrets.

He was so close to her now, holding her. She knew in her heart she wouldn't die. She couldn't. He would never allow it. She could feel his arms lovingly, protectively wrapped around her, cocooning her in the midst of his great power.

Fangs lengthening, Paul leaned down, whispering, chanting in a strange language. She couldn't understand his words, but she felt the great intensity of his hatred and rage. His teeth, searching for her pulse, scraped her throat.

Lightning tore across the sky, and deafening thunder rumbled in Haden's wake. He dropped from the sky and landed in a crouch. Standing upright, his wings shimmered for a few seconds and then disappeared.

Paul jumped up and stood over Caylee. She tried to scoot away, but he was standing on her leg. The ground heaved and rolled as Haden stepped forward.

Hoping Paul was too distracted to notice, Caylee attempted to pull her leg out from under him. He looked down at her and growled, fully baring his jagged teeth and razor-sharp fangs.

"You look terrible, Paul." Haden's voice was serene, nothing more than a whisper, but it held unimaginable power and unparalleled might. His lips parted in a callous smile. Appearing completely at ease, he shrugged. "You've made many mistakes, but I promise this will prove to be your worst." He waved his hand.

Chucked by an unseen burst of power, Paul's body flew several feet and crashed into a brick wall at the far end of the alley. He started to get up, but he was struck in the chest by a bolt of lightning. His body violently convulsed for few seconds and then stopped. He remained, stretched out on his back, completely still.

Haden was several feet away, but Caylee felt him take her arm and help her up.

She looked at him. Actually, she gawked at him. It was impossible not to stare at him. He was a captivating sight, surrounded in a black, glittery mist. A godlike warrior. Her heart raced. He looked different than usual. She would've never thought it was possible, but he looked more merciless and dangerous than ever before. His eyes were unreadable, bottomless pools of something very dark and passionate.

Her thoughts wandered as flames raced through her body. He was a sinful specimen of masculine sensuality. He was a wonderful, delicious fantasy, the most scintillating of all. She could and would secretly dream of spending hot, steamy nights in his arms, touching him, feeling his touch. But that was it. She wasn't the kind of woman to have a man like him.

Haden held her gaze. She was everything wonderful. Beautiful. Sensual. Innocent. Strong. And so much more. She was everything. He allowed his gaze to wander over her picture-perfect body. The right side of his mouth curved upward in a grin. "We've spent many hours together, little love, but I've never see so much of you. Your choice of clothing is causing my mind to conjure up a few naughty thoughts. I do believe I've gained a new appreciation for the rain. When it's wet, your shirt leaves very little to be imagined."

She felt his sinful gaze touching her, slowly spreading over her flesh like a smoldering fire. Before she could blush or scold him, Paul roared. It was a terrible, inhuman sound. He jumped up. Eyes filled with deadly, venomous rage, he rushed toward her. Haden moved so quickly she couldn't possibly see it, but when he gently kissed her brow and wrapped his coat around her shoulders, time seemed to stand completely still. Though his kiss was only a brush of his lips, it sent electrical currents zipping through her veins and over her flesh.

In an instant, Haden turned and slammed into Paul. The impact of their bodies made a terrible, bone-breaking thud. They tumbled back and forth, hurling each other to the ground and against the buildings. Caylee watched in awe. Common sense told her to run and hide, but she couldn't budge an inch. All she could think about was the hot sensation of Haden's lips on her flesh. She wanted to kiss him. Taste him. She needed to feel his mouth on hers. Her stomach was fluttering, and her head was spinning. What was wrong with her? Danger surrounded her, and she was standing there fantasizing. She had been attacked by a ... by a ... *oh, my God! He's a vampire!*

Haden fought fiercely, his strength far greater than any man. Each move he made was perfect. He was elegance and power perfectly combined. Wings? Did she see wings on his back? She shook her head. It didn't matter whether she saw wings or not. Biting her lower lip, she looked up. He'd dropped from the sky. Sure, she had witnessed him do many impossible things. But fly? That was just insane. She shook her head again. Why did she doubt his ability to fly when she'd seen him turn into a dragon?

Pinning Paul against the wall, Haden held him a foot off the ground. He squeezed his throat, his fingers digging deep gouges. He could've ended it right then and there. He could've easily ripped Paul's head right off of his shoulders, but he didn't. A quick death wasn't good enough. Haden threw Paul across the alley. Twisting and turning in mid-air, Paul landed in a crouch and launched himself at Haden. In a wild frenzy, Paul attacked. Haden met the attack with greater force. Bricks and mortar crumbled and rained down on them, but they continued to fight.

Caylee realized car alarms were going off. And in the distance she heard police sirens. She heard people shouting and screaming. Blood was everywhere. What would happen when the police arrived? Or what if, God forbid, an innocent bystander walked into the alley? Her heart raced quickly. Too quickly. Painfully. She couldn't quite catch her breath.

Caylee's distress made it impossible for Haden to focus. He turned to her and forced her to meet his gaze. *I've placed a hedge over the alley. No one will be able to enter it. No one will be able to see what is happening. I need you to be calm.*

From out of nowhere, a knife appeared in Paul's hand. He thrust it forward, burying it deep into Haden's chest, a fraction of an inch above his heart. Caught off guard, Haden stumbled backward.

Caylee's heart stopped. "Haden!" She ran toward him as he yanked the knife out of his chest. His blood spurted everywhere. She was distraught, nearly out of her mind with fear, pressing her hands to the wound, trying to stop it from bleeding.

"What are you doing? Stay back." Pushing her behind the protection of his body, Haden threw the knife at Paul, aiming for his thigh, still wanting to prolong Paul's suffering.

Paul fell to his knees. He growled, his eyes red and glowing. His hunger for blood burned. The agony was intolerable. It was a terrible, fiery pain deep in his gut. "You failed to protect your woman. You used her. You led me to her. It's my right to take her blood." He ripped the knife free, lifted to his mouth, and licked the blood from the cold metal blade. While black, greasy blood seeped from the wound on his leg, he thought of Caylee's hot, sweet blood flowing into his mouth and down his throat, filling him, restoring his strength. He licked his lips. "Her blood is mine!" He threw the knife at Caylee.

Lightning streaks raced from the north, south, east, and west. At the same moment, each bolt struck the knife. The thunder was instant and earsplitting. The knife burst into flames, its ashes falling at Caylee's feet.

Haden wasn't human. She'd known it for some time now. He couldn't be. But what was he? A dragon? Or was he some other mysterious being from a different universe or time? Eyes wide, she stumbled backward, staring at Haden. It was frightening to think about how easily he controlled the most powerful, destructive forces of nature.

Wind blasted through the alley. Caylee felt something terrible and uncontrollable well up in Haden, a horrifying beast, a living creature of rage. His image flashed from man to dragon and then to man again. He growled. It was a deep, animalistic sound.

He'd hunted and destroyed many creatures of darkness to protect humans from distinction. Never once had it been personal. He'd never protected someone he loved. And he loved Caylee; with every ounce of his heart and soul, he loved and cherished her.

Trembling, Caylee slowly backed away. Haden knew she felt the shift in him. He knew she saw the truth. She saw the dragon. A killer with no equal. Ruthless. Merciless. Black flames radiated and leapt out from his body and swirled around him. He was far more than intimidating. He was powerful beyond any human understanding. He was more deadly and cunning than any predator that ever walked the earth.

The ground was shaking violently, heaving and rolling deep below the surface of the earth, so the buildings swayed back and forth. Huge hailstones fell from the sky, shattering windows all around. Several building alarms joined the car alarms. Lightning was striking the ground in several places all at once. Caylee covered her ears to muffle the sounds, but it didn't help. Her body trembled fiercely, and hot tears streamed down her face.

Haden glanced at her. His eyes glowed but were as black as the darkest night. She met his gaze for a moment and then closed her eyes and prayed it was all a terrible dream.

Part of him wanted to wrap her in his arms and take her away. He could easily do it. There was no reason to force her to witness Paul's destruction, but he was too enraged, too frustrated to stop. He fully embraced the cunning, ferocious nature of his kind, allowing the dragon to totally consume all thought. In an instant, he was on Paul, mercilessly attacking.

The sound of flesh being ripped, muscles torn, and bones breaking was so very shocking. Caylee opened her eyes and stared in absolute horror. Breaking apart bricks and mortar,

Haden brutally smashed Paul against the building over and over again. It was a terrible sight. Frightening. Heart stopping. It couldn't be real. It had to be a bad dream. A nightmare. She couldn't possibly be witnessing such horrendous brutality.

Suddenly, Caylee was surrounded by ghouls. She opened her mouth to scream but only managed to release a muffled whimper. Her throat closed so she couldn't take a breath. Snapping their jaws, they snarled, baring their teeth. They were the most hideous dog-like creatures with patches of fur and flesh torn from their bodies. Infection oozed from their flesh. In some places the wounds were so deep bare bones showed.

Haden had placed an impenetrable hedge of protection around her, so he didn't worry about the ghouls. With a closed fist, he hit Paul hard. The impact created a thunderous boom and hurled Paul several feet away, his body slamming against a dumpster. At once, Haden was in front of Caylee.

Whining and whimpering, the creatures turned to face Paul, seeking permission to flee. They would be destroyed if they attempted to attack Haden, but Paul commanded them to do it; they couldn't disobey.

They surrounded Haden. Hesitating, they circled him, whining and shrieking. Then all at once, they attacked. Haden could've destroyed them without ever touching them, but as if they were rag dolls, he ripped each of them apart with his bare hands.

Paul knew he would die if he failed to escape. He watched for a few seconds, and then, using the last bit of his strength, he dissolved into a putrid mist and disappeared.

~ *Five* ~

STANDING IN THE middle of the alley, Haden studied Paul's path. Even after Zack's warning, he'd underestimated the vampire. The situation was so much more dangerous than he thought. He'd never encountered a vampire brazen enough to challenge a fully matured male demon. Not like this. Not using a demon's mate. He should've killed the vampire before taking her home. Why hadn't he? Normally he would've done it. There wouldn't have been any hesitation. Why was it so important to make Paul suffer? Now the vampire was free to strike again. He'd killed numerous vampires, too many to count, but he'd never fought with anger clouding his judgment.

He heard Caylee stumbling over bricks, splinters of wood, and shattered glass to get to him. He turned toward her. "Stay there."

"He stabbed you." She tried to unbutton his shirt, but her hands were trembling too much. "I can't believe he stabbed you."

He took a breath and held it. She was in a state of shock. He needed to comfort her, to say something, anything, but at that moment he couldn't speak. He just stared down at her hands. He didn't move. He *couldn't* move. He didn't want to do anything that might cause her to stop touching him.

Compared to his, her hands were so tiny and delicate, but they wielded such great power over him. In all honesty, he was fascinated by her ability to possess absolute control over his body.

Apparently frustrated, Caylee ripped his shirt open. Haden's heart skipped a beat, and then it thundered. Her assertiveness was unexpected, but it was pure erotic pleasure. His flesh burned beneath her fingertips. His fierce need for her detonated. Enormous waves of lust slammed into him so hard his body shuddered, and every muscle tensed as he struggled to remain in control as she examined the knife wound on his chest.

He'd dreamt of her touching him like this for so long. Her fingers caressed his flesh ever so lightly, mercilessly teasing him, driving him mad. His heart thundered in his ears. He knew she meant to soothe his pain, but her touch was the furthest thing from soothing. It was causing him to experience a delicious form of agony. His heart was going to burst. Her touch was pure torture. She'd never once, in all the time they'd known each other, touched his body so boldly.

She didn't know she was enticing him, tormenting him, rewarding him, and punishing him all at the same time. In fact, at that moment, she would be horrified if she knew how much he enjoyed her touch. But he did. More than he ever thought possible. He'd lived alone for hundreds and hundreds of years, surrounded by people but purposely set apart from everyone, until he met her. He craved her companionship. He needed it. He'd spent a great deal of time gently seducing her, coaxing her a little bit at a time, waiting for the moment she would, without fear, embrace her body's need for his.

Caylee's body trembled, and tears streamed down her face. He knew that, to her eyes, the stab wound would look very bad; his flesh was ripped wide open. Splaying her hand over it, she looked up at him, and he could tell she wished she could take the pain from his body. So much anguish flowed from her heart and soul. It was for him. Every bit of it. It touched him so deeply, so thoroughly. It hurt like nothing ever had before, but at the same time it filled his heart and soul with boundless joy.

"It's okay, little love." He placed his hand over hers. "I'm okay."

He'd endured several wounds in battles, too many to count. Never once, in all of his existence, had his health and well-being mattered to anyone. The people he protected had never shed a tear for his sake. It had never mattered to him. He was a powerful immortal. A guardian. A protector of the innocent and helpless. And yes, the ignorant. His supernatural gifts and great strength were blessings and curses. Mankind, though they were protected by his kind, either feared or hated his kind.

"It looks bad, but it's nothing. It's already healing."

Just then, she felt a burning sensation on her legs. She stepped back and looked down. Even soaked with rain her clothing was smoldering. Confused, she looked up at him. "What's happening?"

"I'm sorry. It's his blood. I should've known it was on you. It burns like acid." Black flames surrounded her and swirled over her, caressing her flesh, touching her everywhere at once. Within seconds the strange flames removed the vampire's blood from her body. "It's gone now. All of it. You'll be fine."

"He's a v-vampire."

"I know." He cradled her against his chest, near his heart where she belonged, safe and protected, shielded from the horrors of the dark world she lived in. He filled her with his healing energy, his strength, and his love.

"How can it be real?" She sobbed. "I don't understand any of it. How can anything that happened tonight be real?"

He felt the warmth of her tears on his chest. His heart shattered into a million pieces. "Why didn't you reach for me?" He wanted to comfort her. He was shocked when his voice sounded harsher than he intended, but he was frustrated and a little bit angry. She should've believed in him. She should've immediately rejected the thought of him raping a woman. She could've been killed. The vampire should've never been able to deceive her and draw her out into the night.

"I did, but I … oh, God." How could she believe he was raping a woman? "He was in my mind … my body." Wrapping her arms around his neck, she cried hysterically, her body trembling.

He pushed his frustration and anger aside, making sure she would only hear compassion and understanding in his voice. "It's not your fault, little love—it's mine. I underestimated him. He's a very strong telepath and an expert hunter. He confused and deceived you, wanting you to believe you were alone and helpless. But you can always reach me, Caylee." He set her down on her feet, and then, forcing her to make eye contact with him, he held her face between his hands. "Always." Embedding the information in her mind, he added, "Be persistent. No matter what is happening, don't give up. Nothing can ever stop you from reaching me at anytime."

Massaging her throat, she stared up at him.

"You're my life." Suddenly, as he watched her massage her throat, he feared he was too late. His heart actually stopped.

He growled. It was a deep, menacing sound.. He didn't try to hide the dark, deadly power radiating from his eyes as he reached up to move her hand from her throat. He examined her throat and neck.

Haden felt her fear, but he ignored it. He wouldn't allow it to stop him. She had every right to fear him—he would kill her if Paul had turned her. He would have no other choice. He would never allow her to suffer the existence of the undead. He couldn't. He loved her too much. He would find a way to do the impossible: he would end his existence to be with her, but he would most certainly kill her. "Did he give you his blood?"

"Huh? What do you mean?" Eyes wide, she stared up at him.

"Did he force you to take his blood into your body?"

"No." Her entire body was trembling so fiercely he suspected she couldn't even see straight.

Relief washed over him, through him. Closing his eyes, he took a deep and calming breath. He opened his eyes and held her gaze captive, forcing her to witness the color of his eyes changing to blue. It was important for her to learn to accept and not fear the things in him that were strange to her.

He moved closer to her, crowding her, caging her between the building and his body. He wasn't trying to intimidate her. He only wanted to comfort her, comfort himself. He wanted to shelter her in his arms forever. He was desperate to make her understand she was safe with him. He would never betray her. He would gladly give his immortal soul to protect her. And yes, he would kill her to protect her. But thankfully, she wouldn't be forced to learn that.

She was a tiny woman. He knew she felt dwarfed by his massive size. Defenseless. Powerless. But he was done pretending. She tried to shove him, but he refused to budge. "What do you think you're doing?" She pushed at him again. "You're such a jerk. Get away from me."

"The skin is broken, and your throat is badly bruised." He wanted her. He needed her, desperately, madly. He gently wrapped his hand around her slender throat. "Why didn't you tell me it hurts to breathe?"

He listened to her heart beat wildly. He knew the heat radiating from his hand was soothing the pain, healing her bruised flesh. But he also knew it was doing so much more. It was heating her blood, sending electrical currents zipping through her body and over her flesh.

Haden was so much more than simply powerful. He was power. He commanded the wind, rain, lightning, and thunder. He made the earth move. He was so much more than intimidating. He was deadly. Mystifying. Sinister. Godlike. Beautiful. Strange.

He brought her hand to the warmth of his mouth.

She tried to pull her hand out of his. "What's wrong with you? Did your head get hit too hard?" Until this night, he'd seldom touched her. He was her friend. Nothing more. He'd never acted so bold, so pushy. She was always safe with him. She knew better now: he wanted her body, her soul, her total surrender. Too much was happening too quickly. "Stop looking at me like that."

"Like what?"

What man looked like him? It was so unfair. So wrong. He made her way too aware of being a woman. Her stomach was flipping, and her head was spinning. Every secret part of her body tingled. He looked so wickedly sexy. She blushed, realizing her panties were damp. He was all man, but he possessed naughty, boyish qualities. He was so very hot. Far too hot in all the right, invigorating, stimulating ways. The heat radiating from his muscular body sizzled over her flesh, caressing her everywhere. His voice was as smooth as the finest velvet. As always, it was flawless. Deep. Seductive. Intoxicating. It wrapped around her like a silk ribbon, tying her to him for all of eternity.

His powerful arms swept around her, dragging her so close her body melted into his heavily muscled frame. She held her breath. Her heart momentarily stopped. He was so powerful. A part of her feared if she needed to, she wouldn't have any chance to escape him. But then, another part of her, a wild, uninhibited part, never wanted to escape. His body was so hot, so wonderfully rock-hard solid against her soft, feminine curves.

"This has been the longest night of my existence, little love." She was shocked when he pressed the swollen, hard length of his cock against her flat belly. "I need you, Caylee. Need me the way I need you. Need me to be inside your body, little love, deep inside your body."

"What is your problem?" She shoved him, harder this time, putting all of her weight into it. "Stop touching me!"

A deep, animalistic growl rumbled in his chest and throat. "Stay still," he whispered between clenched teeth. Her head snapped up so that she met his gaze. Fear pierced her heart deeply. Something dark, aggressive, and threatening burned in his eyes. More terrified of his strength and power than ever before, she stopped fighting him, knowing it was instigating something fierce, knowing he was fighting to harness it.

"Relax," he whispered. She sensed he was struggling to remain in control of something very dangerous. "Just relax."

Hot tears streamed down her cheeks. He was crushing her, holding too tightly. "You're really scaring me, Haden." His arms were like steel bindings; his body was as solid as a boulder pushing her against the building behind her.

"I love you, Caylee."

"If love is your excuse for acting like an idiot and freaking me out, you suck." She considered lifting her knee, hoping that if she did it, he would drop as quickly as the vampire. "Get away from me!"

Chuckling softly, he loosened his arms a bit and shifted his body, giving her a tiny bit of space. "You don't really want to hurt me, do you?"

Her heart was racing. "Yes, I do." she replied. Her body burned against his solid frame. She was terrified. Angry. Aroused. Extremely aroused. His body was remarkable. His strength was amazing. His mysterious abilities were unbelievable. He so easily overpowered her that she felt utterly defenseless in his arms.

"Why do you entertain such thoughts?" His voice was a deep, husky rasp. It thoroughly revealed his lust. It exposed his desire, his need for her, his undying love and his devotion. "Please, don't think the worst of me." He leaned down and tilted his head to the side, as if preparing to kiss her. "With all of my heart and my soul, I love you."

Framing her face with his hands, he gently caressed her lips with the callused pad of his thumb. He wanted to kiss her. He needed to taste her. Once. Maybe twice. "I would never hurt you," he whispered. He wanted to worship her body with his. He needed to give her pleasure she would never forget.

She would never be tempted to stray from him. She would always crave him, only him.

His mouth was too close to hers. She couldn't catch her breath. She needed to get away from him. All at once, she wished he would kiss her and feared he would do it. A delicious shiver raced through her body. Her heart beat frantically. "Please." Her voice was a husky, breathless whisper. "Stop."

Finally able to step away from her, he smiled at her, his black eyes burning with desire. "I need to deal with Paul." As long as the vampire lived, her safety was in jeopardy. "I'll take you home."

"No, don't go after him." She grabbed his wrist as if to stop him, but her fingers were barely able to wrap halfway around it.

"He won't be able to get to you again." He looked down at her tiny, delicate hand holding his wrist, effectively restraining him. "I've no other choice."

"I'm not worried about him getting to me." Stepping closer, she placed her hand on his chest. "You're hurt."

"I'm fine. It's only a flesh wound." He took her hand and held it. He needed to take her home. He needed to go after the vampire. "Every second I wait complicates my ability to find him." He reached out with his other hand and wiped the tears from her cheek. "Please, don't cry."

Her blood heated to a rolling boil, her flesh aching, her heart racing. A wonderful, explosive fire spread throughout her body, blazing through her. Her breasts felt heavier than normal, swollen, full, and so ultra-sensitive, aching for his touch. She closed her eyes and allowed her body's desire for his to grow. She thought of his hands, so strong and yet so gentle. His body was hard and muscular, so perfect in every masculine way. She wanted to fall into the depths of his fierce hunger. She wanted to abandon her fears. She needed to give her body and soul to him, fully and completely. Her pulse raced. Her breaths came in rapid pleas. She longed to feel the heat of his flesh against hers.

Startled by her thoughts, she flung her head up and stared at him. What was she doing? Grinning shyly, she bit her lower lip. It was his fault. It was just simply so wrong for him to be so sexy. She looked down at her feet to avoid his knowing gaze.

He gently lifted her chin, forcing her to look at him. "You've no reason to be ashamed of your desire to be with me."

She tilted her head to the side. "I'm sorry." She looked so sweet. Innocent. Afraid. Needy. Exotic. Damn, the woman was seriously killing him.

"Why?"

"You know why."

He moved closer to her. "Your thoughts don't insult me." She felt his powerful muscles bunching, rippling against her soft curves. He opened her hand and brought it to his mouth. He kissed her palm and then very slowly ran his tongue over it. "They drive me insane, but I'm pleased by them."

She felt the moist heat of his velvety tongue caress every inch of her body. She felt it blaze over her flesh. "We ... oh Haden, we're friends." She could hardy talk. "Haden, I ... you can hear what I'm thinking." She felt feverish and damp. So achy. "You've never hidden it from me." He continued to tease her palm with his tongue. She yanked her hand away from his. "I shouldn't think of you like a man."

"I would be devastated if you didn't." He stood there and studied her for a moment. She believed he couldn't possibly lose his mind over her, but he knew better. He was about to tumble into a state of madness and take her with him. He needed to place a little physical distance between them. If he didn't, he risked causing her to hate him for all of eternity. "We will have plenty of time to discuss this later. For now, I will take you home. I need to go after him."

The color drained from her face. "No!" She stood on the tips of her toes, and, shocking him and herself, she wrapped her arms around his neck and kissed his cheek. "Don't go after him," she whispered.

Her love for him was genuine and pure. It touched him so deeply he could barely breathe. He didn't deserve her love. He wrapped his arms around her. He shouldn't, but he couldn't help it. He was so aware of how easily death could've snatched her away from him. Tears burning behind his eyes, he lifted her up and held her against his body. She was so very precious to him. So fragile. He could've lost her. How long would it take to gain her trust enough to give her immortality? He held her close, trying to alleviate his pain and fear, but his heart continued to ache.

"I can't stand the thought of you going after him." Her body trembling against his, she rested her head on his shoulder. "I'm so afraid for you."

He took a deep breath and released it slowly. "There's no reason for you worry about me." He lowered her onto her feet. He intended to step away from her to put some distance between them, but he couldn't. He needed to hold her for a little while longer. He wrapped his arms around her and pulled her close. Resting his chin on top of her head, a surge of anger entered him. Hatred welled up in him. Paul's days were numbered. No one would ever attempt to harm her. She was the force that caused his heart to beat. He wasn't sure how he'd lived for so many centuries without her. He wasn't sure what kept him going, but he knew he wouldn't survive an hour beyond her death.

When he released her, she looked up at him with tears in her eyes. "I need to go." She turned around to walk away.

Laughing aloud, he captured her arm. "I know you don't really think I'm going to let you go alone." His eyes turned black with strange flecks of silver.

"What are you?" Eyebrows drawn together, she looked up at him.

"What do mean?" He really hoped she wouldn't press him for an answer. Eventually, he would tell her he was a demon. It had been his plan all along. He'd been revealing his powers to her a little at a time. By showing her the dragon he was attempting to further desensitize her to the truth of what he was. But before he confessed to being a demon, he hoped to fully gain her trust. Haden wanted no unnecessary deception between them. Of course, there were things she didn't need to know. Harmful things, like the fact that he'd murdered her father to avenge and protect her. When he'd realized her father had sold her to the men that held her captive, he simply couldn't allow the man to live.

"Why do your eyes turn black when you're mad?" She lifted her chin, and her lips curved up in the sexy, defiant smirk he adored so much.

He smiled at her. "It bothers you," he whispered.

"Well ..." She bit her bottom lip nervously, wondering if she'd offended him. "It's a bit alarming." Not nearly as alarming as witnessing him turn into a dragon, but she wasn't bringing that up. Not yet anyways.

"It's not just anger. My eyes turn black whenever I experience any powerful emotion." He backed her up against the building, moving slowly. "You see them change often because you give life to and stir emotions in me."

Swallowing hard, she shook her head. "Stop it."

"Why do you fear my touch? Your body craves it. Your body needs it. Your body demands it." Gently pushing her, forcing her to face her fear, he used his body to trap hers. "Just as much as my body craves, needs, and demands your touch."

Eyes wide, holding her breath, she stared up at him. "Please," she pleaded, "I want to go home." Her heart beat wildly, pounding in her ears.

Smiling at her, he slowly shook his head. "Not yet, little love, not yet."

"Please, stop." Holding out her hand to stop him, tears filled her eyes. "What are you doing? You're really starting to freak me out."

"You're safe with me." He kissed her softly. "You're always safe with me. There's no reason for you to be afraid of our love." He kissed her again, so very gently.

She placed her palms on his chest. His powerful, well defined muscles tensed and bunched. She had every intention of shoving him, but she didn't. She froze. His heart was beating, steady and strong beneath her hands. Hot electrical currents raced over her flesh. Her body ached. She was on fire, burning up for him. Needing him.

Looking up, meeting his gaze, she whimpered. "Haden?" She was shocked by the sound of her voice. It was a nearly inaudible, husky murmur.

"Don't over-think what you're feeling, Caylee—embrace it," he whispered against her lips. "Just kiss me."

She brushed her soft, satiny lips against his, intensifying the firestorm of passion raging through his body. He groaned loudly, savoring the sweetness of her kiss, the innocence of it. His cock swelled, hardened painfully. Her kiss was more stirring, more erotic than any other kiss. It was so much more sensual, more satisfying than any other. He struggled to allow her to set the pace of the kiss, to control the intensity of it, hoping she would feel free enough to abandon her inhibitions.

Eventually his patience was rewarded, and her kiss deepened as her body melted into his. The delicious, intoxicating scent of her arousal filled his lungs, unmercifully ripping and tearing at his control. His need for her spiraled out of control as her soft moans vibrated against his lips. He parted her lips with his tongue. At first he tasted her, and then he delved deeper, exploring the sensual heat of her mouth more thoroughly.

Lifting her, holding her body against his, he kissed her deeply, aggressively. She wrapped her arms around his neck and her legs around his waist. He shuddered, his control shattering into thousands and thousands of tiny pieces. Every muscle in his body tensed and ached. His cock was unbelievably hard and heavy, painfully pressed far too snugly against the seam of his pants. He was certain he would die if he didn't have her right then and there. He held her up easily, cradling her hips in his palms. Even with the injury he'd sustained, her weight was nothing to him. And even if it were painful, he sure as hell wasn't going to say anything.

He kissed her thoroughly, roughly taking possession of her mouth, her body, and soul. For several moments, he knew she was lost in the sheer ecstasy of it, but then he felt fear welling up in her.

Meeting her gaze, he miraculously found the strength to allow her to retreat. She needed to know she was in control, even if it killed him. "Breathe, little love." She stared into his eyes. He watched as every fear was incinerated in the flames of passion he felt sweeping through her. He savored the way her body was on fire, burning up for his. Needing his. Demanding his. She was kissing him again, timidly at first and then, frantically.

The sweet, intoxicating scent of her arousal filled his lungs. He was seriously going to die. He could easily remove the barrier of their clothing with a thought and bury himself deep inside her body. Her body was so hot and wet, so very ready for him to plunge his cock deep inside her. Merging with her mind, he shared erotic images of their bodies entwined and joined as one. He studied her reaction. He felt her desire for him, but her fear of being vulnerable to him was also present. He was possessive and powerful beyond her understanding. She knew he wasn't human, but that didn't matter to her. She wanted to lose control with him, but was terrified of the consequences.

Despite her fear, he could've coaxed her to allow him to possess her body, but he knew it would be a mistake. There would be no manipulation. At least, not the first time. He loved her too much to rush her. She wasn't ready—her past still haunted her, a past she believed she kept hidden from him. He would give her as much time as she needed. Eventually, she would be free of the fear that stood between them. At least, he hoped she would be free of it.

A black mist surrounded them as he took her through time and space. "Open your eyes, little love." He gently lowered her onto her feet.

Opening her eyes, she looked up him. She turned her head and stared at her bed, Remembering the moment she was pulled out of it, her stomach rolled. She glanced down at blankets on the floor. "How did we get here?" She never thought she would be afraid to be alone in her room. But she was. In fact, she was terrified.

With a thought he waved his hand and lifted, straightened, and pulled the blankets back. He picked her up and carried her over to the bed. He lowered her onto it and then tucked her in. "It's a secret." He leaned down and kissed her brow. "I will share it with you later."

"I don't like secrets."

"I know."

"Haden, I am so … you saved my life two times tonight. I was so afraid. Thank you."

"I love you, Caylee. I will always protect you. You will be safe here. Nothing will be able to enter your room again." He smiled at her. A very naughty, sexy smile that caused her stomach to flutter and heart to race. "But don't thank me. Protecting you is a purely selfish act. I have learned a second without you is an eternity of hell. I need you around. I can't allow anything to happen to you. I won't." She opened her mouth to argue with him, but he continued before she could speak. "Keep your mind merged with mine at all times so he won't be able to use another compulsion." He traced her lips with the tip of his finger, and then he gave her a small kiss.

Eyes heavy with fatigue, she nodded. "You will be safe?"

"Absolutely—I couldn't possibly expect anyone else to keep you out of trouble." Dissolving into a black mist, he vanished.

She stared at the empty spot where he had stood. She was terrified for him. She was tempted to call him back to her and try to talk him out of it, but she knew better. Besides, from now on she needed to stay as far away from him as possible.

* * *

Zack's eyes flashed open. His heart thundering in his ears, he listened to the muffled cries of a young woman in his mind. He felt the fear. No. He wasn't simply feeling it—he was experiencing it as if it were his own. He'd never experienced fear. It had to be a trick. It wasn't possible for him to feel fear of any kind. What would he, a powerful demon, ever fear? Closing his eyes, he attempted to purge the whimpering from his mind and to uncover its creator.

The vision lasted for a second, but he clearly saw a teenager behind Joseph's hotel, cowering in the mud at a vampire's feet. The vision actually caused his entire body to shudder. He didn't take the time to consider that it was very odd for a vampire to kill so close to a demon's property. He was out of his bed and behind the building, fighting the vampire before he actually had a chance to examine the situation. It was a brief but particularly brutal battle. The vampire was surprisingly strong enough to deliver a few substantial blows before Zack killed him.

When it was over, Zack turned and stared at the girl for a moment. He estimated her age to be somewhere around sixteen. She was far too thin and dressed in filthy rags. He figured she was a runaway or an orphan. He didn't look into her mind. He didn't want to know any more. She was too young to be on the street alone. He decided to take her to the police station. They would help her get into a shelter or return her to her family.

She was already so very afraid, and he knew, by the injuries he'd sustained, that he looked as frightening as hell. Plus, she'd just witnessed the killer in him unleashed. He slowly walked over to her, using his mind to hide his wounds to the best of his ability. Kneeling down, hoping to appear less threatening, he held out his hand. "Will you allow me to help you?"

Eyes wide, heart racing, she stared up at him. He remained silent and still, barely even breathing, waiting for her to decide whether or not to trust him. It seemed like an eternity, but within a few seconds he heard her heart slow to a normal, steady rhythm. Then nodding, her thick golden curls bobbing, she placed her tiny hand in his.

He helped her stand up, but her legs gave out. He easily picked her up in his strong arms and cradled her. Wrapping her thin arms around his neck, she hugged him tightly, resting her head on his shoulder, whispering her gratitude in his ear. He couldn't remember a time that a human had actually thanked him for anything. Joy filled his heart in a way he'd never experienced it before. Her genuine gratitude and absolute trust melted his cold, dark heart. It was a powerful moment. A precious moment. A frightening moment. But it was definitely a precious moment.

No! He stopped walking. What the fuck was he thinking? Anger filled him. Hatred and resentment pierced his heart. He wouldn't be duped into caring about any human. Not even the tiny girl in his arms. She meant nothing to him. He almost set her down, but he didn't. He ached to get as far away from her as possible, but he couldn't force himself to abandon her. No matter how much he wanted to do it, he couldn't leave her to fend for herself in the streets. He healed her physical wounds and imparted her with his power. Then, determined to never think about her again, he dropped her off at the police station.

~ *Six* ~

"WHY?" CAYLEE WAVED a twenty-dollar bill in front of Mia's face. "Have you completely lost your mind? I can't believe you told Haden about our bet."

Mia laughed. "You should've seen the look on his face."

"Oh my God, Mia, why?" Caylee shook her head. "Why did you do it?" She plopped down on the sofa facing the dressing rooms and buried her face in her hands. "I've never been so embarrassed in my life."

"Why?"

"Mia, he thinks I believe he's gay. And worse, he thinks I bet on it."

"You do, and you did." She shrugged. "But don't worry, I told him I was the one who thought he was gay." Plucking the cash out of Caylee's hand, Mia laughed.

"It's not funny, Mia." She was far from relieved. She knew Haden could've easily learned the truth by mucking around in Mia's head. Imagining the look on his face, Caylee giggled. "Well, maybe it's a little funny."

"Way more than a little, honey. I have it all captured on the store surveillance camera if you want to see it. I watched it a few times this morning. It's hilarious. Okay. I lied. I watched it several times. It's so funny. It's a miracle he managed to lift his chin up off the floor before he tucked his tail between his legs and ran out of here."

Chewing on her bottom lip, Caylee frowned. "You actually have it on video?"

"I sure do." Mia nodded eagerly. "Do want to see it?"

Grinning, she nodded once. Of course she wanted to see it. Then, she shook her head. "No."

Mia shrugged. "Why not?"

Caylee frowned. "How mad was he?"

"Why?" If he took it out on Caylee, he was going to be sorry. "Of course he was mad, but don't worry about it. It needed to be done. It's his own fault. He's been sending you mixed messages for a year now." Mia sat down next to Caylee. "Don't be upset. How else were we going to find out?"

Caylee took a deep breath and sighed. "I suppose it was his own fault."

"When did he catch up to you?"

"Five thirty."

"Wow. It certainly didn't take him long at all. He rushed out of here at a quarter after."

"Oh, Mia, you wouldn't believe what happened. It was one of the most horrible, terrifying nights of my life."

Instantly, anger flashed in Mia's eyes. "What did the bastard do to you?" She was going to kick Haden's ass.

Caylee shook her head. "It wasn't him. There was a woman in the forest." She paused. "She was dead, Mia. There was so much blood. I couldn't move. I couldn't look away from her. The stench in the air was just awful. It was so foul I couldn't even breathe. I've never seen anything so sickening in my life. I'm so lucky Haden found me. The killer actually returned while we were there."

"Hold on." Mia held up her hand. "I can't believe you actually went out there. I thought you were just trying to teach him a lesson. I wouldn't have let you go if I knew you were going out there." She frowned. "You've seen the news, Caylee. We've all seen it. Four women, now five, have been killed out there. What were you thinking?"

"I wasn't thinking. I know it was stupid. I don't know why I did it. Haden just makes me so mad. He's always bossing me around. He acts like such a jerk. It drives me insane. He makes my skin itch. Sometimes I can't even stand to be near him. I'm serious, Mia—he drives me absolutely insane."

Mia laughed. "It's called sexual frustration, honey. You need to do him and get it over with."

"You know I can't."

"Have you told him about Phillip yet?"

"No." Caylee shook her head. "And you won't say a word to him about it."

"You need to tell him. He's going to find out. It's only a matter of time."

"You're wrong. He won't."

"Eventually the announcement will be in the newspaper," Mia pointed out. "He's a lawyer, so I'm fairly certain he can read. How are you going to keep it from him?"

"Well, maybe he will find out, but it doesn't matter." Tears welled up. "I'm never seeing Haden again." There was a catch in her voice. "I just can't bear to see him again."

"Why?" Mia asked.

A long silence followed. "He kissed me last night."

Mia wasn't a fool. Haden Drake was a chest-beating, annoying as hell, manly man. There was no way he'd just kissed Caylee and walked away. "Just a kiss?"

A blush rose from Caylee's neck to her cheeks. "It was more."

That brought Mia's eyebrow up. "More?"

Nodding, Caylee smiled. "Way more." She paused. "Oh Mia, it was wonderful."

"So you did him?"

"No." Shaking her head, Caylee frowned. "Of course not."

"Of course not?" Shaking her head, Mia smiled. "You can't fool me. I know you want him bad. To tell you the truth, I'm not all that thrilled about this thing you have for him, but it ought to be a fun adventure for you. I mean, I bet he's pretty good at rocking a woman's world in the sack. He obviously takes care of himself. He's in great shape. Some people, mostly men, would lie and say size and stamina don't matter, but trust me, honey, they matter a whole hell of a lot."

"I can't believe you just said that to me." Caylee laughed. "It doesn't matter what I want. What woman wouldn't want him?" Drawing her bottom lip into her mouth, she chewed on it. "I can't have him. Not in this lifetime anyways."

"Why?"

"He's just so amazing. You've seen him, haven't you? He's perfect. He's everything I'm not."

"Stop." Frowning, Mia took Caylee's hand. "I'm not going to listen to you belittle yourself. You're an amazing woman. You're gorgeous. I mean it—you're an absolutely beautiful woman."

"You have to say that."

"Why?"

"You're my best friend."

"Trust me, if you were ugly, I would tell you to date a plastic surgeon." Mia took Caylee's hand. "Are you afraid of him because you were raped?"

Caylee shook her head. "No. He would never hurt me like that. I don't want to talk about it."

"It wasn't your fault. I'm not Haden's biggest fan, but I know he would never think less of you because of it. I also know he would never hurt you."

"Mia, please stop. I don't want to talk about it right now."

"Okay. We will talk later, but I need to take care of a mess at the bank before it closes for the weekend. You need to try on the dress I made for you." Smiling, Mia held up a slinky black dress.

"Oh, no way. Come on, Mia, there's no way I'm ever going to wear this dress." Standing up, Caylee covered her mouth and giggled. "Oh my God, there's hardly any fabric to it. I feel naughty just looking at it and thinking about wearing it." She reached out to touch the dress. "A bikini would cover up more of my body than this."

"You have no choice. You promised. You're not backing out on me this time. You're going to the Fourth of July party with me this year." Mia grabbed her arm, led her to the dressing room, and shoved her inside. "The heels, jewelry, and thigh-highs are yours, too. Don't leave. I'll be back in an hour or so. I want to see it on you. All of it. If you need any help, Julie and Brianna are here." Smiling, she shut the door.

After leaving instructions with Brianna and Julie, Mia opened the door to leave just as Haden was reaching for the door to go inside. "What, now that you're not gay, you're stalking her?"

Nodding, he grinned. "Absolutely."

Her expression softened. "Listen, Haden, I didn't think she would go out there. I wouldn't have let her go. Thank you for finding her."

Frowning, Haden took a step back. The fact that she was being nice was quite scary. Making him feel a little safer, her smile turned into a scowl.

"If you're not serious, if you hurt her in any way, I will hunt you down and I will make you regret the day you were born."

"I would hope so."

"Whatever." Rolling her eyes, she snorted. "I suppose you can go inside and wait for her, but don't bother her. She's trying on a dress." Without saying another word, Mia walked away.

The moment Haden entered, Julie grabbed Brianna's arm. "Oh … oh … my … God, he's back."

"Who?"

"Just stay here." Julie rushed over to Haden. "Can I help you find something?"

"No." He looked down at her, his ruthless, ice-blue gaze causing her to gasp. "I'm waiting for Caylee." When he said her name, his voice deepened, his blue eyes darkened, and lips parted in a sensuous smile.

Toes curling, Julie whimpered. "Oh, okay." He was so damn good-looking. So hot. She was going to pass out; she needed air. "You can sit over there." Turning to rush back to Brianna, Julie tripped. Haden grabbed her arm to prevent her from falling flat on her face, but he released her the instant she regained her balance. Blushing, her entire body trembling, she thanked him profusely and then rushed over to Brianna. "I can die happy now."

Brianna shook her head. "Huh?"

"He touched me." She sighed. "It was more than that. He saved me." Julie placed her hand over her heart. "My God, I've never seen a man look so hot in a suit."

"Who? You know I can't see a thing."

"It's Haden Drake. Oh, oh my God." She turned her head to sniff her arm where he'd grabbed her. "He smells so yummy. I could just lick him all over. And it's not just any suit he's wearing. It's Armani. I bet it's custom tailored. I know it is. It's worth a few thousand at least. He's so tall. Way over six foot." She paused. "He's as buff as they come, Julie. His shoulders and chest are just huge. I would give anything to take a ride on that stud." She took a deep breath and released it with a sigh. "I would give anything to take a ride on any part of that man's body."

"You're so incredibly vulgar." Brianna sighed. "But I almost wish I could see him."

"Want to go over and have a feel?"

"Are you crazy?" Brianna's voice cracked.

"Well, you're blind. It's how you see the world. And I can tell you he's some fine scenery you don't want to miss out on. I don't know how he could object."

"I do." Brianna paused. "Why's he here? We don't have any clothing for men, do we?"

"No. He's here because Mia's friend, Caylee, is here. It's not official, but she acts like they're a couple."

Brianna detected dark note of bitterness in Julie's voice.

Haden took off his coat. Julie squealed. "Oh, oh my God. Now that's a terrific ass. I wish you could see this. I wish he would take a little more off. The man is the most scintillating piece of erotic artwork I've ever seen." She giggled. "Are you sure you don't want to go over and have a feel?"

* * *

Pleased with what she was seeing, Caylee examined her body in the black lacy bra, panties, and thigh-highs for a moment. She felt a little ridiculous staring at her reflection in the mirror, but she was happy to see that most of her scars were so faded they were hardly noticeable. She put the dress on and sighed. Haden was such a handsome man. He had such a very solid, muscular build. His strong arms and broad chest were intimidating, but she savored the sensation of his powerful muscles bunching and tensing against her body as he held her.

Realizing she was daydreaming, she opened her eyes. It was morally wrong to look like him, but perhaps not as wrong as standing there drooling over the thought of him. She shrugged. It wasn't her fault. He could drive any woman insane. Grinning, she remembered his hands cradling her hips as she kissed him and rubbed her body against his. Before she could stop herself, she started to imagine her hands, wandering, touching every inch of his body.

Haden started to hear her thoughts. As if hearing wasn't torture enough, her thoughts were so strong he felt her hands exploring his body. He was instantly, violently aroused. *You're killing me, little love!* His heart rate sped up, and his stomach fluttered. Joy, overwhelming joy filled him. He easily entered and held her mind captive. He sent the sensation of a cold breeze sweeping over her naked body as the warmth of his hands and mouth caressed every lush curve of it. He imagined cupping her breasts in his hands, swirling his tongue over her nipples, taking them between his teeth and nipping and sucking, teasing them.

Caylee's heart rate elevated. The air left her lungs in a startled gasp. She could barely breathe. All at once her body burned and ached for release as moist heat pooled between her legs. She gasped again. *Stop it, Haden!* Biting her lower lip, she blushed.

You started it. With a huge, satisfied smile spread across his face, he reluctantly released her from his fantasy,

Caylee suddenly thought about Emmett, her uncle, and the consequence she would suffer if he ever discovered her friendship with Haden. Her uncle had specific plans for her future, and those plans definitely didn't include Haden. Fear surged through her, and she trembled. Emmett would be furious. He would reveal her secret. Haden would never forgive her. How could he? He would loathe the thought of her.

What am I going to do with you? I could never loathe you. He paused. *What secret do you keep from me?* Of course he knew exactly what she thought she was hiding from him, but he believed she needed to trust him enough to open up to him.

It's none of your business! Stay out of my head! She booted him out of her mind.

He tried to regain entrance to mind, but she continued to block him. He could've easily used more force, but it would've caused her pain. He wasn't willing to hurt her to prove he was powerful. He took a deep breath. Why was she afraid of Emmett? He'd never liked the man, but he believed she was safe with him. Why didn't she tell him otherwise? His heart sank. She didn't trust him to protect her because her self-esteem was shattered. She truly believed she didn't matter to him.

Realizing she could smell his cologne, Caylee turned her head and glared at the door. *You had better not be out there, Haden.*

Why? Are you worried I will come in and see you naked?

I'm dressed. Looking away from the door, she bent over to put her thigh-highs up.

He materialized behind her. She was bent over, and her short black dress was hiked up over her hips. Oh yeah, the view of the black lace thong definitely topped the tight jeans. "You have such a nice ass, little love."

Gasping, she looked up in mirror and saw his reflection behind her. "What are you doing in here?" She started to fall forward.

Laughing, he caught her hips and held her. "It appears I'm helping you keep your balance."

Standing upright, she closed her eyes. Splaying his hands over her belly, he pulled her close, pressing her backside against his body. She tried to convince herself he wasn't there with her. It was her imagination. "Do you really think if you pretend I'm not here I'll just disappear?"

She opened her eyes to meet his gaze in the mirror. "Sure, you appear and disappear all the time—why not now? Now would be a good time for you to disappear." Glancing down at her feet, she thought of falling to the floor and burying herself beneath it.

"I would wait. Sooner or later—I'm betting sooner—you would resurface for air."

"Oh no"—she turned suddenly—"you didn't!" He was so close she stumbled backward. "Enough is enough."

He wrapped his arms around her to prevent her from falling. "What?"

"Don't you dare play dumb." He was grinning like an idiot, looking all innocent, but he wasn't. She was so furious she could feel her checks turning red. She seriously considered slapping him. It would serve him right. "You know exactly what I'm talking about." She pointed at her head. "This is off limits to you!"

"Of course."

She couldn't believe he had the nerve to continue grinning. And was he looking at her butt in the mirror? Yep, he was staring at it. "Stop looking at my butt." Outraged, she shoved him. "I'm serious, Haden." Reaching behind her, she pulled her dress down over her hips.

"I only heard what you hurled at me." Pulling her nearer, he reached out and gently lifted her chin. Leaning down, he kissed her. Just once. A quick peck. "I missed you."

Tilting her head to the side, she smiled sweetly, way too sweetly. "Really?"

Fighting back the urge to laugh, he nodded. "Absolutely."

"You were only gone for one night." She placed her hand over her heart. "And to think only a moment ago you were so close to getting on my bad side. I couldn't possibly be angry now."

Stepping nearer, she reached up and framed his face between her hands. "I missed you, too." She placed her right hand on the center of his chest. "In fact, I nearly didn't survive the night." It took every ounce of her strength to hold back the laughter bubbling up in her, but she managed quite well.

"I appreciate your honesty." Arching his brow at her, he nodded. "Exposing such weakness for a man must be frightening. If I wasn't a man of superior integrity I might take advantage of it by using it to seduce you." He reached behind her and slipped his hand beneath the dress to caress her hips. "You're not only the most beautiful, sexy woman I've ever seen; you're also the most courageous." Taking her hand he brought it to his mouth and kissed it. "I can't stand the thought of you suffering."

Hot flames of retribution danced in her eyes, as she held his gaze. Whatever he could do, she could do better. She brought his hand to her chest and held it over her heart. "I swear my heart just skipped a beat, maybe even two. Can you feel it, Haden?" Her voice was very low and husky, extremely seductive, purposely sounding breathless.

He held her gaze for an entire second, maybe even two, and then looked down at his hand over her breast that was covered by nothing more than thin black lace and silk. His body instantly responded. His breath caught in his throat. His heart thundered in his ears. Every muscle in his body tensed as hot blood rushed to his groin. Startled, he met her gaze.

Knowingly, she smirked. He moved his hand quickly, completely shocked by her behavior. She was playing dirty. He loved it. He should admit defeat and beg for mercy, but he wasn't ready to give up just yet. She was about to seriously mess him up. He couldn't wait. He wanted more—he was a true glutton for punishment. Perhaps he was even a bit demented. "I never meant to distress you, little love."

She stepped nearer and placed her hands on his shoulders, allowing them to slowly slide down his arms. "Oh Haden, you're such a strong, powerful, sexy man." Seductively gazing up at him, she bit her lower lip. "What woman could ever resist such absolute masculine perfection?"

Oh, damn, she'd called him sexy out loud. She was practically naked. He was so swollen, so hard he was about to burst out of his pants. He was in serious danger, but he still wasn't ready to admit defeat. He wanted so much more. Trying to appear as casual as possible, he shrugged. "I've yet to meet one."

"Think again." She shoved him as hard as she could. "No matter how nice you are to look at, I'll always find it easy to resist you. I can't believe how arrogant you turned out to be. I almost believed you were a gentleman. You have the manners of a dog. A nasty, filthy dog. And a terrible sense of humor too. You're so rude."

"A dog?" He laughed.

"A nasty, filthy dog," she corrected, "that's always getting into my head, uninvited. And not to talk me. Oh no, you're not talking. You're sneaking, snooping around. You're probably doing it right now."

"Definitely not. You're talking too fast and making my head spin. Besides getting a terrible headache, I'm finding it difficult to keep up with what you're saying."

"Not surprising."

"Admit it—you're in love with me."

"Not even a little."

"You're lying." He reached out and gently caressed her face with the very tips of his fingers. "I love you, Caylee."

She needed to get as far away from him as possible, before it was too late and she said too much.

He instantly felt fear and saw the change in her countenance. He pushed his mind forward to merge her mind. "Too late for what?"

"Haden, why are you doing this?" Caylee's heart rate sped up as she moved nearer.

He stood absolutely still. Speechless, he looked down at her. His body was a raging inferno of need. The floorboards vibrated as he fought his body's demands. He was in a terrible state. He needed to stay in control. He needed to focus. It was far more convenient to keep a level head when she wasn't touching him. And damn it, she wasn't simply touching him. He might survive a touch. Her body was so snugly pressed against his he could feel every beat of her heart.

He looked furious; his icy blue gaze filled with such terrible darkness. She took a deep breath and swallowed hard. Releasing her breath, she forced herself to smile. "What's wrong?"

She tried to back away, but he held her arms firmly. She struggled for a moment, and then she stopped and stared up at him.

"Stop it. I'm not angry. And I thought my eyes bothered you when they turn black." Looking very naughty, he smiled at her. "I'm just so frustrated. Extremely, painfully frustrated."

He was so big. So close. His body crowded hers. "Why?" Holding his gaze, she paused, secretly battling her desire to embrace the hope his love for her was strong enough to survive the truth. "Oh, Haden, why are you doing this?" Within seconds, her common sense was left gasping for life at her feet as her irrational desire savored the victory.

Enchanted by the love in his gaze, she allowed her safeguards to drop. With him was the only place she wanted to be. Closing her eyes, she remembered their bodies entwined in a passionate embrace. She thought of the warmth and strength of his hands caressing her body. She thought of the enticing masculine scent of his body. The sensation of his kiss on her lips. Suddenly shocked by her wandering mind, she looked up at him. He was grinning from ear to ear. Her face turned red. She couldn't get angry. She'd definitely hurled the thoughts at him.

* * *

"I can't believe he went in there with her," Julie whispered.

"Are you sure he didn't just leave?" Brianna asked.

"There's no way. He would've walked across the store to get to the door. I definitely would've noticed." She tugged on Brianna's arm. "Come on. I want to go listen by the door."

"Nope." Brianna shook her head. "No way. I do not want to hear whatever it is they're doing in there."

"What if he's hurting her?"

"She would scream."

"You don't know that." Walking toward the dressing room area, Julie tugged on Brianna's arm again. "How are you going to feel if you find out he was hurting her? We need to make sure she's okay."

"Julie, you're seriously overreacting. He wouldn't have been able to get in there with her unless she unlocked the door for him."

"Maybe she didn't lock the door."

~ *Seven* ~

"ALL NIGHT LONG I dreamed of your kiss." He bent his head to kiss the corner of her mouth. "I dreamed of your legs wrapped around my body." Lifting her and then holding her up with one hand, he used the other to wrap her leg around his body. "I dreamed of your satiny flesh against mine." He breathed deeply, allowing her tantalizing scent of warm, spiced vanilla to envelope and fill him.

So many thoughts were racing through Caylee's mind. Her body was on fire for him. Her heart was racing so frantically it felt as if it would burst right out of her chest. How long had she hoped for a second chance at life? How long ago had she given up on it? She was so tired of pretending there was any possible way to escape her life. He was promising to pull her out of her silent suffering and take her far away from the endlessness of her dark reality. But why? She wasn't the right type of a woman for a man like him. Was she a diversion? If so, from what? She needed to know as much as possible if she were going to survive the game of seduction he was playing. She couldn't afford to allow him to rip her heart to shreds.

"Your beauty brings me to my knees, little love." It was the truth. Her beauty had always captivated him. "I've never imagined a woman more exquisite than you." She was tiny in stature, with a slender build but with a curvy, womanly figure.

Her long, loose curls of dark brown hair fell to the center of her back. Her eyes were dark green, with shimmers of gold when the light hit them just right. "Your heart is safe with me."

He focused on her lips. While they parted in a sweet, innocent smile, he knew the truth. Her innocent smile doubled as a powerful, intoxicating weapon of seduction. The right corner of his mouth curled upward as he recalled the way she tortured him with her kiss. "I love you, Caylee. I love you with every cell in my body."

"Stop teasing me." Smiling shyly, she bit her lower lip. "You don't have to worry. I'm not stupid. I know we both got carried away last night."

"Damn it, Caylee." His deep, seductive voice, simply saying her name, heated her blood and caressed her soul. "Shut up and lock your ankles together."

Her eyes filled up with tears. "Why are you doing this?" He wouldn't want her if he knew she'd made a terrible decision that led to her being raped by a group of men.

Haden hated that she blamed herself for being raped. He hated that it made her feel unworthy of him. He also hated that he'd allowed her to continue pretending he didn't know about it until it became her reality. He should've forced her to face the truth the night he found her "You're mine. You're my miracle, my angel." He was demon, a soul damned for eternity. "You're everything pure and lovely." He was everything dark and dangerous. "You surpass every fantasy I've ever entertained. My heart and soul belong to you. I'm deeply, insanely in love with you."

She opened her mouth to argue with him, but nothing came out. She had so many reasons to feel not good enough for him, for the love he proclaimed to have for her. But she couldn't deny the truth in his eyes. He loved her more than anything. At least, for that moment she was the center of his universe. His love for her might not last. It probably wouldn't. But she wanted to experience it.

Julie knocked on the dressing room door. "Are you okay in there?"

"Haden," Caylee whispered. "What are they going to think?"

"I don't care. Tell them you're fine," he growled, "and kiss me."

"I'm fine." For a moment, she had allowed herself to believe his love could prevail over the secret she kept from him, but when the moment had passed she knew it was an unobtainable fantasy. She wasn't right for him. He was so amazing. Handsome. Strong.

"Are you sure?" Giggling, Julie covered her mouth.

"Yes." Caylee's heart was racing.

"Kiss me." Several breathless moments passed by as they gazed into each other's eyes. "Damn it, Caylee." His deep, throaty voice richly revealed the depths of his desire for her. "I love you." His words, his voice, caressed her. "I know you're afraid, but I really need you to kiss me right now."

Why wouldn't he leave their friendship alone? She was mesmerized, holding his gaze. He brought her body to life. He made her mind wander to places she'd never dared go before. She needed him. A tiny whimper escaped her throat as the warmth of his breath wisped across her face. His lips were as close as they could get to hers without actually touching. Closing his eyes, he tilted his head to the left. She felt the heat of his mouth barely brushing up against hers, but then she felt a peculiar chill as he pulled back.

Opening her eyes, she gasped, shocked by intensity of the hunger in his black gaze. "Haden?" It was so much greater than ever before. More intense. More fierce. His enormous strength, his mysterious powers, everything about him was so dangerous, so frightening. He wanted her. She knew, without any doubt, he was demanding everything, her complete surrender, body and soul.

"Not demanding. Wanting you. Needing you. But never demanding, little love. You control where this moment will carry us. I will never take anything away from you, but I will gladly receive whatever you're willing to share with me," he whispered, kissing the corner of her mouth. "Kiss me."

She kissed him, timidly at first and then deeply, hungrily. She was on fire, allowing herself to truly experience the exquisite pleasure of his kiss. Her body a raging inferno, she met his tongue with hers, determined to give herself to him.

Experiencing a high like no other ever known to him, his heart thundered in his ears. Something violent, uncontrollable welled up in him, commanding him to take her last breath. It was the only way to ensure her safety. He realized the danger of the situation, but there was nothing he could about it. It wasn't the right time. It was too soon. She would likely die if he tried to give her immortality right now.

He'd just promised he would never take anything from her she wasn't willing to give, but it was lie. He would take her last breath. He was helpless to save her or to save himself. He was no longer in control of his nature. He'd waited for too long. The combination of his lust and love for her devoured his strength, letting loose his true character, demanding he bind them together for all eternity.

For so long, to protect her, he'd been fighting against what he was, but he was done fighting, done denying. She belonged to him. He belonged to her. He needed to dominate, to possess her body and soul. His body ached. Painfully aroused, his cock, impossibly hard, throbbed. He needed to get nearer; he needed to feel the heat of her satiny flesh against his own. He needed to end his agony. He needed to be where he belonged. He needed to plunge deep inside her body.

He slowly, gently lowered her onto her feet. Reaching behind her, he gently but firmly pulled her hair, arching her neck, exposing her throat. "I love you, Caylee. With every cell of my being, I love you. No matter what happens, nothing will ever keep us apart." It was a warning, the only one he could give her. It was promise. If she died, he would do the impossible. He would give up his existence to be with her.

A deep, inhuman growl rumbled in his throat. Leaning down, he breathed in the delicious scent of her body, preparing to take her life. She savored the sensation of the moist heat of his breath on her throat. His seductive voice caused her body to tremble. For an endless moment, he'd not yet touched her with his lips, but she imagined them exploring her flesh. Whimpering, she clung to him, her body pleading for the first touch of his lips. Then, all of the sudden, he was kissing her neck and throat. Her body welcomed his touch. Feverish and damp, every inch of her flesh tingled as her desire for him burned in the core of her being.

In that instant, Haden made a hasty decision. Believing the only hope she had to survive the ritual was to face the truth, he decided to take her through time and space to the place where he'd found her so close to death.

Lost in the pure ecstasy of physical sensations, she wanted the moment to go on and on. She was slightly aware of the black and silver mist surrounding them and the fact that they were moving, floating through time and space.

"Tell me." He so very tenderly kissed her earlobe. "Tell me you know it too, Caylee." Tears burned behind his eye. This was it. It was the moment that would change everything. "We can no longer pretend."

Releasing her hair, he cupped his hands around her face and gazed into her eyes for a moment, and then he slowly leaned down and kissed her lips. "Tell me you know I love you. No matter what happens, you're safe with me."

Unless she believed it, she would fear him and die. And also, quite possibly, hate him on the other side of existence.

All of the sudden, she was silenced by the thought of her secret. Fear slammed into her. Not of him, but of the past. For the first time, realizing they were no longer in the dressing room, she glanced around and immediately recognized the area. Why had he brought her here? She couldn't allow him to learn the truth. Panicking, every muscle in her body stiffened, and she struggled to free herself from his embrace.

The fear, the absolute horror in her eyes, instantly brought him to his senses. He'd come far too close to destroying everything. He brought her here to help her face the past and accept that he knew the entire truth all along. He'd allowed her to pretend that, despite finding her here, he didn't know what had happened to her. He would've allowed her to continue believing he didn't know anything, but he couldn't. It was driving a wedge between them. "Talk to me, little love—tell me why you're afraid."

Her thoughts were jumbled. Why had he brought her here? She was suffocating. Did he know the truth? Her heart beat frantically, painfully slamming against her chest. No. He didn't. He couldn't. It would be too much. She could never endure the shame and rejection. Her chest hurt; clutching it, she stared up at him, her entire body trembling uncontrollably.

"Relax, little love. You don't have any reason to be afraid of anything." Knowing she was about to collapse, he reached out for her.

Taking a step backward, the color draining from her face, she stared up at him. "Please," she said, her voice weak, "leave me alone, Haden." She needed to get away from him. She needed to hide. Her eyes darted around frantically. "Please, just let ... I can't be here."

"It's okay. You're okay." Taking a step forward, he reached out to her. "You're having a panic attack."

Shaking her head, she stepped back. She needed to leave. She needed to get as far away from him as possible.

"Breathe," he commanded, keeping his hand extended, prepared to catch her. "You've no reason to ever be afraid. You're safe with me." Not giving her a chance to back away any further, he took her hand.

Her world was falling apart. She looked down at his hand wrapped around hers. It felt so good, so right to be touched by him. Shaking head, she yanked her hand free. "You had no right to bring me here. I need to leave. I can't be here."

She looked up at him and whimpered. "Please, just let me

go." She desperately searched her mind for a way to escape the moment without revealing the truth. "We're friends, Haden, nothing more." Trembling, she looked away from him.

"Stop lying to yourself." His voice was a low and cruel growl, completely void of the tenderness she was accustomed to hearing. She looked up him, tears streaming down her face. A black mass of strange, translucent flames swirled around him. The ground rumbled deep below the earth. A strong, icy wind picked up. His black eyes reflected unbridled rage. Both eyes, even the whites, were as black as coal with flecks of silver.

Paralyzed by fear, unable to even take another breath, she stood absolutely still and studied him for a moment, wishing she could close her eyes to escape his dark, fearsome gaze.

"Damn it, Caylee, they're just eyes. They change color with my emotions. They can't hurt you." Well, they could, but they wouldn't. Not her. Never her. "I could never do anything to harm you."

He grabbed her hand, pressing her palm against his chest. "My heart beats only for you. You are my life. The reason I breathe. We belong together. You need to trust me. Tell me what you are afraid of."

"You," she lied, her voice was pitiful whimper, but she held his gaze. "I saw you turn into a dragon. I've heard the stories about a demonic phantom killing people in this forest. I know it's you. You're not human. I've seen you do impossible things. How did you bring me here? Being alone out here with you terrifies me." Forced by guilt, she looked away from him. "There's something terrible and dark inside you."

A sudden, terrible burst anger surged through him so that the ground shook enough to cause her to stumble. "The darkness isn't in me." Taking a step closer, he stopped directly in front of her, reaching out to lift her face toward his. "I am the darkness," he growled between clenched teeth.

Lightning erupted, zigzagging in dark, billowing clouds. She gasped, quickly looking away from him. Thunder boomed so very loudly. Bone-chilling terror raced through her veins. Eyes wide, she looked up at him. Black flames swirled around him, engulfing him and engulfing her. He looked wholly evil, his harsh features set in stone, intimidating and cruel. The image of huge, black leathery wings shimmered on his back for a few seconds, and then they became tangible. Very slowly, she stepped backward, looking from the left and to the right, searching for a way to escape.

He shook his head slowly, strange silver flames flickering in his black eyes. "You can't escape a demon, little love—you would have better luck charming him."

Infuriated, she looked up at him and shook her head. Wings or not, she wasn't going to let him frighten her. "Fine—do your worst to me! I've no intention of wasting my time attempting to charm an ass!"

She stepped closer to him, lifting her chin, looking as fierce as possible. "Even if the ass is a demon or a dragon." She paused. "I won't run from you. I won't give you the satisfaction."

Placing her hands on her hips, she shook her head. "You're not a demon." Tilting her head to the side, she chewed on her bottom lip. "I don't know what you are, but I don't believe you're a demon."

Amused by her tantrum, he chuckled. With a thought, his wings shimmered and quickly disappeared. He immediately relaxed, allowing his anger slip away. The atmosphere stilled. She was afraid, but not of him. Even when he tried to frighten her with the truth of what he was, she refused to believe the worst of him. She was lashing out at him because she was safe with him. He was so entirely overcome with joy all he could do was smile at her. He was so very much closer to gaining her trust than he ever truly thought possible.

"I refuse to believe it." Exasperated, she cursed beneath her breath. "And stop smiling at me."

He shrugged, purposely appearing emotionless. "Why do you believe I will not harm you?"

Hesitating for several breathless seconds, she looked to the side to avoid his gaze. "You just wouldn't."

He gently swept his hand over her shoulders, walking in a tight circle around her. "There are many things I would enjoy doing to you."

Grinning, he paused. "With you."

He stopped directly in front of her, firmly grabbed her shoulders, and then slowly leaned down until his lips made the slightest contact with her earlobe.

"Are you absolutely positive I wouldn't enjoy hurting you?" Softly, he kissed her earlobe. "Are you willing to bet your life on it?"

Closing her eyes, she whimpered. "Yes." She was absolutely certain of it. His deep, raspy voice combined with the hot, seductive sensation of his lips caused her body to shudder. A sensational fire burned deep in the core of her being. Breathing heavily, she saw images of their naked bodies tangled together, moving together.

Startled, her eyes flashed open. She needed to get away from him. "Let go!" She struggled to pull away from him, but it was no use; his grip was unbreakable.

Despite her resistance, he pulled her nearer with very little effort. "Not yet." He bent his head to feather kisses along her jaw. "First," he murmured, gently nipping the tender flesh of her neck, "tell me what happened the night I found you here."

He was trying to force her to accept the fact that he'd always known she'd been raped. She needed to admit it aloud to herself. She needed to know he didn't blame her. She needed to know that it didn't make him want her less. She needed to know it wasn't her fault. She needed to believe she was everything to him. She was his life. Nothing could ever stop him from loving her. Nothing was more important than her. He loved her so much that he would gladly give anything, including his life, to protect her,

He was making her crazy. She couldn't possibly take anymore. She needed to get as far away from him as possible. "Let go of me!" She jerked her right arm free and slapped him across the face. Rather than take evasive measures, he absorbed the blow and kept a firm hold of her. "Let go!" Frantic, she struggled to get away.

He lessened his grip but held her firmly. "Answer me." His voice was calm but demanding.

No longer fighting, she took a deep breath and held it, meeting his gaze the entire time. She released her breath and then took slow and steady breaths in an attempt to regain her composure. The only danger she was in at that precise moment was being seduced by him. She needed to get away from him. She needed to end their friendship. She would never be physically strong enough to force him to let her go. She needed to find a different tactic. But what?

"You're making me crazy. I can't think straight. What do you plan to do next?" She glanced from side to side at his hands on her shoulders. "Do you intend to force yourself on me?"

"Damn it, Caylee, you know better." Narrowing his eyes, he clenched his jaw. "I've been your friend, patiently pretending to be some sort of pathetic saint, never expecting too much, always waiting for you to be ready."

Staring up at him, she shook her head. "You've been deceiving me all along?" And for what, sex? How could every minute of their friendship be a lie? Choking on the lump in her throat, she placed her hand over her it.

"Yes, I have. But you're wrong—I would never take advantage of you. It's not a matter of sex. Well, not entirely." He released her shoulders. At the same time, she forcefully pulled away. She started to fall backward, but he moved forward with blurring speed and held her steady.

Pushing him away, she glared up at him, her arms crossed in front of her chest. "Why would you waste your time pretending to be my friend?"

"It wasn't a waste of time." He studied the confusion and rage in her eyes. "You needed time." He couldn't tell her he intended to take her last mortal breath and replace it with the breath of immortality. "You can't fear me. You must have complete faith in my love for you."

She stumbled backward a bit but quickly steadied herself. None of what he was saying made any sense at all. Why had he brought her to this place? If he knew what had happened, he couldn't possibly want her as a lover. And for so long. No. He was lying. He had to be. But why? What was he gaining?

She smiled. He was angry. He was striking back at her for denying him. That was it. He was being cruel. And she deserved it. She'd led him on and then turned him down. He had to know she wouldn't be so gullible. "I just want to go back to Mia's shop. You mean absolutely nothing to me."

"You're lying." Grinning, he looked down at her. "You love me as deeply as I love you."

She turned and walked away from him. "Why are you ruining everything, Haden?" She stopped and looked down at her feet. He took a few strides and stopped directly behind her. She turned and looked up at him with so much pain in her eyes that he struggled against the urge to scoop her up in his arms.

"I hate you." She was trembling so fiercely her voice was nearly inaudible. "I can't be here." Biting her lower lip, she looked up at him. "I never want to see you again."

Lowering her head, she stepped nearer, until their bodies were only a mere centimeter apart. For a moment, she stared at his chest, watching it rise and fall with each breath he took and released. Why would he choose to bring her to where he'd found her? "Haden," she said, teary-eyed as she looked up at him, "why are you doing this?"

He wrapped his arms around her. God help her, it felt so good, so right to be in his arms. She felt so safe, so thoroughly loved and needed. He bent his head and kissed her softly. "You know in your heart we are so much more than friends.

You know our souls are bound together for all of eternity. We've both known we belong to each other ever since I found you lying here, so close to death."

She wiggled out of his arms and stepped back. "Don't say anymore." Why was he bringing up the past again? How could he be so cruel? "We can't be together like that." She frowned, her lips quivering. "And you know it."

Grieving the loss of their closeness, she let the tears stream down her face. Everything was ruined; they could never be friends again. "Why, Haden, why are you doing this?" Her voice was a sad, barely audible whimper.

"I love you, Caylee." Closing the gap between them, he took a step forward, wrapped his arms around her, and pulled her deep into his embrace. "It's that simple. I love you. I happily lived alone for a very long time. I never thought I would want to share my life with anyone, but I need to share it with you. You're everything to me. You're the most wonderful treasure I could've ever hoped to find. There's nothing I value more than you."

He bent his head to give her a slow, sensual kiss, and then, brow-to-brow, he held her gaze captive. "You can't image how desperately I need you." He took a deep breath, kissed her lips, and then leaned down near her ear. "I love you," he said as he kissed her earlobe, "so much."

Kissing her lips, he slowly leaned against her until her back was pressed against the trunk of a tree. For a moment, he hesitated, carefully studying every feature of her face, monitoring her thoughts. "We belong together. You're my heart and soul. I'll never let you go."

She started to argue, but he silenced her with a kiss that went on and on. The wind picked up as they fueled the flames of their desire, but he ignored it until he heard the sound of thunder in the distance. Normally he could command nature at will, but his emotions, if strong, had a tendency to create unpredictable, uncontrollable storms. He reluctantly broke off the kiss. "I will take you back."

"No." Blinking rapidly, she stared up at him. What was she doing? Had she completely lost her mind? "You're right. I'm sorry. We need to go."

He shrugged casually, but there was nothing causal in his eyes. "You're not returning to your uncle's house." It was a fact. He refused to argue over it.

"You have no right to stop me." She glared at him, daring him to try. "You don't own me."

"Damn it, Caylee." His arms enveloped her, holding her tight. "I don't want to own you. I want your love and companionship."

"Make love with me before we say goodbye." The words came out unexpectedly, but she didn't regret them.

Leaning back, he held her at arm's length. "Goodbye?"

Ignoring him, she started to unbutton his shirt. At first he kept his arms locked, forcing her to remain a distance away. Opening his shirt, she leaned forward to kiss the base of his throat, tracing his well-defined muscles with the tips of her finger. The woman was killing him. His arms buckled, allowing her to press nearer.

"Make love with me this one time," she whispered the words against his chest.

The words, *this one time*, tormented him, replaying in his mind over and over again as her soft, satiny lips brushed across his chest. He knew she believed in her heart there would never be another time for them to be together. He didn't want to stop her, but he held her back at arm's length again.

"One time?" Drawn to her, needing to taste her kiss and feel the warmth of her breath, he bent his head to get closer. "One time would never be enough."

Standing on the tips of her toes, pressing her body against the length of his hard cock, she trailed kissed from his neck to jaw. His heart was thundering. She was shattering his control. More than anything he wanted take possession her of body, but he knew better. He wished he didn't, but he did.

"Wait." He stepped back. "Stay right there."

"Haden." She took a step closer. "What's wrong with you? Don't you want to make love to me?"

He held out his hands to stop her, a little alarmed by the way they were trembling. "I can't believe I'm about to ask you to keep your distance, but you've given me no choice."

"Honestly, Haden." She stepped toward him.

"I'm losing control. I could use a little help. I know you're not ready."

She moved even closer.

He stepped back. "I'm serious, I need your help. Stay right there."

"Well, I will admit you have serious issues and for that reason you might need my help. I can't think of a more terrible time for you to be so stubborn."

Lifting her chin, she smiled up at him, arching her brow. "Has it occurred to you I want you to lose control?" Grinning mischievously, she shrugged. "I'm ready, but perhaps you're not ready."

A faint odor wafted past them. He moved closer to her. Crowding her. His body went perfectly still, shielding hers, as he carefully scanned the area and constructed a powerful, magical barrier to prevent the ghouls from getting any closer. What was happening to him? He should've noticed they weren't alone. After all, it was ghouls that were out and about. They were extremely ignorant, literally brainless corpses, completely incapable of doing anything covertly.

A gust of wind came from behind, causing her hair to cover her face. Pulling it behind her back, she look up at him as he looked past her. Lightning raced across the sky, followed by the sound of thunder. Carried by the wind, a terrible, musty stench filled her lungs. Death and decayed flesh. Terror brutally crashed into her heart so it skipped a beat. Her mouth watering and stomach twisting into painful knots, the memory of Paul's insane hatred filled her soul with dread.

"It's the vampire." She moved closer to Haden, seeking his protection, so very thankful that his arms instantly pulled her deep into the shelter of his embrace.

~ *Eight* ~

SEVERAL FEET BENEATH the earth, Paul woke up, confused and disoriented by the thick, heavy mud that covered his body. He seldom went to ground. And he'd never once, during his three hundred years of life, rested in the mud. He was anxious to get out of it but instinctively knew the sun hadn't fully set. Normally he could easily withstand the sun, but his strength was significantly diminished. From the top of his head to the tips of his toes, worms and maggots crawled all over his body. His stomached burned with hunger. His nutrient-deprived muscles ached. He shifted to the left, attempting to find a more comfortable position, but rather than give him relief the movement caused every muscle in his body to spasm.

He was in terrible shape. Haden had nearly killed him, forcing him to choose such an unsavory resting place. He knew Haden wouldn't stop at nearly killing him. He was a particularly hostile demon. Common sense told Paul to flee the area and rejoin the safety of his clan, but anger and pride ate away his ability to entertain any rational thought for any period of time. He wanted Caylee, and he would have her.

The ground rumbled violently. Paul felt Haden reaching for him, searching for his hiding place. He smiled. Demons were unstoppable, hulking brutes, perfectly designed to be victorious in any battle, but they were fools. They allowed themselves to fall so deeply in love they acted like idiots. They devoted their lives to love, willing to sacrifice their immortal souls to protect the ones they loved. Haden tried to hide it, but Paul knew he was afraid for the woman. Choosing a fragile, mortal woman for a mate was a terrible mistake. Keeping her mortal was an even worse mistake. Paul would use her to destroy Haden.

* * *

Watching the torrential downpour head across the meadow toward them, Haden held Caylee close. "You're safe. He's nearby, but he's beneath ground, injured and weak."

"How do you know?"

"I plan to kill him before he's ever able to get near you again," he whispered over her head.

"No." She tilted her head back to look up at him. "How do you know he's here and he's injured and weak? How do you know so much about the vampire?"

"It's my duty to know. It's what I do."

Frowning, chewing on her bottom lip, she stared up at him. She looked so totally confused. Of course she didn't understand. Two nights ago she'd never known vampires existed.

"You know I'm not human. You've accepted it, but you don't know what I am. I possess powers and abilities that you find difficult to comprehend. My kind was created with these powers and abilities to enable us to destroy vampires and other creatures of darkness that prey on humans."

"So," she shivered, "there are more of your kind?"

"Yes," Haden said. "There are many of us. You met Zack and Joseph last night. I was hiding my presence to draw the vampires closer. Zack didn't know I was with you. He was rushing to your aid. He would've saved you if I hadn't reached you in time."

"How did he know I was there?"

"Paul's clan has been killing people in Zack's territory for months. Zack has been hunting them, destroying one vampire at a time. A few vampires, including Paul, fled here to elude him. Zack and Joseph were pursing him the night you stumbled across the dead woman."

"I saw them with my own eyes, but it's still hard to believe there're other men like you." Haden was so incredibly sexy. He looked like a god, but Caylee was certain it was an unpardonable sin to walk around looking so tantalizing. Grinning, she wondered if all of his kind shared his extraordinary sex appeal. She certainly would never want to know another as intimately as she knew him. She giggled aloud. How many other women suffered because of his kind? "One of you is too much for this woman to handle."

"I'm pleased to know I'm appealing to you," he whispered, grinning like a fool. "But it would be best if you didn't envision another man the way you see me. It wouldn't be good for him if another man was even remotely attractive to you." He brought her hand to the warmth of his mouth. "And it would most definitely be better for Zack and Joseph if you didn't handle them. To be completely honest, I am a very jealous man, capable of unpleasant outbursts."

She smirked. "I've known for a long time that you're prone to freaking out over ridiculous things."

"Not until I met you." The rain reached them and was pelting down all around, but Haden prevented it from touching them. The lightning and thunder were rapid, allowing no break between each blinding flash and earsplitting crackle. "It's not safe here," he lied—he had no problem ensuring her safety in the storm. "I will take you to town. Once you show Mia the dress we can go to my place to talk in a more comfortable environment." Meaning, he planned to seduce her and get her into his bed as quickly as possible. Then, she was never leaving his sight.

"No," she said, turning to face him, "I can't go with you. I plan to … oh Haden, you just don't understand. I'm engaged to another man."

Perfectly on cue, a result of Haden's shock, lightning hit the ground a few yards away. The sound of thunder was instant and terrifyingly loud. Her breath rushed in and out of her lungs in startled gasp. Covering her ears, she buried her head against his chest.

"Why didn't I know about it?" Pushing her back, he held her at arm's length. There was no way in hell he was going to permit her to marry another man. "There's no other man for you. You're mine." The menacing tone of his voice was chilling, heart stopping.

A powerful gust of wind pushed her body against his. Terrified and cold, she trembled. A bolt of lightning struck a tree limb directly overhead, and she screamed. With a thought, he raised his hand to toss the limb a safe distance away.

"You're causing it. Make it stop," she pleaded.

"It's not me. It's your doing." Cradling her head against his chest in one hand, he caressed her back with the other. "The storm won't hurt you. It's part of me. I don't know why you would consider marrying another man. You don't want to be with another man. You love me as deeply as I love you." He looked up at the dark, ominous pillars of clouds in the sky. The storm would run its course. Thanks to her unexpected marriage announcement, his emotions were spiraling out of control. There was nothing he could do about the storm for the time being. "Paul will rise soon. Once you and Mia finish the business with the dress, I'm taking you home with me."

"No," she whispered with tears in her voice. "After today, I can never see you again."

Every muscle in his body tensed. No other man would ever touch her and live. No more mental blocks. He'd made a mistake by allowing her to have privacy. From now on, he planned maintain a merge with her mind at all times. He didn't care if it bothered her.

She silently wept against his chest as the rain continued to fall from the sky. What else was she hiding? He needed more information. He needed it now. He found the barrier she placed in her mind and tried to push through it, but it was a solid block. He could use more force to get through it, but at the moment it would definitely cause her to suffer excruciating pain. He would wait until her guard was down, and then he would get rid of the damn thing for good.

Sobbing, she looked up at him. "You're always snooping around in my mind. You know I've imagined being with you." She leaned her head against his chest. "But you also know I've always understood we can never be together." Her voice was a faint whimper. "Come on. Look at me, Haden." Stepping back, she held out her arms and spun around so he could look at her and then, as if her point had been proved, she shrugged. "Anyone can see I'm not the right woman for a man like you."

He let his breath out slowly, searching his mind for the right words, his gaze slowly moving over her. "I can't imagine a woman more beautiful, more desirable than you. Just looking at you takes my breath away. You are more precious to me than anything else. Your existence is a miracle to me. I never thought I would want to share my life with a woman. I certainly never believed I would want to bind my soul to a woman." He wrapped his arms around her and pulled her near, pressing her soft, feminine curves against his solid, muscular frame. "We belong together."

"You're wrong."

"Your heart and soul belong to me, just as mine will forever belong to you." He bent his head and gently kissed her earlobe. "Nothing else matters."

"Love, not even the love you claim to have for me, is strong enough to see us through the secret I've kept from you." She took a deep breath and released it with a sigh. "I plan to marry Phillip in a few months. I must do it. And you need to accept it." She pushed herself out of his embrace. "I need to go."

Like hell she was going anywhere. "Phillip?" He searched his memory. There was only one man who came to mind. "Phillip Wicks?"

Slowly backing away, she nodded. "Please, just forget about it. There's nothing more to discuss. I've made up my mind."

Amused, he smiled. It was an easily fixed problem. If worst came to worst, he would simply kill Phillip. And her uncle too, if it proved necessary. He wasn't going to allow anything or anyone to keep them apart. "I'll take you to Mia's shop." She wasn't ready to live with him, but that didn't mean he couldn't stay very close to her at all times.

"No." She stared at him, studied him. He looked far too guilty, peculiar silver flames swirling in his eyes, to even consider trusting him. "I would rather be alone."

A black mist surrounded him, as wings took tangible form on his back. "Too bad." He reached for her hand. Surely he didn't intend to fly. Grinning, he nodded. "Come here."

His black, velvety wings, like everything else about him, were incredibly massive and intimidating. "No thanks." Shaking her head, she stepped back, her heart pounding in her ears. "I would much rather walk." There was no way she would do it. It wasn't right. She had feet for a reason, and she planned to use them. Nope, she wasn't going to fly. Not with him. Not with anyone. Not for any reason. It was just plain wrong.

"Mia will be returning soon to check on you. Flying will be much quicker than walking." He stepped closer, closing the gap between them.

She started to argue. She was right after all—it wasn't a good idea. He swept his arms around her and bent his head to kiss her. It was a crushing, passionate kiss, stealing her sanity. She moved closer to him, pressing her body against his. His cast-iron, masculine body made her wonderfully aware of her supple, feminine curves. She forgot about his intention to fly with her. She forgot about everything else, as an intoxicating fire of desire spread throughout her body and blazed over her sensitive flesh.

"Wrap your arms around my neck," he whispered against her mouth as he lifted her and then extended and stretched his wings. Without thought, she did as he said, kissing him deeply. Knowing she would panic the moment they were off the ground, he secured her in his arms. He would make it a pleasant experience for her. Well, as pleasant as possible. No sudden moves. "Are you ready?"

Dizzy, breathless from their kissing, she looked up at him from beneath thick veils of lashes. Ready for what? She blinked. She was forgetting something very important. Her mind was a blank slate. She could barely remember her name. She wished he would just kiss her again. She was definitely ready to be kissed again. He bent his head and kissed her slowly, gently, too gently. She wanted more. She wanted him to lose control. She wanted him wild, on fire, burning up for her. With her.

His powerful wings launched them into the sky, high above the treetops.

Startled, she cried out, burying her face against his chest, not too happy to remember what he was planning before he seduced her into a state of ignorant bliss. "I will never forgive you for this." She heard his irritating laughter above her head. "I'm serious, Haden. I will never forgive you."

"Never is a very long time to hold a grudge, little love. Stop being a baby and take a look around."

"A baby?" Her head snapped up, and she glared into his eyes, struggling against the urge to slap him across the face. He certainly deserved a good smack or two. She couldn't believe he was grinning at her as if he were doing nothing wrong at all. Shaking her head, she bit back a few choice names she wanted to call him. Why did he have to look so good? So sexy. Being so attracted to him was a terrible disadvantage when she wanted to hate him.

"Look around and see what you've been missing." He easily took them higher, her weight nothing to him. "The view of the forest is beautiful from up here."

She heard the joy bubbling in his voice. She saw it in his eyes. He was so very happy to be able to share something so special with her. She knew he didn't need to fly to get back to Mia's quickly. He could've taken them instantly through time and space. He wanted to share this with her. "I prefer to enjoy it from the ground." However, curiosity getting the best of her, she looked to the side and down.

Her stomach knotted and rolled. They were so high, the wind rushing past them. Way too high. Everything started spinning. She could feel them tumbling out of the sky, their bodies crashing against the hard ground. She struggled to catch her breath, her mouth watering, her stomach twisting. Perfect—she was going to throw up all over him. She looked up at him and smirked. It would serve him right.

He laughed aloud. Nuzzling his chin in her hair, he took a deep breath, filling his lungs with her sweet scent. "You're not going to fall. You're safe with me." Anchoring her to him with one arm, he lifted her chin with his other hand, forcing her to meet his gaze. "I can hold us up with a thought."

Eyes wide, she stared up at him, slowly shaking her head. She didn't know what he was talking about, but she wasn't going to ask for an explanation. She was certain she wasn't going to like it.

Still keeping her snugly anchored against his body with one arm, he reached over his shoulder and, despite her best effort to keep them clamped around his neck, moved her arms. "Trust me."

"Trust me to do something very awful and painful to you in the very near future."

"Why do I try?" he teased. "That wasn't a very nice thing to say to me." He took her hand in his; it wasn't necessary, but maintaining some physical contact would lessen the shock. He didn't want to frighten her. He wanted to show her his power, his ability to protect and care for her.

She knew he was planning to let go of her. "Don't you dare do it." He'd better not do it. Gripping his hand hard, she buried her nails into his flesh and glared up him. "I swear you'll be sorry." And she meant it.

"Too late." Instantly, she realized his arm was no longer holding her, but his hand held hers. That was it. And it wasn't enough. The air was forced in and out of her lungs in short, violent gasps. She closed her eyes tight, too afraid to look at the ground rushing toward her, but she could feel herself falling. "Don't be silly. You're not falling. I would never allow it to happen. Look at me, Caylee." He purposely, using his supernatural abilities, deepened his voice, making it a hypnotic command.

Struggling to fight it, she vigorously shook her head back and forth. "No way." But she did it. She couldn't help it. Tears burning behind her eyes, she looked up at him. His eyes were solid black, even the whites, except for occasional silver flame like flickers. He filled her with the peace and the strength to accept what was strange to her. He literally flooded her heart and soul with his love.

Everything inside her instantly stilled; even her heart stopped racing. It didn't matter she was so far from the ground. She was perfectly safe. He would never allow her to be harmed. For the first time in her life she felt completely at peace. She'd always love him. She'd always believed he valued their friendship, but that was it. She'd never believed he would fall in love with her. Looking up at him, seeing the hunger in his eyes, she saw everything clearly. He was fiercely in love with her. He cherished her. Some tiny, very rational part of her brain tried to stop her from accepting it. It couldn't be true.

She opened her mouth to argue with him, to set him

straight, but she couldn't speak. She looked past him; his powerful wings moved slowly, lazily pushing against the air. She looked down and realized they were stationary, hovering in one place. Since she was past being scared to death, she couldn't deny he was right. The view was truly beautiful. Looking up at him she gave him her most fierce glare. There was no way she was going to admit it to him.

"Come closer." He wrapped his powerful arms around her, solid and unwavering. He bent his head down and slowly planted a fiery hot blaze of kisses from her ear, down her neck, back up to her ear, and then across her jaw to her lips.

Suddenly, she froze. Something was wrong. "Haden." She looked up at him, her heart stuttering. "What's happening?" A terrible screeching sound filled her ears. Ice-cold hands wrapped around her throat and squeezed, as something vile entered her mind and moved in it. She knew it was the vampire. He whispered to her, threatening to kill her, vowing to do horrific things to her. Gasping, she struggled to breathe.

"No, Caylee." Haden splayed his hand over her throat. "It's not real." She felt dark waves of power flowing from Haden and enveloping her, filling her. "It's a trick. A manipulation. An illusion. He can't touch you."

Instantly, she was able to breathe, and the whispering ceased. "It felt so real, Haden. I'm so afraid. He won't stop. He'll never stop. He's going to kill me. "

"I will stop him." Haden moved suddenly, taking them higher.

Caylee pressed her face against his chest.

He needed get her to Mia and go after Paul. He moved quickly, and as he disrupted the atmosphere, lightning erupted and thunder exploded all around. She felt a brutal gust of wind smash against them, and then it turned and moved with them.

* * *

Hand over her mouth, Julie giggled as she pressed her ear against the dressing room door.

Brianna sat on the couch. "You shouldn't be listening."

"It's so quiet."

"You should give them privacy."

"Shh..." Julie whispered. "They'll hear you."

"You're crazy. They're going to catch you."

"Not if you stop talking. I can't believe he went into the dressing room to get it on with her." Julie giggled again.

Mia walked up from behind. "What are you doing?"

Julie whirled around. "Oh, Mia. I was just ...nothing."

Frowning, Mia looked at the door. "Is Caylee still in there?"

"Yes," Julie answered.

Mia knocked on the door. "Caylee, open the door."

Julie shook her head. "I don't think she wants to."

Mia gaze narrowed on the door. "Why?" She grabbed Julie's arm. "Where the hell is Haden?"

"He's in there with her."

"Oh, hell. Are you okay, Caylee?" Mia pounded her fist against the door. "Open the damn door!" She rattled the doorknob, and then turned to Julie. "Are you sure they're in there?"

"Yes."

"Get me the key."

Julie shook her head. "She said she's okay. I think they're having sex. Besides, I don't know where the key is."

"The key is behind the counter! Get the damn thing!"

Julie nodded. "You don't need to yell at me."

"I'm sorry. I'm not mad at you. I'm just worried. It's too quiet it there. Just find the key." Mia watched Julie walk away.

* * *

One moment they were flying, and the next they were in the dressing room. Caylee looked up at Haden. Fury, deep, violent fury filled his eyes, but she had no fear of it, of him. She placed her hand on his chest to push him back. "Thank you." She felt his heartbeat, steady and strong against her palm. "You were right—it was a beautiful view of the forest."

Blinking back tears, she slowly lowered her hand to her side. She wanted to talk him out of going after the vampire, but she knew it would do no good to try. She knew he would do what he believed was right. And to him, killing the vampire was the only way to protect her. Maybe he was right. She honestly didn't know. But she did know her life wasn't worth his. "Please, Haden, be safe."

He took her hand in his. "Your life is far more valuable than mine." He brought her hand to warmth of his mouth. "But don't worry about me. I will be safe."

Looking down at her feet to avoid his gaze, she pulled her hand free. "Goodbye."

"No. Not goodbye. Never goodbye. Stay merged with me at all times." Forcing her to meet his gaze, he lifted her face. "I'm serious—stay merged with me. I love you, Caylee." He paused for a long moment. "With every ounce of my heart and soul, I love you." He bent his head to kiss her.

* * *

Mia pressed her ear against the door. She could hear Haden and Caylee whispering, but she couldn't make out what they were saying. She knew something was wrong. Caylee would've answered her. Julie handed Mia the key. "Thank you, Julie."

Nodding, Julie sat next to Brianna on the couch. Mia unlocked and opened the door. She was more relieved than embarrassed to catch them kissing. "Caylee, why didn't you answer me?"

Caylee jumped out of Haden's arms and turned to face Mia. "I didn't hear you."

Taking a step back to give them room, Mia glared at Haden as he wrapped his arm around Caylee and led her out of the dressing room. He was smiling, looking far too pleased with himself for her liking. "I seriously doubt it was that good."

"Mia." Caylee shook her head.

"The dress is perfect, Caylee. You look damn hot in it."

"Absolutely wickedly hot." Haden pulled Caylee into his arms to kiss her. *I love you, Caylee. Keep in mind I will come back to you immediately if you don't stay merged with me.* He reluctantly released her and left. He didn't want to leave her there. In fact, everything in him was screaming at him, demanding he take her away by force, but he was certain it would be mistake. She needed to come to him willingly. Using force would cause her to fear him, and he couldn't permit her to harbor any fear of him. He planned to destroy Paul so she was safe and he could fully concentrate on dealing with getting rid of Phillip and Emmett.

* * *

A few hours later Caylee returned home.

"Where the hell have you been?" Emmett shouted. Caylee slowly closed the door, taking a moment to make sure her mind was disconnected from Haden, and then she turned to face her uncle. "I've been waiting for hours."

"I was in town." Her voice was barely audible. Her throat felt as if it had collapsed, so she placed her hand over it. Her pulse raced. She couldn't catch her breath.

"What the hell were you doing?"

Wide-eyed and speechless, she fought to seize the strength and courage to respond.

"Answer me!"

Shivering, she swallowed hard. "I went to see Mia." She took a deep breath.

"Is that right?"

"Yes." Her heart raced madly. Knowing Haden was close by, she kept a barricade over her mind against his intrusion.

He would rush to defend her if he realized she was in danger. She needed to prevent it. In the past, Emmett had physically attacked her, but it had been months since he last struck her because she carefully avoided stumbling onto the triggers of his rage.

Lowering his brow, he was silent for a moment as he glared at her. "Do you've any idea how late it is?"

"I know it's late. I'm sorry, Uncle Emmett."

Nodding, he lowered his heavily wrinkled brow even more. He leaned against the back of the chair. "Phillip was here to see you today." Leaning forward, he rubbed his chin. "He doesn't like you hanging out with Mia. She's trouble."

"She's my best friend."

"Settling for you, Phillip has every right to expect you to honor his wishes. You won't see her again. You know how particular he is concerning you're behavior."

She thought of Haden. Something inside her snapped. "I've given this marriage some thought. I don't want to marry Phillip. We're complete strangers—besides, he's a much older man."

Clenching his fists, Emmett glared at her from across the table. "You don't have a choice." Why? She could feel the color draining from her face. Why had she opened her mouth? She stared into his eyes. For several seconds everything was frighteningly still and silent. She knew it was coming. He sat there glaring at her. The depths of his rage and hatred nearly caused her heart to stop. She wished he would scream or even strike her. Any response, any at all, would've been better than none at all.

He stood up. "You worthless bitch!" Throwing his chair back against the wall, he lunged in her direction. She glanced at the door. Haden would protect her. She reached for the door. Her fingertips grazed the handle as her body was thrown to the floor. She stood up on trembling legs. Emmett slammed his fist against the wall, narrowly missing her head. He grabbed a handful of her hair and pulled her away from the door. Reaching up, she tried to loosen his grip.

He threw her to the ground. With her hair still tangled in his fist, he leaned over her. "You're a filthy, ungrateful whore!" He jerked her head back and forth. "I've taken care of your ass this last year!" He ripped his hand free. "Look at me, bitch!"

Shocked, she gasped and then, reaching for her head, she turned and looked up at him.

"I've kept your secret!" He backhanded her.

Holding her hand over her face, she glanced, tears blurring her vision, at the door and started to stand up.

"You're not going anywhere." He grabbed her shoulder and shoved her down. "Do you want everyone to know what you've done?" Forcing her to look at him, he grabbed her hair. "Do you want everyone to know you're nothing but a filthy whore?" He let go of her hair.

Whimpering, she bowed her head.

"Look at me!"

Looking up at him, she raised her hands to shield herself from another blow.

"Phillip intends to announce your engagement in the next few weeks. You will stay away from Mia, do you understand?" Taking a step backward, he lowered his head and scowled at her.

Nodding, she slowly stood up. He stepped nearer.

"Answer me!" Saliva spewed from his mouth and splattered onto her face.

"Yes." She wiped the moisture from her face. "I understand."

He shoved her to the floor and walked past her. Then, swearing beneath his breath, he stomped down the hall in the direction of his room. She stared at the front door, hot tears streaming down her face. Luckily, she had been able to keep her mind closed to Haden. He hadn't seen the attack—if he had, he would've barged in to protect her. But if he discovered the truth he would despise her. She stood up, secured the lock on the door, turned the lights off throughout the house, and then fled to the solitude of her room.

* * *

While searching for Paul, Haden started to get distracted by a feeling of uneasiness. It didn't help that every time he reached for Caylee's mind, he was blocked. He had an overwhelming feeling she was in danger. Fearing he'd missed something and Paul had managed to get to her, he decided to go to her immediately.

As a vapor, he entered Caylee's house and immediately felt the negative energy of violence. He couldn't identify the origins of it, but he was certain it had something to do with her uncle. She was clever enough to hide it, knowing he would respond and fearing when he did he would learn too much about her past. How could he prove to her she was wrong? He didn't blame her for the past. Did he really need to prove anything to her? He could force her to leave with him. In time, she would learn to trust him, knowing he loved her unconditionally.

He entered her bedroom, walked over to the bed, and looked down at her, sleeping soundly. He couldn't force her to come with him. It would be a terrible mistake. She would fear him rather than trust him. Somehow, he needed to find the strength to wait for a little while longer. He knelt next to the bed and kissed her brow. *I love you.*

She opened her eyes and started to breathe heavily. Shivering, she pulled her blanket up to her chin. Eyes opened wide, she blindly glanced around the dark room. Trembling, she sat up and turned the bedside lamp on; then, leaving the warmth of her bed, she searched every corner of the room. The entire time she felt the sensation of being watched.

I told you to stay merged with me. Blocking me was a very naughty thing to do.

I don't always do as I'm told. Thankful it was Haden only speaking in her mind, she took a deep breath and then slowly released a sigh. *It's late. I'm tired. Leave me alone.* She didn't wait for an answer, figuring it would be best to ignore him.

The moment the thought entered her mind, she heard his soft laughter in her mind. Irritated, she climbed into the bed, turned off the light, pulled the blankets over her, and closed her eyes.

In spirit form, Haden stretched out next to her, listening to distant cries for help. Paul was on a killing spree. Haden knew he should go out to stop the vampire. For the majority of his existence, he would've done it without thought; it was his duty to stop the carnage. But, since Caylee was able to break their mental connection at will, he needed to be near her. The world would have to go on without his help. He was a guardian and protector to no one except for Caylee. She was his only concern now. Nothing else mattered. He couldn't leave her even if he wanted to. She was weak, vulnerable to death.

She slept soundly, embraced by peace for no longer than an hour, and then she started to thrash around and whimper. Regaining physical form, Haden pulled her nearer. Molding her body against his, he wrapped his arm around her, her body fitting perfectly against his. He whispered soothingly in her ear until he'd chased away every last remnant of the night terror from her dream.

~ *Nine* ~

CAYLEE WOKE UP slowly, Haden's enticing, masculine scent filling lungs. She stirred restlessly, her body curiously achy and remarkably warm with his arm wrapped around her and his body so snugly pressed against her backside. "What are you doing!"

She threw her blankets aside, turning to look at him, but he wasn't beside her. It was just a dream. She should've been relieved, but she wasn't, not really. Resting her head on the pillow, curling her body up in a tight ball, she frowned.

Good morning, little love. Haden's voice was a deep, warm, seductive whisper in her ear, a tantalizing caress that spread over her flesh. *There's no need to be disappointed, I was here with you in your bed all night, loving you, holding you in my arms.*

All night? What if my uncle had seen you? She shook her head. *You're making me crazy. Stay out of my head!* Setting her teeth on edge, she heard his laughter mocking her. *I'm serious, Haden!* Nibbling on her bottom lip, she frowned. *You need to find another diversion to entertain yourself.* Silently cursing the sliver of sunlight peeking through her curtains, she sat on the edge of her bed.

You're all the entertainment I can handle. Feeling the heat of his breath on her neck as he whispered, she shivered.

Stomach fluttering, her womb clenched. It was all an illusion. He wasn't even really with her. And he sure as hell wasn't making her panties damp. He was in her mind, tormenting her. She really hated him. She hated the power he had over her. She was a wreck. Her flesh hurt. Her breasts were way too sensitive and achy.

Why are you doing this? We aren't right for each other. We both know it's true. Surely you have other women you could go bother. She waited, but he didn't respond.

He wouldn't. Her comment didn't deserve a response. Besides, at the moment he had his hands quite full dealing with her uncle in the front yard. He'd never had so much trouble gaining a guardian's consent to allow him to date a woman. Not that he'd ever cared to gain consent in the past. In fact, he didn't really care if he got her uncle's consent. He was starting to view her uncle as an enemy. An enemy in need of attention. An enemy he needed to know better.

After several moments, she stood up and walked across the bedroom, and then stared at her reflection in the mirror. Her eyes were red and swollen, and a small, barely noticeable bruise was forming on her cheek. Reaching up, she ran her fingers through her hair, but getting stuck in the snarled mess she was forced to yank them free. She splashed cold water over her face and then brushed her hair until it was free of knots and tied it back to avoid anymore. Her eyes were still a bit red and swollen, but her hair managed to make a complete recovery. A little makeup and she was good as new. Well, ready to start the day anyway.

Exiting her room, she smelled something burning. She made her way to the kitchen and saw Emmett had left a cast iron skillet on a hot burner. She grabbed the handle, and her flesh sizzled. Gasping, she dropped it.

Standing at the end of the driveway, Haden's head snapped up, and his gaze locked onto the house. *What happened, Caylee?*

Using a cloth from the sink, she knelt down, wrapped it around the handle, and picked the skillet up. *Nothing happened, Haden. I want you to leave me alone. I'm not kidding—I want you to leave me alone. I never want to see you again.* Muttering a few curses beneath her breath, she placed the pan in the sink and filled it with water. *And I never want to hear your voice in my head again.*

She searched the house, including his room, but Emmett wasn't there.

Hoping she was alone to go about her day in peace, she decided to look outside. She stepped out onto the porch and shut the door. "Ouch." Glancing down at her blistered palm she took a step and then looked up.

"No way." Mouth gaped wide, she went completely still, too startled to even breathe. Haden and Emmett were standing toe to toe, a few hundred yards away. Emmett appeared angry, but Haden appeared amused. Unable to look away, she reached behind her back and placed her hand on the doorknob. Startled by an instant, sharp pain, she gasped loudly.

Haden lifted his head to make eye contact with her. *Don't lie to me. You're in pain. What happened to your hand?*

How could you do this to me? Wide-eyed, she stared at him for a moment; then, with barely noticeable movement, she shook her head and narrowed her gaze on him. What was he trying to do? Reaching behind with her uninjured hand, she tried to turn the knob. *I told you to stay away.*

Like you, I don't always follow orders. With a thought, Haden held the door closed. *You're not thinking about going back inside, are you?*

She continued to panic; heart bounding too fast, she struggled with the doorknob. *Go away!*

It's not happening. Haden held up his hand to silence Emmett. "Wait."

Emmett frowned. "Wait for what? She's not going anywhere with you."

Haden pointed in her direction. "I want to ask her."

Adrenaline raced through her bloodstream, causing her body to tremble. *What are you trying to do?* Turning on her heel, she rattled the doorknob but was unable to get the door to open up. "C'mon," she said as she struggled with the knob, "just open."

Rage welling up, Haden tilted his head to the side. Her fearful state of mind was unacceptable. He couldn't stand the sight or the feel of it. His frustration grew quickly, causing lightning to erupt and thunder to rumble in the distance. "She will decide." Voice elevated, he pointed in her direction.

A cold wind blasted past Caylee. *Stop it!* She looked up at the darkening sky. *You'd better not make it rain!* She continued to struggle with the door, but the door didn't budge an inch. She glanced over her shoulder at Haden and Emmett. Oh God, no. They were both looking at her. *I know you're holding the door shut. Let go of it now!* Desperate, she looked at the door and tried to open it, but it still didn't budge. "This can't be happening." She continued to struggle with the door. "Please, just open."

"No." Emmett grumbled. "You need to leave."

"Not until I ask her."

"Forget it." Emmett shook his head.

"You want me to leave, right?" Haden rolled his shoulders in a laid-back shrug. "I'm not leaving until I ask her."

"You're leaving now."

"Ask her to join us for a moment."

"You aren't going to talk to her."

The ground trembled beneath Haden's feet, as he walked toward Caylee. Blood pressure rising, Emmett lunged and grabbed his arm. Eyes flickering from blue to black, Haden turned to face Emmett. "Don't touch me." Lightning raced across the sky directly overhead, and thunder boomed.

Emmett released Haden's arm. "Caylee, come here now!"

"No." She stared at the door. "No, no, no, oh God no."

"Get your fucking ass over here!"

Taking a deep breath, she held it as she slowly turned around. Releasing it, she glared at Haden. He appeared far too pleased for her liking. She was so incredibly furious. She actually considered marching right up to him and slapping the smug, satisfied grin off his exceptionally handsome face. He was far too appealing in all the right ways.

Smiling, he nodded. *Not nearly as appealing as you, little love.*

She shook her head. Why did he have to look so good? Glaring at him, she crossed her arms over her chest. He was definitely in serious trouble.

"Get your fucking ass over here!"

Scowling, Haden glared at Emmett. It took every ounce of his strength to restrain the rage building in his soul. He hated hearing Emmett speak to her in such a disrespectful manner, but he decided to hold his tongue for the moment. Besides, he was amused. Even the atmosphere calmed. Besides being angry, she was actually shocked to see him. *You underestimate my resolve to be with you. You've yet to learn your value to me. There is no chance I will ever lose interest in you.*

You're going to pay for putting me through this. She looked up at him from the corner of her eyes. *I promise, Haden, you will be sorry.*

If that was supposed to frighten me away, I should warn you I find the thought of being disciplined by you to be a thrilling adventure. He laughed aloud. He couldn't help it. *I promise you I'll happily receive and cherish any retribution you deem necessary.*

You won't be laughing when I get my hands on you. Frowning, clenching her jaw, she shook her head.

I might not be laughing, little love, but I will be enjoying it.

Looking ferocious, she glared at him. Thoroughly aroused by her display of aggression, he fought to control his body's reaction. But how could he? Waves of lust and desire washed over him, filling him. He tried, but was unable to stop himself from laughing aloud once again.

Why do you keep laughing? This isn't funny. Unless you find torturing me amusing. You're terrible, Haden. You're completely impossible.

Grinning, Haden arched his brow at her. *And I suppose you're much easier to deal with.*

"Tell this idiot you won't go out with him. Do it now. The sooner he leaves the better."

"A date?"

Trying to place her at ease, Haden took a few casual strides in her direction, completely closing the gap between them. "Yes." With a breathtaking, hypnotic gaze he reached for her hand and brought it to his lips.

"Ouch!" She jerked her hand away from him and looked at the burn.

Taking her hand, Haden turned it to see what was wrong. *Damn it, Caylee. I knew you injured it, but I didn't know it was this bad. You're too damn good at hiding things from me.* Studying the burn, he imparted healing energy into it. *It will feel better in few seconds.*

"You son of a bitch!" Emmett shouted. "Get your hands off of her!"

"How did you burn it?" Haden asked, attempting to merge his mind with hers, but she was blocking him.

"On a skillet." She paused. "It's nothing." She felt the warmth of his healing energy. The pain quickly started to subside and was replaced by a strange, tingling sensation until it felt as if a cool, damp cloth was wrapped around her hand.

"It's a bad burn." Ignoring Emmett, Haden continued to hold her injured hand and send healing energy to it as he reached for her other hand and gently kissed it. *I do not like the way you block me from your mind. It's unacceptable. It's dangerous. I should've known before it happened. I could've prevented it.*

For a moment, nothing else mattered to Caylee. They were alone, and the world ceased to exist. It was a moment of sweet madness. She was so powerfully seduced by the warm sensation of his lips on her hand. Her body tingled with unbelievably glorious sensations. Her eyes widened as she stared up at him. Her breasts felt so very achy as her nipples hardened and peaked. Her flesh was suddenly far too sensitive, her clothing uncomfortable, rubbing against it.

Spotting the bruise on her cheek, Haden frowned. *What happened?* From out of nowhere, an unnatural, icy breeze swept past her. Terrified, she started to tremble. Never breaking eye contact, Haden reached up and placed his fingertips on the bruise. "Who did this to you?" Unable to speak, think or move she stared up at him. "Who hit you?" The sky darkened, black clouds billowing. "Who hit you?"

It wasn't a question asked to satisfy curiosity. It was a demand for knowledge that would lead to bloodshed. The ground rumbled. She felt unremitting violence and power coming from him in waves. She felt his dark, untamable rage and knew she was standing before the demon feared by so many. The dragon. And, he loved her. Only her. Fully. Completely. Forever. He loved her. There was nothing he wouldn't do for her. He would, without hesitation or regret, shed the blood of any man for her. And what frightened her the most was that he was capable of it.

She jerked her hand away from him. "No one hit me." She sent Haden a mental picture of Emmett without intending to do it. Realizing her mistake, she instinctively placed her hand over her cheek, as if to hide the evidence of abuse.

Haden turned away from her, prepared to rip Emmett apart. He took a step in Emmett's direction. "You attacked her." Struck by a powerful gust of wind, Emmett stumbled backward.

"No!" Caylee was so terrified her entire body trembled. She struggled to catch her breath, knowing Haden could very easily kill Emmett.

Struck by a wave of her fear, Haden glanced over his shoulder. She was deeply troubled; tears swimming in her eyes, her complexion was so pale it was completely void of color. *Please stop. He's my uncle. You can't just kill him.*

Nodding, he tried to hide his rage, hoping to place her at ease. *Don't be afraid.* It was far from over. He would never allow Emmett to go unpunished for hitting her, but he would wait to deal with it at a more appropriate time. He would kill Emmett. But like when he'd killed her father, Caylee would never know about it.

"Damn it, Caylee, just tell the bastard you're not going anywhere with him. The sooner he leaves the better."

Haden took Caylee's hands. Breathing heavily, she looked at Emmett. Haden reached out and turned her chin, forcing her to look up at him. His eyes were blue again, the amazing, effervescent bold blue she adored. He appeared normal, but she wasn't fooled. She searched for and found the darkness of his soul, the dragon. Oh yes, it was hidden, but it was definitely present.

"What are you doing?" Outraged, Emmett watched the encounter. "Tell him you're not interested in anything he has to offer."

Caylee looked at Emmett. Then, involuntarily giggling, she looked up at Haden. He was so hot. "That would be a lie."

Frustrated, Emmett raised his hand to strike her. "You stupid bitch, there's nothing funny about this!"

"I'm sorry." Stepping back so suddenly she nearly fell, she raised her hands over her face.

The ground rolled and heaved. Haden reached out and grabbed onto and crushed the bones in Emmett's arm with crippling force. "That was a terrible idea." Shaking his head, he glared into Emmett's eyes. "Terrible."

Hearing bones crack, failing to feel the impact, she lowered her hands and looked up, discovering Haden was holding Emmett's arm. *Haden, please stop! Don't hurt him!*

Arching his brow, Haden look at her, shaking his head at her. The woman was impossible. She expected too much. A demon could only take so much.

With Haden distracted, Emmett yanked his arm free. "You bastard!"

Muscles taut, Haden took a step in Emmett's direction. "You will not raise your hand against her again. If you do, I'll kill you." Of course he would anyway; it was just a matter of time. It was obvious he'd been abusing Caylee all along.

Horrified, she gasped. *No, Haden!* She knew with absolute certainty he wasn't making an empty threat. It was a promise. He planned to kill her uncle, and nothing would stop him. Not even her.

By his intimidating stature, Haden forced Emmett to take a step backward. Haden glared into his eyes, daring him to make a move or to respond, but Emmett remained still and silent. *I'm done with you for now. Go inside the house and leave us alone.* Turning, Emmett stormed off, mumbling unintelligibly, in the direction of the house. Haden turned to Caylee, stepped nearer, and gazed into her eyes. "This can't continue. I can't leave you here. You're coming with me."

"I can't."

Frustrated, Haden inhaled deeply, held it, and then released it with an exaggerated sigh. She closed her eyes, but rather than escape the power of his gaze she was more aware of it. She felt the warmth of his body and amazing sensation of his hands caressing her flesh.

"Stop!" Startled, her eyes flashed open. "Get out of my head!" Wide-eyed and breathless, she stared at him, silently begging him to leave and end her torment. "What're you doing here?"

He reached up and placed his hand on her cheek. "How long has he been abusing you?"

"No one hit me."

He reached for her hand. "Let me see the burn again." She reluctantly extended her arm. "I should've known it was this bad. Your ability to block me is extremely annoying." Examining the burn, he imparted more healing energy into her flesh. "I can't believe you're denying it."

"Why are you so upset?"

Groaning, he glanced at her. Clearly, the question didn't deserve an answer.

"Why are you here? You agreed to stay away."

"I never agreed to anything. You're stuck with me forever. The sooner you realize you aren't going to run me off the better." He looked into her eyes and then down at her hand. "When did you do this?"

"Ouch!" She tried to pull her hand free, but he firmly held it. "Don't touch it. You're hurting me."

"You're lying. I've taken the pain from you, and it's nearly healed now."

She looked at her hand. "How?"

"I'll explain later. Right now, I'm taking you home."

"This is my home. You shouldn't have come here." She flinched. "Ouch! Do you really need to touch it? It really hurts. Please, stop touching me."

"It doesn't hurt. You're just panicking because you like the way it feels when I touch you. Do you think I can't feel the need your body has for mine?"

"You're so ... you're a ... you're crazy, absolutely insane." Her face turned bright red. "You need to leave." She paused. "And I need to go inside."

"No." Smiling, he released her hand. "You are coming with me. Why didn't you ever tell me your uncle abuses you?"

She looked down at her feet to avoid his gaze. "He doesn't." She paused for a moment, searching for the right words. "And he really wasn't going to hit me." She looked up at him. "Just go away and leave me alone."

"You're lying. He would've hit you if I hadn't stopped him. You didn't want me to stop him." He framed her face between his hands. "How could you expect me to stand back and allow a man to hit you?"

"Stop!" She turned her back to him. "You're all worked up over nothing. Sure, Emmett has a bad temper, but it's not as bad as you seem to think." She turned to face him but then looked down at the ground. She wasn't completely lying. Her father had been worse in many ways. "He wasn't going to hit me." She looked up at him. "You're the one who showed up here and provoked him. I want you to leave."

"What other secrets are you keeping from me?"

"If you knew you would be disgusted." Her demeanor visibly wilted before his eyes, and his heart broke for her. "I've done things that are more horrible than anything you could ever imagine."

"You didn't do anything wrong. You could never disgust me. We belong together." He drew a deep breath and then released it with a loud sigh. "It's time, little love. We need to talk about the night I found you," "

Taking a quick breath, she gasped. "He's here."

"Who?" He watched a black limo approach.

"Phillip."

Truly pleased, he grinned, but there was no hint of humor in his gaze, only menace, dark, deadly menace. "Perfect." Meeting the dead man was definitely a priority on his to do list.

"I need to go inside. He'll be furious if he sees me out here with you."

"It's too late to hide it from him. If we're able see to him, I'm certain he's able to see us."

"Don't say anything to upset him."

He looked down at her. She was extremely pale and trembling. Shaking his head, he groaned. "I'll be on my best behavior."

From the corner of her eyes, she glared at him. "Sure you will."

"I promise." He had no problem being good for now. Soon enough, he would immerse himself in the pleasure of killing Phillip.

"If not, I will punish you."

"Don't tempt me."

Phillip walked toward Caylee and then gave her a quick kiss on the cheek. Cringing, she glanced over at Haden. *You promised.*

Your lack of confidence in my integrity deeply wounds my heart. Immediately detecting Paul's scent, Haden growled, his body going completely still as he pushed his way into Phillip's mind.

She smirked. *Whatever.* Suspicious, she looked up at him. *Did you just growl at him?*

Phillip looked at Haden and then turned to Caylee. "I didn't realize you were entertaining a guest this morning."

She failed to respond. She was close to panic, her stomach clenching, her mouth watering. She was going to be sick. *It's okay. You're safe.* Fear created so much chaos in her mind she couldn't hear Haden's voice in it.

Sorting through Phillip's thoughts, Haden took control of the situation. "Actually, I stopped by to see Emmett." Paul had placed his scent on Phillip. It was a game; Paul had simply wanted Haden to detect it.

Phillip turned to face Haden. "I've heard you spend a great deal of time at the juvenile detention center in Portland."

"I do."

"I can't believe you spend your time with those wretched creatures to straighten out their legal troubles. It seems to be such a waste of time and energy for such a prominent lawyer. I've also heard they call you a healer. Is it true? Do you believe you can heal the kids? Most of those ingrates will end up being thieves and beggars on the streets."

Deeply enraged, Caylee's fear instantly vanished. She glared up at Phillip for a moment; he disgusted her more than anything could. Shaking her head in disbelief, she glanced over at Haden. *Why are you just standing there? Why aren't you saying anything to defend the children?*

Keeping his temper in check, Haden took a deep breath and then released it with a groan. Being bad was much easier than being good. More fun too. But proud of his self-control, he looked down and grinned at Caylee. *I promised to behave myself. I will always keep my word to you.* Grinning, he tilted his head to the side. *I am always under your command, little love.*

She wanted to hit him, but she settled for rolling her eyes. *You're a liar.* Looking as innocent as sin, he smiled at her.

A promise is a promise, Caylee—I've no other choice but to be nice. Besides, he has a right to his own opinion, regardless of how unpleasant it might be.

Crossing her arms over her chest, she glared at Haden. *You can't be serious!*

"What self respecting lawyer would raise a hand to help the most vile delinquents of society?" Phillip asked.

Haden felt Caylee's anger hit him, as if she'd thrown a large rock at his head. Ditching his resolve to play nice, he took an aggressive step toward Phillip.

"Phillip," Caylee said, "you should be ashamed of yourself. How could you say anything so terrible? They're only children."

Arching his brow, Haden turned to watch Caylee. It was a controlled situation, so he was perfectly content with the idea of allowing her to vent.

"Never mind," she said, glaring at Phillip. "The ass you've proven yourself to be has made a perfectly adequate excuse for your ignorance."

Haden was pleased. He decided to stand back and observe, ready to intervene if his feisty lioness needed help.

"I wasn't speaking to you." Phillip pointed a finger in Caylee's face. "In the future you'll never take the liberty of sharing your opinion without my permission."

Flinching, Caylee hesitated for a few seconds. "I'll never apologize for speaking the truth to anyone. And in the future, you'll never find me silently waiting for your permission to speak my mind."

Phillip glared at her.

Amused, Haden continued to watch Phillip, prepared to intervene at the first hint of unbridled hostility.

Phillip turned to Haden. "Ignore her." He turned to Caylee and waved his hand to dismiss her. "There's a lot she still needs to be taught concerning her place as a woman."

"Ignore her?" Haden openly allowed his lustful gaze to wander over every inch of her body. There was no mistaking

Haden's appreciation for her. "That would be entirely impossible." He made sure his voice was a deep, sensuous purr. He turned to Phillip. "It appears she knows her opinion of you very well. Almost as well as you know the details of my affairs. But I must admit, concerning you, I'm completely in the dark. I'm at a terrible disadvantage. I haven't had the pleasure of hearing any gossip concerning you."

Laughing aloud, Caylee covered her mouth to muffle the sound, but it didn't help.

Turning his head, Phillip stared at her for a moment, and then he turned to face Haden. "I suppose in the long run you do society a great service. The quicker they get out of their cells, the quicker they will kill each other in the streets. There's no sense in forcing the state to pay for their care any longer than necessary."

"I'll sleep much better knowing I've gained your approval."

"Where's Emmett?" Phillip asked.

"Inside the house," Haden said.

"It was a pleasure to finally meet you, Mr. Drake." Phillip extended his hand.

Haden reached out and shook Phillip's hand. "I am certain we will cross paths again."

Phillip turned to Caylee. "We will deal with your behavior later."

"And then perhaps we will deal with your stupidity."

Glaring, Phillip took a step in Caylee's direction,

Haden casually moved nearer until his arm barely touched her shoulder. *He will not touch you.* It was a cold, hard fact. Phillip would die if he so much as reached for her. She maintained eye contact with Phillip for several seconds,

Caylee knew Phillip was struggling with the urge to strike her. She knew he would die if he did it. Haden appeared calm, almost uninterested in what was happening, but she knew his docile appearance was clearly a deception; there was no missing the waves of dark, violent power silently rolling off him. She was certain the earth rolled when Haden moved closer to her. She knew in her heart Haden was prepared to strike with deadly force. She believed Phillip knew it too when he walked away.

"Breathe." Haden placed his hand on the center of Caylee's back. "Everything is okay."

"Don't touch me!" She whirled around. "Look at what you've done!"

"You're the one who called him an ignorant ass."

"I should've kept my mouth shut. I would've if you hadn't been here." She paused. "You help the kids at the detention center?"

"You're wrong." He started to place his hand on her shoulder but then stopped. "Regardless of my presence you would've opened your mouth. And yes, I've helped the children." He shrugged. "C'mon," he said in a calm voice, offering his hand to her.

Smiling, she nodded. The sight of him captivated her every thought.

Feeling a sense of certain victory, he grinned as her fingertips touched his.

"No! Stop it!" She withdrew her hand and brought it to her side. "Please, just leave."

"Enough with the nonsense." He opened his car door. "Get into the car, Caylee."

"No." She backed away from him. "I can't leave with you. I won't."

Groaning, he shook his head. "Come here." Prepared to use force to take her with him, he walked toward her.

"Haden, what are you doing?" She backed away from him.

He captured her arm. "You're not staying here."

"Stop." She tried to pull her arm away. "You're scaring me."

"You're afraid," he said as he pulled her toward the car, "but not of me." He stopped. "Damn it." She would have a right to be afraid of him if he forced her to do anything.

Leaving with him had to be her choice. "If this doesn't end soon the outcome will be disastrous." It wasn't a threat; it was a fact. A fair warning. He wouldn't stand back and allow her to be hurt anymore. People were going to start dying.

"Are you threatening me?"

"You know better." Reluctantly, he released her arm. "The longer you deny us, the longer you're in danger. I will, regardless of the body count, protect you from further harm." He opened the car door and got inside.

"Did you get another car?"

"It's a rental. Mine is being repaired." He took a deep breath. "I will be close by. You will stay merged with me."

Nodding, she lied her pretty little ass off. She had no intention of staying merged with him.

* * *

Phillip walked into the house. Emmett was sitting at the kitchen table, rocking back and forth. "Why is she out there with him?"

Emmett didn't seem to hear him. Phillip grabbed Emmett's arm and yanked it hard. Emmett still didn't seem to notice Phillip was there. Phillip slapped him across the face. "What are you doing?"

Emmett blinked. Placing his hand over his cheek, he shook his head. "What the hell?"

"What wrong with you?"

His memory returning, Emmett shook his head. "The son of a bitch did something to me." He grabbed his head. "My head feel like it's going to burst."

* * *

Haden watched Caylee walk away. She turned to look at him. Assuming she'd changed her mind, he started to get out of the car, ready to gather her in his arms and carry her away. With her hand on her hip, she motioned for him to leave. For a moment, he almost lost control. Leaving her there was nearly impossible. It was so terrifying, but he knew there was no other choice. *Stay merged with me, or I will return immediately.*

Wiping the tears from her cheeks, she stared at the door and took a deep breath. Releasing it, she reached for the doorknob, but before she was able to turn it, Emmett opened the door.

"What the hell were you thinking?" Emmett grabbed her arm, pulled her inside the house, and slammed the door. "What did he say to you?"

Irritated, she jerked her arm free. "Nothing."

Phillip turned to Caylee. "You will never see that man again."

Shaking her head, she rolled her eyes. "You can't tell me what to do." She went into the kitchen and filled the sink with soapy water to scrub the burnt skillet.

A few miles away from Caylee's house, Haden pulled off the road and drove a few hundred feet down a dirt road. He needed to stay close to her. There was no way he would be far away from her at anytime. Deciding it would be great fun to bring Phillip down financially, he called Joseph.

"Haden, what's up?"

"I need your assistance with something."

"Anything."

"Do you know Phillip Wicks?"

"The name sounds familiar. Hold on." Joseph googled Phillip's name. "Sure, there's a lot of information on the web. He's an investment adviser. And it appears he's corrupt as hell. He has several enemies. He has been under investigation for fraud too."

"I don't care about his trouble. I need you to destroy him."

"Done."

* * *

"Damn it, Caylee!" Emmett slammed his fist against the counter. "Don't ignore me!" She whirled around and stared at her uncle. Holding her breath, she tried to recall the question, but she was unable to remember anything. He appeared angry. She glanced around the room and realized Phillip was gone. "I have some business to take care of. While I'm gone, you won't leave the house."

"I have plans to see Mia today."

"You're done with Mia." He took grabbed her arm and pulled her closer. "You will not see her today or any other day."

Nodding, she pulled her arm away. "All right," she lied, "I will stay home." Like hell she wasn't going into town to see Mia.

Muttering, Emmett turned and walked out of the house.

Caylee waited until he drove away, and then she grabbed her keys and headed out to her car. She'd always enjoyed the drive to town. It was a good twenty-mile drive along a deserted road in the middle of nowhere. The wooded scenery was beautiful. It was tranquil.

But she wasn't enjoying it at the moment. Instead, ten miles into the journey, the engine started smoking and making strange knocking noises. She pulled to side of the road, and then the engine stalled. After making several attempts to start it again, she eventually drained the battery. Calling Haden wasn't an option; she was never going to see him again. So, she tried to call Mia, but because there was no cell service, every attempt to call failed. With no other option, she started walking toward town.

~ *Ten* ~

STOP! STARTLED BY Haden's voice, Caylee stumbled, but reaching out for the trunk of a tree she kept from falling. She took another step but then froze the instant she heard a low growl. *They can't touch you.*

Slowly, not really wanting to see what was growling, she turned around. "Oh, no, not again." Wide eyed, heart racing, she stared at a dozen or so mangy dog-like creatures. "This is bad."

Look all around you. There's a hedge surrounding you, protecting you. They can't get through it. They can't touch you.

It's a mist. A black mist. I can't do this. Her thoughts raced wildly, matching her heartbeat. *I can't just stand here.*

The odor of your fear excites them. Take a deep breath. Try to remain calm. They can't harm you. Don't look away from them and don't run. I can see them through your eyes. I need you to stay very still to keep the hedge in place. He was careful to make sure his voice was calm and reassuring. *I'm coming to you now.*

Oh sure, I'll be calm. Maybe I'll even take a nap. Why not? There's a black mist protecting me. Odor? She frowned. *Are you telling me I stink?*

Not at all. He laughed. *I'm telling you that you smell*

yummy. She looked back at her car. She could make it, couldn't she? *No. Don't try it, little love. And don't turn your back to them. I need you to keep your eyes on them so I can see them.*

He was right. She would never make it in time. She returned her gaze to the creatures. She really wanted to look away from them. *I can't do it. I can't just stand here and watch them!* Panic was quickly closing in on her. They were so hideous. So terrifying. She wanted run. The last thing she wanted to do was stand there like an idiot staring at them.

I know they look frightening, but they can't touch you. More than anything he wished he could tell her to look away from them. *I need you to trust me. I need you to be strong.*

Her entire body was trembling. Her breaths were coming in short, violent gasps. Tears welled up and streamed down her face. *This is bad—this is really, really bad.* She tried to take a step back, but her legs felt like rubber. *I can't do it. I can't keep looking at them.*

You're doing it, little love.

Hyperventilating, she watched in horror as they crouched low to the ground and bared their teeth. It appeared they were about to pounce on her, but instead they slowly inched their way nearer. *Oh, God, hurry, Haden!* She turned her back to the beasts, too afraid to look at them any longer.

I'm here. Her ears popped. Pricking her flesh, the atmosphere suddenly electrified. The air was alive with danger and violence. A thousand voices shouted at once. With a terrible, ear-shattering clap of thunder, a strong gust of icy wind blasted past her. The creatures lunged for her, but they were stopped by the hedge surrounding her.

Haden began to regain physical form between Caylee and the ghouls. Opening her eyes, she turned to toward him. Another clap of thunder, and a gust of wind, much stronger, blasted the creatures. Yelping, they landed several feet away. Haden shimmered in the form a black, glittery mist, his wings disappearing as he turned toward her. Extraordinary power flowed from him. Violent. Tremendous. Immovable power. Unable to process what she was seeing and feeling, she stumbled backward.

Black and silver flames danced around him, around her. Everything was moving too quickly. She couldn't make out his form. "Haden." Her vision was blurry. She rubbed her eyes. Not yet fully formed, he reached out for her. Dodging the iridescent image of his hand, she stepped back. The color drained from her face as she placed her trembling hand over her heart.

When the reformation of his flesh was complete, he grabbed her arm to hold her steady. "It's okay."

"I thought you killed them the other night." Everything seemed to darken. She blinked. "I feel weird." Her voice seemed so odd and distant to her. "I can't ... oh, no." She swayed back and forth. "I need to sit down." She tried to back away from him, but everything swirled around her and went black.

Effortlessly catching her up in his arms, he cradled her against his chest. An instant before he dissolved into a mist with Caylee, he glanced over his shoulder and snarled at the severely injured, dying ghouls. Struck by an invisible, thunderous boom, they burst into flames.

Haden was beyond caring about what she wanted. Enough was enough. He knew what was best for her, and it was time for her to trust him. He was taking her home with him. In the blink of an eye he was holding her in his bedroom. He slowly carried her over to his bed and then gently lowered her onto it. Smiling, he stared down at her. She was going to be mad as hell when she woke up, but he didn't care. Let her be mad. She would get over it. She was home now. She was finally right where she belonged. Sitting on the edge of the bed, he watched her sleep, filling her with healing energy.

After several moments, she opened her eyes and she gazed up at him. "I really don't like those things. Where do they come from?"

She suddenly realized she was in an unfamiliar bed. His bed! Panicking, she sat up, determined to get out of it and leave his house as quickly as possible. But she hesitated. What if there were more of the creatures outside? "Are there more out there?"

"Not at the moment. You've been through a horrible ordeal. You need to rest for a few minutes, little love. There's no reason for you to leave right away." Leaning his back against the headboard, he pulled her into his arms. "Come here."

Making a sound of something between a moan and whimper, she halfheartedly pushed away from him, but he gently, with a firm grip, drew her back. "Relax." He kissed the top of her head. "You're safe with me."

She tilted her head back to look up at him, but then quickly, needing to escape the hunger in his gaze, she looked away. "I shouldn't be ... they're so disgusting, Haden. What are they?"

"Animals, mostly dogs, poisoned by the blood of the undead," he stated, still touching his lips to her soft, satiny hair, inhaling her scent.

"You knew they were going to attack me before I did." She tilted her head back to look up at him again. "Most of the time it drives me nuts that you know so much." Grinning, she bit her lower lip. "But in this case, I'm glad. In fact, it's your lucky day, Haden. I'm not going to lecture you about how rude it is to always be mucking around in my head. I'm not saying it's not annoying. To tell the truth, it's extremely irritating."

She pulled away from him and turned her entire body to get a better look at him. "It's so unfair." She scooted to toward the foot of the bed. "I would be happier if I could see your thoughts as easily as you see mine."

"If you want to see my thoughts, I could show you." His voice was deep, raspy.

She stood up and took a few backward steps away from the bed. "How?"

She didn't see him move, but he was standing directly in front of her. "Close your eyes."

She stared up at him. He was so close she could feel the warmth of his body. "Are you teasing me?"

He bent his head and kissed the corner of her mouth. "Not at all," he whispered. "Close your eyes."

Smiling shyly, heart racing, she nodded and closed her eyes. "I'm going to end up regretting this, aren't I?"

He laughed softly. She felt the warmth of his breath, the scintillating moist heat of it across her lips. Waves of hot lust radiated from him, entering her body as he merged his mind with hers. Instantly, she felt the warmth and roughness of his hands on her flesh, all over her body, exploring every inch of it, savoring it, possessing it. She felt his desire and his need for her combined with his steadfast, unwavering love for her.

Leaning back, she opened her eyes and stared up at him. "Why?"

Cradling her face in his palms, he traced her mouth with his thumb and then drew her nearer to kiss her. "Kiss me."

"No." She pulled away from him. "I want you to tell me why you want me." She knew he wanted her to believe they belonged together and he would stop at nothing to convince her of it. But why? She was far from the woman she imagined his type to be. She was certain he could get any woman. Why would he settle for her? He was extraordinarily fascinating. Mysterious. Dark. And way too sexy. He looked too good, more than handsome; he was masculine sensuality perfected. His body was a solid, flawlessly muscled piece of art. He was godlike. He was so powerful in so many ways. Like an ancient warrior. A gladiator. To most people, he wasn't simply intimidating, he was completely unapproachable. And yet, he was gentle with her. So tender, patient, and kind. Well, when he wasn't making stupid demands.

He smiled. "I never make stupid demands." He arched his brow. "I offer advice based on expert wisdom." He shrugged casually. "But anyways, I figured you cast a love spell on me."

"Really?" Drawing her bottom lip in her mouth and chewing on it, she frowned. Well, it made sense. Why else would he long for her? Yep, it had to be a spell. She only wished she knew it, in case it wore off. It would definitely come in handy in the future.

"No." He wrapped his hand around her throat in a bogus threat. "What am I going to do with you? You drive me crazy, little love, and I am starting to believe you enjoy it. I could never imagine a more beautiful woman. You're incredibly desirable. Irresistible. Completely divine." Cupping her breasts, he groaned aloud. The sound was so sensual. Deep. Husky. So full of need.

"Haden." She knew she should stop him, but she didn't want to. "This is a bad idea." Eyes wide, her breaths came in short, labored gasps.

"Your body is perfectly, deliciously proportioned. You're a goddess." Reaching behind her, he grabbed her backside and squeezed. "My goddess. You're so incredibly sexy." He bent his head and kissed her slowly, thoroughly. "Luscious. Addictive."

Moving even nearer, pressing her back against the wall, he parted her legs with his thigh. "Hot." His voice was a deep growl filled with the lust burning in him. Driving him insane, she arched her hips toward him and moved against his leg. "You're so damn hot, little love." He bent his head and nibbled on her earlobe. "You're feisty. Courageous." He trailed fiery kisses from her ear, along her jaw and to the corner of her mouth. "Very sweet. Kind and generous to a fault. But when you're riled, you fight fearlessly, with the heart of a lioness. And you're mine." He held her face between his hands, forcing her to meet his gaze. "All mine."

A blush rising from her neck to her cheeks, she studied his gaze. "You're teasing me." She nibbled on her lower lip, struggling to close her eyes, to look away, to do anything to escape the hunger of his powerful gaze.

"Am I?" He took her hand and pressed it against his swollen cock. It was a mistake! A terrible fucking mistake!

His body shuddering and heart thundering in his ears, he clenched his jaw, groaning aloud. He was so damn hard, impossibly swollen. He released her hand, hoping she would move it. She didn't. Oh hell, he was so damn sensitive.

Her gaze jumped to her hand, and she froze. He was huge. She looked up at him, unable to move her hand away from the fascinating heat of his bulging erection. Even through the material of his pants, she savored and feared the proof of his desire. Her heart beat frantically. Tiny beads of sweat formed all over her body. Her most secret place suffered a peculiar, powerful ache. Knowing and accepting the extent of his need for her was alarmingly. It was shocking, but it was so wonderful it caused fascinating sensations to spread throughout her body and over her flesh, more intense than anything she'd ever experienced.

Turbulent currents raced through his body, electrifying and scintillating, gliding over his ultra-sensitive flesh. Standing on the tips of her toes, she leaned closer to him and feathered kisses along the base of his throat. All the while, her hand remained over his cock. Motionless. Holding him. Driving him insane. Nearly pushing him to the brink of detonation. He couldn't believe how poorly his body was behaving over a simple touch. Her tiny hand was defying his strength, completely and utterly annihilating his ironclad stamina. His cock was impossibly hard. Excruciatingly hard. He needed to move her hand before he burst in his pants.

Of course, he would be damned if she didn't have another idea. She picked that moment to give his erection an experimental squeeze. His cock jerked. His entire damn body jerked. His cock throbbed so damn much. It was swollen way beyond the point of pain. With her palm, she rubbed the full length of him. In sheer, glorious agony, he gritted his teeth, every muscle in his body tensing, trembling from the effort it took to not make an embracing mess in his pants. Pressing her hand more firmly, she continued to explore.

He needed to stop her! "Damn it." He grabbed her hand.

Mortified, she stared up at him, her heart shattering. "I'm sorry." Tears pooling in her eyes, she attempted to hide them by looking down at her feet.

He had a choice. He could either save his ego or her heart. After a brief but intense internal debate, he chose her heart. Lifting her chin, "Caylee," he said as he wiped the tears from her cheek, "there's no reason for you to be sorry. I've dreamed of you touching me, exploring my body for so long. Maybe it's been too long. Words cannot describe how much I enjoy your touch."

She didn't understand. If what he was saying was true, why had he gotten mad? "What do you mean?"

Damn. Damn. Damn. She was going to force him to admit she made him weak. "The pleasure of your touch is more intense than anything I've ever experienced."

She shook her head. "Why would that make you mad?"

"I'm not angry." At least, not at her; his body on the other hand was treading on thin ice. Why couldn't she leave well enough alone? Seriously, did he really have to annihilate his ego? Thankfully, being a demon, he was skilled in the art of deception. He didn't have to tell her he'd nearly prematurely ejaculated in his pants. "I'm overly excited. I don't want to rush, but you tempt me to rip your clothing off and slam into your body hard and fast." He grinned. There—that should throw a bucket of ice on the situation.

She didn't see the problem. Eager was good, wasn't it? "That's a wonderful thing, right? I mean, if we're going to make love, shouldn't you be eager? Shouldn't I be eager?" She grabbed the front of his shirt and pulled him nearer. "I sure hope eager is good. I want you, Haden. I'm very eager to feel you inside me."

"Eager is good." Leaning down he kissed her roughly, passionately. "Very good. It's wonderful." His dominant nature rising, he took possession of her lips. He was on fire, desperate, ready to explode.

She too was on fire, needing so much more. "Absolutely wonderful."

Boldly caressing, almost frantically exploring each other, they kissed deeply, their tongues dueling, their hearts racing. Pressing his body against hers, pinning her backside against the wall, he cupped her breasts in his hands, teasing her nipples with his thumbs. It was too much, but not enough. She needed to feel his flesh against hers; every inch of her body was alive with desire.

She bit his lower lip, tugging on it as she unbuttoned his shirt and pulled it open enough to expose his chest. She stared at his well-defined chest and stomach, so perfectly muscled, a flawlessly sculpted statue except for a faint scar left from the knife wound. She looked up at him, tears in her eyes. It was her fault. He'd been protecting her. He could've died. What if he had died? She couldn't possibly live in a world without him.

"It's not your fault. I've been wounded thousands of times. I'm not easily killed, little love. I'm immortal." Looking as naughty as sin, he grinned at her. "I can't die. I'm too determined to boss you around until the end of time."

Smiling, she traced the scar on his chest with her finger, and then she looked him. "You can try to boss me around all you want, but I promise to do my best to make sure it's never an easy task."

"I never try, little love—I do."

"We will see about that." Standing on the very tips of her toes, she feathered kisses along his jaw and down his neck.

He was in terrible shape. He'd never felt such desperation to be with a woman. She owned him. His body and his soul fully belonged to her. No matter how far back in his life he looked, he couldn't pinpoint a single instant that he didn't have complete confidence in his control over his body. "Yes, we will."

He knew he was in trouble. He was happily at her mercy. It was pathetic. He was pathetic. Pathetic was good. Reaching down, he caressed the backside of her thighs and her hips, and then up her sides, in her shirt; her flesh was so hot, so satiny soft against the rough texture of his calloused hands. Oh yeah, pathetic was wonderful.

Exploring the masculine contours of his chest with her fingers, she continued to kiss the base of his neck and throat. Searing heat radiated from his flesh. His powerful muscles rippled and tensed beneath her fingers. It wasn't enough to just feel his flesh with her fingers. She wanted more, needed more. She kissed his chest, unknowingly teasing his surprisingly way overly sensitive, flat nipples with her fingers.

At first her mouth moved timidly, but eventually she was boldly exploring, savoring every inch of his chest with the moist warmth of her lips and tongue. God save them if she got frightened and tried to stop. He knew in his heart there was no going back. There was no stopping. He was way beyond the point of wanting to bury himself deep inside her body. He needed to feel her heat wrapped around him more than he needed to take his next breath. He grabbed her hips and forcefully pulled her nearer, pressing her body against his.

She gasped, momentarily shocked by the feeling of his swollen shaft pressed so snugly against her belly. "Haden?" There was fear and uncertainty in her voice, in her eyes.

"Trust me." He knew he couldn't allow her to think about it. "It's okay, little love." He bent his head and took possession of her lips, savoring the sweetness of her kiss. "Kiss me."

She was a little afraid, but he was wrong. She wasn't uncertain. She wanted him as badly as he wanted her. The passion they were sharing was much better than okay. It was astounding. Her breasts, pressed against his well-muscled chest, tingled. A tantalizing sensation spread over her most feminine place so she had no other choice but to seek relief by helplessly moving her body against his.

The sensation of her body moving against his and sound of her soft, whimpering pleas for more was more than he could take. He took her mouth more aggressively, pinning her against the wall, exploring every lush curve of her body with his hands.

Eventually, he couldn't take anymore. Scooping her up, he cradled her against his chest, kissing her deeply as he carried her across the room. Gently, he lowered her onto the bed. His heart thundering, creating an intense roaring in his ears, he gazed down at her.

Staring up at him, she held her breath, her eyes wide with the wonder of the powerful sensations racing through her body and over her flesh. She looked like a sexy seductress and an innocent young virgin all at the same time. She was everything to him. She was the substance of his most cherished dream. But if she knew what he was, if she knew the entire truth, she wouldn't be in his bed.

What right did he have to claim her now? She wasn't the only one keeping a secret; he too was keeping one, and it was enormous. He hadn't thought about it much lately, but now it was weighing down on him. She deserved to know the truth. He could've prevented her from being forced to endure a lifetime of violence, but he'd decided to walk away from her. Yes, he'd known she was to him many years ago, he'd known she was living in violence, but he'd abandoned her. He'd failed her. He'd allowed her to suffer, and she didn't even know about it. She might forgive him, but he would never forgive himself.

Standing up, he pulled his shirt on and walked to the other side of the room, keeping his back to her as he buttoned his shirt. Rendered speechless, she watched him for a moment, and then she got up from the bed and walked up behind him. She reached out and turned him around. Terrible pain and sadness filled his eyes as he reached out and placed his hand on the side of her face. "I'm so sorry."

She turned her head and kissed his palm. "For what?" She took his hand in hers, needing to feel the warmth of it as she gazed up at him. "Please, Haden, tell me what's wrong."

"There are things you don't know about me. And I'm convinced that if you did, you would be appalled. In the very least you would have second thoughts about being intimate with me." He wasn't certain how to continue the conversation without revealing he knew the secret she was keeping from him. Stalling, he brought her hand to his mouth to kiss it. "I want you to be sure this is what you want. No. I need you to be sure. We need to slow down."

The last thing she wanted was to slow down. "I have no doubts I want to make love with you." Chewing on her bottom lip, she studied him. "And, unless you're hiding another woman on the side, I'm certain there is no way anything I don't know about you is going to change my mind in the future." She smiled up at him. "Is there another woman, Haden?"

"No, absolutely not." He couldn't allow her to have doubt in his faithfulness. And yet, he couldn't avoid telling her he knew her secret if he revealed his. Maybe it was time to further introduce her to the truth of what he was. Surely that would throw a bucket of ice on her desire to be with him at that moment. It would give her more time to share her secret with him. It would definitely give her a lot to think about. "You know I'm not human, but you don't know what I am."

"I don't care," she replied quickly, refusing to give it too much thought.

Taking a deep breath, he pulled her into his arms and nuzzled his chin in her hair. "What if I tell you I've kept what I am a secret from you because the truth would terrify you?"

"Is it more alarming than seeing you turn into a dragon?" She giggled. "I honestly believe I could never fear you for what you are or what you are not." She tilted her head to look up him. "I know you're good at heart."

Releasing a sigh, he feared the worst and hoped for the best. He knew telling her wouldn't be enough. She wouldn't truly believe he was a demon unless he showed her. Taking her hand he led her toward the bed. Then, sitting down on the mattress, he pulled her onto his lap and cradled her in his arms. "I'm going to show you." He kissed the top of her head, as he summonsed the power within him to come forth.

A chilly breeze drifted into the room as a black, glittery mist surrounded them.

Nervous, she looked up him. "You don't need to do this. I know you're not human. It doesn't matter to me."

He cradled her head against his chest. "Close your eyes, little love." He merged with her, but rather than enter her mind he brought her into his and showed her many of the things he'd hidden from her. She felt his presence with her, studying her reaction to the discoveries she was making, but he remained silent, allowing her to sort through and absorb the information, one moment at time, at her own pace.

Eventually, she panicked. She didn't want to see anymore. She didn't want to know what he was. It didn't matter to her. She struggled to pull her mind from his.

Don't be afraid, little love. With very little effort, he held her mind captive. *You must see it to know the truth.*

Yielding to him, she took a deep breath and released a sigh as he brought her into a space of utter darkness.

A wave of dizziness struck her hard. She felt as if she were alone and floating through time and space. Fear slammed into her heart, and it raced so frantically she was certain it would burst. She felt a need to run away to escape the truth.

He placed his hand over her heart. *You're not alone. I'm with you. You must know the truth, and you must not fear it.* Heat flowed from his hand and penetrated her heart, forcing it recover before it stopped. *You're always safe with me. I love you, Caylee.*

He took her through the many years of his existence, showing her many of the wars he'd fought. He went so far as to take her through a few of the terribly gruesome bloody battlefields he'd left in his wake. He wanted her aware of the violence and brutality he was capable of committing. When he took her last breath and replaced it with his immortal breath, she would see and feel it. Showing her now would lessen the shock. If she survived, she needed to believe he would never harm her no matter what was happening. He wanted her to feel his lack of remorse when he destroyed the creatures that threatened his kind and mankind. He showed her the limitless dark powers that filled him and aided him. He was a powerful demon, created for war, nearly indestructible. He was a force of darkness, dangerous and deadly.

Once again Caylee felt the nauseating sensation of moving through time and space. She clung to him, afraid of being swept away and lost forever. Regardless of how he saw himself, she knew he was good at heart. He showed her the worst of himself, but all she saw was the best. On many occasions, far too many to count, he'd risked his eternal soul to protect helpless strangers. How could she ever doubt her safety with him? She was no stranger to him. He loved her deeply, completely. How much more would he give to protect her?

When the sensation of moving stopped, she opened her eyes and looked up at him. He was staring down at her, tears pooling in his eyes, obviously expecting her to reject him for what he was. "How old are you. Haden?"

"Over nine hundred years."

She wiggled out of his arms and stood up. "Really?" She took a few steps away from him and then turned to face him. "You hide it very well."

He looked guilty. He was hiding something. Grinning, she tilted her head to the side. "How many more than nine hundred?"

Lowering his brow, he frowned. "A few hundred more."

She crossed her arms over her chest. "How many?"

"A thousand."

"Holy smokes, you're nineteen hundred years old?"

He nodded. "Give or take a few years."

"Wow. You're an incredibly old man, Haden." Grinning, biting her lower lip, she took a step toward him. "But you're not evil."

"I'm a demon."

"I know." She nodded once. "That's why I'm getting a big spray bottle to fill with extra blessed holy water as soon as possible."

"Interesting." Tilting his head to the side, he smiled at her. "What are you planning to do with it?"

"Squirt you whenever you try to tell me what to do." She narrowed her gaze on his. "Think of it as a tough love training tool."

He was struggling to keep from laughing. He wasn't prepared for her to accept it so quickly, so easily. But she was so accepting of it she was teasing him. Making fun of him. Of course, teasing or not, he had no doubt she intended to use the holy water on him in the very near future. He didn't have the heart to tell her it wouldn't have any effect on him. Water was water. Holy water was just another invention designed by mankind to make them feel more powerful. For some it was a tool used to alleviate their fear of the mysterious unknown. But in truth, it was only water.

"I've always known you're not a human. It was confirmed when you turned into a dragon. You've mucked around in my head enough to know that." She grinned. "You should also know it has never mattered to me. You've protected me. You've risked your life for mine. I love you, Haden. I want to make love with you."

He stood up. "No." His reply shocked him. What was he doing? He realized at that moment he didn't believe she could truly love him because of his failure to protect her. It was shocking to think that perhaps his insecurities rather than hers had prevented him from giving her immortality. But there was definitely some truth in it. He'd never suffered from a lack of self-worth. It was something he would definitely take a look at in the near future.

Reaching up, she framed his face with her hands. "Do you think I do not know what I want? There are things about you that startle me, but I'm not afraid of you. Am I wrong to believe you would never hurt me?"

"I am what I am."

"And?"

"I can kill anyone with a thought."

Looking far too serious, frowning and chewing on her bottom lip, she remained silent for several moments. "You're right." Grinning mischievously, she shrugged. "You are what you are."

He should've been pleased, but he wasn't. "You agree with me?"

"Of course." She tilted her head back to meet his gaze. "You could think me dead at any moment."

His blood pressure skyrocketed. "I wouldn't."

She laughed so hard her eyes started to water. "Oh Haden." Her face turned bright red as she struggled to catch her breath.

Tilting his head to the side, he studied her for a moment. He was appalled. He couldn't believe she was laughing at him over such a serious matter.

Her sides ached. She tried, but couldn't stop laughing. Wrapping her arms around her stomach, she bent over, struggling to catch her breath.

Hesitantly, he stepped forward. Perfect. She was having a mental breakdown. "Caylee?"

Fighting to pull herself together, she straightened up to meet his gaze. Within a few moments she was able to subdue her laughter, but she continued to giggle. Her hands trembled as she wiped her tears dry.

Mental breakdown or not, she was seriously irritating the hell out of him. "Damn it, Caylee, what's wrong with you?"

"Nothing." She pulled his shirt from his shoulders. "I'm finally not the one making excuses."

She was right. He couldn't think. He couldn't move. He couldn't respond. Holding his breath, he stared into her eyes.

"You love me, right?"

"Yes." He nodded, squinting his eyes warily, fearing what she would say or do next.

Slowly, watching him watch her, she unbuttoned her shirt. She took it off and tossed it at his feet. Heart pounding, he made a deep growling sound, his dark gaze briefly jumping to hers before he lowered it to savor the sight of her perfect, round breasts. Next, she unbuttoned her jeans and slowly pulled them over her hips and down her legs. She stepped out of them and kicked them aside. "It's the duty of a man to meet the needs of the woman he loves." She flashed him a wickedly sexy smile and then turned her back to him. "I've needs you must not ignore any longer. Regardless of your excuses, my body is suffering." Watching his reflection in the mirror, she waited.

He stepped closer, his body nearly touching hers, towering more than a foot over her. Looking up at him in the mirror, fear stabbed at her. He stood absolutely still, waiting for her to recover, fearing she might not. He knew she felt very small compared to him. And she was. His large, muscular frame was intimidating. He was stronger than her. He could easily overpower her. He could hurt her. She needed to believe he wouldn't.

He watched as she took a deep, calming breath to clear her thoughts. He knew he would never use his strength against her, and eventually she would know it too. For the first time ever, he allowed his gaze to feast on her naked, flawless body as he waited for her to work through her fears. He couldn't force her to trust him. It was up to her. But he needed to touch her. Meeting her gaze in the mirror, he gently drew her long hair to his face. He bent his head and inhaled deeply, savoring its sweet aroma and the silky texture of it against his flesh.

Breathing deeply, she closed her eyes, savoring the tantalizing heat of his hard body against her flesh. Every inch of her flesh tingled with delicious sensations. She felt so feverish. She felt restless. Empty. Wanting more. Needing him to touch her.

Breathing in the exhilarating scent of her arousal, his heart started to thunder painfully. His hunger for her was ravenous. The atmosphere exploded. Lightning zigzagged across the sky, and thunder shook the house. The wind howled, and dark clouds billowed outside, turning daylight in to darkness. He caught her tiny waist and dragged her close, pressing her body against his as he leaned down and kissed her neck. "Open your eyes, little love." Meeting her gaze in the mirror, he feathered kisses along her neck and shoulders.

She wanted him to stop, but she was terrified he would. Ashamed, she tried to look away from his dark gaze, but she couldn't. Stark hunger burned in his gaze. A shiver ran down her spine. She took a deep breath and held it for a few seconds as she watched his hot, sensual mouth move over her neck and shoulder.

"My every thought is of you, little love. You're a treasured miracle to me. You belong to me. I belong to you. I will forever love, cherish, and protect you with all that I am." He lightly feathered kisses from her ear, his tongue swirling over her flesh, filling her with his fiery passion. From behind, he pulled her into his arms and held her close, taking a moment to savor the warmth of her body against his.

Tilting her head back, she looked up at him. He smiled at her, but there was no hiding the agony in his eyes. She loved his smile. He had such a strong, masculine face, his warrior like features set in stone. Most of the time it was impossible to read his mood, but whenever he smiled at her like this, his harsh features softened, revealing the goodness of his heart. Perhaps it was wrong, but she secretly loved the misery so often apparent in his eyes when he smiled at her. Deep down, she'd known all along it was a symptom of his lust for her and his resolve to wait until she was ready.

He laughed softly. "It's not wrong, little love. It's good for you to know what you do to me. I do want you, but ... oh, damn it." He wanted to assure her there was still no rush, but he couldn't lie to her while his erection pressed so snugly against the small of her back. "I really need to be inside your body." His voice was a deep, lusty whisper. "I love you. Do now know that I love you?"

Her lips curved in small smile. She believed him, truly believed he loved her. But she knew his love would never last once he knew her secret. Her large eyes stared up at him, fiery tears spilling over. The thought of having his love only to lose it hurt her like nothing else could. "I know it." There was catch in her voice.

He couldn't bear the pain he felt in her. He lowered his head protectively over hers. "You will never lose my love." He made the statement, despite knowing she wasn't able to believe it just yet. One day she would know her place with him. Moving his hands slowly from her belly to her breasts, he caused her temperature to rise and her pulse to skyrocket. He unclasped the front of her bra and pulled it from her shoulders.

She was on fire, her body burning up with need. It was so exhilarating to be needed so thoroughly, so completely that nothing would ever satisfy him more than her. He cupped her breasts, causing her breaths come in short gasps. Knees weak, she leaned heavily against him. He gently massaged her breasts and teased her nipples, listening to her soft, husky moans, allowing the sound to hurl him into a massive, violent flood of desire.

Blazing kisses along her neck, he reached down and cupped the entrance of her body. He caressed her nipple with the thumb of one hand as he slipped the fingers of his other in her silk panties to rub her swollen clit. Her body was so sensitive. Too sensitive. She restlessly, seeking her own pleasure, rubbed her sex against his hand. He was so swollen and hard, throbbing and aching. It was the perfect torture, her eager response to his touch nearly causing him to burst in his pants.

She was so hot, dripping wet with desire. He'd waited for so long. His need was violent, brutal. He needed to slam into her, to take her hard and fast, but he knew better. She needed him to be gentle with her. His fingers, coated with her hot, silky essence, stroked her clit, shattering her body and mind. Her heart raced wildly as her breaths came in short gasps and soft moans. The pleasure of his touch was setting her ablaze, incinerating every shy inhibition, driving her insane. Nearly frantic, she moved against his hand, attempting to soothe her body's wild, urgent need for more

In all of his existence he'd never even imagined a more desirable woman. She was so beautiful, flushed with need, eyes wide with wonder. Watching her reaction to his touch in the mirror, monitoring her thoughts, he leaned down near her ear. "I love you, Caylee." Teasing her nipple, he stroked her hot, wet sex. "I really need to be inside your body."

It happened all at once; the sensation of his touch, the sight of his hands on her body and the sound of his deep, lusty voice caused her body to detonate. A sudden and powerful surge of marvelous sensations raced through her entire body, striking her core with a vengeance and smoldering there for several mind-blowing seconds. Stroking her, taking her further, he brought her to a state of ecstasy she'd never known. Erupting, she cried out, her knees buckling, but he easily held her upright, her body firmly pressed against his cock, allowing her to experience several enormous waves of hot pleasure.

When she was able to stand on her own, he released her and stepped back to turn her around. But he stopped. How had he missed it before? He stared at a large bruise on the back of her shoulder. Shaking his head, he ran his fingertips along the bruise. A demon could only take so much. Sensing something was wrong, she looked up at his reflection in the mirror. He looked furious. She felt his anger. Raw. Lethal. A terrible, icy chill of terror race up her spine, causing her to shiver.

~ *Eleven* ~

THE ATMOSPHERE DARKENED. A frigid wind swept into the room. It would've knocked her off her feet if he weren't holding her. Her breath caught in her throat. Her heart stopped. Turning her around, he stared into her eyes, forcing his way into her mind. There was nothing gentle about his intrusion; it created an excruciatingly sharp pain directly between her eyes.

Caylee clutched her head as tears filled her eyes. "You're hurting me, Haden" She intended to scold him for so brutally invading her mind, but she only managed to release a tiny whimper.

Haden saw everything. He saw Emmett attack her and shove her to the ground. He saw her cowering on the floor. It wasn't the first time. Emmett had abused her many times. Haden felt her fear, and it ripped his heart right out of his chest.

Caylee trembled uncontrollably. She knew what Haden was seeing. She tried to back away from him, but her knees buckled.

With little effort, he held her tiny frame upright, forcing her to meet his gaze. "Emmett attacked you last night." Haden's voice was harsh, his gaze crueler and darker than ever before, as he held her in a grip that was too tight. "It will never happen again." And it wouldn't.

* * *

The wind picked up from out of nowhere, tossing debris in every direction. Dark, ominous clouds billowed above the bank, releasing torrential rain. The people on the street ran for cover. The sky turned pitch black seconds before vivid lightning erupted and thunder boomed.

Waiting in line for the next available teller, Emmett turned his head to look out the window as the lights flickered off and on a few times. Emmett felt something slam into his chest. The pain was unbearable. His heart felt like it was going to explode right out of his chest. He clutched his chest and fell to his knees.

The building shook violently; it felt like an earthquake. The lights went off and stayed off, and chaos broke out. The entire building, as if it was being ripped from its foundation, continued to shake. Pushing and shoving at each other, attempting to flee and find shelter, people were screaming.

The pain in Emmett's chest was more intense than any other pain he'd ever experienced. He knew he was dying. It felt as if his heart were being crushed. He could literally feel fists gripping it, squeezing it. In the darkness he saw Haden approach in the form of the dragon. He blinked once, and the dragon was gone. Haden stood in its place.

Emmett tried to close his eyes to escape, but Haden's cold, black gaze held his captive. He struggled for enough air to speak, frantically gripping at his throat, attempting to plead for his life.

Haden laughed. He walked to Emmett, looked down at him, and laughed.

* * *

Caylee's mouth went dry, and her stomach clenched. Haden looked mad, mad enough to hit her. "You're scaring me." He was staring into her eyes, holding her too tightly, but she sensed he wasn't really there with her. A few seconds went by, but it seemed like decades.

"I would never hit you." Lifting her chin, he forced her to meet his gaze. "And you know it." He took deep breath and released with a heavy sigh, struggling to regain his composure, searching for the right words. "You blocked me from reaching you last night. You purposely prevented me from discovering you were being attacked. It's entirely unacceptable." Tilting his head to the side, he studied her for a moment. "You will never do it again, Caylee." Realizing his grip was too tight, he released her. "You will never block me when you're in danger."

Taking a step back, she stared up at him for a moment. She turned away from him and was faced with her reflection in the mirror. She needed to get away from him. Seeing herself naked in the mirror, feeling the dampness between her thighs, suddenly made her feel uncomfortable and, even worse, ashamed. Reaching down she grabbed her shirt to cover up her body.

His heart broke, shattered into a million pieces, at the sight her trying to hide her body. In an instant he had destroyed her dignity. He was an idiot. Cursing beneath his breath, he took the shirt from her and tossed it onto the floor. "I'm sorry." He gently, sending healing energy into it, placed his hand on her bruised shoulder. "I love you, Caylee. I can't bear the thought of anyone laying a hand on you, harming you in any way. I have such a powerful, violent, driving need to protect you. It's who I am, what I am. You're everything precious to me. There's nothing, no one I value more than you. You knew I would protect you, didn't you? Why didn't you call out to me?"

She started to take another step away from him, but then she stopped.

He moved nearer, unable to do anything else. He needed to touch her. Comfort her. Comfort himself.

Leaning her back against his much larger, muscular body, she took a deep breath and released it with a long sigh. "I only want to forget about last night, Haden." Turning to face him, she looked up at him for a moment. Then, resting her head against chest, she listened to the strong, steady sound of his heart beating. She searched for the strength to walk away from him. It would've been for the best, but she couldn't find it. Honestly, there wasn't a part of her that truly wanted to find it. "Help me forget."

Wrapping his powerful arms around her, holding her close, he lowered his head protectively over hers. From the beginning he'd failed to protect her. He'd turned his back on her. He'd left her alone and vulnerable. When he'd finally came to his senses and realized she was his life, he continued to neglect her. If he hadn't allowed her to block him from her thoughts, he would've known Emmett was abusing her. It shouldn't have happened. It would never happen again. He would never fail her again.

He held her back at arm's length, allowing the heat of his gaze to explore every inch, every lush, feminine curve of her body. "You're perfect in every way, little love. You're the substance of my most cherished dream."

She felt his gaze touching every inch of her flesh, slowly spreading over her. She was burning up, her heart pumping liquid fire through her veins; the hunger in his gaze was awakening greater passions in her. She felt his need, the aching, unrelenting intensity of it.

She slowing, devouring the sight of him, lowered her gaze. Then, nearly breathless at the sight of his arousal, she stood perfectly still. Even through his pants she studied the shocking evidence of his terrible need, the heavy, bulging heat of it, so swollen and on fire for her. She looked up at him, shyly biting her lower lip, her cheeks flushed.

Leaning down, he kissed her long and thoroughly. She trembled, her body eagerly anticipating more, as he parted her lips with his tongue.

He savored the sweet taste of her kiss, his passion violently crashing into hers, their needs erupting into a fierce firestorm of lust that burned through their bodies as he lowered her onto the bed.

She reveled in the exquisite sensation of his hands wandering, exploring every inch of her body. Her flesh was so soft, hot and satiny against his. Pushing her thighs apart, he lowered his body over hers, kissing her deeply. Suddenly, the weight of his body created a reminder of the past. Though gentle, Haden's touch felt as if it was the touch of a violent assailant. Her body tensed to the point of pain, and her flesh turned cold and clammy, her lips rigid, completely void of desire.

Violence enveloped her. She was powerless, chained to a cold stone altar. Men mocked and threatened her. She was trapped. She couldn't breathe. She was pinned down beneath the weight of a man, unable to move and unable to defend herself. She was suffocating. Her desperation grew. Her entire body ached. There was no escaping the inevitable. There was no reason to hope. Pain, agonizing, unthinkable pain was inflicted on every inch of her flesh. Fear far beyond understanding stole her breath. Her heart labored. Her body absorbed vengeful blow after blow. She prayed for death to deliver her from the brutality of violent, lustful hands all over her body and around her throat. Death was the only possible escape. Chains bruised and tore the flesh on her ankles and wrists, holding her captive. Her entire body ached and throbbed.

Backing away, Haden looked down at her, his mind remaining deeply merged with hers. With a blank expression, she stared up at him. For the first time ever, he was able to study the entire memory. Despite knowing what had happened the night he found her, he had never been able to access detailed memories in her mind without causing her pain. Now, he saw faces of all of the men her father had sold her to. He would hunt each and every man down.

The pain was too much. It was too great. She needed it to end, but her assailants were far too powerful to fend off, and death lingered just out of reach. Left to die, she prayed for a miracle, she prayed for death to deliver her, but she knew death was no longer an option the moment Haden showed up. He was a stranger, but her heart and soul knew him, knew he would never permit her to die, knew he would never hurt or betray her. His resolve was unshakable.

Holding her close to his heart, allowing her to be soothed by its steady, strong rhythm, he healed her physical and emotional wounds. There was no mistaking he was powerful beyond human comprehension. For a man like him there was no hiding it. She knew then he wasn't human, but it didn't frighten her as it should have. He was so gentle. Caring. Kind. Being in his arms was like being in the arms of an angel. He spoke softly, his magical, healing voice a warm, loving embrace. He made her feel protected and loved. He made her feel joy. True, heartfelt joy. And even more surprising, he made her want to embrace life for first time since her birth.

Realizing she was allowing her mind to wander, she closed her eyes in an effort to censor her thoughts. In doing so while their minds were so deeply merged, she revealed to Haden how she was able to block him. For now on he would know the instant she tried to block him, and he would be able to get through it without hurting her.

He placed his hand over her heart. "You need to breathe, little love." He forced his rage down, successfully keeping it from showing in his eyes. "You're safe with me." Revenge would come, but for her sake he needed to remain calm for the moment.

Slowly, she opened her eyes and looked up at him. Studying him, she found no hint of anger or disgust. Relieved, she smiled up at him, choosing to believe he still didn't know her secret. For the moment, it was easy to believe she'd managed to keep it from him. She was amazed by him, by the way he made her feel, and by the way he made her body ache for his touch and burn for the wild intensity of his kiss. She knew he loved her. It was there, his love for her. She saw it so clearly she actually felt how deeply he loved her. Everlasting.

Unconditional. For one precious moment, she felt the intensity of his enormous, never-ending love for her. It filled her like the spicy, masculine scent of his skin filled her lungs with each breath she took. Thoroughly. Completely—though she still believed if he knew she'd been raped he couldn't possibly love her.

Rolling over onto his back, he reached for her and dragged her nearer. Pulling the blanket over their bodies, he encouraged her to rest her head on his chest, immediately applying more healing energy to her deep emotional wounds. "It's okay." Gently caressing her shoulder and arm, he was tempted to take another glance at the memory, but he wasn't entirely sure he could handle any more and contain his anger. He needed to focus on her. Heal her.

She was shaken by the way the past had revisited her. It had never happened before. Sure, she had dark memories, but she'd never relived them so vividly. How could intimacy with Haden compare to violence? She tried to rationalize the condition of her mind, but she couldn't focus on herself. What if he had seen it? He would never want her as a lover. How could he? She was dirty. Filthy.

Haden was sure that the instant she confided in him, her past would no longer have the power to enslave and torment her. Pretending he didn't know wasn't easy—he'd much rather tackle a problem head-on—but his love for her enabled him to wait for as long as she needed. He brought her hand to the warmth of his mouth. Still, it wouldn't hurt to encourage her to open up to him. "Tell me what happened a moment ago." He opened her palm and kissed it. "Why were you so afraid?"

"I'm not afraid of you." And she wasn't. She knew he was nothing like the men that had chained her to the altar, tortured her, raped her, and left her for dead.

"I know." Nuzzling his chin in her hair, inhaling her sweet scent, he kissed the top of her head. "But there's something you're hiding, something you're afraid of. What is it?"

Perfect. She frowned. Absolutely perfect. She'd ruined everything. Taking a deep breath, she released it with a frustrated sigh. "I'm so sorry, Haden. I don't know what's wrong with me. I don't blame you for being mad."

She heard him chuckle softly above her head. "I'm not even a little mad. I won't deny being frustrated. But it's okay. Frustrating is good. There's no need to rush into anything." He wrapped his arms around her body, battling a powerful urge to go after the men that had hurt her. He didn't want to wait for revenge. He wanted to rush out and find them. He wanted to kill them immediately. He needed to do it. But he couldn't. Not yet. She needed him, and her needs would always come before his. "Rest with me for awhile, little love."

"You want to sleep?" Chewing on her bottom lip, she frowned. She'd certainly screwed things up. The last thing she wanted to do was sleep.

"Not really." Attempting to stop the visions of death and destruction from moving through his mind, he closed his eyes. "I want to hold you." He forced his voice to remain calm, wanting to hide the rage building in him, knowing it would alert her to the fact that he knew what had happened to her.

Driving him insane, massaging and tickling his chest and stomach with her fingertips, she snuggled up closer to him. He grinned and, with barely noticeable movement, shook his head. If she was purposely trying to torture him, she was succeeding.

She believed her time with him was running out. Remaining with Haden wasn't an option. She had one chance to be with him. One chance to make love to him. Haden would never make the first move. He knew she was frightened, and he would wait for her to make the first move. Gradually, she started to explore his body with her hands, timidly at first, and then more boldly.

He knew she was planning to return to her uncle's home, but it didn't matter. Emmett was dead. One way or another, no matter the body count, she would never be abused again.

His blood pressure soared; his entire body was responding to her touch, but he remained completely still, holding her in his arms, allowing her the freedom to explore his body at her own pace.

His body was so solid. He was a magnificent man. His well-defined chest and abdominal muscles were tight, trembling as she moved her hand lower. She heard him take in a sharp breath and hold it in anticipation. He was such a strong and powerful man. His response to her touch intensified her desire, flooding her body with such sinfully intoxicating pleasures that she couldn't stop touching him. She didn't want to stop; she wouldn't stop.

Time seemed to drag on and on; her touch was slowly pushing him over the edge of control. She made him feel so weak. So needy. The torture she was forcing him to endure was bittersweet. During his entire existence, he'd never resorted to begging for anything, but his entire body was desperately pleading for hers. He thought he would go mad when her hand briefly brushed against the hot, ultra-sensitive flesh of his swollen cock.

Through clenched teeth, he made a sound of something between a growl and a groan. Horrified that she'd done something wrong, she lifted her hand. He ached to plunge himself deep inside her body, so deep nothing could ever separate them. He needed to feel her womanly heat tightly wrapped around his cock. Before he could stop himself, he took her hand and guided it back to his erection. With his guidance, she stroked the length of it. Groaning, he released her hand. She continued to stroke the length of him. Tightening her grip, she repeated the motion over and over again as drops of his hot essence seeped onto her hand.

His eyes flashed open. "Caylee." Her name came out a breathless, desperate plea. A fierce fire burned deep inside him. He needed to stop her before it was too late, before he couldn't stop her. She'd suffered too much. She wasn't ready. He knew he should get out of the bed, but instead he turned onto his side and faced her.

She wrapped her arms around him. "I can't believe I'm in your bed." She giggled. "It's easier to believe you can turn into a dragon and you have wings and can fly."

Pulling her nearer and wrapping her leg around his body, he pressed his cock against her belly. Taking her breast in his hand and stroking her nipple with his thumb as he kissed her lips, he pumped his hips, unable to stop moving against her.

"Haden." Every inch of her flesh burned. She felt completely empty, desperately wanting him to fill her, needing to feel his cock deep inside her body.

"What's wrong?" He trailed kisses down her throat to her breasts. "Do you want me to stop?" Lightly, he swirled his tongue around her nipple.

She took sharp breath. "No." The wonderful sensations that spread throughout her entire body startled her, but her body wanted more, needed more. "Never stop."

He chuckled. "Are you sure?" He drew her nipple into his mouth, holding it between his teeth and swirling his tongue over it. "Absolutely sure?"

"If you stop, I'll never forgive you." Tangling his hair in her fingers, she held his head to her breast, his hot mouth on her breast causing moist heat to pool between her legs.

Leaning back, he gently, splaying his hand over her chest, pushed her flat onto her back. "Never?"

Opening her eyes, she looked up at him and shook her head. "Never."

"Perhaps we should wait," he whispered so softly she could barely hear it.

"I'm tired of waiting."

He gazed into her eyes for several seconds, delving deep into her mind, searching for a hint of fear or reservation. "There's no reason to rush." And there wasn't. Not really. He might die, but he was willing to sacrifice his life for her.

"Are you in my mind now?"

"I would never want to trespass." Looking far too innocent, he nudged her legs apart, making room for his body.

Meeting her gaze, studying her reaction, he positioned his body between her thighs.

"You can't hide it from me, Haden. I can always feel you. I know when you're in my mind." She allowed her hands to wander down the contours of his back muscles and then upward along his sides. "You know what I want. You know what I need. What are you going to do about it?" Biting her lower lip, she let her hands slide downward along his sides and to the center of his lower belly, her hand brushing up against his erection. "Or would you rather wait?"

Lowering his body, he kissed her, and his heart thundered, roaring in his ears. Conflicted, he backed away and looked down at her, and then he closed his eyes as he lowered his head to rest it on top of her flat belly. Guilt? He groaned. He was actually feeling guilty for seducing her. "To be honest, I would rather not wait." He paused for a moment. "But I would wait."

"I want you, Haden. I need you. I don't want to wait any longer. I can't." She ran her fingers through his thick hair. "Look at me," she whispered. Lifting his head, he met her gaze. "I've never wanted anything more than I want you to make love to me, Haden."

Their minds were so deeply joined he knew she meant it. So, why the hell did he still feel guilty for wanting to share something so natural with her? It wasn't as if he were going hurt her. Sure, he possessed the skills and knowledge to make sure she experienced many mind-blowing pleasures. But what if he wasn't to her liking?

Really? Was he seriously doubting his ability to perform well enough for her?

At first Caylee didn't realize what was happening. She could hear his voice in her head, but it was slightly different than when he was talking to her. But then, studying his worried expression, she realized she was hearing his thoughts. She giggled aloud.

He arched his brow at her. The grin on her face spoke volumes. She'd just heard his thoughts. Sure, she was his true mate, so once the ritual was complete she would have the ability to read his thoughts at will unless he prevented it, but not now, not in her mortal state. But, by the grin on her face, there was no denying the fact that she just heard what he was thinking.

Looking very naughty, his lips curved up in a wicked smile. "Caylee, after all the lectures you've given me, are you actually mucking around in my head?"

"No," she replied too quickly, her smile instantly disappearing, her eyes filled with fear as if she expected him to hurt her.

He bent his head to kiss her. "I was only teasing you, little love. I'm not mad over it," he whispered against her lips. "I want to be as close to you as possible for all of eternity. It's a wonderful thing, a beautiful thing for you to merge your mind with mine." She opened her mouth to deny it, but he silenced her with a long, slow kiss so tender, so loving it stole her ability to entertain any other thought than the taste and feel of his mouth claiming hers.

She wasn't sure exactly when it happened, but eventually his possession of her mouth elevated into something more urgent, more demanding. She wasn't afraid of the change. In fact, just the opposite—she welcomed it, embraced it. When he reached down between her legs to place his palm against her hot, silken mound, he was pleased she lifted her hips and moved against his hand. Rewarding her eager response, he gently stroked her clit and bent his head to suckle the hard bud of her nipple. Moaning, she arched her body, pressing herself more firmly against his hand, her fingers tangled in his hair, holding his head to her breast.

Slipping a finger inside her, he stroked her most sensitive spot with his thumb. Her inner muscles clenched tightly around his finger as he moved lower, slowly kissing, licking his way from her breasts to her navel and then lower, until he arrived at the hot, savory entrance of her body.

"What are you doing?" Violently arching her body, nearly throwing herself from the bed, the air burst out of her lungs in a startled gasp. "Haden, you can't!" Her nails dug deep into his shoulders.

"But I am." Grinning wickedly, he looked up at her for a moment, and then he bent his head and licked her once. It was just a quick stroke of his tongue, but it sent wonderful, powerful shock waves through her entire body. She squirmed restlessly, her body trembling. He grabbed her hips and brought her closer, pinning her to his mouth so his hot breath seductively caressed her most intimate place. He suckled greedily, tasting her, feasting on her, savoring her, devouring her sweet essence.

The pleasure was agonizing and wonderful all at the same time. Her body shuddered. Her thoughts shattered. What he was doing to her was so wrong on so many levels, but her body was responding wildly to the forbidden act. A million thoughts raced through her mind, but none made sense. None mattered. She should stop him. She couldn't stop him. She didn't want to stop him.

Wanting more, needing more, she pressed her body against his mouth. Groaning deeply, he stabbed her with his tongue, gripping her hips more firmly. Opening her thighs wider, pressing her against his mouth, his tongue delved deep. Her hot, creamy essence prepared her body for his. Suckling her clit, he slid two fingers inside her. She was so hot and slick, her inner muscles clenching tightly around his fingers. She was so damn tight. He imagined his cock, buried deep, releasing his seed inside her body. He groaned loudly, his cock nearly bursting as he continued to feed on her.

Delicious, explosive sensations spread throughout her body, centering between her legs, burning at her core. "Please." She was desperate, her body feverish, needing his, demanding his to fill hers. Her heart was racing. She had to struggle to catch her breath. "I need you, Haden. I need you inside me now."

He spread her legs to make room, moving slowly, watching her closely, covering her tiny body with his.

"Caylee, are you sure?" It was more of a desperate plea than a question. He heard the torment in his voice. There was no hiding it; she had to have heard it too. There was no mistaking it for anything else. He could scarcely breathe; his heart literally stopped. Lingering at her hot entrance his erection grew even harder, throbbing so very painfully.

Eyes enormous, she stared up at him, her palms caressing the contours of his heavily muscled shoulders and biceps. How could she not be sure? She felt the heat of his cock pressed against the entrance of her body. The sensation alone nearly brought her to a powerful climax, her need building into a raging storm. She ached to feel him inside her body. Deep. Filling her. "Absolutely." She opened her legs further, cradling his body in her hips, allowing the broad head of his cock to enter her body.

Gasping her name, he pushed deeper, stretching the soft, satiny corridors of her body, but then he stopped to gain control. Her body was so tight. He wanted to thrust harder, deeper. The pleasure of being inside her body was so great it was painful. She was so hot and tight, wrapped around him, annihilating his control. Restless, she wiggled beneath him, needing more.

Reaching behind the nape of her neck, he lifted her head to share the erotic view of his cock partially buried in her. Lightning whipped through their bodies, and thunder rumbled in their ears. Digging her fingernails into his shoulders, she arched her body to meet his, watching as he ventured further, plunged deeper.

She felt her body stretching, but willing to take him, wanting more, needing more. She savored the sensation as he pulled out slowly. Eyes wide, she stared in wonder at the glistening length of him, amazed she was able to take so much of him into her body.

"We fit together marvelously, perfectly." He kissed her deeply, thoroughly savoring it, his tongue tangling with hers, his teeth nipping at her lips, the head of his cock buried just inside her entrance.

"Oh, Haden." Whimpering, she squirmed beneath him, nearly frantic, her body burning up, needing so much more.

Releasing her neck, he bent his head and kissed her throat, slowly working his way lower. "You're so beautiful, Caylee. Perfect in every way." Cupping her breasts, he flicked his tongue over each nipple.

Arching her body, breathing heavily, she tangled her fingers in his thick hair, holding him to her, pressing her breast against his mouth.

Sucking her nipples, taking them between his teeth, he pushed slowly forward, burying his erection deep inside her body. She closed her eyes and moaned huskily, head thrown back, savoring the sensation of him stretching her.

Hesitating, he looked down at her for a moment to make sure she was okay. It was easy to enter her mind. Every block was removed, leaving her thoughts completely open to him. For the first time, her violent past was a forgotten memory. Her only thoughts were on the physical, spiritual pleasures of their joining. She was focused on the glorious sensations racing through her body, igniting wild, unstoppable flames, driving her insane, devouring her natural defenses.

"Look at me." He kissed her lips, softly. "Open your eyes, little love." He wanted to see her hunger for him, but holding his breath, he hoped to see her love for him.

She opened her eyes and smiled up at him. Her eyes were so wide, gazing up at him, her love for him obvious. She was so damn beautiful beneath him, too beautiful, her pale flesh flushed and long, dark brown hair cascading over the pillows. Moving slowly, maintaining a steady, erotic rhythm, creating delicious friction, he made love to her gently. He had hoped for this moment for so long, never fully able to imagine it. How could he? He'd never loved a woman. He'd never cherished a woman. And he'd certainly never needed a woman to make him whole. She was a priceless miracle, an entirely undeserved miracle, one he would never relinquish.

The sensations of pleasure grew in each of them as they stared into each other's eyes. He instantly knew she was far better than just okay. Every trace of her fear was gone. She was in the same state of complete enchantment he was experiencing. The sensual and spiritual pleasure was shockingly more than he'd ever dreamed it would be. The combination of the heat of her body and taste of her flesh was completely overwhelming to all of his senses, unleashing his dark nature. No longer in control, he began to thrust deeper. Harder. Faster. His pace was as ferocious as his need for her. There was no past to contend with and no future problems to solve. Only the present mattered. Feeding the hunger and fanning the flames of their desire was all that mattered.

In the past, she'd often imagined the way he would feel and the hungry, passionate look in his eye, but she was far from being prepared for the pleasurable sensations that were riveting throughout her entire body. Gasping, struggling to catch her breath, she called out his name, her voice desperate and hungry. Her body gripped his cock, mercilessly squeezing it, as he entered her again and again, thrusting deeper and harder, creating the most delicious friction as it stretched her. Arching her body, meeting his every move, her body was on fire. He whispered her name in her ear, along with many indiscernible endearments, his voice a raspy, barely audible whisper.

The pleasure was too much; it was too great, bordering on pain. He felt his control slipping away. He struggled to catch his breath, his pleasure growing with every thrust of his hips. Her fingernails were digging into his back, scraping his hips. He slowed the pace, wanting to draw it out. He finally had everything. He was finally alive. They were finally one. He would never allow anything to come between them. He kissed her deeply, putting every ounce of his love for her in to it. For several moments time stood completely still.

Feeding on his love, she returned the kiss, and all of her love for him, so pure and abundant, poured into it. Her thighs quivered against his sides as she met his powerful thrusts with her own.

Suddenly, she went completely still, shocked by the fire burning in her core. He kept moving, creating hot friction, building the fire, pushing her further, taking her far past pleasure. *Don't leave me, little love.* Rejoining him, she frantically met his thrusts with her own, holding onto him, her nails biting into his shoulders, terrified she was going to shatter into thousands of tiny pieces. The explosive climax he brought her to was alarming, but so wonderful.

He felt his body quickly losing all control, his erection swelling, growing impossibly hard. He couldn't succumb to the pleasure before her, but the more he fought the more he was desperate to succumb to it. Just in the nick of time, he heard her cry of ecstasy muted against his chest. Her body tightened and released in powerful spasms around his cock, pushing him far past the point of control.

He released a roar, his body shuddering, every muscle tightening to the point of pain that turned to intolerable pleasure, as his orgasm violently ripped through his entire body. In a very strange state of shock, his focus remained fixed on the sensation of his cock pulsating, jetting his seed into her body. He'd never seriously entertained the thought of having children, but he wanted his child inside her body. He tried to stop the thought, knowing his kind had control over whether or not they reproduced, but it was too late. He knew a child had been conceived by their lovemaking. His arms buckled, and he fell full weight, in a helpless state of awe, on top of her.

She wrapped her arms around him, trying to hold him even nearer, her legs trembling against his body. His flesh was damp and feverish, droplets of sweat covering him. After several moments, he lifted his upper body and looked down at her. Perhaps he should warn her. Better yet, he was still hard and swollen; there was no reason to deny either of their bodies any pleasure. He decided it would be better to wait. There was no reason to tell her now. It might dampen her mood.

Smiling, she reached up and caressed his face. "Why do you look so guilty?"

Lowering his head, he kissed her. Tears slowly welled up in her eyes and trickled down the sides of her face. "Are you okay?"

"I never imagined it would be so wonderful." Blushing, she giggled. "And I've imagined it many times."

"Me too." He leaned down and kissed her as the intensity of his desire grew once again. "I love you, Caylee." He would never get enough of her. He wanted and needed to make love to her again and again.

She kissed him deeply. "I love you with all of my heart and soul, Haden."

Rolling off her and onto his back, he sat up with his back against the headboard. "Come here." He reached for her and encouraged her to sit over his lap. Tilting his head back, he looked up at her.

Feeling shy, she crossed her arms over her breasts. "Forget it." He grabbed her wrists and pulled her arms to her sides. "I want to see you." He framed her face with his hands and drew her nearer. "You're absolutely beautiful."

Looking into her eyes, anger filled him. He would seek justice for her. He needed to kill the men that had hurt her.

"You look mad." She leaned back. "What's wrong?"

Laughing softly, he pulled her closer. "Everything is finally right."

They kissed. It was a deep, sensuous kiss that went on and on. She wasn't sure when it ended, but she became aware of it as he kissed the warm, soft flesh of her breasts and drew her nipples in his mouth. Her body tingled in response to his mouth and tongue on her sensitive flesh. Reaching around her hips, he lifted her and then lowered her until the heat and tightness of her soft sheath enveloped his cock. They made love for hours, worshipping each other, until they collapsed in each other's arms.

~ *Twelve* ~

CAYLEE STARTED TO fall asleep, but then she panicked. It was too late to leave Haden. Opening her eyes, she turned and looked over her shoulder. He would never allow her to leave. Not now. Not after they'd made love. Oh God. He was going to discover her secret.

Haden knew why she was panicking. He slowly allowed his hands to slide down her arms.

Savoring the flicker of hot desire racing through her body, her breaths came in short gasps. What was wrong with her? Her life was about to be ruined, and her flesh was tingling and her sensitive breasts ached, craving his attention.

He turned her around. He looked so sexy, wickedly hot, his sensuous lips curved in a naughty smile. One thing was for sure: he was pure sin, she was addicted, and no patch would ever get her through the withdrawals. "You have nothing to fear." He gently pulled her against his body. "I've allowed you to keep a secret from me for a very long time now, but I've decided it's time for you to tell me about it."

She bit her lower lip, chewing on it. "When you discover the truth you'll never look into my eyes as you do at this moment. Your love for me will be replaced with disgust." She looked down to hide the shame in her eyes. "You will never forgive me."

He lifted her face, but she directed her gaze away. "Look at me, Caylee." Whimpering, she met his gaze with tears streaming down her face. "My love for you could never turn into disgust. Trust me." He kissed her. "Tell me your secret."

Taking her life was the only plausible way to end the agony. It was too painful and exhausting, always knowing that each second they spent together was a second closer to the moment she would lose his love.

He held her against his body. "Don't even think about it."

She needed to get out the bed. She tried to get free, but it was no use. His arms were like steel bindings, holding her captive. Desperate, she whimpered. "You're hurting me."

"I'm not hurting you."

She buried her face against his chest. "You've no idea what I've done."

"Look at me." He wanted to tell her he knew everything, but he knew it would devastate her. She needed to trust him. She needed to tell him. She needed to have absolute, blind faith in his love for her. There could be no doubt in her mind when it was time to give her immortality.

She met his gaze. "Please." Gasping for a breath, she sobbed desperately, her eyes pleading with him to stop. "Don't try to see it." Tears streamed down her face. Heartbroken, he reached up and gently wiped her tears. "Please," she gasped, her throat closing. "I can't tell you."

"Breathe." He wrapped hands around her throat. "Nothing will ever come close to destroying my love for you."

"Please," she pleaded, "don't make me tell you." She knew in her heart he would never let her go until she told him. Taking a deep breath and holding it, she looked up at him for a few seconds. Ashamed, she turned her head to look away from him.

He waited for a few moments, and then he turned her face toward his. "You can tell me."

"I lived in Portland with my father. He was a very cruel man, worse than my uncle. I tried to run away. I never made it very far out of the city." After a few moments of silence she looked up at him and shook her head. "Please." She paused for several seconds. "Don't make me tell you."

"Tell me what happened."

"It was late," she said, her voice weak, "but I kept going through the night. I wanted to get as far away from the city as possible. My father would come after me in the morning. My car broke down. I was in the middle of nowhere. My first thought was to go back to the city. But I couldn't. My father would've kept such a close eye on me."

Pausing for a moment, she took several deep breaths. "I kept walking until the sun came up, and then I left the road. I didn't want my father to find me. I walked several hundred yards into the forest, and then sat down and leaned against a tree and waited for nighttime. I fell asleep. I heard their voices. When I opened my eyes they were standing over me." She buried her face against his chest and wept heavily.

Maybe he was wrong. Maybe he should've never hidden from her that he'd known all along what had happened. Taking a deep breath, he tightened his embrace around her and caressed her back.

"You'll despise me once you learn the truth."

"No." He leaned back and held her face in his hands, forcing her to look up at him. "I'll love you forever."

She whimpered, her body trembling, as she took several rapid breaths. "You don't understand. Please don't make me do this. I can't live through it again." She paused for moment. "Not with you." She shook her head. "I would rather die than watch your love for me vanish."

"It will never happen. I will always love you. You need to tell me." His voice was calm and soothing. He felt her body tense, as she struggled with the past. He waited, holding her against his chest.

The tension in her body eased up as she listened to his steady, strong heartbeat. She closed her eyes and thought of the love they'd shared in his bed. He was right. She needed to tell him. She owed him the truth.

"I knew they intended to harm me." She paused for a few moments, gathering enough courage to continue. "I tried to run away, but they chased after me. Someone hit the back of my head. I lost consciousness. I woke up chained to a stone altar. My head hurt. I couldn't see straight. I kept going in and out of consciousness. Eventually, I remained conscious and I was more aware of my surroundings. I tried to get free of the chains, but it was impossible. The chains were so tight. They dug into my flesh."

She was thankful for the way he was caressing her back, quietly allowing her to take as much time as she needed. "They raped and beat me so badly they thought I would die. Before I lost consciousness, I heard them discuss what they should do with me. They planned to bury me. But when I woke up I felt the warmth of the sun, of your touch. You were holding me, healing me, whispering to me, willing me to live." She was silent for several moments. "At first I was so very angry with you. I wanted to die." Biting her lower lip, she frowned. "I knew you wouldn't allow it."

He'd made sure she'd never learned she had been buried in a shallow grave when he found her. He gently lifted her face to his.

She closed her eyes to avoid the anger and disgust she was certain to find if she met his gaze. Bending his head, he kissed her lips tenderly. "Look at me, little love."

She opened her eyes. Tears were streaming down his face. Shaking her head, she reached up and placed her hand on the side of his face. "I'm so sorry, Haden. Now you know why I never wanted to tell you." She sat up. "I'll go home."

He captured her arm. "You're not going back there."

She looked up at him and saw no sign of anger or disgust in his eyes. Instead, she saw love, sadness, and pain.

He leaned toward her and gently kissed her lips. "I'm deeply, completely and forever helplessly in love with you." He gazed into her eyes for a few seconds. "I'm afraid you'll be stuck with me for the rest of your life."

"How can you still love me? You've made love to a woman that has ... oh, Haden."

It was time. She needed to face the truth. "Deep down, you know I've always known what happened. I found you. I healed you. I let you pretend I didn't know. I knew you weren't ready for me to know. I knew we belonged together." He paused. "Caylee, I made love today to the only woman I'll ever love."

"You knew?" She shook her head. It couldn't be true. She got up from the bed and paced back and forth. "You're lying." She sat down on the floor. Leaning her back against the wall, she rested her forehead on her knees. "How could you want to be with me?"

He kneeled down in front of her. "None of it was your fault."

"I should've known better. I never should've tried to do it."

"You were trying to escape abuse." He pulled her up with him as he stood, and then he gently wiped her tears.

Perplexed, she looked up at him. Was it pity? The thought frightened her. His attitude was completely opposite to what she expected. "Why are you doing this?"

"What do you mean?" Reaching behind her and pressing her body against his, he leaned down and kissed her deeply and passionately.

Pulling away from him, she stared at him for a moment and shook her head. "What are you doing? I was raped over and over again by group of men. How can you act as if the thought of being with me doesn't make you sick? Tell me you resent ever knowing me, but don't you dare do this. I don't need you to feel sorry for me. Don't pretend it doesn't matter."

"I love you, Caylee. You're everything to me. I can't image a woman more beautiful than you. I can't even begin to imagine a life without you." He took possession of her mouth roughly, passionately pouring every ounce of love into the kiss. "I can assure you my love and desire for you has nothing to do with pity."

Waving his hand, he caused flames to ignite in the fireplace. "I need you more and more with each breath I take." Kissing her deeply, he wedged his body between her thighs. "I could spend the rest of eternity making love to you and still need and want more of you."

A fire spread from her breasts to her most feminine place between her legs where his cock was pressed so snugly. She arched her hips in invitation, her body weeping for his to wash away the pain and loneliness she'd endured for her entire life. She needed him to take her farther away from her past. Only he could heal every wound that her mind and body had sustained since her conception. Her flesh tingled. Her breasts, overly sensitive, ached for his touch.

His lips brushed her breast, his tongue swirled over her nipple, sending fire blazing through her body. Flesh to flesh, he was so hot and hard, pressed against her opening. She wiggled restlessly beneath him, arching her body toward his, needing him to fill her. Starting from the center of her throat, he rubbed his calloused fingertips down the center of her chest, down her tiny flat belly, and lower to the soft mound between her legs. Savoring the satiny texture of her warm flesh, he parted her feminine folds, and then he pushed the head of his cock inside her.

Cupping her breast, he swirled his thumb over her nipple. He took her mouth, his passionate kiss driving her insane. She wanted more. Needed more. Her nails dug into his shoulders, her body trembling with the fiery sensations racing through it. She tried to arch her hips to get more of him inside her, but he captured her hips and pinned her down. "I love you, Caylee. I will love until the end of time. Do you believe it now?"

She reached up to his face. "I know it now. I know you love me. I know you'll always love me, no matter what."

He bent his head and kissed her. "And?"

"I will love you forever, Haden."

"Good." His fingers digging into her hips, he pulled her closer. "Now, wrap your legs around my body."

The moment she locked her ankles around his body, he slammed deep and hard. She cried out, her body tightly, mercilessly clamping down on him. He thrust harder and faster, stretching her tight muscles, filling her, creating the most sensational flames of pleasure. She moved with him, lightning ripping through her body, as she took pleasure from his fierce lovemaking. She loved that he was wild and out of control. He continued to pound into her over and over again, thrusting wildly.

Finally, after hours of lovemaking, they collapsed in each other's arms and slept in front of the fire. It was the end of life as she knew it and the beginning of a new, eternal life. Together until the end of time they would share a love too few would ever know. Very soon, she would be ready and he would take her last mortal breath and replace it with his immortal breath.

~ *Thirteen* ~

STANDING NEXT TO CAYLEE'S car, Paul lifted his head and drew in a deep breath from his nostrils, allowing the intoxicating scent of her fear to fill his lungs. He opened the driver side door and climbed inside. Settling into the seat and gripping the steering wheel, he tilted his head back and closed his eyes. Her sweet aroma was so concentrated in the confined area that it wrapped around him and would no doubt cling to him for hours. Groaning aloud, he savored the lust consuming him.

It went against Paul's nature, but Caylee was no longer just a source of entertainment and nourishment. Fangs lengthening and mouth watering, he imagined what it would be like to take her hot blood into his body. Oh yes, he would drink her blood, but not until he was buried deep inside her body. His need for her was driving him crazy. He knew he was tumbling into a state of madness, but it didn't matter. He didn't care. He couldn't contemplate a future without her.

He wasn't sure why he was so obsessed with her. At first he thought it was caused by her attempt to fight him in the alley, but it was more than that. She was different. She was extraordinary. He actually ached to bury his cock deep inside her body. She was meant to be his. No other woman had ever ignited such a violent fire of raw lust inside his soul. No other woman could ever quench the flames. She was the only woman that could ever give him relief. He was so certain of it he planned to share his blood with her to bind their souls together for eternity.

Unable to resist the need to touch her mind, Paul reached for Caylee's mind. The image of her naked body wrapped in Haden's embrace filled him with murderous rage. His eyes snapped open, and he jumped out of the car. There was no way in hell he would allow a demon to go unpunished for defiling, for stealing what was rightfully his. She would also pay for betraying him. He wouldn't allow her to get away from him. She belonged to him.

Wrenching herself out of Haden's arms, Caylee screamed.

Heart pounding, Haden's eyes flew open. Pulling her close, he instantly, brutally pushed Paul out of Caylee's mind. He placed a wall around her mind, but Paul continued to reach for her, desperately attempting to merge his mind with hers once again.

"He's here." Caylee trembled in his arms. "He's going to take me from you."

"No," Haden whispered. "He isn't here, little love. He touched your mind. He can't take you from me." Something was terribly wrong with the vampire; it was entirely unnatural for one to provoke a demon in such a blatant manner.

"He was in my car. I saw him. He's so mad at me. I don't understand. Why did he say that I belong to him? He said that I will pay for betraying him." She whimpered, clutching her head. "He's calling me to him." Eyes wide, she shook his head. "Do you hear him? He's still in my mind. I don't understand. Why does he want to give me his blood? Why does he want me to be like him?"

Searching her mind for the vampire's presence, Haden tilted his head to the side. "You can still hear him?"

Caylee nodded. "He's so mad at me." She paused. "What did I do to him? Why is he so mad at me?"

"You didn't do anything wrong, little love. Don't blame yourself for his insanity. None it's your fault." Finally, Haden found the path Paul was using to enter her mind and was able to block it with minimal effort. Relieved, he took a deep breath and released it with a heavy sigh. "He's entirely evil. He's sadistic. There's no good in him."

"How did you do it? He's gone." Smiling, she gripped her head. "I don't hear him at all." She frowned. "He's gone, right?"

"Yes." Standing up, easily lifting her, he carried her over to the bed.

"What if he takes me? What if he gives me his blood? He said I will be your enemy. He said you, your kind, will hunt me down to kill me." Tears welled up in her eyes. "I can't bear the thought of being like him."

If it happened Haden would save her from the curse. He would kill her. But she would never be his enemy. He smiled at her to place her at ease, but he couldn't hide the cold, dark death in his piercing blue gaze seconds before his eyes turned black. "You will never be like him, little love. I wouldn't allow it. And you will never be my enemy. You are my life. I will always do whatever it takes to protect you." He kissed her brow. "There aren't and never will be any limits to my love and devotion to you." He gently lowered her onto the bed.

While the realization of what he was saying was sinking in, she stared up at him. He wouldn't allow her to suffer the endless demise of the undead. It would destroy Haden, but he would kill her. He would always place her welfare above his own. She should've been terrified. He had just told her he could and would take her life. She knew there was no one powerful enough to stop him if he decided to do it. But she wasn't afraid of him. How could she fear the man that loved her enough to take her life to save her?

"I have hunted and killed his kind for centuries." He brought her hand to the warmth of his mouth. "I'm going to destroy him. He will never touch you again."

"You plan to go after him tonight." She grabbed his hand. "Please, don't do it. He wants to kill you. Stay here with me, Haden."

She was worried about him. He smiled. "There's no reason for you to worry about me." He took a deep breath and released it with a sigh. "I'm not easily killed, little love." Gently wiping the tears from her cheeks, he tilted his head to the side and smiled at her. "Trust me to protect you." Leaning down, he kissed her brow as he pulled a thick blanket over her body. "I need you to have faith in my ability to take care of you."

"I do." She frowned. "But I have a bad feeling. I don't think you should go after him tonight. He's waiting for you. He has a plan. A trap. He wants you to rush out after him tonight. He has set a trap for you. I don't know how I know it, but I do."

Haden smiled at her. "A vampire could never construct a trap able to hold me. I am a demon. I need to end the threat he presents to you." He gazed into her eyes for a moment. "Everything will be ok ay." Standing upright, he started to turn away from her.

"Wait." Sitting up, she reached for his arm. "Please, don't leave me here."

"You will be safe here." He hesitated and then sat down next to her. The last thing he wanted to do was leave her. He studied her face; her every feature was so beautifully illuminated by the moonlight seeping through the window. Her eyes were very heavy with fatigue as she gazed up at him. "I won't be gone long." Leaning down, he kissed her. It was a quick peck, nothing more. "You will stay here and wait for me."

Sitting up, she shook her head. "Oh no, you don't. You aren't going out there without me. You can't go alone, Haden. It's too dangerous. I'm going with you."

"No." Framing her face in his hands, he slowly leaned down and deeply, passionately kissed her. "You will stay right here and wait for me."

"Why won't you listen to me? I know you're making a mistake. He plans to kill you tonight."

"He can't," Haden growled. Revealing his growing irritation, he narrowed his gaze on her. "I have destroyed his kind for hundreds of years. Why do you always think the worst of me? It's way past time for you to have an ounce of faith in me."

"I do have faith in you. I just don't want you to go alone. Take me with you."

"Absolutely not. It's too dangerous." He kissed her lips gently.

Too gently. Coldly. She sensed he was struggling to contain his frustration with her, with the situation. She knew he was getting angry, but she couldn't let him face the vampire alone. She needed to stop him. "If it's too dangerous, why are you going?" She chewed on her bottom lip. "What if he kills you?"

"There's no way I would allow him to kill me." He laughed aloud, attempting to make a joke of it. "Especially with you in our bed waiting for me to return."

Her mouth twitched as she smiled, but then she forced herself to frown.

Kissing her, he leaned against her, pushing her down onto the bed. "You will stay right here." He pulled the blankets over her, tucking her in. "Now get some rest." He turned and away from her.

"I'm not staying here." Tossing the blankets off of the bed, she started to get up.

He turned and locked his cold, black gaze onto hers. "What?" A demon could only take so much. She wouldn't defy him. Not now. He wouldn't allow it.

"I'm not staying here." She felt an icy breeze sweep by her, and fear enveloping her, she shivered. "I will follow you." She swallowed hard. "You can't stop me." The moment she said the words, she knew she'd made a mistake. Heart racing, she held her breath.

A muscle twitched in his jaw. He smiled at her, but there was no warmth, no love in it. She quickly realized it wasn't a smile at all. His lips were curved upright and parted in a silent, threatening snarl.

Stepping toward her, he glared down at her. "You will do what I tell you to do." His voice was a deep, menacing growl.

Her breath caught in her throat. He was threatening her. But with what? Did he plan to beat her into submission? Teary eyed, she stared up at him for a moment but then looked away from his terrifying gaze.

Framing her face between his hands, he forced her to meet his gaze. "You will stay right here in this bed," he commanded between clenched teeth.

Too afraid to respond, she remained silent. Too afraid to follow the instinct of flight, she remained absolutely still. No. Wait. It wasn't fear. Her body felt incredibly heavy. She tried to move her legs. Nothing. She tried again. Nothing. He'd done something to her. She tried to lift her arm. Nothing. She couldn't move. She was paralyzed.

He smiled at her. "I won't allow you to place your life in danger." He saw her fear, he felt it, but it didn't matter. "I won't allow you to defy me." He turned away from her.

"Please." Her heart was pounding. "I won't leave. You're right. Please, don't do this to me." She was only a little relieved when he turned to look at her. He appeared to be deciding whether or not he should release her. "I promise to stay here." She paused, tears streaming down her face. "Allow me to move."

Suspicious, he narrowed his gaze on her. She was giving in to him far too easily.

"You're right. I won't follow you. I promise. Don't leave me like this, Haden. It's too much. I can't stand it."

Releasing her, he walked over to her. "I won't be gone long." He leaned down and kissed her. "I love you," he whispered.

"I love you too." Stretching her arms, she yawned, purposely exaggerating the sound of it.

Pulling the blankets over her, he smiled down at her. "Get some sleep, little love. I will be back soon." He turned and walked out of the room.

Enraged, Caylee lifted the blanket to her mouth and vigorously wiped his kiss right off her lips. She couldn't believe he'd taken control of her body. He'd actually paralyzed her. How had he done it? She shook head. It didn't matter. He would never make her a prisoner in her own body again.

Stepping outside, Haden hesitated to leave for a few seconds. She'd given into his demands too easily. He almost went back to apologize to her, but he didn't. He wouldn't. He hadn't done anything wrong. There was no doubt in his mind that she'd finally realized he was right. Well, maybe there was a little doubt. But even if she hadn't realized he was right, it didn't matter. He refused to feel guilty. Let her be mad at him. Let her think the worst of him. It didn't matter as long as she was safe.

Taking the form of the dragon, Haden took to the sky. His heart was heavy. He knew he'd hurt Caylee's feelings. He'd seen it in her eyes. Worse, he'd scared her by taking away her ability to move. For that he would apologize. Once the vampire was out of the way he would have plenty of time to smooth things over with her. Eventually she would come to terms with the fact that he knew what was best for her.

It wouldn't take long to track Paul down. Haden headed toward Caylee's car. From there he would be able to easily track the vampire.

* * *

Knowing she didn't have much time, Caylee got dressed quickly. Carefully guarding her thoughts, she made her way through the house. When she reached the front, she hesitated for a few seconds. She wanted to make sure Haden was gone. She didn't want him to stop her. She planned to run as far and as fast from him as possible. She opened the door and stepped outside. Standing on the front porch, she waited for her eyes to grow accustomed to the moonlight. She could hear the terrible howling and shrieking sounds of ghouls in the distance. She didn't care. She wasn't staying there. She didn't understand how Haden could treat her so badly. She would never be bound to another man that thought frightening her and forcing her into submission was acceptable.

He'd hurt her more than anyone else could've hurt her, but she wasn't going to sit and cry over it. She wasn't a baby. It was her own fault. He was only able to hurt her so deeply because she was an idiot. She knew better than to allow him to convince her he cared about her. She couldn't believe that, after all she'd been through, after all she'd learned, she'd actually allowed him to convince her he truly loved her. Taking a deep breath, she stepped off the porch. Prepared to face whatever gruesome fate was awaiting her in the ever-darkening forest, she started to run.

The physical exertion felt good. Allowing herself to just be mad as hell at Haden felt wonderful. It felt absolutely marvelous. She knew he would eventually come after her. She didn't how she would ever be able to escape him for good, but she would find a way. "Arrogant bastard," she whispered. He was just another cruel, arrogant bastard. She was so mad that she unknowingly opened her mind to Haden.

Haden had just left her car and was following Paul when Caylee's anger slammed into him. *What's wrong, Caylee?* She was running from him. *What are you doing?* There was no reason for him to ask. He knew she was doing everything in her power to leave him. He'd seen the look of horror in her eyes the moment she realized he was preventing her from moving. He'd felt the change in her kiss. He'd heard it in her voice. He knew he'd pushed her too far. He'd shattered her fragile trust in him by using his power against her. *We need to talk, little love. I know I made mistake. Please don't run away from me.*

The forest was dense. It was too dark too see much of anything, but she continued to run as quickly as she could. *I don't want to talk to you, Haden. I'm done. We don't belong together. Being with you today was a mistake. A terrible, horrible mistake.* Her heart beat so frantically it felt as if it was going to explode. *I will never be with you again. I don't want you. I don't need you. I don't love you.* Struggling to catch her breath, she continued to run.

You're mad. You don't mean it. We belong together, and you know it. A warm breeze swept passed her, touching her intimately, as if Haden were there with her, softly caressing her flesh. *We can work this out. Stop running away from me.*

She kept running, desperate to escape him.

Refusing to give up, he continued to toy with her. He flooded her with his desire for her. *The love we shared was marvelous. It wasn't a mistake.* He heated her blood with vivid imagery of their lovemaking.

Infuriated, she stopped running. Sensing he was flying, she lifted her face to the heavens. *Stay away from me! And stay the hell out of my head!*

The ground vibrated. *Damn it, Caylee, stop being so difficult. I made a mistake. Get over it.* His anger and frustration washed over her, momentarily startling her to the point that her breath caught in her throat.

"Oh that's it, Haden, be your big, bad demon self and throw a fit! Get as mad as you want! I don't care! Just leave me the hell alone!" Caylee shouted. She glanced around. She couldn't see anything. She didn't know which direction to run, but she needed to get as far away from him as possible. Completely blinded by darkness, she started run again.

Paul was so close he could've reached out and touched her. He was intrigued by the fact that Caylee was running away from Haden. It confirmed Paul's belief that she belonged to him, that she was his salvation. He was so insanely tempted to do it, but he didn't. He knew better. Haden was too close. Paul wouldn't be able to get away with her. It was better to wait for Haden to move deeper into the trap he was preparing. Once Haden was confined in it, Paul would be able to easily take her. Remaining silent, Paul watched Caylee for a few more moments and then he left to finish his trap when he realized Haden was close.

Irritated, Haden scowled. Perhaps the truth would convince her to behave more sensibly. *The vampire is stalking you. He's waiting for you to get further away from me so he can take you away from me. You need to stop before he succeeds.*

Startled, she tripped and fell, but she stood up and started running again.

Damn it, Caylee, you need to stop now!

* * *

Caylee sensed something stalking her, but it wasn't the vampire. It was something far more powerful and dangerous. She turned around just in time to see a dragon swoop down from the sky. She took a step back. A black, swirling mist surrounded the dragon. She blinked and the mist was gone, but Haden appeared, his large, muscular frame intimidating as he moved toward her. She glanced from the left to the right, but there was nowhere to run. She backed away a little further.

Haden stopped. "Don't move."

Wide eyed, she stared up at him, wanting to scream at him, but she couldn't even breathe. She wanted to run, but she knew he would easily catch her. And then what? Would he hurt her? Or would he simply take control of her body to prevent her from moving?

He was shattered by the sight of her cowering before him. She truly believed he planned to attack her. "Oh, Caylee, come here." Stepping nearer, he reached out and wrapped his arms around her. "I'm not going to hurt you."

She was so mad. So was so incredibly sick of being bullied by men. "Don't touch me!" With every ounce of her strength, she shoved him. Of course, making her even madder, he didn't budge an inch. "Let go of me, Haden!"

"I can't," he whispered. "You're too close to the edge, little love. Move away from it, and I will let go of you."

"Stop telling me what to do. Let go of me now." Tears streamed down her face, her eyes pleading, begging him to let her go. "Please, Haden, I can't stand being touched by you."

"I was wrong." He'd intimidated her just as so many other men had intimidated her into submission. He'd wanted to protect her—he'd needed to know she was safe in his home, in his bed. He'd bullied her because he was desperate to stop her from following him, but he should've handled it better. "I was wrong, Caylee."

She turned her gaze away from his. The ground shifted beneath her left foot. She looked down and realized she was standing on the edge of a cliff. For the first time, she noticed the sound of rushing water below.

"I feel so trapped. We don't belong together." She didn't really want to die, but she was so very tired, and death promised to give her rest. "I'm tired of fighting for the right to be free. I don't want to be anyone's possession. I want to free." In a state of turmoil, she looked up at him again. "I can't be with you. I'm so tired, Haden."

"Calm down, little love, just calm down." He knew she was asking him to allow her jump to her death. "I don't want to own you, but I could never stand back and allow you to hurt yourself." He released her to make her feel a sense of control, but there was no way he would allow her to jump. "I would give you anything, but never the freedom to take your life."

There it was. The cold, hard truth. "I was so close to knowing freedom, but you took it from me." Just like every other man in her life, Haden believed he owned her. "My greatest wish is that you never found me a year ago." She turned away from him and jumped.

He lunged forward and wrapped his arms. Turning her around, positioning his body between her and the cliff, he held her for several moments before he gently lowered her onto her feet. "Destroying yourself won't give you freedom." Holding her face in his hands, he gazed deeply into her eyes, attempting to absorb her pain and fill her with healing energy. His entire body was trembling. He couldn't believe she'd actually attempted to jump. "Earlier, when I frightened you, I was wrong. I was frustrated. I should've handled the situation differently."

"Yes, you frightened me." She turned her back to him. "You wanted me to be so afraid of you I wouldn't challenge you. You wanted me to believe you would hurt me if I dared to defy you."

She turned to face him again. "I trusted you, Haden. I knew you were mad at me, but for first time in my life I wasn't afraid of what an angry man would do to me." She paused to catch her breath. "I just didn't want you to go. I didn't want you to get hurt. I stood up to you because I believed you wouldn't hurt me. I wasn't frightened of you until you took my ability to move away."

"I would never hurt you. I know I was wrong. You must understand that I was only trying to keep you safe. There're no words to explain my driving need to protect you. I'm a dragon, a demon. It's what I am. It's what I'll always be. I have a bad temper at times, but I would never harm you."

"You don't get it! I wasn't afraid you were going to hurt me. Huh. God. You're such an egotistical jerk, Haden!" Glaring, looking quite fierce, she took a step closer to him. "How can you justify your actions by claiming you couldn't help yourself because of what you are? You took control of my body. I couldn't move. It's too much. You have too much power. I can't deal with it." Shocking herself, she reached out and shoved him. "I won't be your puppet."

He tilted his head to side, struggling to understand why she would be upset over something so ridiculous. It wasn't as if he'd hurt her. He was taking charge because he knew what was best and she wasn't cooperating. "That's why you're upset?" He took a step toward her. "There's no reason to over-dramatize it. I returned your control to you when I believed you'd realized you were wrong."

Jaw dropping, her eyes widened. "Are you being serious?" Holding up her hand, she shook her head. "No. Don't answer that." Clenching her fists at sides, she took a deep breath and released it with a sigh. "Haden, it would be in your best interest to turn around and get away from me as quickly as possible."

Failing to heed her warning, he took a step closer to her. "Being mad at me isn't going to help anything, little love." He caressed her cheek with the tips of his fingers. "I won't apologize for doing what was necessary to protect you. You weren't listening to me. You were being irrational." He shrugged. "It's okay. I understand being irrational at times is in your nature. It's what you are. You're a woman." He smiled at her. "My woman. And I am your man. It's my responsibility, my right to make decisions to ensure your safety."

Shaking her head, Caylee stared up at him. "Huh?"

"Stop being so stubborn, little love." He bent his head to kiss the corner of her mouth. "There really is no reason to be so overly dramatic. I mean, is it really so terrible to have a man love and cherish you so deeply he would do anything, go to any length to protect you?"

"Control is not love. I refuse to deal with your inflated ego anymore. I've always known I'm not the right type of a woman for a man like you. I don't want to be in love with a man that possesses so much power and such a great need to control. As far as I'm concerned, it would be better to never fall in love than be in love with a man that has the ability to force me to obey his every command. You don't need me. There're women like you, right? Strong women that are worthy of your respect. Just get away from me and stay away from me, Haden. I don't want you. Go out and find a rational woman that is your equal."

Powerful emotions washed over him. Through him. Hatred. Love. Sadness. Joy. Fear. Courage. Pain. Pleasure. Frustrated, he grabbed her shoulders and shook her. "I am the one unworthy of your respect and your love."

He suddenly looked wild and ferocious. He was more beast than man. His voice, a shocking, inhuman growl, revealed such terrible agony. She felt his pain. His self-hatred. His loneliness. She wanted to remain mad at him, but her heart was shattering into a million pieces. It didn't make sense, but it was true. He honestly believed he was unworthy of her love and her respect. A sudden gush of tears streamed down her face. Unable to respond, she lifted her chin and stared up at him.

He closed his eyes. It was time. He needed to tell her the truth. He didn't deserve her tears. His rage built quickly, violent and ravenous. Incandescent flames, ignited by his self-hatred, swirled around his body. The atmosphere came alive with his rage. For an instant, the ground beneath their feet trembled. "I abandoned you." Lightning flashed across the sky, followed by a loud clap of thunder.

Startled, she jumped back, nearly out of her skin. "What are you talking about?"

Lightning streaked across the sky, each blinding streak followed by a deafening boom. Large hailstones pelted down all around them, but not one came near her. She wasn't afraid. It wouldn't hurt her. It couldn't. The storm was a physical manifestation of his emotions. It was a part of him. It was him. The ground shook violently, and trees groaned and creaked eerily, threatening to topple over.

~ *Fourteen* ~

THE STORM WAS building too quickly. It was getting dangerously out of control. He closed his eyes and commanded the violent forces of his emotions to return to his soul. A powerful gust of wind slammed into his chest. He stumbled back a bit. Caylee reached for him, but he pushed her away as he bent over. For a few moments, feeling helpless, she watched as he struggled to breathe. Once he caught his breath, blood-red flames flickering in his black gaze, he stood straight and squared his shoulders. "I turned my back on you. I allowed you to suffer a loveless, violent childhood."

"No. We met a year ago." She stepped forward and placed her hand on the center of his chest. "Your eyes. They're red. Whatever you're doing, you need stop. You're hurting yourself. Your heart is beating too hard, too fast."

"We first met when you were five years old. You were flying a kite on the beach in Astoria. I was talking to Nikolas, my brother, when you ran straight into the back of legs."

"Wait," she interjected. "I remember. I lost my kite when I fell." She smiled at him. "I was so upset. I loved that kite. You kneeled down next to me and took my hand in yours." She giggled. "You raised my hand toward the kite and told me to call it back. It was so amazing, so magical. It came right

back to me. I didn't know how, but I knew that you did it."
Returning her smile, he nodded. "I was so sad. I turned to
thank you, but you were gone. One second you were there,
and the next you were gone."

"I didn't leave. Not right away. I watched you for a few
hours. I knew you were my other half. I was shocked. I'd
searched for you for hundreds of year. You were my miracle,
but because you were human I refused to be bound to you."

"I don't blame you." Forcing herself to smile at him, she
stared up at him. "I understand." And she did. The truth was
painful, but he was right. They clearly weren't equal. They
were so very different. Turning her back to him to hide the
tears welling up, she stepped away from him. "We don't
belong together."

"You're wrong. I was being an idiot, Caylee. I will forever
regret my actions that day. I should've taken you under my
protection. I failed you. I allowed you to suffer. I could've
stopped your misery before it ever started, but I didn't. I chose
to remain detached from you, from your suffering." He felt so
cold and alone. He deserved her hatred. He deserved to be
cold and alone. "The only reason I finally returned to you a
year ago was because I could feel you dying. I couldn't allow
you to die."

She turned to face him again. That was it. For the past year
she couldn't understand why he'd chosen to be around her all
the time. Guilt had been forcing him to remain by her side.
She needed to let him go. She needed help him find peace
with the fact that they didn't belong together. "Why did you
stay away, Haden?" It was too painful to continue looking at
him. She turned away from him.

"You're wrong, little love. I was a wreck. When we met on
the beach I was too full of hatred and resentment for your
kind to think clearly. I've stayed by your side because I can
never get enough of you. I'm helpless to do anything else. I
love you. I need to be near you. I need to feel your touch. I
need to touch you. You're the most perfect woman ever born.

I could never even hope to imagine a more amazing, beautiful woman."

He didn't make a sound, but she knew he was moving closer. She took a deep breath and held it. She could feel the warmth of his body reaching out to her, wrapping around her. Slowly, she turned to face him. "Do you really think I'm your true love?"

"No," he whispered. A terrible chill ran up her spine. She shivered. He removed his coat and draped it over her shoulders. "I know beyond any shadow of a doubt you are my one and only true love." He pulled the collar together. "I know I will love you with every fiber of my being for the rest of eternity." He smiled. "But what about you, little love? Despite the fact I failed to protect you, can you still love me until the end of time?"

A mischievous glint in her beautiful green eyes, she moved closer to him. "Yes." Shrugging the coat off her shoulders, she wrapped slender her arms around his waist and held him tightly. "I know I'll love you forever, Haden." Tipping her head back, she stood on the tips of her toes and nipped his chin, and she then soothed the sting of it with a soft, sensuous caress of her tongue. "Forever is a very, very long time."

Still standing on the tips of her toes, she kissed the corner of his mouth. "It should be plenty of time to punish you for being an arrogant, know-it-all jerk." She nipped his lower lip, and then parted his lips with her tongue.

Passionately, raging fires of lust and love merging, they kissed. Devouring. Tasting. Savoring. Teasing. They dined on each other. Blood rushed to his groin and pooled there, making him hard and heavy with need. Clutching her soft, curvy backside, he pressed her body against his. Savoring the sensation of the heat of her body, he moved his hips, rubbing his hard cock against her belly.

Trailing kisses along his jaw and down his neck, her hands worked quickly, unbuttoning his shirt. Pushing it from his shoulders and down his arms, she kissed his chest. Her lips, teeth, and tongue tested his reaction to her curious exploration of his body. "I want to taste you."

"What do mean?" His husky voice deeply revealed his desire.

She rubbed the length of him from outside his pants. "I want to taste you." She unbuttoned his pants and slipped her hand inside to stroke his cock. She thought of his mouth and tongue, working together, sucking and licking, driving her insane. His teeth nipping, pushing her over the edge, stealing her sanity. She needed to experience him full and hard in her mouth and against her tongue. She wanted him at her mercy. No. She needed him at her mercy.

Dropping to her knees, she pulled his pants down to his ankles and looked up at him. "Will you like it?"

Helpless, he stared down at her, unable to respond. The heat of her breath caressed the ultra-sensitive flesh of his erection, sending ferocious waves of pleasure through his body. He couldn't speak. He could barely breathe. His heart raced, pumping more blood to his groin. He was so hard. So swollen. He feared he would lose control. Experimenting, she held the base of his cock; retrieving tasty drops of his essence, she swiped her tongue over the broad head of it.

He wrapped his fingers in her hair, his jaw aching from clenching his teeth together. She drew the head of his cock in mouth and swirled her tongue around it as she gently suckled. His fingers, now tangled in her hair, trembled. He wanted to thrust forward and bury his cock in her throat. She took him a little deeper, licking and sucking.

His control was quickly fading. He'd never experienced anything so wonderful. He was going seriously hurt her. He wanted her faster and harder. He wanted to ram his cock down her throat. "Caylee." His voice was raspy. He could barely breathe. "You need to stop."

Showing no mercy, she relaxed her throat muscles and took him deeper. He involuntarily thrust forward. Trembling, he stopped. He was so terrified he'd hurt her. He remained absolutely still, barely breathing. She moved again, taking his cock even deeper, her lips squeezing it. Her throat muscles were so tight. Agony and pleasure mingled. Hot. Moist. Teeth gently scraping. She kept taking him deeper. She was devouring him. It was so wonderful. It was perfect. Too perfect. He lost control. Holding her head, he plunged deeper.

She wanted more. She needed his release. She needed to force him over the edge. Her mouth and throat eagerly accommodated his cock with each thrust of his hips. Her breasts tingled and ached, yearning for his touch. Heat, delicious, scintillating heat spread throughout her body. Pleasurable sensations fluttered over her flesh. She was burning up, set ablaze by the combination of lust and love, moist heat pooling between her legs. Her sex was red-hot and slick, needing him to slam into her, thrusting deep and hard, taking possession of her body and soul.

Suddenly, he froze. Their minds were deeply merged. Her desire, her need for him added to his pleasure. It was too much. He released her head, tugging on her hair as he struggled to untangle his fingers. She moved impatiently, her teeth grazing his overly sensitive flesh. If he moved, if she continued to suck on his cock, he would burst. She would hate him. He opened his mouth to warn her, but he couldn't speak. He couldn't even breathe. *You need to stop now!*

She looked up at him, her lips still tightly wrapped around him. Her eyes shimmered, revealing her mischievous intent. He heard her giggling in his mind. She was doing it on purpose, pushing him to the brink of mindless bliss. She wouldn't stop until she hurled him over the edge. He tensed, so that every muscle in his body ached, as he fought for control. Toying with him, she slowly slid her tongue over the crown of his cock. Throbbing, his cock swelled even more. His body shook. He gritted his teeth, holding on, refusing to allow his body to let go. He nearly collapsed from the strain of it. She took him deeper, sucking harder, her throat muscles tightly clenching him, drawing him deeper. Her tongue teased. Swirled. Fondled.

Stop being so stubborn, Haden. I want to taste you. Lose control. Come for me. And he did. He threw his head back and shouted her name. His orgasm was so violent he felt it surging throughout his entire body. It was thousands of times more powerful than any other before it. He expected her to pull away from him, but she didn't. She savored each and every drop as his cock pulsated inside her mouth. She sucked greedily as his hot essence flowed from his body.

He was wild and ravenous, and her scent of arousal heated his blood even more, forcing it to pool at his groin. He was desperate for more, still so very hard, impossibly swollen with need. Lifting her up, he removed all of their clothing with a thought. "Wrapped your legs around me." He held her, gripping her hips, her sex poised over his cock. "That's it." He tilted his head back to look up at her. "Now, look at me."

She opened her eyes and met his gaze. She felt such complete joy in that moment. Tears filling her eyes, she shivered, her body weeping for his, needing to be joined with his. She felt his thick, hard heat pressed against her. Her sex clenched tightly. Hot, beckoning fluid rushed from her body, bathing his erection.

"I love you, Caylee." He lowered her, just enough to immerse the head of his cock inside her heat. "Never doubt that I love you." He lowered her a bit more and then held her still. "I'm not perfect. I know I will make many more mistakes with you, but I will never abandon you again. I will never fail you. And you must never fear me. No matter how mad I get, I could never hurt you. You must believe it. You must know I could never hurt you."

"I know." He didn't need to tell her anymore. She didn't want to hear anymore. "I know." She was way beyond needing to talk. She needed action. She needed his cock buried deep inside her body.

Looking quite extraordinarily fierce, she glared at him. "I love you too."

Knowing he was tormenting her, savoring the fact he was the man that was able to torment her, he groaned aloud. "Why do look so angry, little love?" He lowered her just a bit more, making sure that it wasn't enough.

He was holding her too firmly, restricting her movement, using his strength to rob her freedom. She wanted to move. She wanted hot friction. "I don't want to talk anymore." Her flesh was too sensitive. It actually hurt. She needed him. She was going to burst into flames. "I need you inside me now." She wiggled restlessly, seeking pleasure, grinding her body against his.

All at once, he lowered her and surged upward, thrusting hard. Lightning hit the ground all around. Immersed deep in her slick, hot passageway, he paused to savor the tightness of her body.

She wanted more. Needed more. She immediately took over. She was on fire. She didn't want slow and easy; she needed fast and hard. Riding his cock, she took him fast and hard.

He easily supported her weight, his fingers gripping her hips, as she rode him. "You're so hot. So damn tight."

She was a blazing inferno. She was beyond words. Desperate for release. Her ultra-sensitive breasts rubbed against his rock-hard, muscular body. A persistent delight swept from her breast to her sex, until her body clamped down around him, constricting his cock. Crying out, she burst. Wave after thrilling wave of turbulent pleasure raced through her, but she needed more. Her body fastened tightly around his as she ferociously took more pleasure from his body.

She was climbing another glorious peak and taking him with her. Pushed too far, he took charge. Holding her steady, he savagely thrust upward—again and again he impaled her. Moving constantly. Burning up. Creating scintillating friction. Burying his cock deeper. Then, her body gripped onto his with a powerful vengeance. Squeezing tighter and tighter. Mercilessly strangling his cock, holding him deep, drawing out his seed. They both shattered. He threw his head back and roared. She screamed out his name, her nails digging deep into his shoulders.

His knees buckled, and he collapsed, taking her down with him. He held her tightly, her legs straddled over his lap. He was silent for several moments, just holding her close. Savoring the moment. "That, little love, was by far the single most amazing experience I've ever had."

Drowsy, she nuzzled his neck. "Truly amazing." Teeth chattering, she started to shiver.

"You're freezing."

She yawned. "It's a very small price to pay."

He kissed the top of her head. "I suppose you're right." Standing up, he lifted her, and then gently lowered her onto her feet. "But we need to get you warmed up." He replaced their clothing with a thought.

"For the end of June it's a little too cold out here, don't you think?" Smiling, she looked up at him. Her heart stopped. The sight of him, the change in his posture and expression, told her something was seriously wrong.

~ *Fifteen* ~

TAKING CAYLEE'S ARM, Haden dragged her to his side, and his wings momentarily shimmered and then solidified. Expanding his mind, black eyes glittering, he stood completely still, barely breathing, receiving and sorting through the hidden information in the night air.

Caylee felt subtle movement under her feet. It was barely noticeable, but something beneath the soil groaned.

"Haden." Lowering her gaze, she studied the steady movement of the forest floor. "What's … oh, God." It wasn't him. Whatever was beneath the ground was evil. Pure evil. Murderous. An icy shiver started at the soles of her feet and ran up her spine to the back of her neck. "It not you, is it?"

"No." The situation was unlike any Haden had ever encountered. He was too old, too experienced to be caught unaware by an enemy. They were under attack, and he hadn't seen it coming. This didn't happen to him.

Caylee saw something move above the trees. "Haden!" she screamed, pointing toward something that swooped down and moved quickly toward them. He threw her to the ground and, using his body to shield her from the impacted, landed on top of her.

A scream welled up, but she bit it back. "What was that?" Holding her breath, she stared up at him, waiting for but not particularly wanting further enlightenment.

He stood and helped her up. "A ghoul." He was already creating a barrier around them to prevent further attacks from above.

"With wings?" She shook her head. "But you said they're dogs. Dogs don't have wings."

"Mostly dogs, little love, not always."

Why had she asked? She didn't want to know. Taking a breath, she choked. A noxious, ammonia-like odor burned her nose, throat, and lungs. Eyes watering, she coughed and gagged, struggling to get air to pass through her throat.

With his hand, he turned her head, pressing her face against his chest. "It's okay. Breathe." It instantly helped, and she filled her lungs with his addicting scent. She opened her mouth to ask him what was happening, but she was silenced by a high-pitched scream.

It quickly escalated, becoming a blaring outcry of fury that echoed all around. She covered her ears, but it did nothing to muffle the sound. She beyond afraid. She was terrified. Her legs turned to rubber. Her heart raced frantically. She would've collapsed if Haden weren't holding her up. The pressure and pain were so intense. She'd never experienced such extreme agony. Her skull actually felt as if it were in the process of imploding. It was impossible to determine where the sound was coming from. It was generating from every possible direction. It seemed forever, but within seconds, Haden took the pain from her, closing her ears to the sound before her eardrums ruptured.

All senses on alert, he studied the black vapor rising and extending in every direction for as far as he could see. It swirled a few feet above ground. Waving his hand, he created a hedge, preventing it from getting close enough to touch them. It was a form of black magic. He was unfamiliar with it, but he knew its roots were human. And he knew it was only the beginning of the attack; there would be more. Much, much more.

Something very powerful was aiding the human's magic. Paul was part of it, but the energy thrumming through the air was a thousand times more powerful than any vampire could ever hope to produce. It was demonic. He quickly realized it was Demetri's energy. Demetri was thousands of years older, and he possessed greater power and knowledge than any other demon. Why would Demetri help Paul? It was shocking. Until now Haden hadn't believed Zack's accusations against Demetri. It didn't make sense for one as great as Demetri to unite with the living dead.

Holding Caylee as close to his body as possible, he slowly spun around, scanning the forest, sorting through his centuries of warfare knowledge. They were surrounded. Completely surrounded. A low, threatening growl rumbled in Haden's chest and throat. Violence and hatred lurked just out of sight, hidden in the shadows, encompassing them. They were in the heart of a deadly trap. The essence of pure evil was pulsating in the atmosphere. Sadistic. Ferocious. It was everywhere, below ground and above the treetops. But what exactly was it?

The temperature was rising quickly. Caylee was completely out of her element. The air was so sweltering hot that, besides sweaty profusely, she felt weak and a little lightheaded. This didn't happen in her world. She didn't know what to do. She knew they were in a bad situation, but she didn't have the slightest clue of what was happening and what would come next.

She looked up at Haden. He appeared confident and strong, silently searching the area, assessing the enemy, preparing for the battle. There was no doubt in her mind he could and would do anything to keep her safe. Closing her eyes, she thanked God for Haden, for the way he held her so close, shielding her with his body.

He kneeled down, taking her with him. He placed his hand on the ground and whispered in a strange language. She didn't have a clue of what he was saying, but his voice was beautiful, hypnotic. The ground rippled in response to his touch and voice. Without any warning, a snake burst out of the dirt.

Caylee would've screamed if she could've breathed. Standing up, Haden pulled her closer, keeping her hand in his. "He's a friend. He won't hurt you. He can tell us what is happening below ground."

In denial, she shook her head. Oh sure, the giant snake was a friend.

Why hadn't she thought of it sooner? None of it was real. Not the snake. Not Haden. And definitely not the vampire and flying ghouls. They were all figments of her demented imagination. She smiled. Yep, that was it. She was in an asylum, curled up in corner, her mind fried beyond the point of repair.

Lifting her chin, she looked up at Haden and smiled. "Well, at least my alternate reality includes the most amazing, mind-blowing sex with tall, dark, and yummy as hell."

He laughed aloud. "You're not losing your mind, little love. This is real. I'm real. And the amazing, mind-blowing sex is most definitely real."

His deep voice was a seductive caress, touching her everywhere at once, causing her body to ache. She frowned. There was no way in hell she was going to let him know his voice was wreaking havoc in her body. Not when he could've and should've warned her about the snake before it popped up out of the ground. Cursing beneath her breath, she rolled her eyes at him. She was definitely getting a spray bottle of holy water in the near future.

He bent his to kiss her, and then he turned to face the snake.

Head raised, seemingly prepared to strike, the snake swayed from side to side, its body rapidly growing in length and width. It was huge—larger than any other she'd ever seen. A shiver ran through Caylee's body. And she'd recently started watching Animal Planet, so she'd seen a quite few large snakes.

Glowing, blood-red eyes locked onto Haden's gaze, venom dripping from sharp fangs, the serpent hissed. "I smell your mate's fear of me." Suspicious, the serpent moved closer to her, locking his gaze onto hers.

Caylee felt it moving in her mind, searching for information.

"Interesting." Looking amused, he met Haden's gaze. "She has no idea who you are."

"Leave her alone." Growling, Haden glared at the snake. "I called you to the surface because I need to know what lies beneath us."

"You know very well what's happening here. This vampire is obsessed with your mate. He's driven by lust. Why have you entered his trap with your mate? She's mortal. You know you can't escape this with her."

"You know what I'm asking. I need details."

"This is an ancient burial ground. Its occupants, unable to rise, have remained in turmoil for a very long time. They're violent savages. Murderers. And now, the blood of the undead flows through their bodies. They thirst for blood."

"How many?"

"Thousands." The snake looked up at the ghouls circling the treetops, and then it moved closer. "Since when have demons and vampires united? Any fool can see this uprising is far too great a feat for any vampire or human. A demon is either behind or least in some way supporting this attack."

Sighing, Haden nodded. "I've been told Demetri is lost to us."

"You believe Demetri is behind this?"

"I feel his energy." Chanting in a strange language, Haden waved his hand. The snake shimmered for a few seconds, and then it disappeared.

Considering his options, Haden turned to face Caylee. His first urge was to scoop her up and take her through time and space to a place of safety, but he knew better than to try. She was mortal. Fragile. Vulnerable to death. The snake was right. He would never be able to safely take her through the spells surrounding them. She wouldn't survive it. He couldn't fly with her. She would be ripped to shreds by the ghouls. He needed to fight. He needed to win. There was no other option. He needed to destroy the evil, or she would die.

Zack, I need you now!

What the hell have you started? Joseph and I were searching for your vampire when we felt the disturbance. We're coming as quickly as possible, but there is much opposition all around.

It's a rising. There're too many for me to defeat on my own. Demetri is aiding the vampire, enabling it to bring thousands of warriors to the surface to fight. Caylee is here with me.

Zack froze midair. Not because he was shocked Caylee was there. He already knew. He was shocked because he'd never heard Haden plead for anything before. And Haden was pleading. He was begging for help. The woman had made him weak. She would be his demise.

She's still mortal, Zack. We're trapped.

You're not trapped. She is. And you'll stay right by her side and die with her rather than leave her. Zack didn't even try to hide his disgust. *We know she's with you. We will fight with you to protect her, but once this is over, you must either give her immortality or leave her with no memory of your existence. This cannot continue.*

Joseph connected with Haden. *Demetri is powerful, but he's very far away. It's odd, but I don't believe he's even aware of what's happening. We won't arrive to aide you before it starts. Demetri's spells are reproducing as quickly as we destroy them. Keep her in one place. We will combine our powers with yours to create a sturdier hedge of protection around her.*

Haden framed Caylee's face between his hands, forcing her to focus on him. "I won't lie to you, little love. I need you to trust me. It's going to get bad. You're going see, hear, and feel horrible, frightening things your mind has never conjured up."

She blinked. Obviously, he didn't know about the nightmares that haunted her.

"I know every dream and every nightmare you've ever experienced. What's happening here is worse than any thought that has ever entered your mind." Taking her hand, he brought it to the warmth of his mouth. "I love you, Caylee. Forever and completely, I will love and cherish every breath you take. Know that you're safe with me. Trust me. I won't allow you to be harmed."

"Haden." Eyes wide, she stared up at him. "I trust you. I really do. But I don't want to be here for another minute. Take me somewhere else, anywhere. I don't even care how we get there. I'll fly with you. I won't complain about it. I promise. Please, Haden, I want to leave now."

She was breaking his heart, shattering it into thousands of tiny pieces. He rubbed the bridge of his nose, forcing himself to think with his brain and not his heart. Every fiber of his being wanted … no, needed to give her everything she wanted, but he couldn't this time. It was simply too dangerous.

He bent his head to kiss her. "I'm sorry, little love. I can't. It would be too dangerous. There are too many waiting to ambush us in the sky. I should've known better. I never should've stayed out here with you long enough to be trapped like this. Please, Caylee, forgive me." He kissed her once more. "We will survive this together. I know this is all strange to you, but it's not strange to me at all. This is what I was created for. I've fought many battles like this one, and I've never experienced defeat." He wasn't bragging about his power and strength; he was stating a fact, hoping it would give her peace.

Hot tears streaming down her face, she took his hand and placed it over her heart. He needed her to have faith in him. He was begging her to believe in him, in his love and devotion. He needed her cooperation to do what needed to be done.

"I love you, Haden. And I trust you to protect me." Looking so sexy that his heart skipped a beat, she smiled at him. "But I refuse to forgive you. As I remember, it's my fault we remained out here." Savoring the memory of the taste and feel of him, hard and swollen, helplessly surging into her mouth, she bit her lower lip. "I owned you for a moment. You cannot be blamed for it. I was simply too tempting for you resist. Admit it, I seduced you into a state of ignorant bliss."

Jaw dropped, he lifted his eyes brows at her, his black gaze smoldering. *Well, isn't this a lovely situation.* Maybe not lovely, but it was certainly a new one. An interesting one. In all the long years of his existence, he'd never sported a raging hard-on during a battle.

"Oh come on, admit it." Doing her best to look as fierce as a five-foot-three-inch, hundred-pound woman could possibly look, she glared up at him. "If you know what's good for you, you'll admit it."

"Woman, you're pure evil." Joy filling him so entirely his heart felt as if it would burst, he smiled at her. "And I love it. Yes," he said, nodding, "you seduced the hell out of me then and now. But, you're wrong about one thing, little love. You didn't own me for a moment."

Lowering her gaze, she frowned at her poor choice of words. Of course she didn't.

He lifted her chin. "You have always and will forever own my heart and soul." Just then, the ground rumbled violently. "It's happening."

He took a step back. "You will be safe. Stay right here." He walked away from her.

Raising his arms to the heavens, he altered the atmosphere, commanding a storm to come from out of nowhere. The wind instantly picked up, slamming into the flying ghouls. Lightning zigzagged, illuminating the ominous black clouds billowing overhead, chasing the monstrous birds. Thunder echoed all around. Fascinated, oblivious to the rain saturating her, Caylee watched Haden. He was so sexy, so perfect in every possible way. She was ordinary, nothing even close to the woman he should've picked, but he loved her. He was the most remarkable man and lover she could ever hope to dream up, and he truly loved her. He chose to love her. He was powerful beyond belief. He could easily possess any woman's heart, but he chose hers. She belonged to him in every possible way. She knew that now. She truly belonged to him. She would never feel the pain of being alone again.

I will never know how I survived for so long without you, Caylee. You're my life, my heart, my soul. I will forever need you more than I need to take my next breath. She literally felt the warmth of his breath on her earlobe, and his arms, still defying the distance between them, held her even closer to his body. Smiling, she closed her eyes, remembering the passion, the firestorm of desire and pleasure they shared. Nothing could ever taste better than his kiss, his flesh. His masculine scent drove her wild. His rough, calloused hands were so demanding, so powerful, and yet they so gently touched her everywhere, causing desire to burn in her. His cock was so hot and hard, filling her, stretching her, thrusting wildly into her again and again, creating the most scintillating hot friction imaginable.

His laughter filled her mind. *Serious foul, little love. Now, when I'm unable to do anything about it, is not the time to torment me with delicious thoughts of being buried deep inside the tight, silky heat of your body.*

The ground burst open in hundreds of places all at once, but he didn't seem to notice. He held her gaze captive, letting her know he wouldn't do anything to defend himself until she relinquished her mind to him. She immediately opened her mind to him. Not because she was afraid of him, but because she knew beyond any doubt he wouldn't focus on the battle he was about to face until she did.

She blinked once, and he was surrounded by grotesque human-like ghouls. "Oh, God, no. What are they?" she whispered.

Mouths gaped wide, flesh torn from their bones, and their bodies unbelievably twisted and contorted, they closed in on him. She tried counting them, but there were too many. There were hundreds and hundreds of them, and he was their sole focus. How could he fight off so many? He couldn't. He would die if he tried.

No. It's okay, little love. These creatures cannot harm me.

Once again, she could feel the warmth of his breath on her ear. She was so grateful he possessed the ability to make her feel the heat of his large, solid frame against her back and his powerful arms protectively, lovingly holding her close when he was so far away. He might believe he was a demon, but she believed she was in the arms of an angel.

I am never far away from you, Caylee. I am always with you. A part of you.

A burst of brilliant colors and an explosion of light illuminated the woods as Haden took the form of the dragon. Oblivious of the danger he presented, the ghouls continued to move closer to him. The dragon's warrior heart thundered with excitement for the battle at hand, for the victory it would claim. While Haden had fixated his attention on Caylee for the past year, the beast had been denied the pleasures of war. Rising onto his hind legs, the dragon fanned his massive wings, creating flames that spread out to devour the ghouls and encompass Caylee.

The dragon swung its head around, capturing her gaze. *Keep your mind open to me. You're protected. Nothing will touch you.* He shot straight into the sky, but the instant he cleared the treetops, he was bombarded by monstrous birds of prey. Caylee stared in horror. They were all over him screaming, biting, and digging their talons deep into his flesh. Lightning struck the ground a few feet from her. The thunder was instant and earsplitting. Caylee jumped back, her focus now on the ground. She watched ghouls attempting to walk through the flames surrounding her. Most were burned to a crisp before making it through. A few managed to make it through, but they were instantly incinerated by lightning.

She looked up, her gaze searching the sky for Haden. At first, she couldn't find him; then, to her horror, she realized why: he was completely covered with the winged ghouls and was falling out of the sky. Flames surrounded them, burning the creatures from his body. He was falling way too fast. She held her breath. Her heart actually stopped. He landed hard, flat on his back, his body creating a hole in the ground. Roaring, he jumped to his feet, destroying the remaining birds with flames, and then, without showing any signs of pain or weakness due to the fall, he shot straight into the sky to fight once more. Finally breathing, her heart beating, her gaze followed him.

Another dragon appeared in the sky. She watched it closely, fearing it would join the birds and attack Haden. Within seconds, she realized a third dragon was approaching. Her heart beat so quickly she feared it was going to burst.

Feeling her distress, Haden reached for her to soothe her. *They're friends, little love, Zack and Joseph. You remember Zack, right? He helped us before. They've come to help us now.*

Chanting, Paul approached Caylee; believing Haden was too distracted to notice, he worked to unravel the protection surrounding her.

She stared at him. He was so very close—only a few feet away. She looked up. She could still feel Haden's arms holding her, but she doubted he was really with her. It was an illusion to make her feel safe.

Engaged in battle, the dragons fought so fiercely the monstrous birds were falling like stones from the sky.

She wanted call out to Haden but feared distracting him. She didn't know what to do.

Haden froze, his fierce gaze locked onto hers. Tucking his wings close to his body, he dived toward her, the other dragons following his lead. She looked for Paul, but he was gone. The human like ghouls were also gone. The dragons landed hard, the ground shook, and she fell to her knees.

~ *Sixteen* ~

RETURNING TO HUMAN form, Haden turned to face her.
"Damn it, Caylee, you always call out to me when you think
you are in danger! That is what you do! You do not hesitate!
You call out to me!" Breathing heavily, walking toward her,
he looked as ferocious as he was.

She didn't stand up, knowing her legs were too weak to
support her weight.

"You arrogant son of bitch!" Zack slammed into Haden. In
disbelief, Caylee watched as they fought.

Chuckling, Joseph walked over to Caylee. "Don't worry.
They're both a little hotheaded. They'll work it out. They
always do." He nodded. "Caylee, right?" He leaned down,
offering his hand to her. "Joseph Payne."

Staring up at him, she took his hand and stood up.
Wonderful. Absolutely, magnificently, wonderful. She
pointed toward Haden and Zack, still pummeling the hell out
of each other. "This is normal behavior for them?"

He shrugged. "It's a cousin thing."

"They're related?"

"I know they don't look alike, but I assure you it's true."

"I don't doubt it. They both seem prone to throwing
extreme tantrums." Zack hit Haden's face with a closed fist,
knocking Haden off his feet. Caylee winced. "Ouch." That

was going to leave a mark. "I can't believe after all that has happened he could forget I'm here watching him behave like a toddler."

"Trust me, regardless of his immature behavior he knows you're here. He knows every breath you take. What I find amusing is that as far as our people are concerned they're two of the most feared, legendary warriors of all times."

Caylee giggled. "Well, legend or not, one thing is certain, Haden's behavior is about to get him into serious trouble with me." She paused. "What happened? I mean, where did all of those creatures go?"

"The vampire left," Joseph said. "He was the fuel that enabled them to attack. Without him, the human army he raised had no power to remain above ground."

Caylee pointed at Haden and Zack. "How long does it usually take for them to work out their tantrums?"

"It depends. It could be minutes, or we could be here for quite some time. Some say they've fought too many battles to ever be anything other than warring brutes."

"What do you say?" Caylee asked.

"They have unresolved childhood issues."

She looked at him. "Joseph, are there many battles like the one today?"

Frowning, he looked worried. "To be honest, the magnitude of what happened today hasn't happened for centuries. The vampire hunting you is powerful, but even so, it's odd for one such as him to provoke a matured male demon. Something is off kilter." He paused for a moment. "Demetri, one of our own, joined the opposition today. None us know why Demetri is siding with our enemy, but it's a serious threat to mankind and our kind. Demetri is extremely powerful. He has been around for thousands and thousands of years. No one really knows his age. It's rumored he has no equal."

Such a terrible blast of fear slammed into her that it caused her heart to skip a beat. Haden felt it and stopped fighting with Zack. Staring at Joseph, he walked toward them. *Why did you upset her?*

Grinning, Joseph pointed. "Take a look."

"What?" Caylee turned to see what he was pointing at. She took a step back. "He looks mad."

"Not at you."

"Huh?"

"He plans to kick my—sorry," Joseph said. "He's mad because I told you about Demetri and it frightened you."

"Are you serious?"

Joseph nodded. "Unfortunately."

"Unbelievable." Stepping past Joseph, she marched right up to Haden and shoved him. "What are you doing?"

Zack walked up from behind and smacked the back of Haden's shoulder. "One word—neutered."

Seething with rage, she turned her gaze toward Zack. "Just ... oh, damn it ... shut the hell up!"

"Be careful, woman," Zack growled between clenched teeth, giving her a look of disgust.

That was all it took. Haden turned on Zack, and they were fighting again, rolling around on the ground, punching each other.

"Fine. Just ... oh, God, whatever." Caylee looked up at Joseph. "Let the kooks beat each other up. I'm done." Exasperated, she turned and stormed off, muttering explicit curses beneath her breath.

"Where do think you're going?" Haden pushed Zack away and stared at Caylee.

Stopping, she tried to count to ten to gain her composure, but only managed to get to three before she turned to face Haden.

"Oh, how sweet." Looking way too innocent to ever be considered anything other than guilty as hell, Haden and Zack were standing side by side as if they couldn't possibly be guilty of any wrongdoing. They, well over six feet tall and built like warriors, had the nerve to attempt to look sheepish.

Fuming, she rolled her eyes. Clearly, attempting to manipulate a situation by faking innocence was a family thing. Fire burning in her eyes, she slowly walked toward them.

"Damn, Haden, I think you really pissed her off." Joseph chuckled. "This is going to be great. I wouldn't miss what's about to happen for the world. I hope when she's done with you she kicks Zack's ass too." He fumbled inside his pockets. "Oh shit, I forgot my phone. This would've made a damn great status update for both of you."

Zack's eyebrows shot up. "She wouldn't." He swallowed hard.

Watching Caylee walk toward them, Haden grinned. "She would."

Joseph nodded. "Zack, I don't think she likes you at all. After she's done with Haden, I've a hundred bucks that says she'll take you down in five seconds."

Zack shook his head. He wasn't going to stick around to get his ass kicked by a woman. "How the hell do keep figuring out our passwords, Joseph?"

"You're predictable, and Haden never changes his."

Zack looked a Haden. "Never?" Looking worried, he took a few steps back. "Well, good luck, Haden. If there's anything left to you after she get done with you, I'll see you later." He turned with blurring speed, wings forming on his back, and leapt into sky.

"Don't keep her out here. Bring her to your penthouse. We will be able to aid you, should you need us. And after witnessing the strength of your opposition today, I have no doubt you will." When Caylee reached them, Joseph bowed at the waist. "It was nice to finally meet you, Caylee. I hope to see you soon."

"It was quite refreshing to meet a civilized gentleman." Smiling at Joseph, she nodded once. "Thank you." Then, she turned to glare up at Haden, fury burning in her green eyes.

Thinking she looked way too damn sexy when she was mad, Haden grinned, his gaze feasting on her. "You look angry, little love." And it was driving him insane, filling him with lust, heating his blood, making him yearn to immerse himself in the solace and pleasure of her body again and again.

Clearly able to hear his thoughts now, she smirked. Who did he think he was? He demanded she keep her mind open to him at all times, but he felt he was justified in closing his mind to her at will. Tilting her head to the side, she glared at him, biting back a few choice words and fighting the urge to kick him. "You think I look mad?"

Looking as naughty as he was, and way too sexy, he held out his hand for her. "We should get going, little love."

"Little love?" Shaking her head, she forced herself to frown. "Tell me, Haden, is that endearment designed to get you out of trouble?"

He arched his brow. "Is it working?"

His voice was a deep, flawless purr, a weapon of seduction. Yep, she was definitely getting her hands on a bottle of holy water.

"I won't stop you, but I don't believe spraying me will make you feel any better. You're not mad at me. I know what's troubling you. It's troubling me too."

Gee. Should she or should she not? She shrugged. Why not open his stinky can of worms? "Really, what's troubling me?"

"Sexual frustration."

He wasn't actually touching her, but she felt hands wandering, exploring her body. His mouth and tongue teasing, tormenting her.

"What you really need is to get naked and wrap your sexy legs around my body."

He looked way too proud of himself for her liking. Two could play this game. "Serious sexual frustration," she whispered, her voice purposely breathless, husky. Parting her lips in a mysterious, sexy smile, she closed the gap between them. Standing on the tips of her toes, she wrapped her arms around his neck and her leg around his thigh. "Silly me."

Pressing closer, intimately rubbing her body against his, she tilted her head back and kissed his chest and the base of his throat. "Why didn't I think of it?" she whispered against his flesh.

He knew she was using her body as a weapon of revenge, but it didn't matter. He couldn't resist her. He bent his head to take possession of her mouth. She bit his lip, a teasing, erotic nibble that drove him insane. Then, when she was certain he'd forgot about the revenge she was seeking, she bit him hard and shoved him.

Caught off guard, he fell flat on his ass.

"I can't believe you actually thought you could use sex to turn me into a mindless twit when I'm so mad at you." Hands on her hips, she stuck her tongue out at him. "Who's the mindless twit now, Haden?" Smiling, savoring the victory, she turned at walk away from him.

Roaring with laughter, he jumped to his feet and followed her. "Where are you going?" He was still laughing.

"Stop laughing," she warned as she turned to face him, "or I will kick you." She turned away from him and started to walk. "I'm going to the city."

At her side, still laughing but attempting to control it, he matched her pace. "You're going the wrong way, little love."

Mumbling obscenities, sounding quite fierce, she spun around and stared up at him. "Which way is it?"

"Kiss me."

"Hell no!" she shouted.

He pointed. "It's a day's walk." Moving closer, forcing her to press her back against a tree to avoid touching him, he grinned at her. "But I could get us there in a few seconds." He moved closer, his body crowding hers, touching hers, heating hers. "Kiss me."

Palms pressed against his chest, savoring the yummy masculine contours of his hard, heavily muscled body a little too much, she tried to shove him, but he didn't move at all. He was as solid as the tree behind her. She lifted her chin, smirking up at him defiantly. "I'm never flying with you again, Haden Drake," she promised, saying his last name to prove a point. Although, after saying it aloud and hearing the longing in her voice, she wasn't entirely sure what point it proved. Well, that was a lie. It clearly proved she wanted to rip his clothes off of his body and ... no! She shook her head. She wouldn't think it. His ego didn't need to get any bigger. If it did she would be forced to toss him into a pool of holy water.

"Flying would take too long." Capturing her waist, he easily picked her up and held her against his body. "I wasn't planning to fly tonight." His black, hungry gaze held hers captive. "I need you now." He smiled at her. "And you will fly with me many more times." Before she could argue, he whispered, "Wrap your legs around me."

Needing him, wanting him as desperately as he needed and wanted her, she did it instantly, without thought.

"Now, please, kiss me."

Completely swept away by her desire for him, unaware he was taking her through time and space, she kissed him.

When he lifted his head, she realized they were no longer in the woods. He was walking, carrying her across a room. She looked around, but it was too dark to see much of anything. "Where are we?" She gasped. "Where are my clothes?" Then, she realized they were flesh to flesh. "Where are yours?" The air was moist, warm and sweet smelling.

"Gone." He took three downward steps.

She heard the sound of water swishing. "Why?" Hot steam enveloped them.

He took another downward step, and hot water lapped at her backside and legs. "They were in the way." Waist deep in the water, he lowered her onto her feet and pulled her close. "I need to feel every inch of your flesh against mine." He waved his hand, lighting several candles.

Turning, she moved away from him, taking in the beauty surrounding her. They were in a huge, oversized hot tub. No.

It was more like a pool. In the far corner was a waterfall, and the walls and ceiling were made of granite and decorated with ancient carvings. Several mirrors on the walls reflected candlelight. "It's so beautiful, Haden."

He picked up a bottle of oil and slowly made his way to her. Never in his life had he seen anything as beautiful, as perfect as her tiny, slender body. It amazed him that she didn't know. That she didn't have a clue about how incredibly gorgeous, how sexy she was. She closed her eyes. His mind was open to her, sharing his desire, his need to worship her body with his, to convince her of her beauty, of her value to him. There was and never could be another woman for him. She alone could make him drop to his knees and beg for one more taste.

Tears burned behind her eyes. It was all too wonderful to be real—it had to come to an end. This wasn't her; she didn't belong with him. Gathering her hair, he pulled it over her shoulder to expose her back to his admiring gaze. She turned her head to look up at him. He bent his head to kiss her shoulder, her neck, and her ear. Breathing deeply, he inhaled her scent, savoring it. There were no words to describe his need for her, his love for her at that moment.

He massaged her shoulders and back, softly caressing the oil into her skin. His hands trailed from her sides to her hips, touching her everywhere, tracing her feminine curves, adoring her body, every inch of it. "Turn around, little love."

When she did, he was right there, solid, real, larger than life. Her man. His gaze was feasting on her. He was touching her, loving her, needing her, massaging her. Her gaze wandered. His body was built to perfection. Tall. Powerful. Muscled like a god. Men like him didn't exist. Not in her world.

Biting her lower lip, she looked up him. "Haden?" She was breathless, hot tears streaming down her face. Yes, he loved her now, but would he eventually grow tired of her? He'd live many lifetimes, shared many lifetimes with women he loved.

"What if you … Haden, I'm afraid of the way you make me feel. Of having you only to lose you."

"Caylee." Tossing the oil, he dragged her close. "See yourself as I see you. Know what you mean to me. We are one. There was, is, and never will be a me without you. Yes, I lived many lifetimes, but I've never shared my life with a woman. It would be impossible. For a long time I waited for you, hoping you would come, but eventually I no longer had the strength to hope." He closed his eyes, searching for best words. "No matter what happens, I will never allow us to be separated by anything or anyone." Looking very naughty, he smiled at her. "I have a small confession to make, little love."

That brought her eyebrow up. "What?"

"You're going to have my child."

She nodded. "Maybe eventually, but it's a little soon for us to even think about having a child."

"You conceived the first time we made love."

"No, I didn't." She frowned. "I'm taking birth control."

"It failed."

"How would you know?"

"I wanted you to conceive." He shrugged casually. "My kind has the power to choose whether or not a child is conceived."

"You did it on purpose?" She splashed water in his face. "You got me pregnant and didn't even ask what I thought about it?"

"Yes." He smiled, looking quite proud of himself. "What do you think about it?"

Caylee stared him for several seconds. She'd never really thought about bringing a child into the world. She'd never wanted to be responsible for raising a child in such a sick, twisted, and loveless world. But the world didn't seem so sick and twisted anymore. It definitely wasn't loveless. She had Haden. Their child had Haden. He was serious. She was pregnant. And he was very happy about it. To her surprise, she was happy too. She smiled at him. "It makes me very happy."

~ *Seventeen* ~

"THIS ISN'T RIGHT." Caylee took a deep breath and released it with a sigh. "What's wrong with me?"

"There's nothing wrong with you," Haden said. It was a fact he wasn't going to argue.

Looking down at her feet, Caylee frowned. "I'm standing at my uncle's gravesite, and the only thing I feel is relief."

Taking her chin, forcing her to meet his gaze, he said, "Good."

"I should feel some form of sadness, shouldn't I?"

"Nope. No way," Mia blurted. "Why should you? The bastard was absolutely terrible to you. He's lucky to be dead. If I would've known he was blackmailing you into marrying that nasty little weasel of a man, Phillip Wicks, I would've made his life a nightmare. He would've wished he was dead."

"You don't understand," Caylee explained. "I know he wasn't a good person, but he was my uncle, my flesh and blood."

"Stop it, Caylee. I won't allow you to beat yourself up over your lack of tears for the man. It doesn't matter if he was your uncle or a stranger. There's no reason for you to feel any sadness over his death at all." Haden wrapped his arm around Caylee and pulled her close to his side. He didn't regret killing Emmett, but he felt a little guilty because of how negatively the man's death was affecting Caylee. "Of course you feel a sense of relief. He was treating you badly, abusing you. Why would you feel anything but relief?"

"He's dead, Haden. His life is over. It's done. He will never have another chance to change, to be a better person. They just lowered his casket into the ground, and I couldn't force myself to shed a single tear for him if my life depended on it."

"Oh come on, Caylee. You need to focus on the facts. Emmett was a dirty, rotten bastard. And don't you dare try to deny it," Mia said. "Listen, I hate to admit it, but Haden is right."

She paused to glare at Haden. He'd better never use the fact that she'd agreed with him against her. Just the thought of being like-minded with Haden nearly caused her to hurl her breakfast. "There's no reason for you to waste any time crying for him. The world is a better place with Emmett six feet under. Honestly, when you asked me to come here with you today, I was shocked. I tried, I really did, but I didn't and still don't understand why you wanted to come here."

"I never wanted to be here. I didn't have a choice. I'm his only living relative. I need to be here. Just take a look around. There's no one else here to mourn his death." Caylee looked up at Haden. "It was a heart attack, right?" She knew he could and would kill, but she didn't want to think he'd killed her uncle. Especially if he'd killed Emmett on her behalf.

Mia's gaze shot straight to Haden. Maybe she'd judged his character too soon. If he had killed Emmett, she would be inclined to like him a little.

Grinning, Haden nodded at Caylee. "That's what the autopsy report indicated," he said.

Mia smiled. Haden had killed Emmett. Maybe she would like him a lot. She shook her head. Nah. There was no reason to get carried away. He was still a man. Liking him a little was more than enough.

Eyes filled with suspicion, Caylee tilted her head to the side and studied his way-too-innocent, naughty schoolboy grin. She, like Mia, instantly caught on to the fact Haden had used his words carefully to avoid lying. "Yes, it did." Haden had killed Emmett. The only doubt she had was that she could live with her uncle's blood on her hands.

Haden bent his head to whisper in her ear. "How could you forget I was with you, little love?" His deep, sexy voice caused images of their lovemaking to flood her mind. Hot desire raced through her body, heating her blood and causing her heart race.

Haden wasn't sure why he was attempting to convince her he hadn't done it. He had every right to kill Emmett. It was his responsibility to do it. Killing Emmett was the right thing to do. It was a good thing. It was the only thing to do.

Mia looked up and saw a man approaching them from the far side of the cemetery. She pointed. "Do you know him?" She instantly knew she didn't like him at all. Studying him closely, she couldn't decide what really bothered her, but there was something very dark and threatening about him.

Caylee looked up. "Oh sure, that's Haden's friend, Joseph." She grabbed Haden's hand. *What's happening, Haden? What's wrong?* She knew Joseph and Zack were hanging around the cemetery in case there were any problems with Paul, but they were supposed to stay out of sight.

Haden brought her hand to his mouth and kissed it. *There's nothing for you to worry about. Paul is nearby observing us. We knew it would happen. I told you it would, remember? We haven't been able to pinpoint his exact location. Joseph is just letting him know we're aware of his presence as a preventative measure. Zack will continue to watch from a distance and wait for Paul to slip up and reveal his location.*

In truth, there was plenty to worry, but as far as he was concerned, she didn't need to know about it. Joseph and Zack had spent two days and nights searching for Paul, but they were unable to find him. He was always close, but he always managed to hide. The vampire's ability to continue hiding his exact location from the demons was strange. They knew

Paul's ability to elude them had something to do with Demetri and Mary Tate. But what? Mary wasn't a huge concern. She was only a problem as long as Demetri remained loyal to her, but why was Demetri remaining close to her? How was he aiding the undead? Why was he doing it? More importantly, how could they stop such a powerful demon?

Vampires naturally preferred a variety of sexual partners, never lovers, but possessing and keeping Caylee was all that mattered to Paul. It went against his nature, but he knew he would enjoy her company for a number of years. Unable to stay away from her, he remained as close to her as possible at all times. His obsession with her was growing every minute of every day. She should've remained nothing more than a source of nourishment and entertainment, but it was impossible to listen to the voice of common sense when she was his obsession.

Caylee was always surrounded by demons. If not Haden, Zack or Joseph were near her at all times, but Paul refused to give up. Why should he? He believed he had the upper hand. It was only a matter of time before the demons slipped up. The demons were confused and acting accordingly. They didn't know how to handle a vampire with his extraordinary powers and abilities. They feared him—and for good reason. Paul was in the process of altering the unfair balance of power that for thousands of years enabled demons to nearly wipe out the existence of vampires. He was the first of his kind to wield the ancient demonic and human spells that were enabling him to stay one step ahead of demons. Word of Paul's certain victory was spreading like a wildfire. Soon, many more vampires would rise up to stand by his side to annihilate the demons that nearly destroyed them.

Joseph walked straight up to them. He glanced at Haden and then took Caylee's hand in his. "Good morning. I'm very sorry for your loss, Caylee."

Mia was extremely irritated Joseph would add to Caylee's guilt. She snorted indignantly. "It isn't a loss." She smiled up at Haden, secretly letting him know that she approved of the fact he'd killed Emmett and that she had his back. "The man was a no-good asshole. He deserved to die."

Frowning, Caylee shook her head at Mia.

"What? It's the truth. The man was a worthless asshole."

"Thank you, Joseph," Caylee said.

What's going on? More than a little perplexed, Joseph glanced at Haden. *How does Caylee's friend know you killed Emmett?*

She's assuming.

Well, at least she approves of it so much she was just trying to let you know she has your back.

Thanks for the warning, but I already caught onto it. Trust me, I'll be extra careful to watch my back from now on.

Joseph looked at Mia. *You don't trust her.*

I would rather turn my back on a pack of rabid pit bulls than a wolf. She's a vicious, man-hating woman.

Lycan? Shocked, Joseph glanced at Haden and then returned his gaze to Mia. She didn't appear to be vicious. As a matter of fact, she was quite petite. *I don't see it.* Smiling in appreciation, he opening allowed his gaze to wander over every inch of her tiny but curvaceous body. He studied her from the top of her head to her toes. Oh yeah, he liked what he was seeing. The woman was hot as hell.

She was orphaned. Her wolf is dormant. I don't even think she knows she's lycan. Haden grinned. *Trust me. You'll see it if you make her mad enough.*

There was a long and awkward silence. Caylee glanced up at Haden. *What's wrong with Joseph?*

I'm not sure, but Mia is not liking it. I suppose it would be best to introduce them before she gets any madder and knocks him on his ass.

"Oh. Oops. I'm sorry," Caylee said. "Mia, this is Joseph Payne, and, Joseph, this is my best friend, Mia Harte."

Taking a step closer to Mia, Joseph held out his hand for her. "It's a pleasure to meet you, Mia Harte." He loved the sound of her name and feel of it on his lips.

Mia wasn't even slightly impressed. Her only thought was to get him the hell out of her personal space. He needed to back off. She sure hell wasn't going take a step back. She didn't even try to hide the fact that he made her sick; she didn't like him at all, and there was no reason to pretend otherwise. She glanced down at his hand and then, locking her gaze onto his, she smirked. "Gee, you bet. It's so totally nice I can hardly stand the excitement." Rolling her eyes, she reached for his hand.

The instant his hand touched hers, Joseph's mind merged with hers. Deeply. Completely. He wasn't expecting it to happen. Normally, it wouldn't happen without exerting some sort of effort. To say he was shocked was a serious understatement—he was completely blown away by it. He was drawn so deeply into her mind and body he actually felt her physical and emotional pain. It was so severe and it hit him so hard his entire body shuddered. Her flesh was so fragile and weak, but her spirit was as strong as any ferocious, fearless lycan spirit.

Joseph couldn't believe she was standing there as if nothing was wrong. The pain threatened to bring him, a powerful immortal, to his knees. Her strength and resolve amazed him. Absorbing her pain into his body and imparting healing energy into her body, he continued to hold her hand. He had to help her. He simply didn't have any choice. He had to do all he could to give her relief.

Mia felt heat penetrate her hand and spread up her arm. At first it was a tingling sensation, and then it turned into a magnificent burning sensation that spread throughout her body. She liked the way it felt, and that irritated the hell out of her. She also felt Joseph's powerful presence in her mind. She didn't know much about her father and mother, but she knew they were murdered by vampires. Given the way Joseph was able to enter her mind, he must be a vampire. "Let go of me!" She yanked her hand out of his. "What the hell do you think you're doing?"

She's dying. Looking shattered, Joseph met Haden's gaze. *She has been in a great deal of pain for a very long time. I'm serious, Haden. The pain she lives with is so bad it nearly knocked me on my ass."*

From what? Haden looked over at Mia. *I've never sensed any illness or pain in her.* Now, looking at her, it was clear she was a bit thin and pale skinned. He had noticed her complexion was pale before, but he'd never looked too deeply at her health. For the most part she appeared to be healthy. She definitely presented herself as being a healthy woman. As a matter of fact, he was quite certain she would get into the ring with Mike Tyson if he pissed her off.

It's an extremely aggressive form of bone cancer. Does she behave irrationally?

Haden shrugged. *She has an explosive temper. She doesn't seem to have the ability to control it.*

She's taking high doses of morphine.

That's not good. It explains a lot, but it's not good, In fact, Haden knew it was extremely dangerous because of her lycan blood. Over time morphine would cause her to go insane. She would eventually become a sadistic murderer without remorse.

"I'm sorry, honey." Mia took Caylee's hand. "I don't want to leave you right now, but I've never left the girls alone this long. You know how Julie behaves when I'm gone. I don't want her to run Brianna off. You know how shy and withdrawn Brianna is." She turned to glare at Joseph, and then she looked up at Haden. "Just in case you didn't already come to the conclusion yourself, your taste in friends suck."

Grinning, Haden nodded his agreement. "He has several flaws, but what kind of a friend would I be if I used his imperfections as an excuse to discard him? Wouldn't it be better to guide him, to show him the error of his ways?" Haden patted the back of Joseph's shoulder. *Thanks for acting like an idiot, Joseph. Now you can be her chew toy. Life will be much easier and safer now that Mia hates you more than she hates me.* It was difficult, but Haden managed to keep a straight face.

Mia shrugged casually. "In most cases, but sometimes it's better for a person to face the facts and act accordingly." Pressing her lips together to keep from laughing at the stunned look on Joseph's face, she glared up at him. "I always say it's best to throw the trash out before it stinks up the entire house."

That brought Joseph's eyebrow up. *Holy shit. She just called me trash.*

Haden smiled. *Stinky trash.*

She didn't mean it. Not really. She thinks I'm a vampire. Besides, she's taking morphine.

Haden opened his mouth to respond to Mia, but Caylee shut him up by jabbing his ribs with her elbow. "Ouch!" He hunched over and held his side. Looking way too heartbroken for her to even consider feeling sorry for him, he asked, "What did I do?"

Rather than waste her breath on a response, Caylee rolled her eyes at him. She couldn't blame Mia for being mad. Joseph was acting weird. The way he looked at Mia was downright creepy. But Caylee wasn't going to allow Haden to enjoy Joseph's verbal beating. "Oh Mia, don't apologize for needing to leave." She hugged Mia. "I'm so grateful you came here with us today."

"I'll always be here for you, honey." Mia smiled at her. "And don't forget about tonight. There's no way I'm going to let you back out on me. Make sure you get to my place no later than eight so we have plenty of time to get ready for the party."

Blushing at the thought of wearing the very skimpy, super-revealing dress Mia'd made her for at public event, Caylee nodded. "I'll be there."

Mia turned and walked away quickly. She knew it sounded crazy, but she knew Joseph had somehow entered her mind and her body. She had no idea how he'd done it, but he'd taken her pain away. He knew she was dying. She'd seen it in his eyes. He pitied her. The thought of it made her feel nauseous. She didn't want anyone feeling sorry for her. She didn't want anyone to know she was dying.

Caylee noticed that Joseph was watching Mia walk away. Actually, she noticed that he was gawking at her with a goofy grin on his face. She looked up at Haden. *What's wrong with him?*

Raising his brow, Haden shrugged.

Mia pulled her hair back and put her helmet on.

Joseph's jaw dropped. "What's she doing?"

Mia lifted her leg to get onto the bike.

Frowning, Joseph shook his head. "No." In seconds the engine roared to life. "That's way too much of a ride for a woman."

Caylee laughed. "She has been riding a motorcycle since her teens."

Joseph was still shaking his head. "That's not good." Clearly, Caylee realized, he wasn't hearing her. "I don't like it at all."

Mia respectfully, slowly made her way through the cemetery, but the second she got to the exit she sped off. "She didn't even look for traffic." Mia was out of sight, but the sound of engine roaring as she shifted through gears echoed loudly. "She's going way too fast. She doesn't belong on that bike."

Haden chuckled. "I dare you to tell her that the next time you see her."

"I will." Joseph nodded. Then grinning, he turned to face Haden and Caylee and held a newspaper up. "Have you read the paper this morning? A local millionaire, Phillip Wicks, has been charged with tax evasion and money laundering. It's such a shame. The poor guy has absolutely nothing of worldly value left to his name. It appears all of his assets have been seized."

Caylee snatched the paper away from Joseph. "I can't believe it." Giggling, she started to read it. "Did you do this, Haden?"

"No." Pointing at Joseph, he said, "It's all his doing."

Caylee turned to Joseph. "How did you do it?"

"The less you know the better," Joseph teased, but he maintained a very serious, matter-of-fact expression. He almost looked angry.

Drawing her bottom lip into her mouth and chewing on it, Caylee frowned. "Oh." Feeling uncomfortable, she moved a little closer to Haden. Immediately wrapping his arm around her, Haden glared at Joseph.

"I'm only kidding." Smiling, purposely gentling his expression, Joseph shrugged. "I just rearranged of few of his assets to expose several of his dirty little secrets. It raised a few red flags. Uncle Sam did the rest."

Squealing, she flung her arms around Joseph neck and kissed his cheek. "You're absolutely brilliant, Joseph." Not wanting to get his ass kicked, Joseph respectfully, looking more than a little worried, didn't return the hug or the kiss. Haden quickly moved forward and wrapped his arm around Caylee's waist and pulled her to his side where she belonged.

Leaning against Haden, Caylee asked, "Will you be coming to the party with us?"

Looking over Caylee's head to where Mia had exited the cemetery, Joseph smiled. "I wouldn't miss it for anything." And he wouldn't. He was eager to see Mia again. "It has been a little while since I've gone out."

"A little while?" Haden laughed aloud. "You've been playing dead for nearly two years now."

"Has it been that long?" Joseph shrugged casually. "I didn't notice. I guess time flies when you're having fun."

"You've been playing dead?" Caylee asked.

Joseph shrugged. "My wife and her lover killed me."

"How sad, but you're like Haden, right?"

"It was little depressing. And yes, I'm like Haden. Since I can't really die, I decided to play dead until I could figure out what to do next."

Haden laughed. "He's lying. He has been playing dead so he can haunt them."

"If people recognize you it will be over. Aren't you just a little worried that if you go to the party someone will recognize you tonight?" Caylee asked.

"Not at all," Joseph said. "I have the ability to control my appearance."

"What do you mean?"

"Our kind has the ability to take the form of just about anything or anyone at any time," Joseph explained.

"I can understand how playing dead would be fun, but the thought of taking another form is just a little bit freaky." She smiled. "I'm still struggling to grasp the dragon thingy." She looked up at Haden. "If you ever take the form of a woman, we're done."

"There's no reason to worry about that." Haden shook his head. "I don't think playing dead would be fun at all."

Caylee giggled. "I don't know. His wife and her lover tried to kill him. They believe they succeeded. I think haunting them is very funny. When I die, I plan to haunt you."

Clearly irritated, Haden frowned. "Don't say that."

"Why?" She smiled up at him. "Are you afraid of ghosts?"

"It's not funny, Caylee." Haden took a deep breath and released it with a growl.

"Are you seriously growling at me? Don't it again, Haden. It's so unattractive."

While Haden and Caylee argued, Joseph took out his phone and got onto Facebook. He searched for Mia and found her right away. He read her profile and checked out her pictures and then, unable to resist the urge, he requested a friendship with her and poked her. Was the poke immature? Absolutely. But he just couldn't resist the temptation of doing it. Just the thought of how mad she would be caused him to smile. He put the phone in his pocket and then interrupted their argument. "So Haden, do you still plan to go out and talk to Nikolas today?"

"Yes." Haden turned to face him. "He has always been the closest to Demetri. There's a chance that he knows more about what is going on. We need more information, and we need it now."

"Sounds like a plan. Zack will follow you to make sure Paul doesn't get too close to you. I'm going to follow Mia to make sure Paul doesn't follow her." Joseph smiled. "Enjoy your day." He certainly planned to enjoy the day. "I'll see you later tonight." Turning to walk away, he dissolved into a mist.

Caylee took Haden's hand and looked up at him. "Do you believe Mia is in danger? I mean, do you think Paul plans to go after her?"

Haden shrugged casually. "It's possible, but I doubt it. I think Joseph is following Mia because he takes pleasure in her company."

"Oh no. I sure hope not. Mia didn't seem to like him at all." She paused. "Maybe you should warn him to leave her alone. She definitely won't like him following her around."

"I would be wasting my breath. He knows she doesn't like him, little love." He wrapped his arm around her to lead her toward the car. "He's not accustomed to being so quickly and entirely rejected by a woman. Tragically, in a twisted sort of way, he liked being cast off by her."

"Why? That's just sick. He has serious issues. Well then, if he bugs her too much, I guess he'll get what he deserves. I won't feel bad at all when she puts him in his place."

There was a subtle shift in the atmosphere. Haden stopped right next to the car and opened the door for Caylee. Studying the disturbance, he glanced all around. He knew that Paul was deeply enraged. He wanted to snatch Caylee, but he didn't dare. Not yet anyways. The vampire was using ancient spells to prevent Zack from finding him. The vampire was way too sure of himself. He knew Paul would've attempted to attack and snatch Caylee if Zack wasn't nearby, ready to intervene.

Settling in her seat, Caylee looked up at Haden. "We're actually going to drive?"

"Yes." He smiled at her. "It's a short drive to my brother's place."

"Are you going to tell me where it is yet?"

"No. It's a surprise, little love." He leaned down to kiss her, and then he shut her door and walked over to the other side and got in.

"What did Joseph see when he was holding Mia's hand?" Caylee asked. "And don't you dare try to tell me he didn't see anything. I saw look on his face. He was shocked. Maybe even a bit worried about something."

Haden took a deep breath and sighed. "Mia has been keeping something very serious from you." He paused. He was hoping to wait to tell her until he was certain Joseph could heal her. "I suspect that she's kept it from everyone."

"What?"

"She has bone cancer, Caylee." He turned his head to look at her. "It's very serious. She's dying."

"No. It isn't possible. Joseph is wrong," Caylee said. "She doesn't have cancer. She isn't dying."

"He isn't wrong." Mia's illness was a terrifying reminder of Caylee frailty. She was still mortal, and danger was all around. Haden was failing her. Where the hell was his courage, his confidence? Why did the method of transforming her need to be so frightening, so brutal? "Joseph is already attempting to heal her, little love." Haden paused. "It's why he's following her right now. We hid her presence today. There was no way Paul or any other vampire could've known that she was with us."

"He lied?" Caylee whispered, sounding hurt and confused.

"He's a demon, Caylee." Haden's voice was a low, threatening growl. He couldn't hide the fact he was jealous.

Believing her pain and confusion was caused by her faith in Joseph, he was irritated.

Caylee leaned back in the seat and closed her eyes. "I can't believe she's dying."

There was such deep sadness and pain in her voice it actually caused him to feel physical pain in his heart. He was a selfish idiot. Thankful she hadn't heard the jealously in his voice, Haden placed his palm on her thigh to impart peaceful, healing energy into her.

"She's such a good friend, Haden." She knew that by touching her leg he was trying to comfort her. She was thankful but felt guilty because it was working. How could she feel better when Mia was dying? "What if Mia makes Joseph so mad she pushes him away?"

"It won't happen." He smiled at her. "Joseph is a very stubborn man. The meaner she is to him the bigger the smile he'll be sporting. I know that he'll do everything possible to help her. We will all help her. We won't give up."

"What if it's too late?"

"It's never too late, little love."

Tears welling up in her eyes. "I should've noticed." The catch in her voice broke his heart. He knew she felt as if she'd failed Mia. "I don't understand. She's my best friend. Why didn't I notice, Haden?" She closed her eyes and swallowed hard. "Why did she hide it from me?"

"She loves you. She didn't want you to know about it. She didn't want you to worry. She's an extremely strong, stubborn woman. She was determined to hide it from everyone."

"Mia is such a good person. She took Julie and Brianna in off the street. Julie was prostituting, and Brianna's entire family died in a fire last year. Brianna is blind. She didn't have anyone. Julie didn't have anyone. They were without a hope until Mia intervened. I know that everyone dies, but I can't stand the thought of her dying so young."

"We won't allow it happen, little love."

~ *Eighteen* ~

"GET THE HELL out of here!" Backing away, Mia gripped her forearm to slow the blood seeping from it. Damn it. She was bleeding all over the place. And damn it, her favorite leather jacket was ruined.

"You think that you can run from me?" Chad moved toward her. "The only way out of here is death."

She was thoroughly pissed off. If the son of a bitch wanted a fight, he was going to get one. She didn't run away from anyone. She took a deep breath and squared her shoulders. "Well, Chad, if you want to die, I'll happily arrange it for you."

"Oh come on, you don't really believe that you can kill me, do you?" He laughed aloud, mocking her.

The sound of his laughter made her want to strangle him. She tried to keep her eyes on the knife, but he was swinging it all over the place. How the hell had he taken the knife from her? He wasn't a very large man, but he was strong. Too strong. She'd never allowed a man to disarm her. She was so pissed off at herself. She knew better than to allow him to corner her. She was losing too much blood. Her head was fuzzy. But damn it, if she was right, he was going to send her to hell. Well, she wasn't going alone. She would take him down with her. Her thoughts were racing. She needed to focus. She needed a weapon. But what? She was way too far away from her gun.

Chad tossed the knife a few feet away from them. He lunged and reached for her so quickly that his movement was a blur. "You're going to die today, bitch!" He was so close, cornering her, that his saliva spattered all over her face.

"Huh? Yuck. What the hell? You nasty little freak. Try brushing your teeth." She wiped her face with the back of her hand, unintentionally smearing blood across her lips. "And you're going to die first, asshole."

The enticing scent of her blood and alluring sight of it excited Chad. Fangs bursting, he inhaled deeply as he stared at the crimson-red blood smeared across her lips. His mouth was watering with anticipation, and his stomach clenched tightly. "I'm going to suck you dry."

Fangs? Oh, crap. A vampire. Yep. She'd suspected it a few weeks ago when they had their first encounter. She'd hoped for conformation, but this, being cornered, wasn't the confirmation she was searching for. "Gee." She rolled her eyes, pretending to be unconcerned. "Thanks for the offer, but not on our second date."

He squeezed his hands around her throat so hard she was certain her eyes were going to pop right out of the sockets. "You want a date, bitch?" His voice was angry, lustful hiss. It was definitely inhumane.

She fought for air but couldn't get any. She didn't panic. She refused to give him the satisfaction. He doubled his fist and hit her face hard. The back of her head banged against the wall. She was seeing stars. He still had one hand wrapped tightly around her throat. He moved closer, crowding her, using his body to press hers against the wall. He closed his eyes and groaned, savoring the sensation of her hot body pressed against his. Then he opened his eyes and held her gaze captive with his while grinding his cock against her belly.

She was so shooting his mother-fucking ass as soon as she could figure out how the hell to get to her gun. "Are you serious? If that's all the fucking dick you have, wake me up when you're done." He was squeezing her throat with so much pressure that she could barely get the words out. But damn it, she got them out.

"You goddamn fucking bitch!" The scent of her blood was making him so crazy his entire body was trembling. "You're going to regret interfering with my whore."

He was getting madder. She was definitely getting madder. "She isn't a whore." She braced herself, gathered every ounce of her strength, and kicked him in the balls. "And you don't own her." Stumbling back, his fingernails dug into her throat. He released her, but he quickly reached for her throat again. His hands were squeezing her throat. It was badly bruised and bleeding now. He yanked her head to the side to expose her neck. Leaning closer, he savored the scent of her blood.

"I've should've known better. Kicking a man without balls is a total waste of time and effort." Her voice was barely audible. Her vision was darkening. She was in serious trouble. She gasped. If she didn't get some air she was going to pass out.

Enraged, his gaze was locked onto hers. Snarling, he slowly leaned forward. He breathed deeply, inhaling her scent of her blood. It took a lot to freak Mia out, but she was freaked. She knew that she saw fangs. And his eyes had a strange red tint to them. He was a vampire. Her biggest problem wasn't passing out. She was going to die if she didn't fight. She was probably going to die anyways, but it would be much more satisfying to take him with her. She started to fight. She didn't know how it happened, but she managed to get away from him. She dove for the knife, grabbed it, and rolled over onto her back. He pounced full weight on top of her. She thrust the knife into his back. He yelped, but he didn't back up off her. He yanked the knife out of her hand.

Chad pressed the knife against her throat. He leaned

forward and licked the blood from her cheek. She twisted and turned. She kicked and hit him, fighting with every ounce of her strength to get out from underneath him, but he was too strong. He grabbed a handful of her hair and yanked her head to the side.

She felt his teeth scraping her throat. She fought like hell and managed to squirm out from underneath him. "You son of a mother-fucking bitch!" She jumped onto him, doubled her fist, and hit him hard. "Keep your fucking hands off of me!"

Chad threw her across the room and pounced on her again.

Ready and eager for round two, Joseph walked into Mia's Clothing Boutique. He immediately sensed the presence of a vampire. He glanced around quickly, taking in the information seen and unseen. He saw Mia's purse and its contents scattered across the floor. He immediately scented sweat, human blood, and the foul odor of vampire blood. He felt waves of lust, fear, and rage. He used his mind to reach out and pinpoint Mia's exact location in the building.

Using supernatural speed, Joseph ran to the back of the boutique. In one swift, violent move he yanked Chad off Mia and slammed the vampire against the wall. He glanced at Mia, quickly but thoroughly assessing her condition. She was okay for the moment. Hurt, but okay.

Mia rolled over and tried to sit up. Her heart was racing. She couldn't quite catch her breath. Hands to her throat, she scooted back to lean against the wall. She recognized Joseph immediately. Her eyes were so heavy. Her lungs burned. She watched in a dazed state. Joseph seemed to have the upper hand, but she knew that it could change at any moment. She needed to warn Joseph that Chad was a vampire. She needed to help him. She needed to get to her gun. She tried to stand up, but her head was spinning and she couldn't get up. Her body was too heavy. She tried to talk, but she couldn't get a sound out. Her throat was so badly bruised it felt as if it was crushed.

She knew she wouldn't make it to her gun. She saw the knife a few feet away. She could do it. She could get to the knife. On her hands and knees, she tried to get closer to it. Chad screamed. The sound of it was so inhuman, so frightening that her head snapped up to look at him. Hand around Chad's throat, Joseph was holding him against the wall. Covered by iridescent black flames, Chad's entire body was twisting and contorting. He kept screaming, his arms and legs flailing. The sound of his scream was like nothing she'd ever heard. It was so loud Mia had to cover her ears.

Suddenly, Joseph wrenched Chad's neck to the side. Mia heard it snap. The vampire's head fell from its body and landed on the floor at Joseph's feet. Joseph tossed the vampire's body next to its head and then lifted his hands. Within seconds, vivid currents of electrical energy engulfed Joseph and then the vampire's remains. It seemed like a short eternity, but within seconds the vampire's remain burst into flames. Mia blinked, and there was nothing left of it. No ashes. No burn marks on the floor. There was absolute nothing.

Mia looked up at Joseph. What the hell was he? She decided it would be a good idea to get the hell out of there. If Joseph was a vampire too, he was a hell of a lot stronger than Chad. She tried to stand up, but her head was fuzzy, and her knees simply buckled.

Joseph turned to face her.

It happened so fast she didn't see him move. He was on his knee in front of her, touching her all over.

Swallowing hard, reaching for her throat, Mia closed her eyes. "He's a vampire," she whispered, her voice hoarse.

Joseph forced her eyes open to look at her pupils. He knew she had a slight concussion. It was nothing serious, but it needed attention. "Was a vampire." He was already sending healing energy into her body while wrapping one hand around her arm to stop the bleeding. "Did he cut you anywhere else?"

"No. I don't think so." Mia opened her eyes. "Who the hell are you?" Her vision was blurry. She blinked to bring his face into focus. "And why are you here?"

"Joseph." Amused, he looked up to meet her furious gaze. "And it's a good thing I stopped by for a visit. Your vision will get better in a minute or two. You have a slight concussion, and you've lost a lot of blood."

"I know that you're Joseph, you idiot. What are you?" He wasn't human. "You snapped his neck off of his body like it was a twig, and then you burned him. How did you do it?" Taking a deep breath, she closed her eyes. "I know you're not human." The pain was subsiding. "You'd better not be a damned blood-sucking leech." Her body was filled with a peculiar but soothing warmth. "And I swear that I will kick your ass if you ever try to friend me or poke me again."

"You take a great picture. I noticed your single status." He smiled at her. "I'm still waiting for you to accept my friend request."

Her eyes flashed open. Narrowing her gaze onto his, she glared up at him. "It's never happening."

Grinning, Joseph shrugged casually. "Why not?"

Mia blinked a few times. He was way too good-looking. She wanted to beat him for looking so hot. Men like him were just way too confident. And worse, he was cocky. No. He was just plain annoying as hell. She tilted her head to the side. "I never asked you to come here. I want you to leave."

"You needed me here." The knife wound on her arm was closed, but he was still healing the wounds on her throat and face. "I'm not leaving just yet. You're a wreck. You still need me here."

"I had everything under control." One way or another she would make sure that he regretted being a cocky, annoying son of bitch. Realizing her arm no longer hurt, she looked down at it. Her leather jacket was no longer torn. "What did you do to my jacket and my arm?"

"It's your favorite jacket so I fixed it, and I healed your arm." He paused. "And for your information you didn't have anything under control. He nearly killed you. Why was he here?"

She got mad. He was right. She didn't have anything under control. Chad would've killed her if Joseph hadn't arrived. She didn't like it. Clearly, she'd needed him. She didn't want to need anyone; she hated seeing herself as needy. She couldn't stand the sight of Joseph. She needed to get away from him. She tried to stand up, but her legs were like rubber. "Let go of me."

"Just relax. There's no reason for you to get all bent out of shape. You need to calm down."

"Get your hands off of me and get away from me." Looking as if she planned to rip his head off, she glared up at him. "I want to get up."

"Let me help you." He took her arm.

The second she was on her feet, she shoved him. "I told you to get the hell away from me."

It was easy enough to hold her up without touching her, so he released her arm and turned his back to her. "You're very rude." He walked around, acting as if he was checking the place out as he weaved healing and protective spells throughout the boutique. "Why are you such an angry, bitter woman? In case you didn't notice, I just saved you. You should at least thank me for your life. You're too young and too beautiful to be so bitter. Surely you know that acting so ungrateful is quite unattractive."

Mia narrowed her gaze on him. "Who the hell do you think you are?" She walked up from behind, grabbed his arm, and yanked it. "Get your ass out of here!"

"Sorry, angel, but you're wasting your time and energy." He very slowly turned to face her. Locking his gaze onto hers, he smiled and winked at her. "A simple, immature temper tantrum won't run me off. You're marked. If one vampire came after you and failed to kill you, another will take its place and attempt to kill you. I've no intention of allowing you to die. In fact, whether you like it or not, I intend to protect you."

"Huh?" She shook head in disbelief. "What did you just say to me?"

"I intend to keep you safe."

"No." She clenched her fists at her sides. "What the hell did you call me?"

"Angel." He smiled, clearly pleased with himself. "It's a lovely pet name." Grinning, he winked at her. "It fits you very well."

"Really?" Well, that was lie. If she had a halo it would be shoved up his ass so far he would be choking on it.

She smiled, but there was no humor in it. It sort of reminded him of a panther's snarl. A very irritated, cornered panther.

"Well then, to be polite it's only fair if I come up with a special pet name for you."

Clearly hearing her thoughts, it was very difficult to shrug casually, but he managed to do it. "I agree."

If she were blind she might not notices his muscles rippling beneath the thin material of his shirt. The man was hot. He had it going in all the right places. He was a fine specimen of his gender, a fine specimen to take down. She figured she could have great fun with him in bed if she didn't hate him so thoroughly. She openly gave his entire body a good and thorough visual inspection. Yep. He was going down. Purposely attempting to make him feel as uncomfortable as possible, she allowed her gaze to linger on his crotch for several seconds.

"See anything you like, angel?"

Smiling way too sweetly, she slowly lifted her heat to look up at him. "Nope. Not at all." Then, forcing herself to yawn and covering her mouth as if to hide it, she locked her gaze onto his. "Imbecile." Lifting one brow and tilting her head to the side, she smirked. "Yep. That's it. It's a perfect fit for you.

And now you have a perfect pet name it's time for you to leave, imbecile."

Ouch. The woman was vicious. He was certain she'd reduced many men to blubbering fools. Lucky for him, hundreds of years of discipline enabled him to keep his expression void of emotion and pretend she hadn't just hurt his ego. "No. Why would I leave when I know that deep down in your heart you're happy I'm here? I saved you. I'm your knight in shining armor. Being a control freak with anger management issues, you're just too afraid to admit it."

Oh yeah, that did it. The idiot had a big mouth. Her blood was way beyond the boiling stage. Literally seething with rage, she glared up at him. "Get your ass out of here now!"

"Don't worry. I understand your fear of getting too attached to me. I've always been cursed with having that affect on women. I will leave eventually, but first I would like you to answer one question."

He was kind of funny in an annoying sort of way. She almost cracked a smile but managed to keep a straight face. Suspicious, she tilted her head to side. "What?"

"How long have you been sick?" His voice was different. It was deep and far too smooth. It was hypnotic.

She'd had many encounters with vampires in the past. She knew he was trying to use his voice to force the truth from her. Was he a vampire too? Cheeks turning red with renewed anger, she pointed at the door. "Get the hell out of here!"

"I'm not a vampire." Shaking his head, he stepped closer to her. "How long have you had cancer?"

He'd read her mind. She was outraged. He didn't have a right to be poking around in her head. Lifting her chin, she scowled at him. "You really are a pathetic imbecile." She refused to be intimidated by him. She refused to back away from him. Vampire or not, he was going down if he took one more step toward her. "I don't care if you're Haden's friend. If you don't get out of here right now, I'm going to kick your ass."

"You're such a naughty, temperamental little angel, aren't you? If I didn't know any better, I would start to think you don't particularly like me. It's a good thing I know better." Smiling, he winked at her. "And trust me, I would truly love to wrestle with you." Enjoying the idea of it a little too much, his voice unintentionally turned into a deep, throaty growl. "But first, I must insist that you tell me how long you've been suffering so I'll be able to more effectively help you."

The man was insane. Where was her gun? She glanced around. Spotting it, she smiled. She was going to prison. She glared up at him, refusing to look away until she walked over to her gun. She picked it up. Yep. She turned toward him and aimed. She was definitely going to prison. She was shooting his ass. Why was he concerned about her being sick? It was none of his business. He didn't even know her. She shook her head. How did he know about her illness? It was stupid question. He'd read her mind earlier. And he'd killed a vampire with his bare hands. He wasn't human. She believed he was a vampire, but the vibes around him were all wrong. What was he?

He knew she was extremely knowledgeable about the existence of vampires and was trying to figure out what he was. Her gut was telling he wasn't a vampire, but he was definitely not human. She was sizing him up, trying to strategize the best way to overpower him and bring him down on his ass. She was so damn feisty. She was completely irresistible. He was amused until he saw pain flash in her eyes. At the same moment her flesh turned frighteningly pale. He instantly reached out to touch her, to pull her into his arms.

"Don't touch me." She smacked his hands away. She stumbled to the side and dropped the gun, struggling to remain upright.

He could hear her heart beating too hard, too fast. Every cell in her body was immersed in pain from the cancer, but she didn't flinch from it. He needed to touch her. He needed to hold her. He needed to take the pain away from her.

"Stop looking at me like that." She was determined to hide her distress. He wasn't going to leave. She needed her pain medication. She was so desperate to get away from him. She needed to back down. It was her only option. She didn't even care if it meant he would win.

"Please. I'm so sorry. I upset you. I was wrong. Just try to calm down."

She tried to take a step back, but the pain was so intense her head was spinning and she felt nauseous. "Oh no." She needed a plan. She needed to get rid of him. She blinked; her vision was fuzzy. She needed to get rid of him now. She couldn't see anything. She blinked again, but it didn't help. "Oh crap." She couldn't focus her eyes on anything. The pain in her body was so intense, worse than ever before. She struggled to remain on her feet. She turned to walk away from him, but before she took one step she blacked out.

Joseph easily caught her up in his arms. He carried over the dressing room area and lowered her onto the couch. It was his fault. He'd pushed her too hard. He knew that she would fight him if he backed her into a corner. He'd wanted her to fight. He'd wanted her to get mad. Any why? He'd wanted to see the fiery nature of the wolf. Attempting to rile her temper when she was so weak was uncalled for. It was downright inexcusable. Maybe he was the imbecile that she'd named him.

Kneeling down next to Mia, he pulled her extraordinarily thick, dark blonde curls away from her face. "I'm sorry, angel." He took her hand, brought it to his chest, and held it over his heart. Closing his eyes, he released his healing power and allowed it to flow into her body and mind. He admired her strength, integrity, and courage. He would do all he could do to heal her, but because she wasn't his mate and her illness was terminal, there was a high probability it wouldn't work. If she'd been his mate, he could give his eternal breath to her.

Hopefully, she would learn to tolerate him, because if there was any hope, it would likely take several months to a year to heal her.

Allowing her to sleep, he stayed with her, healing her and absorbing her pain into his body for over an hour. With a thought, he set the entire boutique in order. When he realized Julie and Brianna were returning from lunch he bent down to kiss Mia's brow. "No more picking fights with vampires, angel. I know you don't want the girls you've taken under your care to see you like this. I would rather you rest for a little while longer, but wake up now and feel refreshed." The instant her eyes fluttered, he dissolved into a mist.

Awareness hitting her hard and fast, Mia's eyes flew open and she jumped up off the couch. She was disoriented, but she felt good. There was no pain anywhere in her body. She remembered fighting with the vampire. She remembered Joseph barging in and destroying the vampire. Oh crap. It wasn't real. Somehow the imbecile had gotten under her skin enough that she'd dreamed of arguing with him.

Taking a deep breath, she shook her head. No. She lifted her arm to her nose. It wasn't a dream. She could smell Joseph's cologne on the sleeve of her jacket. Confused, she searched the store. There was no visible sign of a struggle. Chad wasn't there. Joseph wasn't there. Had they ever really been there? Joseph could've contaminated her with his cologne earlier. He'd touched her at the cemetery. She couldn't be sure. Sometimes the medications she was taking for pain messed with her head. She didn't have much time to worry about it. A few moments later, Julie and Brianna returned.

~ *Nineteen* ~

HADEN OPENED THE car door and held out his hand for Caylee. "It's about a twenty-minute walk to my brother's place from here." Looking way more than a little hopeful, flashing a devilish smile, he asked, "Would you rather fly? It would be much quicker than walking."

"Gee, Haden, I'm not sure. Hmm. Let me think about it." Meeting his gaze, looking too sweet and innocent to believe, she tapped her finger on her chin, pretending to seriously consider it. "Nope. No way." She smiled at him. "Nice try, but I would much rather walk." Taking his hand, she got out of the car. "We're close to the ocean, aren't we?" Closing her eyes, she took a deep breath. "It smells wonderful, doesn't it?"

"Yes, we are, and it does." Pulling her close, he tucked her head beneath his chin and wrapped his arms around her. It was such a blessed relief to be able to hold her in his arms without fear, without anything standing between them. His eyes flashed open. He still needed to take her last mortal breath and replace it with his eternal breath. "I love you, Caylee."

"I love you," she whispered against his chest.

His heart was fuller than ever before. This was the miracle he'd waited for nearly two thousand years to experience.

"You are my miracle, little love. Holding you, touching you, having your love and loving you is my greatest dream come true."

Tears of joy burning behind her eyes, she tilted her head back to look up at him. "I feel so free, so at peace, so thoroughly loved. Sometimes I think that what I'm feeling is too good to be true. I don't want this to ever end. Being with you is like living in the most wonderful dream. A dream I never before dared to dream before." She smiled. "If I'm asleep I hope I never wake up. I've never been so happy to be alive."

Flooded with desire, Haden bent his head to kiss her. Caylee was instantly, completely swept away by his desire, his need for her. There was nothing more exquisite, more exciting than feeling his hunger for her as he kissed and touched her. It was hard at times to believe she could be so loved and needed by anyone, but it was impossible to doubt his love for her when he was touching her everywhere in her mind and body. The man was talented. He definitely knew how to make her feel like she was the most desirable woman in the world.

"You are, little love, you are the most desirable woman ever born," he whispered against her lips. "And you are mine. I will never have enough of you." He wanted to get lost in the moment. He wanted to show her just how desirable she was to him, but he knew they needed to go. Paul was close by. Not close enough to do any real harm, but a little too close for comfort. He wouldn't take chances with her life. Groaning, he pulled away from her. "We should get going before there's no stopping."

Pouting, she looked up at him. "I vote for not stopping."

Staring at her full, lush lips, he was so tempted to kiss her once more, but he fought the temptation. "You make me crazy."

"I try." Reaching up, she traced his lips with her index finger. "Do you have any idea what you do to my body when you kiss me, Haden?"

Clenching his jaw, fighting to control his body's response to her touch, he took her hand and placed it over his heart. "Do you feel my heart?"

She nodded. "I do."

"It's going to burst right out of my chest if you keep tormenting me, little love."

Moving a little closer, she smiled up at him. And he would be damned if it wasn't the most wickedly sexy smile he'd even seen on a woman. "Oh Haden, please forgive me. I never meant to afflict your heart." Her voice was a breathless, seductive purr.

He was still holding her right hand over his heart, but his focus was on her left hand as it slowly moved up his thigh. His body shuddered. Eager for her touch, hot blood shot straight to his groin. Her hand was so close, only a fraction of an inch from his cock. It was so hard, so impossibly swollen, pressed far too painfully against the seam of his pants. He wanted to remove his clothing, her clothing. He wanted to feel her flesh against every inch of his body. He wanted her to touch his cock. No, he was beyond want. He needed her to touch his cock, to wrap her hand around it and squeeze.

Giggling, she stood on the very tips of her toes and kissed the underside of his chin. "Just kidding."

"What?" Eyes wide, jaw dropped, cock still hard and aching like a son of a bitch, he stared at her.

"I was only teasing you." Grinning, she glanced down at his groin. "Oops." Looking up to meet his gaze, she nibbled on her bottom lip. "I'm so sorry. I guess that I got a bit carried away with the teasing."

Lifting his eyebrow, he tilted his head to the side. "You know you're pure evil, right?"

She shrugged. "Maybe a little." She giggled. "But I couldn't possibly be as evil as you."

"Why?"

"You're a demon."

"Which is why you can trust that I will retaliate," he vowed.

"You can try. I really hope you do," she whispered, her voice sounding husky and breathless.

"I will succeed."

"Well then," she murmured as she licked her lips, "I guess that I have some spectacular retaliation to look forward to."

He brought her hand to the warmth of his mouth to kiss it. "In the near future." He led her off the main path.

"The very near future, I hope." The trail was dark and heavily wooded. It was nothing more than an animal path with deep grooves from motorcycle tires. "Are you sure this is the right way?"

"I never get lost," he stated. His voice was a little too serious. And? She glanced up at him. Yep. He was annoyed.

She laughed. "Discussing the topic of you getting lost is going to be great fun in the future."

He shook his head. "No, it won't."

There was a bold, unambiguous rush of demonic energy in the atmosphere. A copper-colored mist formed directly in front of them. Pointing toward it, Caylee froze. "Oh, God. What is it?"

"It's only Zack," Haden said, obviously not surprised.

Caylee pinched his arm hard. "Jerk."

"Ouch." He rubbed his arm. "What was that for?"

"You did the same thing to me with the snake. You knew that Zack was going to pop up out of nowhere. You should've warned me."

"You were distracting me."

Zack stepped out of the mist and walked toward them. "Paul isn't able to step foot onto Nikolas' property. He has another vampire with him. A young male. They're trying like hell to get closer. And it is as we suspected. They're using ancient forms of Demetri's spells combined with Mary Tate's magic. It's odd. If Demetri is truly aiding them, why is he helping them with older spells? Wouldn't newer spells be more effective? And why would he allow his power to be polluted and weakened by a human's touch?"

"I don't believe that any influence from Mary would hamper Demetri's power. And, I don't believe any older form of magic is any weaker than anything current. Yes, we know the origin of them, but they're foreign to us. Demetri knows ancient spells will be more time consuming and difficult for us to unravel and defuse."

"You're right." Zack nodded. "He's truly lost to us, isn't he?" Pain and fear filled his voice.

Caylee's gaze shot straight to Zack. She could understand the pain, but the fear puzzled her. It was deep. She could see it in his eyes. It was as if he expected the worst to happen. It was as if he had no hope. She looked up at Haden.

"The past won't be repeated," Haden wrapped his arm around Caylee and pulled her closer. The possessive, protective way he held her frightened the hell out of her. Did he expect the worst too? Did he believe that something terrible was going to happen to her?

"What's your plan? You know that I'll stand by your side, Haden. You know that I'll give all that I have to help you, but we both know that this situation is massively fucked up. You say that the past won't be repeated, but it's already repeating. You have a vampire hunting your woman, and we can't stop him."

The sky darkened, and the ground rumbled. Caylee rolled her eyes. She was really getting tired of being drenched with rain whenever Haden lost his temper. "I won't allow it to happen." Haden's voice was a deep, menacing growl.

"Damn it, Haden, stop lying to yourself. You fucking know that living in denial will get her killed a whole hell of a lot quicker. I was there. You were there too, damn it. Your father said the same fucking thing. How do you intend to stop Demetri before it's too late?"

Caylee wasn't rolling her eyes anymore. Zack was really freaking her out. They expected her to be killed.

Hit by Caylee's rising fear, Zack glanced at her. Closing his eyes, he took a deep breath and held it. He knew he was causing her fear to build. He didn't want to care about her. He didn't want to feel guilty, but he did. He released his breath with a groan. "Just tell me what the hell you want me to do, Haden."

"We need to talk to Nikolas. He's older. He has fought side by side with Demetri for thousands of years. He has greater knowledge of him than we do. He also knows the ancient forms of dark magic as well as Demetri knows them."

Caylee didn't really want to draw attention to the fact she was still there, but she had to know. "How old is your brother?" It was hard to believe anyone was older than Haden.

"You think I'm old?"

"No. Extremely old."

"Demetri and Nikolas are about ten thousand years old," Zack explained, looking down at Caylee as if she disgusted him.

Shocked by it, she tripped on her own feet. Thankfully Haden was there to grab her arm and steady her or else she would've fallen flat on her face. "Dang." What else could she say? She couldn't even fathom the thought of living a thousand years. How was she supposed to imagine anyone living for ten thousand? From the corner of her eyes, she stared at Zack. Why did he dislike her so much?

Haden brought her hand to his mouth and kissed it. "It's not that Zack doesn't like you, little love. He would never admit it, but he cares very deeply. He's here with us today because he wants to ensure your safety. If I were ever unable to protect you, he would be the first to rise up and defend you."

Zack glanced at Haden. He knew Haden was saying it out loud to make sure Zack knew he was causing Caylee distress. Zack looked at Caylee. "I'm not a people person. My social skills need work." That was it. The woman wasn't getting an apology.

They walked out into a small clearing then veered off onto a path that led through a small cemetery. It was surrounded and filled with beautiful, lush foliage. Flowers. Trees. Vines. There were several smaller headstones with a twelve-foot high monument in the middle.

"Who's buried here?" Caylee asked.

"Family," Zack said.

Taking Caylee with him, Haden stopped in front of the monument. She immediately realized that it was a headstone. Seth and Ella Drake. "My mother was murdered by a rogue demon. Our father followed her. He couldn't continue in this life without her."

Zack turned to Caylee. "Knowing his mother, she probably kicked his father's ass for leaving Haden. He was her little baby. She was a tad bit overly protective of him and would've been mad as hell when she realized he'd been left without a parent."

Caylee looked at Zack. He was teasing Haden. It seemed so cold and callous for Zack to tease him about losing his mother and father. She looked a Haden. Clearly, by the smile on his face, he was remembering the past. "You were a baby when she died?"

Still smiling, Haden looked at her. "Not really."

"How old were you?" When Haden didn't answer, Caylee looked up at Zack.

Ready and eager, Zack grinned. "Well, he was nearly weaned." He was more than pleased to continue the conversation. "You were somewhere around fifteen hundred years old, right?"

"Give or take a few years." Haden smiled. Caylee sensed he didn't mind being teased. He seemed to like it. It seemed odd that he could smile over their deaths.

Haden brought her hand to his mouth and kissed it. "They aren't in the ground, little love. This is a place for reflection. They're together in the next realm of existence. It's a good thing he followed her. My father loved my mother too much to be apart. She loved him too much to be apart, too. It's common for our kind to follow their mates." What he wasn't telling her was that they'd shared his father's eternal breath. His mother had been mortal at one time too. When she died his father followed because of it.

That was it. That was why Zack didn't like her. She would eventually die, and Haden might follow her. She tilted her head to the side. "I wouldn't want you to follow me if I died!"

"Nothing could stop me. But there's no reason to worry about it. I would, but you're not going to die."

"No. She isn't." The deep, masculine voice came from behind. Haden and Zack moved so quickly that it was a blur. They shoved Caylee behind them and turned to face the threat.

"Nikolas." Haden brought Caylee to his side. "Not funny."

Nikolas didn't show any emotion. "I thought it was extremely funny." Caylee stared at him. She tried to look away, but she couldn't. Nikolas looked quite a bit like Haden. His hair was a lighter medium brown color. His eyes were a strange, golden brown. But he had the same smile and facial structure as Haden. He had a very dark, dangerous aura. "You're both still neglecting your backsides." Folding his arms behind his back to appear less threatening, he met Caylee's gaze and bowed his head slightly. "It has been a quite few years since you've been back here. You've grown into a beautiful young woman." He smiled at her. "It's a treat to see you again, little sister."

Eyes wide, Caylee moved closer to Haden. Nikolas' presence was so intense, so powerful. It was downright terrifying. He wasn't acting in a threatening matter, but it didn't matter. He was intimidating as hell. She opened her mouth to say something, but she didn't know how to respond to him. She'd never been to his home. She didn't understand what he was talking about.

Smiling, Nikolas held out his hand, and a kite appeared in it. "Perhaps you were too young to remember the first time you were here."

She immediately recognized it. "Oh, wow." It was her long-lost kite.

"You left it down on the beach." He pointed toward the cliff overlooking the sea.

Smiling, suddenly more at ease, she took it from him. "I can't believe you have it." She examined the kite and looked up at Haden. "It really is the same kite." She pointed at a name written in barely legible print. "Look, Haden, my mom put her name on it." She flipped the kite over. "So did I. We made it together just a few weeks before she disappeared."

"It's a beautiful kite." Haden touched the kite, bittersweet memories flooding him. "A beautiful memory of your mother."

Nikolas looked at Haden. "Do I want to know why you've brought vampires with you today?"

Zack pointed at Caylee. "She's being hunted by one."

Nikolas looked at Haden. "Why is it alive?" He didn't show any sign of anger, but there was an unmistakable sound of accusation in Nikolas' voice.

Haden frowned. "It's complicated."

Zack nodded. "The vampire is being helped by a powerful demon."

"What?" Nikolas paused. "Who?"

"Demetri."

"No." Nikolas shook his head, immediately rejecting the accusation. "You're wrong. Demetri would never aid a vampire."

"Perfect," Zack growled, "you're both in denial." He glared at Caylee. "She's as good as dead."

Caylee gasped.

Haden lunged forward and shoved Zack against a tree. "Stop scaring her."

"Stop acting like idiots." Lowering his brow, Nikolas clenched his jaw. "Nothing will happen to Caylee. And denial has nothing to do with my opinion, Zack. You're wrong. Demetri wouldn't side with a vampire, and he sure as hell wouldn't do anything to harm a woman."

"You're wrong. Demetri is helping the vampire. He's using ancient spells. Haden, tell him about the trap. You almost lost her."

Nikolas looked at Haden. "What trap?"

Haden explained the entire story. Caylee was more than relieved that he left out the fact he'd stumbled into the trap because he was distracted by having the best sex ever.

"An ancient human warrior rising?" Nikolas was reaching for Demetri, demanding an answer, an explanation, but Demetri wasn't responding. Nikolas knew that performing such a feat without help from a demon would be impossible for a vampire. In the past there had been instances when demons joined with vampires, but Nikolas couldn't believe Demetri would commit such a vile, treasonous act against his kind. He believed there had to be another explanation, but he couldn't deny that something was terribly wrong. Why wasn't Demetri responding to him?

"Demetri must be destroyed if he's united with any vampire. But I just can't get beyond the idea something else is going on. Demetri is too honorable to do something so wicked. I just can't believe he would do this, but I can't deny your vampire is using a form of Demetri's spells not used for thousands and thousands of years."

Zack said, "Believe or not, it's true."

"Do not doubt that if it's true, if Demetri has become a threat to Caylee, I will destroy him." Nikolas locked his gaze onto Haden's. "You should've come to me immediately."

"I underestimated the vampire, the entire situation." Haden took a deep breath and released it with a heavy sigh. "I thought I could handle it. I never thought Demetri would do this."

"When Paul fled, the rising just ended, right?" Nikolas asked.

"Yes. And it bothers me." Haden nodded. "The moment the vampire disappeared so did Demetri's power."

That brought Nikolas' brow up. "Totally?"

"Yes."

Deep in thought, Nikolas rubbed the bridge of his nose. "I have an idea. Stay here for as long as you want. Don't go back to your car. The vampire has set a trap for you. Zack and I will go and have a talk with Demetri." Nikolas took Caylee's hand again. "You will be safe. No one will ever harm a hair on your head. For years, I've looked forward to the day I would see you again, little sister. I hope you will come by again soon." Nikolas looked at Haden. "It's way past time to take care of a certain matter. You can't keep putting it off."

"I know," Haden said.

Haden's voice sounded more than a little annoyed. Caylee sensed Nikolas had just reprimanded Haden. But why? Caylee's questioning gaze darted from Haden to Nikolas. Zack and Nikolas turned away from them and slowly dissolved into a mist. She was starting to get used to the disappearing and reappearing thing, but the fact they were all dragons was a little bit too much to comprehend. Not that she didn't believe it. She'd watched them turn from man to dragon and dragon to man. It was just shocking. No. It was strange. Haden was strange.

Haden took Caylee's hand and walked her over to the cliff. "What was your brother accusing you of putting off?"

"Nothing important," Haden lied. "And I'm not strange."

"I agree. You are extraordinarily strange. Tell me the truth, Haden—does your brother think you shouldn't be with me?"

"No." Haden stopped walking and turned her to face him. "Absolutely not." He shook his head. "Why would you think that?"

"No matter what you say, I know Zack doesn't like the fact that we're together." She shrugged. "Nikolas is your brother. He would naturally want what's best for you. Family generally looks out for each other. You have so much power, so much potential. I'm an ordinary woman. I just thought maybe Nikolas might believe you're slumming it by being with me."

"You're wrong. They know you're the best thing that has ever happened to me. They know you are my heart, my soul, my life. Zack is irritated because he believes I'm not taking care of you properly. He's worried about you. Nikolas shares his concern and his belief that I'm not doing all I can to keep you safe."

"You're not serious, are you? I mean, you're extremely protective of me." She narrowed her gaze on his. He was lying. But why? She held his gaze for a few seconds, and then, deciding to ask Nikolas or Zack later, she looked down at the beach. "Haden, I want to go down there."

"I would kill any man that ever tried to convince you to leave me. Especially, if that man tried to convince you that you're not good enough for me." For a moment he looked dangerous, like the demon he was. But then, thrilled over the idea she might willingly fly with him, he was smiling at her, his eyes shining with joy and anticipation. "Oh, I'm sorry. We can't. I wish we could, but the only way down there is to fly, and it's your least favorite form of transportation."

"Actually, I've a little confession to make." She smiled up at him. "I've grown quite fond of the idea of flying with you again."

He was so very hopeful, but he was also way more than a little suspicious. "Are you teasing me?"

Flashing a way too sweet, innocent little grin, she asked, "Do you really believe I would do something so cruel?"

"Yes," he replied.

"What do you want from me? Should I beg?"

"Never."

"Well then, will you take me?"

"Absolutely." He definitely wasn't going to wait for her to change her mind. He loved to fly. He hoped one day she would love it too. He immediately, waving his hand, created a cloud of fog for cover.

In awe, she watched him. The sight of him took her breath away. He was so good-looking. So amazing. So powerful.

And he was her man. He loved her. His black, leathery wings shimmered for a few seconds and solidified. "You're so beautiful, Haden."

Growling, he pulled her into his arms. "Women are beautiful. Men are not beautiful." He bent his head and took possession of her lips roughly to prove his masculinity.

Struggling to catch her breath, Caylee giggled against Haden's lips. When he stopped kissing to look at her, she tried to pout, but her pouter wasn't working so well. He looked so appalled, so mortified. She couldn't stop smiling or giggling no matter how hard she tried. "But you are ..." Struggling to get the words out, she continued to giggle. "So very, incredibly beautiful."

He captured her tiny waist and easily picked her up. "Wrap your legs around me." And she did it without hesitation. He tilted his head back to look up at her. "Now, take it back," he growled.

She wrapped her arms around his neck. "No way." She smiled at him teasingly. "It's the truth. You're absolutely beautiful."

"Take it back." He glanced down at the ocean and then returned his gaze to hers. "Or you're getting wet."

"So what?" Wiggling, she moved her body against his while nibbling on his ear. "It isn't a big deal to me. Really, it isn't." Her voice was a breathless, husky whisper that caused his entire body to shudder. "To be completely honest, you're such a beautiful sight that my panties are already quite damp." Rubbing her body against his, she teased his earlobe with her tongue. "In fact ..." She paused, still moving her body intimately against his, and trailed hot kisses from his ear to his jaw. "They're so uncomfortably damp that I would like to take them off."

Lust. He groaned. Oh yes, he loved her more than anything, but raw, violent lust was what slammed into him so hard at that moment he could hardly catch his breath. He needed her now. She kissed him, her tongue spiritedly wrestling with his. He savored the wild taste of her kiss and the erotic sensation of her body moving against his. The need growing in her was exploding in him. Without warning, he extended his wings to full length and launched off the cliff. She stiffened for an instant. Before he could say anything to assure her that she was safe with him, she was kissing him again. Wasting no time, he took them straight down to the beach.

The moment his feet touched the sand their clothing disappeared. She was ready for him. He thrust inside her body so fast and hard that he didn't even think about hiding his wings. His only thought was of the pleasure that her body alone could give his, that his alone could give hers. Nothing in the world could ever compare to the satisfaction of burying his cock inside her body. He was wild, ferocious. He was just barely mindful, only enough to prevent him from harming her, of his great strength and her physical weakness.

Multiple orgasms ripped through her entire body. It was so amazing, so wonderfully exquisite that she was near tears. She could do little else but hold onto him, her nails digging into his shoulders.

Finally, he lost all control. There was no holding it back, no fighting it. With a beastly roar he thrust one last time, burying his cock deep as possible. His entire body shuddered. Her inner muscles violently and tightly clenched his cock as his hot seed spurted inside her body.

Candice Stauffer *Eternal Breath of Darkness*

~ *Twenty* ~

IT WAS EARLY afternoon. Wicked Sensations, Mary's strip club, wasn't officially open for business. Nikolas got off his motorcycle. He immediately knew Demetri was expecting him. Several annoying traps had already been set in place. None were deadly. None were strong enough to stop him. It was clear Demetri wanted Nikolas and Zack to come inside the building. "Can you feel it?"

"Of course," Zack said. "How did he know you were coming?"

"I told him."

"Why?"

"Why not?"

Walking across the parking, Zack asked, "Are you sure this is the best place to pick a fight with Demetri?"

"He's the one instigating a fight. And I sure as hell don't intend to waste my time chasing after him to fight." Nikolas smiled. "He wants a fight, he's got one. He certainly doesn't like his woman being threatened."

"This is a very bad idea. His presence is extremely strong here. We should lure him somewhere else."

Nikolas shook his head. "He's too smart for that."

"In case you haven't noticed, he's got an entire army of vampires here."

259

"Stop whining." Opening the door, Nikolas glanced over his shoulder. "Leave if you're afraid of the damn mosquitoes. But stop whining."

Zack followed Nikolas inside. "Mosquitoes supercharged with Demetri's power."

Nikolas walked toward the very center of the establishment and took a seat. Within seconds a waitress walked over to them. She had deep, dark circles around her eyes, and her face was pale and gaunt, making her look much older than her true age. She looked overused and reeked of dirty, nasty, old sex. Obviously unaware of her unappealing appearance, she seductively leaned over the table, allowing her breasts to hang out of her tiny tank top. "What's your pleasure?"

"Mary Tate rotting in her grave," Nikolas said. The waitress, obviously believing it was a joke, laughed. "I'm not kidding," he said, allowing his eyes to turn black and ripples of his dark power to wash over her. The waitress stepped backed away from the table slowly, and then she turned and ran toward the bar.

Zack laughed aloud. "And I thought my people skills needed work."

"Beating around the bush will just waste time."

"You've never been one to waste time."

Nikolas sensed the presence of danger. It was affecting him to the extent that his blood pressure elevated, and he couldn't control it. It was odd. Of course there was danger. Walking into the bar he knew he was instigating a fight with Demetri. Why would his body react to the presence of danger? It had to be a spell. What else could it be? He'd never experienced fear. And yes, it was fear in him that was causing his blood pressure to soar.

"You aren't looking so good," Zack said. "What's wrong?"

"I don't know." Reaching out with his mind to search for the source of the spells affecting him, Nikolas glanced around. "Something is off. Do you feel it?"

"No." All senses on high alert, Zack also reached out to examine the atmosphere.

"I think you're right, Zack. Demetri is lost to us."

The fact that Nikolas had admitted it shocked Zack. "What do you see?"

"It's not what I see—it's what I feel." Nikolas locked his gaze onto Zack's. "Go now, find Haden and tell him to not let Caylee out of his sight for even a second. No matter what happens, do not let either of them out of your sight."

"Haden is with her. He can take care of her. I'll go later—I'm not leaving you here alone."

"No." Nikolas shook his head. "I will be fine. Go now."

* * *

Julie led Brianna by the hand toward the back entrance. Deep down Julie knew she was making a mistake. Coming to the strip club was the last thing she should be doing, but she was desperate to make contact with her younger sister, Emily. It had been several weeks since she'd heard from Emily.

Brianna had such a bad feeling that it was making her feel physically ill. "Something is not right. We shouldn't be here." She stopped walking. "We need to leave. I think we're being watched."

Julie glanced around. "No one is back here right now. No one knows we're here. Come on. I can't leave yet. I need to check on her." Julie saw the fear on Brianna's face, and she mentally kicked herself. "I knew this was too much for you. Bringing you was a mistake. I told you to stay at the boutique."

"There's no way I would ever let you come here alone. I just think we should've told Mia. She would've helped us. Coming here alone isn't safe. What if Chad is here? What if someone else recognizes you?"

"No one will notice me. I've been wandering around this building ever since I was old enough to walk. Trust me, I know how to get around without being seen. And you know better. I can't wait for Mia. She left Emily here. She gave up on her. I don't blame her, but Emily is my sister, so I can't just turn my back on her."

"You know that isn't true. Mia hasn't given up on her. She never gives up on anyone. She just knows that your sister must want to get out of this place. I have absolutely no doubt that when Emily is ready, Mia will be there to fight for her."

"Maybe, but I can't wait." Julie led Brianna into a vacant room. "Stay here. I'll find her and then come back for you."

"No way. I'm not staying anywhere in this place alone."

"It will be quicker for me to search for her alone. No one will find you in this room. You'll be safe here."

Brianna started to argue but stopped when she heard the door close. "Julie?" Of course there was no answer; Julie was gone. The air in the room reeked of stale cigarette smoke, sweat, cheap perfume, and sex. No way was she staying in the room alone. She reached out to search for the doorknob, but before she found it, she heard the lock on it click. She grabbed the knob and tried to turn it. It was locked. Her heart raced. Her mouth went dry. She lifted her arms to pound on the door but stopped. She wouldn't panic. She couldn't. Drawing attention to the fact that they were there would get them killed. Julie would come back for her.

* * *

Nikolas was close to panic. Something terrible was happening. Something life altering. He couldn't believe the way fear had gripped onto him. He reached up and wiped his brow. When he lowered his hand he realized he was sweating blood.

He knew the moment Demetri walked up behind him. Struggling to regain his composure, he didn't turn to look at Demetri. "I was wondering if you would come out of hiding."

"You know better." Demetri walked over to the other side of the table and pulled a chair out. "I was a little disappointed when you sent your boy away to protect him. Oh, I mean, to help your brother. I was hoping to have a little fun with Zack today. I hate to admit it, but he was right. You aren't looking well at all, old friend." He sat down. "You're always so quick to strike. I'm assuming your poor condition has something to do with the fact that you still haven't learned the meaning of the word caution." He shrugged. "So, why are you here?"

Nikolas immediately noticed that Demetri had undergone a physical change since he'd seen him the year before. He'd aged. It was odd. Their kind never physically aged beyond thirty-three unless they were suffering some form of extreme anguish. The signs of it were so subtle it could've easily been missed: creases on his face, a few streaks of gray in his raven-black hair, and his normally vibrant golden brown eyes dark and dull.

"Playing dumb isn't like you," Nikolas said.

"What a pity," Demetri replied in a sarcastic tone. "I guess you aren't in the mood for small talk."

"Tell me why you're helping a vampire hunt my brother's mate."

"Your brother is an idiot. Haden left her to suffer for years. He doesn't value her life as he should. For some demons, they must first lose their mates before they learn to value them. He needs to learn a lesson. If it's her life, it's her life. It would be no real loss in the scheme of things. She's a weak, wretched human. Even now, he fails to take care of her. He has no right to leave her vulnerable because of his pathetic insecurities."

"You cannot truly believe that my sister is vulnerable." Nikolas laughed, but there was no humor in it. "We've known each other for a very long time. I've considered you my closest friend for more than ten thousand years, but since you're planning to harm my brother's mate you've become my greatest enemy."

"Fantastic." Grinning, Demetri nodded. "I would expect no less from you. I hope you expect no less from me." He took a deep breath and released it with a long sigh. "Fear is an interesting emotion, is it not? Tell me, what does it feel like to sense a woman's fear? Does it make your heart feels as if it might pound right out of your chest?" Narrowing his eyes, he smiled. "To be honest, I admire her. Imagine being so weak and walking into a place like this hoping to save another person. Oh yes, for all of her physical limitations, your beloved is a very brave girl. Foolish, but she's brave, is she not?"

Outwardly, Nikolas remained as still as a mountain. Inwardly, he was trembling uncontrollably. He knew Demetri could sense his distress. No matter how hard he fought against it, he couldn't break free from the fear gripping his heart. "She isn't here. She isn't weak. She has many willing to stand and fight for her." Lowering his brow, Nikolas frowned. "You will die for threatening my sister, Demetri."

"Your sister?" Leaning back in his chair, Demetri stretched his arms behind his back. "I thought you knew me better. Do you truly believe I would waste my time harming your sister to punish you for walking in here to threaten my woman? Your sister means nothing to me. The vampire will take care of your brother's woman for his own reasons." Lifting his brow, he smiled. "It isn't your sister that I've targeted, Nikolas. It isn't your sister that's already suffering for your ignorance. It isn't your sister's fear you're feeling right now."

Nikolas knew there was some truth in it. He felt the presence of a female in the building. She was reaching for him, and she didn't even know it. It couldn't be his mate. He didn't have one. He would know his mate. He sure as hell would know her before Demetri would. He was tempted to do it, but he knew better than to extend his mind to reach for the woman. Demetri would sense it and see it as an affirmation that he was concerned about the woman. Nikolas glanced at Mary. "Why do you defend the murderous whore?"

Demetri laughed aloud, mocking Nikolas. "You've grown cold in your old age. It seems that neglecting one's mate is a family trait. After waiting for her for so long, I can't believe you would rather talk about my woman than do anything to stop your mate's terrifying ordeal."

Narrowing his eyes, he shook his head. "No. That isn't it, is it? You want nothing more than to reach for her, comfort her, protect her. What does it feel like to know she's reaching for you, needing you, and you must ignore her to protect her? Do you truly believe that by acting disinterested you will keep me from harming her?" Clenching his jaw, he leaned forward and whispered, "It's too late. She already tastes my vengeance."

It was instant. It had been thousands of years since Nikolas lost control of his temper, but there was no containing his dragon's rage. Shattering several windows, powerful gusts of wind arose from out of nowhere. Black clouds gathered, lightning streaks exploded, and baseball-size hail pummeled the building. Jumping to his feet, Nikolas tossed the table away and lunged for Demetri.

It was a violent fight like no other. Every vampire and every human in the bar, including Mary, fled the building. Nikolas and Demetri ripped the place apart. They were equally matched. Neither could win. If they continued, both would die.

The sounds of thunder and hail were so loud that Brianna's ears ached. The room was quickly filling up with smoke. She couldn't get the door to open. Smoke was burning her eye, nose, and throat. For a few minutes she heard people screaming and fleeing the building. It sounded as if the building were being torn apart and ripped off its foundation. It didn't matter. She knew it was over. The smoke was too thick. She couldn't breathe. Even if she managed to open the door, she was dead—she couldn't remember the way out of the building. She fell to her knees.

Uncaring that he was leaving his body exposed to any attack from Demetri, Nikolas froze and stared at the back of the building, expanding his mind to search it. The instant he found Brianna's exact location he waved his hand to place a protective barrier around her.

"Now, only after you allow your mate to feel distress, you decide to reach for her. Tell me, did you pick up the habit of neglecting your mate from your father? It's okay. Go fetch your mate, and I'll go fetch Zack. We will have plenty of time to play later."

Nikolas' gaze darted to Demetri. It wasn't a bluff. Demetri had every intention of going after Zack. What if the woman wasn't real? She could be an illusion; Demetri possessed great power, and Nikolas knew she wasn't his mate. It could very well be a trick. But if she was real, if she wasn't an illusion, he couldn't allow her to suffer and die. Zack was one of the most capable, most powerful warriors. He had a chance. The woman didn't. Nikolas turned away from Demetri and started down the hall toward the end of the building.

"Wise decision." Laughing, Demetri dissolved into a mist.

Nikolas didn't rush. He had no reason to; the woman was perfectly safe. Making his way toward her, he was racing around in circles in his head. He walked down the burning hall with no regard for the flames or falling debris. Deep down in his soul, he knew he was about to meet his mate, the other half of his soul. How had Demetri known about her? Why would he harm her? Why would Demetri harm any innocent woman? The closer he got to her, the more his heart thundered.

Face down on the floor, Brianna felt a cool breeze wrap around her. The smoke that was suffocating her, burning her nose, throat, and eyes, was replaced by a pleasant, masculine scent. While pushing herself up onto her knees, she heard the door open and then close. Slowly, she turned toward the sound.

Nikolas stood in front of Brianna, towering over her, unable to look away, unable to move, unable to speak. There was a powerful stirring like no other in his body, his heart. She was his mate, his life. Dark, murderous rage filled his soul so he couldn't prevent a low, animalistic growl from rumbling in his chest and throat. Demetri had just signed his death certificate.

Eyes suddenly going wide, Brianna gasped. She was trapped in a room with an animal. Its hatred and hunger for vengeance struck her to the core. Trembling, she stood up and took a step back.

"Don't be afraid, little one," he whispered. "I would never hurt you. I'm here to help you."

"The building is on fire, isn't it?" She'd had no doubt it was on fire a few minutes ago, but now she couldn't even smell the slightest hint of smoke.

"Yes, but don't be afraid. We're going to make it out of here together."

"My friend?"

"She's safe," he lied. At the moment he didn't know, but he didn't care. She was his only concern. "I know you can't see me." Taking a step closer, he closed the gap between them. "Don't be startled—I'm going to take your hand."

Nodding, she held her hand out for him. "Are you sure we can make it out?"

"Absolutely." The instant his hand closed around hers, her pulled her to his side and wrapped his arm around her. "Stay close to me." He expanded his wings and wrapped one around her to shield her from the heat of the flames—not that keeping her close to him or using his wing to shield her was necessary. He could've been thousands of miles away from her, and she would've been safe. The powerful protective barrier surrounding her would have prevented even one hair on her head from being singed even if the building had burned to the ground around her. Keeping her close, using his wing as an unnecessary precaution, felt so good he couldn't resist doing it.

The moment Nikolas opened the door, Brianna heard the fire crackling and debris falling all around. But that was it. It was like before when her family's home burned to the ground.

She was walking side by side with a man through flames, but there was no trace of smoke in the air and no heat.

Nikolas easily monitored her thoughts. He knew the only being that would ever be able to take her through a fire was a demon. Because she was blind, she didn't have any visual memory, but Nikolas knew the man who had saved her was Demetri. After meeting with Demetri today, Nikolas knew better than to believe it had been out of the goodness of his heart. Demetri planned to kill her, but he wanted to make sure Nikolas knew her first.

With a thought, he opened the back door. "We're out now."

"I feel bad to ask you to do anything else for me, but would you please help me find my friend?"

"No. I'm sorry. I would if I could," he lied. He wasn't taking her to anyone. He led her across the parking lot. He wasn't letting her out of his sight. "Everyone is gone," he lied again.

"Are you sure?" She swallowed the lump in her throat. What was she going to do? How was she going to get home?

"Yes. Everyone fled to seek cover from the storm."

"I heard it, but it's over now." She paused. "I really need to find my friend."

"Don't worry. I've no intention of leaving you here." He stopped next to his motorcycle and placed her hand on the back of his bike. "I'll take you home." It wasn't a lie. Not really. His home was her home. And even if it was a lie, so what? He was a demon. He sent Zack a quick text message to warn him about Demetri, and then he unzipped his leather jacket and took it off. Zack replied almost instantly, assuring Nikolas that he could handle Demetri.

"No." Realizing that she was touching the back of a motorcycle, she shook her head. "This is a bad idea."

He wasn't taking no for an answer. "It's a bit chilly." He put his phone back into the inner pocket of his jacket and then put the jacket on her. Before she could argue, he zipped it up.

Taking a moment to admire the sight of her, he smiled down at her. She was such a sweet, lovely sight. She looked so tiny and delicate in his jacket. Once he was able to rip his gaze off of her, not an easy feat, he got onto the motorcycle and then turned to take her hand.

"You don't understand," she said, her eyes wide, pleading with him to come to his senses and realize it was a bad idea. "I've never been on a motorcycle."

"Well then, it will be a memorable adventure."

Grinning shyly, she lifted her chin as if to meet his gaze. She opened her mouth to argue with him, but he was right. And deep down, she yearned for adventure.

He felt her hunger for adventure and excitement. "You know you want to give it a try." He knew that, besides dealing with its natural limitations, her blindness had forced her to be overly cautious in just about every situation. "Get on up." Good thing for her inner wild child, he wouldn't know how to be cautious if his life depended on it.

She frowned. Was he guessing, or was it that obvious? Suddenly remembering that she was wearing a rather short dress and nearly nonexistent panties, she shook her head. There was no way she was going to lift her leg up and climb up behind a man she didn't know when she was so under-dressed. "I don't even know you."

A shudder running through his body, he closed his eyes. Thinking about her panties was a bad idea, but he couldn't help it. Hot, wild desire shooting through his body, he opened his eyes, quickly realizing that envisioning them was a worse idea. Turning his head, narrowing his gaze, Nikolas stared toward the front of the building. He knew Julie was looking for Brianna and was about to walk around to the back of the building. He wasn't about to allow her to interfere. "You have nothing to fear." He took her hand and placed it onto his shoulder. "Get on." It was a powerful command, utterly impossible to ignore.

Nodding, she got up behind him and attempted to pull the dress down. It wasn't working out so well since his jacket was several inches longer than her dress. Normally, she would never even consider wearing such a revealing dress, but Mia had insisted on making her the dress for the party tonight. For the past few weeks Julie had vowed that she would get Brianna to dance, but Brianna had no intention of doing it. Dancing in public was not the best activity for a blind woman to attempt. Secretly, she really wished she could dance, but it just wasn't going to happen. Wait! What was she doing? Why did she get onto the motorcycle with him? He'd lied to her. Julie would never leave her. She was crazy, completely insane.

He smiled. It just so happened that demons were very good at dancing. So, he quickly decided that he was taking her dancing. First, he needed to make stop at his home to see what he could find online concerning the fire that burned down her family's home. He was hoping to figure out how Demetri was linked to it. He reached behind him, took her hands, and wrapped her arms around his waist. "Scoot closer." When she didn't move closer, he said, "Lean on me, little one."

"No." Panicking, she struggled to get off of the bike. "I want to get off now." She couldn't take off with a stranger. "Let me get off." He was probably a disgusting, nasty pervert or rapist. There was no telling what he was doing at the strip club. Everyone knew it doubled as a brothel. There was no telling what he was capable of doing to her.

"It's okay. Normally, I would never suggest you jump onto the back of a bike with a complete stranger, but I happen to know that you're safe with me." He internally laughed at his need to explain, to make her believe he wasn't a nasty pervert or rapist. He wanted to tell her he hadn't been with a woman in over six thousand years, but he knew that was a confession she'd never be able to comprehend. He wanted to make her believe she was the only woman he ever wanted. She was his heart, his soul, his life. Luckily, being ten thousand years old gave him the wisdom to know that professing his undying love for her so soon after meeting would most likely make her think he was a deranged stalker or serial killer. "You need to scoot closer and hold on tight." He certainly needed her to hold on tight and never let go.

Nodding, she reluctantly moved closer to him. When the engine roared to life, her heart jumped. Yep. She was in serious trouble. She was truly headed off on the back of a motorcycle with a complete stranger. She considered jumping off, but even after they were moving he kept one hand was over hers to ensure she stayed close and held on.

The air was crisp and cool, but his body was so warm, and the jacket he'd put on her seemed to be holding heat, generating it. It didn't take long for her to relax enough to enjoy the experience. She breathed deeply. He smelled so good, so addictive. His body was so strong and solid. One thing was certain: the man worked out. There was no missing his roped abdominal muscles against her palms. She had no idea how fast they were traveling, but she knew they were passing cars and swerving in and out of traffic. She had enough sense to know she should be scared to death—she wasn't even wearing a helmet, and she knew he was leaving the city—but she'd never felt safer. In fact, as crazy it was, she really wanted him to go faster.

In seconds, they were thundering down the highway at an insane speed. If she wanted faster, she was getting faster. He would do anything to please her. When he heard her squeal of excitement and felt her arms squeeze his waist tighter, he went even faster, using his powers to push the bike far beyond its natural limits.

Pressing her face against his back, struggling to catch her breath, she laughed so hard tears welled up and her sides ached. Something powerful shifted deep inside her soul, flooding her body with the most invigorating, delicious sensations. Her hormones were spiraling out of control because he wasn't simply holding her hand, he was caressing her hand with his thumb. How could such a simple touch wreak such havoc in her body? She didn't even know him. It was frightening and exhilarating all at the same time.

Feeling her arms around him, feeling her body pressed so snugly against his, and hearing her laughter made him feel so alive. Even after seeing Haden with Caylee, the thought of one day finding his mate had never entered his mind. He'd given up all hope so very long ago. If fact, he'd actually accepted the fact he'd failed to find his mate during her lifetime. He'd never seen this moment coming.

Ten thousand years was a hell of a long time to wait to experience the peace, joy, and excitement that were now thrumming through his soul. It was too long. More than enough time for him to lose his appetite for sex. And now, his body was on fire, burning up with lust. He was so full of need. For the first time in … damn. He couldn't remember his last hard-on. How long had he existed without living? It didn't matter. His cock was as hard as rock. The brutal agony of needing to bury himself deep inside her body and knowing he needed to court her for a little while before taking possession of her body was the sweetest pain. Oh yeah, it hurt so damn good. He was alive again, truly alive. Grinning like fool, he glanced down at his cock. And better yet, he was quite incapable of controlling his body's reaction to a woman, his woman.

She felt a strange sense of weightlessness when he created a thick fog to take them through time and space. One second they speeding down the highway, and the next they were traveling slowly down an uneven gravel road. She lifted her face off his back and took a deep breath, filling her lungs with the unmistakable scent of ocean air. There was no way they could be by the ocean. There was no way they'd been traveling for over an hour. Maybe she was wrong about the distance. What she really needed to worry about was the fact that she was alone with a stranger on a secluded road and they'd just stopped.

Without saying a word he turned and, shocking her, lifted her off the bike and gently set her down on her feet. She stood there for no more than a second before he took her hand and started to walk. "Where are we?"

He stopped at the front porch. "It's fifteen steps up."

She yanked her hand out of his. She wasn't going anywhere else with him. "Where are we?" All of the color drained out of her face.

Fuck. He knew a panic attack when he saw it. "My house."

She was an idiot. Heart racing, tears welling up, her entire body started to tremble. "Why would you bring me to your house?"

"Forgive me for being so thoughtless." Sending peace into her, he took her hand and slowly brought it to his mouth. "I'm Nikolas Drake."

Instantly recovering from a nearly full-blown panic attack, she smiled. "Do you know Haden?"

"He's my brother. How do you know him?"

"I don't really know him. He comes to where I work to see his girlfriend, Caylee."

Nikolas took his cell phone out and called Haden. "Put Caylee on." He turned the speaker on.

"Hello."

"Hello, little sister. I need a favor."

"Okay."

"I've put you on speaker. I'm with Brianna Larkin right now, and I'm attempting to convince her to allow me to take her to the party at the Grande tonight, but there's a small problem."

"What?"

"She's rightfully a little apprehensive about taking off with a stranger."

"Oh, I understand. It's okay, Brianna. You're safe with Nikolas. He's a good guy." It was everything Caylee could do to keep from laughing when Haden stopped the car, swung his head around, and commanded her to give him the phone.

Feeling more than a little embarrassed, Brianna giggled. "Thanks, Caylee."

"Anytime." Caylee giggled, struggling to prevent Haden from taking the phone out of her hand. "I'll see you later."

Knowing Haden was attempting to wrestle the phone away from Caylee, Nikolas ended the call and turned the phone off. "You have no reason to be embarrassed." He took her hand. "It's fifteen steps up. I just need to change my clothes, and then we will leave for the party."

* * *

"Here you go." Caylee handed the phone over.

"He hung up." Haden tried to call Nikolas back. "He turned the phone off." He frowned. "What did he say?"

"Sorry," Caylee teased. "I wish I could tell you, but I can't. It's a secret."

Growling, he lowered his brow. "Tell me."

Nibbling on her lower lip, she grinned up at him. "Say pretty please."

"Do you know what happens when you play with fire, little love?"

"Nope. I've never really considered fire to be a toy." Pressing her palm against his cock, she winked at him. "But I'm getting very knowledgeable in what happens when you get naked and play with a fire-breathing dragon."

"Did you just call me a toy?"

She giggled. "My favorite toy."

"You really are pure evil." Frowning, he pulled the car back onto the road and started driving again. "You don't fight fair." He glanced over at her, and he'd be damned if she wasn't smiling up at him, waiting for him to say it. He wasn't going to say it. There was no way. Imagine how impossible she would be to deal with it he allowed her to win this one.

"Pretty please," he growled, between clenched teeth.

"Nope. No way. No growling." She crossed her arms over

her chest. "And I really didn't think we were fighting, but now that I know, I'm not telling you unless you say it very nicely."

Blood pressure skyrocketing, he pulled the car into the only available parking spot anywhere close to the boutique. Struggling to keep his composure, he got out of the car and walked over to the passenger side. He opened the door and reached for her hand to help her get out of the car. Without thought, he wrapped his arms around her and pulled her close. He bent his to head. "Pretty please, little love, tell me." he whispered in a deep, seductive voice that sent shivers of desire racing through her body.

"Pretty please?" Joseph walked up from behind. "It must not be all that earth shattering if she makes you beg for it."

"Oh, damn it." Haden brought Caylee to his side to face Joseph. "What are you doing here?"

"Picking Mia up for the party."

"Does she know?" Caylee asked.

"Not yet." Joseph smiled.

"She won't go with you. She doesn't even like you," Haden growled.

Joseph shrugged casually. "Maybe I'll try saying pretty please."

Before Haden could hit Joseph, Caylee blurted, "Nikolas is taking Brianna to the party tonight. She's with him right now."

"Huh?" Haden glanced at Joseph and then looked down at Caylee. "That's what he said to you?"

"Yep."

"I don't think I've ever seen your brother with a woman," Joseph said. "What about you?"

"Never." Haden replied.

~ *Twenty-One* ~

NIKOLAS TOOK HIS jacket off Brianna, and then he pulled out the chair and guided her into it. He leaned down next to her and turned the computer on. She lifted her chin and turned her face toward him. Feeling the heat of her breath on his neck made every muscle in his body go rigid. He looked down at her and stared into her unseeing blue gaze. She was almost too beautiful, too perfect in every way he could ever imagine. Her lips were so close. He was tempted to lean down a little further and kiss her. It took every ounce of his strength, but he managed to force himself to look away from her and focus on the computer screen.

It didn't take Nikolas long to find the story of the fire that claimed her family. Following one clue after another, he eventually found a picture of Demetri with a young woman. She could've been Brianna's twin. He studied picture and realized that Mary Tate was standing in the background, watching Demetri. "Brianna, do you have a twin sister?"

Visibly shaken by the question, Brianna attempted to rest her hand on the desk, but ended up placing her hand on his. "Sorry." As if she'd just touched a flame she jerked her hand back and held her breath.

He got down on his knees and slowly turned the chair so that she was facing him. He took her hands in his to send waves of healing energy into her. "There's no reason for you to be sorry, little one. You didn't do anything wrong," he whispered. He took a deep breath and released it with a sigh. "I upset you by asking if you have a twin sister, didn't I?"

Hot tears burning behind her eyes, she nodded.

"Why?" He continued to send healing energy into her as he waited for her to recover and respond.

"My sister, Sara, disappeared after our home burned down." She swallowed the lump in her throat. "The authorities believe she started it."

"Tell me why they blamed her," he whispered.

"She didn't do it," she blurted, her unseeing gaze pinning his, her voice and expression fierce with her love and loyalty for her sister.

"I know." He reached up and gently wiped the tears from her face. "But why do the police suspect her?"

"She hears voices," Brianna whispered. Why was she telling him anything? She didn't know why, but she felt as if she could tell him anything. "Sometimes, she hurts herself. She has violent outbursts. They believe she's insane."

"I'm sorry. Thank you for trusting me." Nikolas brought her hand to the warmth of his mouth. "How did you get out of the fire?"

It was just as Nikolas had suspected. He watched a dark spell of fear, intended to silence her, grip onto her and squeeze hard. He immediately recognized Demetri's power in it. He placed his hands on her shoulders. "The only way to break the fear is to defeat it. The only way to defeat it is to challenge it. I'm here. I will protect you. Nothing bad can happen to you. Tell me how you managed to get out of the fire." He didn't need her to tell him. She needed to tell him. It was the only way to break the spell. Well, he could easily get rid of it, but it was better for her to do it. It would empower her and make her less vulnerable to Demetri's power.

Somehow, she knew it was true. She didn't how, but it didn't matter. She believed him. "It was the same as when you rescued me today. A man I'd never met took me out of the house. Then the moment we stepped off the front porch, he told me that if I ever told anyone he'd helped me he would ... oh, God."

"Would what?" Nikolas asked, careful to hide his anger.

"Kill me and whoever I told."

"I know him," Nikolas said. "He can't touch you."

Brianna nodded, but she wasn't truly convinced. She believed Nikolas was attempting to make her feel better.

Nikolas was having a difficult time containing nature. He was a powerful immortal, a fierce warrior, and his anger was growing. "Did he hurt you?" He attempted to hide his rage, but his voice was so dark and menacing it sounded as if he'd growled the words.

Brianna nearly jumped out of the chair. She would've if he weren't holding her down. "No." Her heart was racing frantically, painfully.

"Forgive me, I didn't mean to startle you."

Nodding, attempting to smile, she swallowed the lump in her throat. "Do you think he hurt Sara?"

"I don't know, but I promise to find out what happened to her." Regardless, Nikolas was killing Demetri. He released Brianna's hands and stood up. "It's getting late. Give me a moment to put something more presentable on, and we will get going."

Changing his clothing with a thought, Nikolas walked over to the window. Staring out at the setting sun, he ran his hand through his hair and took a deep breath. Slowly exhaling, he glanced at Brianna over his shoulder. Demetri had killed his own mate. It was the worst, most vile crime his kind could ever commit. What would drive a demon to kill something so exquisite, so fragile? He closed his eyes and leaned forward to rest his forehead against the cool window. Some would say Demetri's power was his downfall. It was believed ultimate power was the only thing that could so completely destroy a demon's sense of honor and loyalty.

Nikolas opened his eyes to gaze out the window once more. He wasn't worried Demetri would ever be able to harm Brianna. He had every intention of doing whatever it took to protect her, and he had faith in his abilities to do so. By the end of the night he would secure her future and walk away from her for forever. Ultimate power had corrupted Demetri. He didn't want to believe it was true. He'd lived just as long and possessed just as much power as Demetri, and he wanted to believe he would never commit such a despicable sin. But it was inevitable. Guilt crushing down on him, he took a deep breath and held it. He wouldn't take any chances with Brianna's life. For hundreds of years he'd felt the influence of utter darkness building in his soul. It was why he'd kept his distance from everyone. He was warrior. He was a killer. It was far too late for him to claim his mate. Resisting the urge to shatter his reflection in the window, he closed his eyes once more. If he tried to hold onto Brianna, he would eventually use his powers, his strength to destroy her.

Brianna felt the crushing waves of his agony. She stood up. "Nikolas?" He didn't answer. She felt drawn to him in a way she'd only ever experienced with her sister. She didn't hesitate. She took a step away from the desk and then, following the waves of his sadness and pain, she kept taking one step after another until she was standing directly behind him. Just as she had with her sister so many times in the past, she reached out and touched his back, hoping to ease his pain. "Nikolas?"

His head snapped up. His deep pain and sadness instantly vanished, leaving him feeling so at peace that tears of joy burned behind his eyes. He didn't need to ask how she'd made her way across the room. He saw it in her mind. They shared a connection. And it was stronger than he'd ever imagined it would be. He was hurting, his heart was breaking, he needed her, and she came to him. He placed her hand over his heart and held his hand over it. Despite being unable to see her unfamiliar surroundings, she came to him without any hesitation or fear because of the powerful connection she'd shared with her twin.

Feeling his steady, strong heartbeat beneath her palm caused her to shiver. "I never thanked you." Lifting her chin, she smiled up at him.

Mesmerized by her smile, he stared down at her, his breath harsh, his body shuddering with need. "You're welcome, Brianna." He bent his head so his mouth was so close his hot breath tickled her ear. "But you don't need to thank me." His voice was deep and husky, his breaths ragged.

She stepped back. The heat of his breath, the deep, lustful sound of his voice when he'd whispered in her ear heightened a sexual hunger in her she'd never known existed. More than anything, she really wished she could see him. Not seeing his gaze, but feeling it on her, she lowered her head. She folded her arms behind her back to resist the temptation to touch his face.

"I would love it," he whispered. Then leaning back to look at her, he softly trailed the backs of his fingers up her neck and kept going until he forced her chin up.

Brianna gasped at his touch. "Huh?" She held her breath. She knew exactly what he was saying, but she was so embarrassed. It wasn't his words that brought color to her cheek; it was the way his touch caused her body to ache.

He felt her desire. "I would love for you to touch me." His voice was a low, lustful growl.

She felt the heat of her blush deepening. She struggled to take even, steady breaths. His nearness, the warmth radiating from his body, was wreaking havoc in her body. She fought to steady her nerves, but it was no use. Hands trembling, she reached up and placed them on his face. Electricity arced between them, through them. For a moment, startled by the fiery, intoxicating sensations racing through her body and over her flesh, she froze. Finally able to move, she started to explore his face.

Nikolas thought his heart was going to explode right out of his chest. Her tiny fingers caused lightning to rip through body and thunder to rumble in his ears. It was nearly impossible to resist the urge to wrap his arms around her and pull her closer. He'd never known such a desperate need to feel a woman's body against his. Every muscle in his body ached from the strain it took to remain still so she could finish her exploration. It was the most perfect form of torture imaginable. He never wanted it to end. It was a good thing she couldn't see the color of his eyes turn to black. She would be horrified. She would know he wasn't human.

Tilting her head to the side, she smiled up at him. "I don't need to see the color of your eyes to know you aren't human. I don't need to see the power in and around you." She paused. "I can feel it."

"What did you say?"

"Oh no." She immediately removed her hands from his face. "I'm so sorry, Nikolas. I didn't mean to intrude. Sometimes when I use my hands to see a person I can hear their thoughts." She frowned. "Sometimes I don't know it's happening. It sounds as if the person is talking to me. It usually only happens when I have a strong connection with the person. Mostly Sara."

Turning away from him, she quickly took a few steps to put some distance between them. As luck would have it, she ran into something solid and tripped. Thankfully, it was right into his arms instead of flat on her face on the floor. "You think I'm a freak, right?" Besides commenting on his thoughts, attempting to walk away from him was just about the dumbest thing she could've done. Thoroughly humiliated, she buried her face against his sternum and didn't move.

"No," he whispered, smoothing her hair, holding her as close as he dared to. "Not at all." He was shocked. He was too well guarded for most of his kind to ever freely hear his thoughts. "You're the most intriguing woman I've ever met." Resting his chin on the top of her head, he breathed deeply, filling his lungs with the sweet scent of her soft, silky hair. "I've always had the ability to hear the thoughts of other people. It can be confusing. The fact that you're able and willing to merge your mind with mine is the most fascinating feeling."

"You're a liar. Why would you want me in your head?" She giggled at his attempt to make her feel better. "You don't even really know me."

Normally, he would've it shrugged it off. He was a demon. Being called a liar was no big deal. He'd been called worse. He gently pushed her out of his arms, and then he took her hands and brought them to his face and opened his mind fully, hiding nothing from her. "I belong to you, little one. From this day forward until the end of time I will be watching over every breath you take and every move you make. Though we're apart I will always be aware of every beat of your heart. I will do whatever it takes to make sure you're safe."

Brianna's head was spinning. Being so deeply merged with him there was no doubting his sincerity, but it didn't make sense. It was wrong for him to have such deep feelings for her, wasn't it? He didn't know her. Love at first sight was a fairytale. It wasn't real. It couldn't be real. Then she realized it wasn't real. He wasn't real. Duh. He hadn't existed until she'd passed out from smoke inhalation. He was a figment of her imagination. He was a fairytale lover that came to sweep her off her feet while she was in a coma.

"Will you do something for your fairytale lover, Brianna?"

It didn't bother her that he referred to himself as her fairytale lover. It was no mystery how he was able to hear her thoughts—he was a figment of her imagination. "Sure." She smiled up at him. "Why not?"

Reaching behind his neck, he removed his most powerful possession. Then he took her hand in his to show it to her. "I want you to wear this necklace."

It took her a minute, but she eventually figured out what it was. "It's a dragon, right?"

"Yes." Nodding, he smiled.

There was too much power in it. Dark, deadly power. It actually felt as if there were a life force in it. "I can't take something so valuable from you."

"It was made for you a very long time ago." Refusing to take no for an answer, he turned her around slowly and pulled her long, reddish brown hair over her shoulder.

It hit her hard. She knew what was happening at that moment was real. "This isn't a fairytale, is it?"

"No." He placed the chain around her neck, and then he bent his head to trail kisses across the back of her bare shoulder and up her neck. "This is real," he whispered in her ear. "I'm real." He turned her around to face him. Then he looked down at the dragon nestled between her breasts for a few seconds. Leaving her was inevitable. It was the only way he could ensure her safety. And hopefully, he would find Zack before it was too late. He framed her face in his hands. "It's a part of me. The power you feel in it is me. It won't harm you. It's protection. Never take it off."

"Why are you giving it to me?"

"I told you that it was made for you." Nikolas wrapped his arm around her and started to walk. "We need to get going, or we'll be late."

~ *Twenty-Two* ~

"OH GOOD, YOU'RE here. Caylee is finishing up. She'll be out in a minute." Mia turned her head to glare at Joseph, and then she looked at Haden. "Please, tell me that he isn't coming with us."

Grinning, Haden nodded. "Sorry, I tried, but I couldn't get rid of him."

Mia rolled her eyes. "Wonderful."

Haden turned to Joseph. "I don't think she likes you."

"Duh." Shaking her head, Mia took a deep breath and released it with a sigh of frustration.

Completely capturing Haden's attention, Caylee walked out from the back of the boutique. His closed the distance between them immediately. He'd dropped her off only an hour ago and had waited right outside, but the physical separation from her had been torturous. Naturally, he couldn't stand to be away from her, but the fact that she was being hunted made his need to be near her more insistent. He wrapped his arms around her and kissed her as if they'd been apart for days.

Joseph reached for Mia's hand. "It's wonderful to see you again."

Mia glanced down at his hand and then glared up at him. "Get the hell away from me, Joseph."

Undeterred by her hostility, he took her hand, brought it to his mouth, and kissed it. "Stop being so difficult, angel."

Glaring up at him, she yanked her hand out of his. "One warning. That's it. Touch me again, and I'll shoot your ass." She turned to walk away from him.

"You're all talk and no action. I've already told you I would be thrilled to wrestle with you."

She spun around. "Are you mocking me?" Looking as if she could to do some real damage to him if she wanted to, she took a step toward him.

"Me, mock you? Never." Rather than take a step back, he took a treacherous step toward her while openly allowing his eyes to explore every inch of her body. "You look beautiful tonight, angel."

"It's never happening." Turning her back to him, Mia snorted indignantly. "You're such an imbecile, Joseph." Fumbling with her bracelet, she attempted to close the clasp, but it fell. She bent over to pick it up. And so did Joseph. He won. When she reached out to take it from him, he grabbed her arm and helped her stand up. Once she was standing upright, she tried to yank her arm out of his hand.

"Why do you always feel the need to act so mean? I'm only trying to help you again." Touching Mia, taking her pain, attempting to impart healing energy into her and to remove the morphine from her blood, Joseph pretended to struggle with the clasp he could've easily closed with a thought.

"Get away from me." She reached over the counter to grab her pepper spray, but, as luck would have it, it wasn't there. "Let go of my arm." Wrapping her fingers around the handle of her gun that was there, she smiled.

"Stop being so difficult, angel." Finally closing the clasp, he let go of her arm and looked up to meet her gaze but instead he found himself staring down the barrel of a gun.

Apparently, there was a lot of morphine in her blood. "Oh, damn." Holding his breath, he locked his gaze onto hers. She had a crazy, wild look in her eyes. She'd snapped. He knew it was the morphine heightening the ferocious, unpredictable temper of her lycan nature. And her belief that he was a vampire didn't help.

"You don't really want to shoot me?" She nodded slightly. "Fuck." She did. He couldn't even put up a protection shield. They were standing too close. The bullet would likely bounce off it and hit her. The bullet wasn't going to kill him, but it was about to give him one hell of a headache. She was going to squeeze the trigger. It was going to hurt bad, real bad.

"No, don't do it, Mia!" Caylee shouted.

Casually wrapping his arm around Caylee and holding her close so he could shield her if Mia fired and a bullet ricocheted, Haden smiled. "Joseph, what did you do? I thought you were going to be on your best behavior tonight." *I'm thinking you're going to regret playing with a lycan under the influence of morphine.* Haden focused on the bullets in the gun and used his mind to remove them. It wasn't an easy thing to do. In fact, few of his kind could do it as quickly. But it was a special talent Haden possessed. Also, *if you plan on playing with her again in the future you should consider letting her know you're not a vampire.*

Joseph turned his head slightly to glare at Haden. "I just helped her put the bracelet on."

Lifting his brow, Haden nodded. "Did she ask for your help?"

"Not really."

"What? Not really?" Mia cocked the gun. "I told you to get away from me. I told you to let go of me."

"What do you expect? One minute you're trying to get me to wrestle with you and next you're pretending you don't want me to touch you." Growling, Joseph flashed his most sexy, devilish grin. "You can't blame me for being confused with all the mixed signals you're giving me." He shrugged casually and then opened his arms wide. "There's no need for you to get all frustrated and worked up. This isn't preschool, angel. We're not playing tag on the playground. We're both adults. If you want me, take me."

"Mia," Caylee said, "I'm sure he didn't mean any harm by trying to help you. You can't shoot him because he didn't get away from you or because he's acting like idiot."

"Well," Haden said, "she can, and I wouldn't blame her, but I don't think she wants to deal with the mess in here. It would be bad for business."

Caylee stared up at Haden. "Huh?"

"Don't worry," Haden whispered as he opened his hand to show her the bullets.

Narrowing her gaze, Mia squeezed the trigger. Click. "Damn." She squeezed it again. Click. "Oh, damn it."

"You knew it wasn't loaded, right?" Jaw dropped, Joseph stared at Mia. He saw the disappointment and frustration in her eyes and knew beyond any shadow of a doubt that when she'd squeezed the trigger, she'd believed the gun was loaded. "Damn, woman, you're just … you're so … you're vicious."

Mumbling obscenities, Mia set the gun down behind the counter. She smiled up at Joseph. "It will be in your best interest to stay the hell away from me. I never make the same mistake twice. Next time it will be loaded." She headed toward the door. "We're going to be late."

Joseph was right on her heels. "You will dance with me tonight, right?"

Mia whirled around and took a step to close the tiny gap between them. Hands clenched at her sides, looking quite ferocious, she glared up at him. "Screw you, Joseph."

Pinning her gaze with his, he smiled. "Anytime and anywhere, angel."

Mia didn't hesitate; she certainly didn't give him a chance to savor the fact that he was getting under her skin. Without saying a word, she doubled up her fist and punched him right square on the nose.

* * *

Brianna was thankful for the way Nikolas kept his arm around her as they entered the crowded building. This particular party wasn't just a yearly event—it was *the* event. Hundreds of people attended it. She'd always stayed away from it. In fact, until Julie and Mia had convinced her to attend it, she'd never even considered it. She'd been blind from birth, so she didn't really understand what she was missing by not seeing her surroundings, but she did understand that to avoid bumps and bruises from embarrassing collisions with animate and inanimate objects, avoiding crowded gatherings was a good idea.

Feeling as if his life had purpose for the first time in thousands of years, Nikolas led Brianna toward a table. He pulled a chair out and guided her into it. Hands on her shoulder, he leaned down near her ear. "I need to go and talk to my brother."

Oh, great. Her heart skipped a beat and then fluttered. He'd finally come to his senses and was dumping her off. Preparing herself to be left alone, she tried to remember the way they'd walked. She frowned. It was going to be a challenge. Besides the fact that they'd made several turns since they'd entered the building, she hadn't focused on anything other than the fabulous ways his large, heavily muscled body felt against hers. She really hoped Julie would show up.

He chuckled softly in her ear. "Silly woman," he whispered. "You don't have a chance in hell of getting rid of me tonight." He kissed her cheek.

"I'm fine." She felt the growing heat of a deep blush growing on her cheeks. She decided to get it over with before he noticed. "I don't need a keeper."

"No," he whispered, this time his lips brushing her ear, "you don't, but there's no other place I would rather be than as close to you as possible."

Suddenly he realized his mistake. She hadn't seen Julie jumping up and down and waving her arms to get their attention. She had no idea Julie was frantically shoving her way through the crowd to get to them. "Forgive me. I should've explained. Your friend is rushing over here to talk to you. I need to talk to my brother. I would take you with me, but your friend appears to be quite desperate to speak to you. I thought you might want to talk to her."

"Julie?"

"Yes." Standing upright, he placed his hand on her shoulder. "I will be back in a few minutes. Miss me, little one."

"I've been searching all over the place for you. I was so scared. I saw you leave on the back of a motorcycle. You weren't even wearing a helmet." Julie shook her head at Nikolas just before he turned and walked away. "Oh my God, Brianna, I'm so sorry."

"It's not your fault. I'm fine. Did you find Emily?"

"I did." Julie took a deep breath and released a heavy sigh. "She's really messed up."

"I'm so sorry, Julie. I'm sure she will come to her senses and stop using drugs."

"I hope so," Julie replied. "I promised to take you out on the dance floor. Do you want to go now?"

"No." Brianna shook her head. "I really don't want to dance. Go ahead. Have fun."

"Are you sure?"

"Yes," Brianna lied. Of course, more than anything else, she wanted to be normal; she wanted to dance. But being blind, she'd never actually danced in public.

"He's watching you."

"Who?"

"Duh. Your Harley Davison stud." Julie said. "He's talking to Haden Drake. They look a lot alike."

"They're brothers."

"That must've been one heck of a ride on the back of his motorcycle. You're such a lucky girl. I can't believe you got to have a prime piece of Drake beef between your legs." Julie leaned down and whispered. "Double thumbs up. He's like totally hot."

"What does he look like?" Brianna whispered.

"Well, do you remember when I told you about Haden?"

Grinning, Brianna nodded. "It was a description I'll never forget."

"That's what he looks like. Well, his hair's a bit lighter, and his eyes are a brownish color. He's a tall, dark, muscle-bound god. Basically, the man is the perfect picture of yummy, hot sex. A lot of the women here are checking him out and glaring at you. When he walked away from the table, a nasty-ass bitch swooped in and tried to wrap her arm around his to drag him out onto the dance floor, but he shrugged her off and kept walking without saying a word. He didn't even look at her."

"Stop teasing me." Frowning, Brianna lowered her brow. "You know that I can't see anything. I hate it when you exaggerate."

"I swear it's the truth. He's all yours for the night. I'm sure of it." Julie leaned down to kiss the top of Brianna's head. "Have a blast with him, but I want details in the morning." Giggling, she walked away.

Brianna felt a sudden rush of excitement so strong it caused her entire body to shiver, and then it felt as if her entire body were submerged in warm water. It was as if the warmth embraced her.

Julie was telling you the truth. Perhaps it was wrong to monitor their conversation, but Nikolas couldn't help himself. He was thankful for Julie's description of him, but it was the fact Brianna had asked that thrilled him. *I will never allow another woman to touch me. Your touch is the only touch I want. Your love is the only love I need. For so many years I never thought I would find you. I'm yours forever more. I belong to you, little one, only you.*

Brianna felt the heat of Nikolas' breath on her ear, but she knew that he wasn't next to her. His voice was in her mind.

Seeking him out, she turned in her chair and quickly locked her unseeing gaze onto his. She smiled. *I'm missing you.*

I'm missing you too. His heart melted. *If you're done with your friend, come over here and meet my brother, little one.*

No. She turned away from him.

Why not? He waited for a moment, knowing she was struggling with wanting to do it and fearing what would happen if she dared to try it. *Merge your mind with mine, and you'll have all you need to do it.*

Haden was having a difficult time accepting the fact Demetri had gone after Zack. "You're sure?" Haden asked. There was no reason to ask. Nikolas wouldn't claim it unless it was true.

A muscle ticked in Nicolas jaw. "Yes." He felt some degree of guilt for sending Zack out of the club. He should've kept Zack close. He'd truly believed he was protecting Zack by making him leave.

"We shouldn't wait." Joseph said. "We should go after him now."

"No." Nikolas shook his head. "Zack is strong. He can hold his own against Demetri for a while. Demetri wants us to rush after him and leave our women unprotected. He will grow tired of waiting. By the end of the night he will show up. When he does, I'll deal with him and you will stay with the women." He narrowed his gaze on Haden. "You will take my mate under your protection while I'm away. You will be my connection to her while I'm dealing with Demetri."

"Of course." Haden took a deep breath and released it with a sigh. "You're sure she's your mate?"

Smiling in a way Haden had never seen him smile, Nikolas nodded. "There's no doubt in my soul." Then rage flooding him, he frowned. "Zack was right. The past has returned to haunt us, but this time we won't fail. Demetri killed Brianna's sister, his own mate, and now he plans to kill Brianna. The night he killed his mate, he saved Brianna. I suspect he did it because he wanted to make sure I knew her before he kills her."

"I never would've imagined Demetri would fall so far into the darkness." Haden pushed his hand through his hair. "Did you already restore Brianna's sight? She's walking over here."

"No, I didn't. She has been blind from birth. It will be a long process. I want you to continue it for me." Nikolas smiled. "Demetri and I are equally matched. There will be no end. There will be no true victor, I will not return,"

"Why? You're overreacting. You haven't given this enough thought. You can't just give up on the future. Don't go after him now," Haden said. "There's no reason for you to make such a terrible sacrifice. You've found your mate. You belong with her. We will come up with another way to stop him."

"I do not wish to have a future with Brianna," he lied. "There's no other way. When I leave here tonight, I won't maintain any connection with her."

Haden lowered his brow. "Why?"

"Look at what she's doing." Watching and adoring every move she made, Nikolas smiled. "She has powerful telepathic abilities."

"She's only human," Joseph blurted. "You're leading her, keeping the people out of her way."

"So what if she'd telepathic? The majority of our kind can't poke around in your head," Haden said. "You can easily block her from any part of your mind."

"I can't unless I completely, purposely block her," Nikolas replied. "And I'm not leading her or keeping the people out of her way. She's finding her way to me by taking the information on what's surrounding her from my mind. I've no desire to be with her. Cutting our connection is the most merciful thing I could do for her. She effortlessly enters my mind at will. She so quiet I can't always feel her presence. Our connection is so strong she will likely suffer the pain of any injury I sustain, and she will attempt to come to me, to help me if I don't shut her out."

In stunned silence, Haden watched as Brianna finished making her way to Nikolas' side. He couldn't understand why Nikolas would chose to walk away from her. He was amazed when Brianna tilted her head as if to look up at Nikolas and even more amazed when he saw the tender way Nikolas wrapped his arm around her to kiss the top of her head. The pride and admiration he felt for her was so powerful his countenance shined with it. *What are you doing? You cannot lie to me, brother. You do not want to leave her.*

You know nothing. You will watch over her. Nikolas wasted no time making introductions; instead, he led her toward the dance floor. "Dance with me, little one."

"No." Shaking her head, she tried to pull her hands from his, but his grip was unbreakable. "I can't dance."

He laughed. "You just walked the full length of this crowded building alone."

She wanted to run away and hide. Dancing in public was so entirely out of her comfort zone. There were too many people, and she couldn't see any of them. If she tried to dance, she was going to be tripping and bumping into every one of them.

"No, you won't." He brought her hand to his mouth and kissed it. Then, with no warning, he spun her around, and then he dipped and kissed her. She was laughing, nearly hysterical, when he pulled her into his arms. "You liked that, didn't you?"

"I did." She continued to laugh.

Pressing her body against his, he started to move, forcing her body to move in perfect sync with his. "So did I." And that was the truth. His only problem, if you could call it a problem, was controlling his body's reaction to the glorious sensation of feeling her body pressed up against his.

At first his motive was unselfish. He wanted to give her this experience, but he quickly realized that he needed this moment, this dance with her, more than he'd ever needed anything. He didn't know how he would find the strength to walk away from her, but by the end of the night he wouldn't have a choice. She'd done well getting by on her own, but she would never face the world alone again. In his absence, Haden and Joseph would watch over her.

Brianna was amazed by Nikolas' strength, his ability to lead her and prevent her from bumping into anyone when she couldn't see anything around her. But she was even more amazed by the hard evidence of his desire pressed against her belly. The fact that he wasn't even attempting to hide it was exhilarating.

Nikolas knew the chemistry between them was building, and it was explosive. Their dance was more like making love and could easily get out of control. Dancing with her was more sensual than any other experience he'd ever had. No past sexual encounter could ever compare to feeling her body moving against his. He knew she was scared, but she wanted him to kiss her. He wanted to kiss her too. He needed to feel her against his lips, taste her, claim her. With a thought, he placed a privacy hedge around them as he bent his head so his lips lightly touched the corner of her mouth. "Brianna, kiss me."

She hesitated to move, to breathe, to do anything. She wanted to kiss him, but she'd never kissed a man. She knew they were surrounded by people. Swallowing the lump in her throat, she took a breath and held it. Her body was pressed so snugly against his, intimately moving with his. What was she doing?

"I've taken care of it. No one can see us." Nikolas lifted her chin and leaned down to softly press his lips against hers. When she would've backed away, he held her firmly. "Kiss me." He knew she wanted to believe him, but she could hear people all around.

"We can hear them, but they can't hear or see us." He didn't give her a chance to hesitate. His mouth was on hers;

his tongue parted her lips and delved deep, completely silencing the voices and sounds of the crowd.

* * *

Being very beautiful women, Caylee and Mia were getting a lot of male attention on the dance floor. Dancing together, they ignored the men trying to move in on them as best as they could.

"How can you stand it?" Joseph asked.

Remembering how crazy it used to make him when he stood back and watched Caylee dance, Haden smiled. Over the past year, watching over Caylee from a distance, he'd learned to enjoy it. It wasn't difficult. He loved to watch the way her body moved to the music. "Why would I mind as long as none of the men touch her?"

"That's your mate out there." Clearly disgusted, Joseph scowled. "You're seriously screwed up. The entire building reeks of lust."

Just then, a man moved in on Caylee, pressing way too close for her comfort. He was tall and heavyset. He was dressed in an expensive suit, but he reeked of sweat and old beer. He kept stumbling and grabbing her to steady himself.

"Well ..." Joseph didn't hide the anger in his voice. "Is that enough to warrant an intervention?"

Narrowing his dark gaze, Haden growled. "What the fuck do you think?" He walked toward Caylee.

At first Caylee tried to ignore the man, but she quickly realized it wasn't working. She tried to move further away from him, but he followed. She shoved him, but he didn't back away.

Mia shoved the man. "Get your ass away from her."

"Shut the fuck up, bitch." The man shoved Mia hard enough to cause her to stumble.

Beneath his breath, jaw clenched to the point of causing him pain, Joseph whispered, "Oh, hell no." He headed out onto the dance floor.

Caylee didn't see Haden, but she knew the instant he was behind her. She saw fear in the man's eyes as he backed away. From behind, Haden reached around her waist and pressed her backside against him.

Giggling, Caylee lifted her arms. "What took you so long?"

Haden bent his head and rested his chin on her shoulder so she could wrap her arms around her neck. "You're so naughty, little love. Getting all of these men worked up."

"I've no idea what you're talking about. I didn't do anything wrong."

Haden whirled her around and kissed her. "No, you didn't. You did everything perfectly, magnificently."

* * *

Once Mia was satisfied Caylee was safe with Haden, she moved away from them and continued to dance. Experiencing a sudden wave of excruciating pain, she stumbled. At the same time, the man who'd shoved her grabbed her arm and yanked it. He held her body against his too firmly, hurting her. She pulled to get away, but the pain in her body weakened her and nearly brought her to her knees.

Joseph came up from behind Mia and wrapped one arm around her waist to support her weight and lesson her discomfort. Then he reached over her shoulder and grabbed the man's throat. "She's dancing with me now."

She glanced over her shoulder. "Kiss my ass, Joseph!"

Joseph shoved the man hard. Then, flashing her a devilish grin, he leaned closer to whisper in her ear. "There's no reason to beg for it. Bend over—I will happily kiss your ass, angel." He turned her around slowly, gently, careful to not cause her any pain as he sent waves of healing energy into her body.

Mia glared up at Joseph. He was a vampire. She hated him. She couldn't believe he had the nerve to continue harassing her and pretending he was anything other than a bloodthirsty murderer. There was no way of knowing how many people he'd already killed to satisfy his thirst for blood. It was possible he'd killed her parents. One way or another she would find a way to kill him to stop him from killing. Maybe seduction would work; relaxing, allowing her body to move with the music, she danced with him.

Before Joseph knew it, Mia was dancing very seductively with him, kissing him, touching him, driving him absolutely insane. Her body was so hot, suggestively moving, rubbing up against his, and her hands were touching him everywhere. He was lost, forever lost. During the entire time he'd been married to Teresa he'd never felt such an intense sexual hunger. All along, he'd believed that he loved Teresa. She'd paid special attention to him and made him feel like he had a purpose. It broke his heart when he discovered that Teresa was having an affair and planning to kill him. Dancing with Mia, feeling the heat of her body, was such an exceptional feeling. He knew that he was holding the best he ever had. It was healing experience. His soul, filled with joy, was alive. His body, hard with need, was alive.

Mia allowed Joseph to pull her closer. She didn't resist even though he was holding her a little too firmly. She wanted to kick him in the balls when he bent his head to kiss her, but she resisted the urge. She was a smart woman. He was a very large, physically fit man. Taking him down wouldn't be easy. She needed to make sure he wasn't clear headed when she made his move. Pressing even closer, allowing her body to melt against his, she kissed him. Once she was certain he was solely focused on the taste and feel of her kiss she, using an exceptionally well-learned self-defense move, knocked him flat onto his back. "You son of a bitch!" She glared down at him, pressing her six-inch heel against his chest. "No means no, asshole!"

Blinking, he looked up at her. Not a bad move for a dying woman. He was so stunned that he couldn't move, couldn't do anything except stare up at her. Something shifted deep within his soul. She wasn't simply a wolf; she was an alpha female, and she would naturally only accept the strongest of the strong as her mate. He wasn't her mate. But she wanted him. Her aggression was a test. It was intensified by morphine and distorted by her belief that he was a vampire. He was so incredibly moved by the knowledge he didn't even care that he was flat on his back, surrounded by so many people.

A primal, lustful growl rumbled in his throat as he lifted his chin to look at her heel pressed against his chest. It hurt so incredibly damn good. He slowly moved his gaze up her leg. More than anything, he wanted to feel her legs wrapped around his body.

She heard the dark lust, the sinful intent in his growl and saw it in his eyes. "Be careful, Joseph." She smiled down at him, her lips parted in a way reminiscent of an angry wolf baring its teeth. "There are certain things the devil would regret attempting to do."

Smiling, savoring the threat, he lifted his hand to caress her leg. Sure, he experienced a certain amount of pleasure in touching her, but pleasure wasn't his immediate focus. He was studying the bone cancer that was attempting to kill her. There was no way in hell he would allow it to win. He sent waves of healing energy through her body. He sent it deep into the marrow of her bones.

She felt the heat of his healing power; she felt the relief. "What the hell are you doing?" Getting madder, she pressed her heel harder.

"Oh, yeah." He couldn't prevent the lusty growl from rumbling in his chest. Her temper was spurred by hatred and lust for him. She was so damn hot in every way imaginable. Locking his gaze onto hers, he grinned. Then, the gravity of her illness struck him, and he frowned. Rage filled him and caused the floor and walls to shake.

A large-framed man in a security uniform grabbed her arm and yanked her to the side. She tried to hit the man, but he let go of her arm. Losing her footing, Mia stumbled. "Shit." She fell to her knees, coming down hard on Joseph's chest. The man grabbed a fistful of Mia's hair to pull her off Joseph. Before Mia could reach for the man's hand he let go and Joseph was on his feet. And so was she. Joseph had moved so fast. She didn't know how it happened, but he'd managed to bring her up with him as if she weighed nothing.

Joseph kept one arm tightly wrapped around Mia's waist while he wrapped his other hand around the security guard's throat. "Don't fucking touch her again!" People were gathering around. It was only a matter of time until someone else tried to intervene. Mia's heart was racing. It was her fault. She needed to stop Joseph before he killed the man. But the moment the thought entered her mind, Joseph released the man and turned her to face him. "Are you hurt anywhere?"

"What the hell is wrong with you? You could've killed him. He was trying to help you!"

"I didn't ask for his help. I didn't ask for him to touch you. Are you hurt?" His voice was a deep, ominous growl. It sent chills from her feet all the way up to the top of her head. It definitely wasn't a human sound. And his eyes were so dark, nearly black, but tiny red, flame-like flecks were burning in them. "Let go of me, Joseph." She tried to sound firm, but there was a tremor of fear in her voice.

He felt Mia's body trembling against his. He heard fear in her voice. He saw it in her eyes. He felt the pain deep in her bones. The constant, terrible pain she'd lived with day and night for far too long.

He was aware they were surrounded now. It wasn't easily missed. People were openly gawking and whispering. He was aware of a camera flashing. He knew it was a reporter. When he'd jumped up to deal with the security officer he'd inadvertently revealed his true identity. He heard his name and Teresa's name, but he didn't care. It didn't matter,

"There's no reason for you to be in pain." Catching the nape of her neck, he bent his head. Needing to taste her, he pressed his lips against hers as he sent healing energy into her body and transferred her pain into his body.

He was so deeply merged with her that he knew she wanted to rip his flesh from his bones, but first she wanted to rip his clothing off his body and take as much pleasure from him as he was willing and able to give. Unconsciously arching her hips, allowing her body to move against his, she kissed him deeply, savoring the feel and taste of his kiss. No. She wasn't simply savoring his kiss. She was loving it, needing it, her body demanding it.

One second, he felt the rush of her desire merging with his, and then she pulled away him. Growling, he forced her back. He dipped his head. He wasn't done. He needed more. So much more of this woman. She made his blood boil.

Mia was lost in the pure, erotic pleasure of the moment. She returned his kiss, helpless to do anything else. Her body was burning up. She wasn't supposed to want this. He was a vampire. A murderer. She stepped back and stared at him.

"It's never happening." Needing to put more distance between them, she took a few more steps back. "Stay the hell away from me. I don't want anything to do with you."

She turned and walked away.

He was surrounded by people. The reporter was in his face taking pictures. He heard questions being shouted, but he ignored them as he watched her walk away. Then one voice shouted above the rest. "Does your wife know you've returned?"

Mia turned and locked her gaze onto his.

Joseph saw the intense anger of Mia's wolf flash in her eyes. He expected her to come back and beat the hell out of him. He looked forward to it. But she didn't. He was so deeply saddened by the pain and disappointment that hid just behind the anger in her eyes. He'd hurt her deeply. Shaking her head, she turned and walked away. He needed to go after her and explain. He started to push his way through the people surrounding him, but he was swarmed by more.

~ *Twenty-Three* ~

HADEN TOOK CAYLEE outside to get fresh air. He quickly realized that something was wrong. It was too quiet. Too still. Too dark. He sensed Paul's presence, but there was no tangible evidence of the vampire, only a subtle presence of black magic, wrought by a human, in the air. He immediately recognized the foul vibes of it. Mary Tate was the creator. They were being hunted by the vampire. He scanned the surroundings to get an idea of where Paul was lurking, thoroughly studying their surroundings for something out of the ordinary.

"What's wrong?" Caylee whispered.

"I'm not sure." Just then, Haden picked up on Paul's scent. But where was he? He knew the vampire was out there somewhere, but he still couldn't pinpoint his exact location. Under the circumstances, his best option was to take to the sky. Securing his arms around Caylee, his wings began to take form. "We're going to fly."

A spilt-second before his wings were fully tangible he heard a loud bang. Haden felt a bullet slice through the back of his shoulder and exit through the front. Rapidly losing blood, he was having trouble holding his body up upright. What was happening to him? For a moment, struggling to right himself, his body leaned to the side, weighing heavily against Caylee's shoulder. He shouldn't be so weak. Something was wrong—something more than blood loss.

In his desperation, Haden tried to reach for Nikolas. Nothing. He struggled to straighten and lift the weight of his body off her, but it was nearly impossible. Where were his strength and power? Where were his wings? The answer came suddenly. He felt poison burning through his bloodstream. "Damn it." He felt the rapidly growing warm and wet sensation of it on his back and chest. His body wasn't replenishing it as it should. He was losing too much blood, too quickly. His head was spinning.

His vision blurry, he tried to reach out to Joseph, but he failed. He tried to send another call out to Nikolas, but once again he failed. He had no powers. None at all. His eyes refused to focus as he struggled to remain upright and fight off the poison. He was losing consciousness. He struggled to remain in control of his body, but the blood loss was too rapid. He pushed Caylee toward the building. "Go inside!" Internally cursing his body, he forced it to cooperate. Haden's vision started to darken. Unable to see anything, he fought to remain upright and conscious, his weight pulling Caylee to the right.

He was too big, too heavy; she tried to hold his body upright, but within seconds they fell.

"Get up, Caylee, and go inside."

"No." She climbed off him and tried to pull him upright.

Seeing their struggle, Mia ran toward them. "What happened, Caylee?"

"Haden!" She tried to help him upright, but he was too heavy. "Mia, help me. He's been shot."

He felt the women trying to lift him. He opened his eyes, but he could barely see her.

He stood up, everything swirling around him, but he stumbled to the side. He would be damned if Caylee wasn't trying to hold his weight upright. "Damn it." No one had ever cared so deeply for him. He knew she was willing to die for him. He couldn't allow it to happen. Forcing his body to function, he pulled her in front of him and shoved her toward the building. "I love you, Caylee. You need to leave me. You need to get inside. You need to find Nikolas or Joseph." Haden stumbled and fell to the ground. Once again she was trying to help him. "I can't die. It's impossible. You need to leave me, Caylee. You need to get inside. Mia, take her now. Find Joseph or Nikolas."

It was too late. Caylee felt someone watching her. She sensed danger. A foul odor filled her lungs. Her mind shrouded in layers of a heavy fog, she struggled focus her eyes. "No!"

Reaching out, Paul touched her face. "You're not disappointed to see me, are you?" He turned her around so her back was to him. Pulling her nearer, he wrapped his arm around her neck. "We're leaving now." She cringed as he pressed a kiss on the side of her face.

"Let her go!" Mia struggled to pull Caylee away from Paul.

Paul hit Mia in the face with a closed fist and knocked her to the ground. Her head hit the pavement hard. Unconscious, she lay absolutely still.

* * *

Joseph swung his head around. He growled, instantly placing a hedge of protection around Mia. His image was a blur as he moved toward the front the building. He pushed and shoved his way through the crowd. As with any male of his kind, he didn't care if hurt anyone.

Haden managed to get up. He looked into Caylee's eyes. He couldn't merge his mind with hers, and that terrified him. He couldn't let her out of his sight. The fear in her eyes mixed with his and stirred a powerful rage in his heart. "Let her go!"

Invisible flames burned Paul's hand. Snarling, he exposed his fangs. "There's not a chance in hell of that happening." He nuzzled his chin in her hair. "I've grown very fond of her."

Haden completely transformed. He was more demon than man. The poison was still inside his body, but his anger was momentarily fighting its effects on him. Dark, deadly power surged through his body as Caylee's fear rushed over and through him, overwhelming his senses. Lightning raced overhead, and thunder echoed loudly. Black storm clouds billowed overhead. A thunderous noise rumbled in Haden's mind as large-size hail pummeled the ground a few hundred yards away. He couldn't process a coherent thought. The poison took his control.

Tears filled Caylee's eyes. A terrible pain stabbed inside her skull; crying out, she made eye contact with Haden.

A black mist swirled around Haden as his appearance changed. His flesh turned ashen gray. His eyes briefly flashed red before returning to black. Seething with rage, he glared into Paul's eyes. "Let her go!" he commanded as he thrust forward a surge of energy.

Caught off guard, Paul and Caylee stumbled backward, but Paul quickly regained his balance. "You have no control over your power. You have no ability to harness it. If you follow us, it'll be her death."

Haden's body was hurled backward by an unseen force. He couldn't get up. He lifted his head, but he couldn't get up; he couldn't get her.

Pulling Caylee nearer, Paul forcefully kissed her, bruising her mouth. "Your demon has offered you nothing. I offer you immortality." He ripped his wrist open with his teeth, and then he forced his blood into her mouth. "He refuses to give it to you. What future would you have with him? You'll age while he remains the same. You can't hide it from me. I know you want me." Pulling her hair he yanked her head back, forcing her to meet his gaze. "Now you are his enemy. He will hunt you until he kills you."

Nikolas and Brianna materialized behind Paul. Nikolas created a barrier to temporarily block Demetri's power from Paul. Paul instantly released Caylee and fell to his knees. It was too easy. Demetri's power could've easily penetrated the barrier. It was obvious that Demetri hadn't even tried to stay connected to the vampire. Demetri was playing a game. A dark, deadly game. It was only a matter of minutes before Demetri showed up to finish it.

Caylee's body started convulsing violently. Barely conscious, Mia managed to crawl to Caylee's side. Haden's unknowing gaze locked onto Mia. Some small portion of Mia's brain warned her that Haden viewed her as a threat to Caylee. Waves of rage rolled off Haden's body, causing lightning and thunder to erupt. Deep below the surface, the earth shook violently.

Joseph moved quickly, his image a blur. Haden towered over Mia; his fury was as explosive as the storm raging. As Mia stared up at him, a cry of terror welled up in her, but she held it back. Joseph pulled Mia out of Haden's way. Powerful gusts of wind tossed dangerous, deadly debris all around. Lightning struck the ground, and torrential rain fell from the sky. Joseph pressed Mia against the building, using his body as a shield from the storm.

Covering her ears, Mia looked up at Joseph. His eyes were black. He looked inhumane, murderous. But he wasn't a vampire. He was too strong. His wings were spread wide, shielding her. "What the hell are you?" She struggled to get away from him, but she was unmovable.

"Stay still." His voice was a low, angry, threatening growl. Attempting to calm her, he cradled her head against his chest. He immediately felt the warmth of blood on the back of her head. He sent healing energy into her to close the wound.

"No! We need to help Caylee!" Crying hysterically, Mia struggled to get away from him, but then her body went limp.

"Haden will help Caylee." Joseph lifted her chin, forcing her to meet his gaze. "He's the only one able to help her." Mia was breaking his heart. He felt her pain, her love for her friend, and her need to take care of her friend.

Mia turned her head to look over her shoulder. The sight of

Haden towering over Caylee terrified her. "What's wrong with him?" He looked wild and ferocious, surrounded by strange, black, incandescent flames. She felt enormous waves of rage and hatred rolling off him.

Studying the poison in Haden's system and searching for a spell to eliminate it, Nikolas held Haden in a trance-like state with his gaze. "Haden, we don't have much time. Stop fighting me. Allow me to take the poison from your body so you can help your mate."

Haden fought to break the power of Nikolas' gaze, but his effort only caused him pain. He was unable to move or speak. He saw it. He knew Caylee had ingested Paul's blood. All he could do to save Caylee was to kill her.

"You're right. The vampire has turned her, but as long as she's with your child she won't fall victim to the curse." Nikolas was already taking the poison from Haden's body. "Long before your birth I witnessed such a thing as this. If it's necessary, you must force her to take your blood. Your blood is powerful. It will destroy the vampire blood in her, but after she takes your blood you must take her breath. You can't put if off. Your blood will kill her if you don't immediately give her immortality."

"You believe it will work?" Haden asked.

"I won't lie to you. It's only been done once before. It's considered impossible. As a vampire, she is your natural enemy. When she takes your blood you will need to fight the dragon. Its first and greatest instinct is survival. It will attempt to use you to kill her."

"I would never harm her."

Nikolas nodded. "Well then, the poison is gone from your body. When I release you, kill the vampire first and then take care of your mate."

"She belongs to me," Paul hissed, rising to his feet.

Nobody else made a move, so Mia wrenched herself out of Joseph's arms and smacked the back of Paul's head. "You're an idiot!"

Joseph managed to get between them before Paul was able to strike her. "You're going to be big trouble, angel"

Mia glared up at Joseph. "Haden had better kill the bastard."

Paul glared at Mia. "You're going to die too, bitch!"

Joseph grabbed Paul's arms and held them behind his back, and then he turned Paul around to face Mia. "Go ahead"—he nodded at Mia—"but make sure it hurts."

And Mia did. She kicked Paul in balls as hard as she could. Paul buckled over, but Joseph tossed him to the ground. Mia looked up at Joseph. She didn't say a word, but Joseph knew she was thanking him.

Calm, Haden slowly turned to face Paul. "You'll beg me to end your suffering long before I kill you."

"You can't save her. She belongs to me now."

Haden released a surge of power in the form of a powerful, icy gust of wind forcing Paul to his knees, and then he took a single step toward Paul. "Stand up."

"It's not possible." Under a strong compulsion Paul obeyed the command and stood. "You will never do it."

"You will not die until you know the pain and fear you've caused my mate." Haden could've used his mind to destroy Paul, but he needed to take his life with his hands. Taking a hold of Paul's throat, he hurled him across the parking lot.

"I'll take her again!" Paul struggled to move, but he couldn't break the invisible shackles holding him captive.

Surrounded by black and silver glittery flames, Haden tortured and burned Paul. Paul screamed and begged for mercy, but his agony and desperation meant nothing. Haden had no intention of letting him off easy. He dragged out the destruction of Paul's body, as slowly and as painfully as possible. He wanted him to suffer even though no amount of suffering would satisfy Haden's hunger for revenge. Gaping wounds covered the vampire's body, but it wasn't enough. Tainted blood and foul fluids began to ooze from every wound until the atmosphere was filled with the terrible stench of rotting flesh. Haden raised his hands, and a swirling mass of black flames grew in his palms; he allowed it to intensify, and then he hurled it toward Paul's tattered body.

Nikolas lifted his face to the sky. Demetri was coming. He looked at Brianna. He didn't want to leave her, but there was no other choice. He looked at Haden. "Demetri is near. I need to stop him. I'm holding Caylee's pain—are you strong enough now to take over for me?"

"I am." Haden knelt down next to Caylee and leaned down near her ear. He lowered his voice to a deep, hypnotic tone. "There is no pain—I'll not allow it to touch you. There is no fear—I forbid it to enter your mind. I'm here with you to protect and to heal you."

Nikolas took Brianna's hand and brought it to his mouth. "I will miss you."

"No." Brianna couldn't see him, but she lifted her face as if to look up at him. Deep in her heart she knew he was saying goodbye. She started to reach up but then folded her hands behind her back. She wished she could see him. She knew he was facing danger and that he wasn't sure he would survive. Tears welled up in her eyes.

Nikolas bent his head to whisper in her ear. " I love it when you touch me." He reached behind her and took her hands, and then he brought them to his face. "I've waited to meet you for a very, very long time. I will always be missing you." He bent down and kissed her ear. "Miss me, little one."

Brianna wrapped her arms around him. "I already do," she whispered against his chest.

Demetri, in the form of the dragon, stepped out of a cloud of smoke. His gaze moved over the crowd and then settled onto Brianna. Grinning, he walked toward them.

Nikolas led Brianna to Joseph. "Keep her close to you until my brother is done with Caylee."

"I will." Joseph knew if anything happened to Brianna, Nikolas would hold him responsible.

Nikolas handed Joseph his keys. "Take them to my place and keep them there tonight." He bent down and gently, softly kissed the top of Brianna's head. "You will be safe." It was the hardest thing he'd ever done, but he walked away from her, blocked her from his mind, and took the form of his dragon. Using an ancient spell Nikolas instantly transported himself and Demetri to another time and realm.

Haden knelt down and picked Caylee up in his arms. He cradled her close, and his heart thundered, pumping adrenaline through his body as his wings briefly shimmered and then solidified.

Caylee opened her eyes and stared up at Haden. "Help me."

"No." Haden knew she was asking him to kill her. "You're not leaving me."

"Don't make me live like this." She was gasping, eternal death taking a hold of her flesh and her soul.

"You will not die." Dark, limitless power surged from Haden's body and filled hers. "Breathe for me, Caylee." Staking his claim on her, he violently shoved the spirit of eternal death out of her body.

Caylee's throat opened, and a breath was forced into her lungs. She automatically released it and took another. Her body was too damaged and weak to survive, but it didn't have a choice. It obeyed Haden's powerful command. Her heart stuttered as she took another breath. Within seconds she was breathing easier, and her heart began beating in a strong, steady rhythm. "What are you doing? It's too late. Haden, please, let me die."

"I will never allow you to leave me." Haden took to the sky, and they dissolved into a black mist.

In a matter of seconds, Haden was carrying Caylee through Nikolas' house. The house was dark and cold, but he knew her eyes would be super-sensitive to light. He waved a hand, causing a fire to ignite in the fireplace.

Startled, Caylee shrieked and buried her face against his chest to shield her eyes. She wept so hard her body trembled.

"Keep your eyes closed, little love," he whispered as he slowly lowered her onto the bed.

"Please, Haden. I can feel death in my blood. I don't want to live like this. Please, Haden, I want to die." Her voice was hoarse and desperate. "I can't live like this." Her hand trembled as she grabbed at his shirt, but she was too weak to take a hold of it.

Devastated, he lifted her hand to his mouth and kissed it. "You're my life. I need you more than I need my next breath. I'm not leaving you, little love. You will not die." He gently lowered her hand. "I love you."

His soul filled up with rage. The transformation was happening so quickly. She looked so very pitiful. Her flesh was pale. Her face was gaunt, and her body was far too thin. Her flesh was filled with infection. It was hot to the touch. There wasn't an inch of her flesh spared. She had dozens of burn-like wounds. Her body was so ravaged by the tainted blood that her organs had already started to decay.

Sensing his rage, she tried to open her eyes, but the light from the fire hurt them. No matter how hard she tried, she couldn't get her vision to focus. She just wanted to die. She needed to convince him to save her, to kill her. Breathing heavily, she tried to speak, but she had no voice.

Listening to the steady rhythm of Haden's pulse, Caylee's heart raced. Her stomach clenched as fangs exploded in her mouth and pierced the inside of her cheek. She wanted his blood. She needed his blood. She would do anything to taste his blood. "No!" She leapt from the bed and backed up against the dresser. Eyes wild and glassy, her gaze darted around. "Haden, you need to leave me." She felt intense fear, hunger, and lust for his blood.

He advanced slowly, cautiously. "You need to be calm." She was in a dangerous state; he wasn't worried about his safety, but if she attacked him she could easily harm herself and their daughter. "Don't be afraid."

She turned away from him and looked at her reflection in a mirror. She looked wild and downright hideous. She looked like death. "You said you would do it." Her vision grew darker, and a terrible buzzing filled her head. She was felt so weak and faint. "Why won't you help me die?"

Standing behind her, he wrapped his arms around her and held her upright. Meeting her gaze in the mirror, he slowly leaned near her ear to breathe in the scent of her body. It was a mistake. She reeked of vampire. "How could you ask such a ridiculous question?" His voice was low, angry growl.

She turned around to argue with him, but instead she nestled her face against his chest. His heartbeat was strong against her cheek. Instinctively, she knew his blood offered her nearly limitless power and immortality. His blood promised to satisfy the hunger that burned in her.

Leading her by the hand to the bed, he sat and pulled her down on her lap, and then he cradled her in his arms as if she were an infant. He opened his shirt. "Take my blood." He held her face against his chest. "Trust me—it will destroy the vampire's blood. You'll never hunger for blood again. You and our daughter need my blood to survive the night."

Gently caressing her back, he whispered soothing words, his hands and words working magic, calming her. She tilted her head to look up at him. She knew in her heart he would never allow her to die. His resolve, as usual, was unshakable. He would force her to take his blood if it proved necessary. When he leaned down to take possession of her lips, her sharp, elongated fangs pierced his lip.

Some small part of her brain was telling her that she should be repulsed by it, but moaning, she savored a drop of his blood on the tip of her tongue for an instant, and then she was attacked by a violent lust for blood. Her body trembled as she greedily sucked on his lip.

"Do it now." Growling, he tilted his head back to expose his neck and chest. "Take my blood," he whispered between clenched teeth. He made sure it was a command she wouldn't have the strength to defy. Her fangs punctured deep into his flesh. A low, menacing growl of warning escaped his throat as he wrapped his fingers around her neck. A swift and violent force of rage raced through his veins.

The walls and floors trembled. His body shook as he struggled to subdue the urge to snap her neck. He felt power leaving his body. He felt it strengthening her. He snarled, baring his teeth. His blood was sustaining her life, the life of a vampire. The thought of it was entirely unacceptable. He needed to stop her. She was his enemy. Her life meant nothing compared to his. His fingers tightened around her neck.

An instant before he took her life, he was reminded of his love for her. His grip loosened a bit. She had freed him from his dark nature long ago. He was a demon, a dragon. A feared warrior with no one willing to love him. Now, he was the man she loved. He smiled as she continued to feed. He was the man who loved her. He wasn't a slave to his dark nature. He was a willing servant of his love for her. He would do anything for her. He would give her anything.

In a tender display of affection, he started to caress the nape of her neck with his fingertips. Despite learning the truth of his identity, she loved him deeply and completely. Loving her was always against his nature, but since the day they met he'd loved her far more than his own life. Her love was the most amazing treasure he could've ever been given. He would forever cherish and protect it. He was a fortunate man. Too few would ever experience such a powerful connection with another.

When Caylee stopped feeding, Haden cradled her as he stood up, and then he slowly lowered her onto the bed. She looked so much better. He was incredibly relieved that his powerful blood had instantly, completely healed her. "You've no reason to be afraid." He feathered kisses along her chin and then kissed her lips. "There is one more thing we must do."

She didn't know what he was talking about. She was fairly certain by the serious look in his eyes that she wasn't going to like it, but it didn't matter. How could she not trust him with her life? Before she could even think to question him about it, he was kissing her into a mind-blowing state of ignorant bliss.

Terror rose swiftly when she realized he was suffocating her. She opened her eyes and met his black, icy gaze. Frantically writhing, she tried fight him, kicking her legs and swinging her arms wildly. But it was no use. He was too strong. He held her firmly, his grip like steel. Her heart slammed against her chest, struggling to beat. He was killing her. Suddenly, peace washed over her. No matter the situation, she trusted him to do what was best for her. He was setting her spirit free. Why would she fight him now? Her body went limp and completely still. Her mind was numb, a strange fog shrouding it, as she accepted his gift of mercy and closed her eyes.

When he was certain her heart was no longer beating, he was so relieved. Taking a life had never been more difficult. He knew it needed to be done, but he'd almost failed to complete the act. *I give you my immortal breath.* He breathed into her, filling her lungs, her body. *You belong to me, as I belong to you.* Her heart stuttered irregularly for a few seconds and then started to beat regularly. *You are my heart and my soul.* Startled, she opened eyes and looked up at him. *I will never leave you or betray you, Caylee. I will protect you with my last breath. I vow to love and cherish you with every fiber of my being for eternity.*

Rendered speechless, she stared up at him for several moments. Never had she hoped to find a love like his. As a young child she craved love but was surround by hatred. She always hid in the darkest corner of her father's home, alone and shivering from fear, hoping to escape his cruelty. Reaching up, she touched the tears streaming down Haden's face. She would never be alone again. She would never live in fear again. She would very likely be forced to face the cruelty of hatred in future, but she would always be embraced and protected by Haden's undying love for her.

* * *

"Where did he take her?" Mia asked

Joseph glanced at Mia. "We're going to meet up with them right now."

Mia grabbed his arm. "I'm not going to ask how the hell you guys have wings or how the other guy turned into a dragon, but is she okay?"

"Yes." Joseph led Mia and Brianna across the parking lot toward Nikolas' car.

Just before they reached the car Joseph stopped. He felt the unmistakable presence of a strong male predator. A lycan. He reached out with his mind and discovered that there was more than one. It was pack of more than thirty. He looked at Mia. The pack was there to take her. Her mate, the alpha male, was there to claim her.

Surrounded by his pack, Eli crouched low to ground as he watched from the shadows. Mia belonged to him. The union had been arranged long before her birth, and he'd been searching for her ever since the night her parents were murdered by vampires. He would've never found her if the vampire hadn't tried to take Haden's mate. Lycans and demons generally tolerated each other, but they never formed friendship though they fought side-by-side in many battles against vampires and other dark creatures that murdered mankind.

Eli knew very little about Joseph, but he knew the demon wielded great power and strength. Getting Mia away from Joseph wouldn't be easy. There would be many casualties, but Eli was willing to pay any price to take possession of his mate.

About Candice Stauffer

I live in Zeeland, Michigan, where half the year is winter and the other, much shorter half, is summer. It's a wonderful place to live as long as you own a four-wheel drive vehicle and happen to get a kick out of measuring the snowfall in feet rather than inches.

I write paranormal romance because I love to explore and manipulate the limitless possibilities of the genre. To be completely honest, I'm also very fond of taking a totally hot, powerful, immortal hero and using a strong, confident, beautiful heroine to turn his world upside down and make him fight like hell for a victory that seems impossible to achieve. Some might call it torture. I call it entertainment and character building. Regardless, it's great fun!

I have a strong aversion for helpless heroines. Though she's afraid, a heroine must always be willing to fight like hell—and, yes, even if the fighting is against the hero. I'm not sure why, but I tend to really enjoy it when the heroine fights against the hero. Putting a hero through the wringer builds personality, right?

I'm often accused of being a little bit naughtier than nice and slightly rough around the edges. Okay, I lied—very rough around the edges. Life has been a challenge. But I'm grateful for every challenge I've faced. Through them, I've learned to focus on the goal rather than the walls surrounding it. Basically, I figure that as long as I enjoy life and do all I can to encourage and help the people around me enjoy life, it's all good.

To find out more about me, please visit my website *http://www.candicestaufferparanormalromanceauthor.com,* and for the latest news, check out my Facebook page,

　http://www.facebook.com/pages/CandiceStauffer-Paranormal-Romance-Author/135025903252623.

Made in the USA
Charleston, SC
03 November 2012